THE ARCHANGEL TRILOGY

"Magazine Clip"

Comprises the Archangel trilogy:

Archangel
Raven
Archangel: Raven's Card

Ed Adams

a firstelement production

IT HAD TO BE DONE

There are individual 'Thanks' pages for each of the three novels that follow in this Trilogy/ 'Magazine Clip' edition. Archangel was envisaged as a novella, but then reader John suggested a sequel. Terry, on a Zoom call, added that it could have something to do with Freemasons. And so Raven appeared, with cliff-hanger ending. I received emails asking for a sequel, which is Raven's Card, written with the aid of tarot.

Thanks also to Caroline, Richard, Georgina, John, Melanie, Julie, and Elizabeth for hugely varied cover design suggestions.

So, here we are with:

1 Archangel
2 Raven
3 Archangel: Raven's Card

And thank you, dear reader, for at least 'giving it a go'.

Published in Great Britain in 2020 by first element
Directed by the six twenty
Copyright © 2020 Ed Adams

10 9 8 7 6 5 4 3 2 1 All rights reserved.

ISBN : 978-1-913818-02-9
Ebook ISBN : 978-1-913818-03-6

Printed and bound in Great Britain by Ingram Spark

Ed Adams
an imprint of first element rashbre@mac.com

Mailing list: https://mailchi.mp/9f0b30712620/ed_adams

Books by Ed Adams include:

Triangle Trilogy		About
1	**The Triangle**	Dirty money? Here's how to clean it
2	**The Square**	Weapons of Mass Destruction – don't let them get on your nerves
3	**The Circle**	The desert is no place to get lost
	The Ox Stunner	The Triangle Trilogy – thick enough to stun an ox
		(all feature Jake, Bigsy, Clare, Chuck Manners)
Archangel Trilogy		
1	**Archangel**	Sometimes I am necessary
2	**Raven**	An eye that sees all between darkness and light
3	**Card Game**	Throwing oil on a troubled market
	The Archangel Trilogy	the above three in one heavy book.
		(all feature Jake, Bigsy, Clare, Chuck Manners)
Stand-Alone Novels		
1	**Coin**	Get rich quick with Cybercash – just don't tell GCHQ
2	**Pulse**	Want more? Just stay away from the edge
3	**Edge**	Power can't be left to trust
	Now the Science	the above three in one heavy book.

About Ed Adams Novels:

Triangle Trilogy	About
Triangle	Money laundering within an international setting.
Square	A viral nerve agent being shipped by terrorists and WMDs
Circle	In the Arizona deserts, with the Navajo; about missiles stolen from storage.
Ox Stunner	the above three in one heavy book.
	(all feature Jake, Bigsy, Clare, Chuck Manners)
Archangel Trilogy	
Archangel	Biographical adventures of Russian trained Archangel, who, as Christina Nott, threads her way through other Triangle novels.
Raven	Big business gone bad and being a freemason won't absolve you
Card Game	Raven Pt 2 – Russian oligarchs attempt to take control
The Archangel Trilogy	the above three in one heavy book.
	(all feature Jake, Bigsy, Clare, Chuck Manners)
Stand-Alone Novels	
Coin	cyber cash manipulation by the Russian state.
Pulse	Sci-Fi dystopian blood management with nano-bots
Edge	World end climate collapse and sham discovered during magnetite mining from Jupiter's moon Ganymede
Now the Science	the above three in one heavy book.

ARCHANGEL

Book 1 of the Archangel Trilogy

Ed Adams

a firstelement production

First published in Great Britain in 2020 by firstelement
Copyright © 2020 Ed Adams
Directed by thesixtwenty

10 9 8 7 6 5 4 3 2
Archangel Second Edition
All rights reserved.

Every effort has been made to acknowledge the appropriate copyright holders. The publisher regrets any oversight and will be pleased to rectify any omission in future editions.

Similarities with real people or events is unintended and coincidental.

A CIP catalogue record for this book is available from the British Library.

ISBN 13 : 978-1-8380146-4-3
Ebook ISBN : 978-1-8380146-6-7

Printed and bound in Great Britain by Ingram Spark

rashbre
an imprint of firstelement.co.uk
rashbre@mac.com

Mailing list: https://mailchi.mp/9f0b30712620/ed_adams

"þetta reddast"

things always have a way of working out in the end

Icelandic credo

THANKS

A big thank you for the tolerance and bemused support from all of those around me. To those who know when it is time to say, "step away from the keyboard!" and to those who don't.

To thesixtwenty.co.uk for direction.

To anyone who has read any of the Triangle trilogy

And, of course, thanks to the extensive support via the random scribbles of rashbre via http://rashbre2.blogspot.com and its cast of amazing and varied readers whether human, twittery, smoky, cool kats, photographic, dramatic, musical, anagrammed, globalized or simply maxed-out.

Not forgetting the cast of characters involved in producing this; they all have virtual lives of their own.

Cover photo credit: Luca Giordano 1666: The fall of the rebel angels

And of course, to you, dear reader, for at least 'giving it a go'.

TABLE OF CONTENTS

ARCHANGEL

ARCHANGEL - RAVEN'S CARD

Your Cards   **928**

PART ONE

Author's Note

This book is an attempt to piece together the story of Christina Nott, variously known by a multiplicity of other names in her past.

We sat together while this was being created and much of what is written is exactly as it was spoken into the Philips Voice Tracer and then transcribed into Dragon Dictate.

I've cleaned up the wording somewhat and occasionally skipped a graphic moment, but most of what is in the following pages is as Christina intends it to be. I guess you'd call it an autobiography, although Christina sometimes thinks of it as notes on part of a life.

She's changed identity again now, so there's no direct way to pin her to this and I've been asked by lawyers to describe the whole thing as a work of fiction, which gets around several matters, which will be resolved as the story unfolds.

Starting Out

"WHAT YOU WON'T FIND IN HER CLOSET

- *Three-inch heels. Why live life halfway?*
- *Logos. You are not a billboard.*
- *Nylon, polyester, viscose and vinyl will make you sweaty, smelly and shiny.*
- *Sweatpants. No man should ever see you in those. Except your gym teacher – and even then.*
- *Leggings are tolerated.*
- *Blingy jeans with embroidery and holes in them. They belong to Bollywood.*
- *UGG boots. Enough said."*

— Anne Berest, How To Be Parisian

Agnes Örnólfsdóttir

We are in Iceland at the start. Agnes was born to the Örnólfs and gained the name Agnes Örnólfsdóttir. On Iceland, the last names of everyone reflect their family and so Örnólfsdóttir literally means Örnólf's daughter.

It shouldn't be mistaken for Guðmundsdóttir, which is famously the last name of Björk Guðmundsdóttir and is probably the only Icelandic person who many can name.

Christina continues: I guess there's a couple of footballers too, Gylfi and Kolbeinn. Then I could list Vigdís Finnbogadóttir as president of Iceland in 1980. She was the first female in the world to win a national presidential election. She was re-elected a further 3 times.

Or Hafþór Júlíus Björnsson, best known as 'The Mountain' in the Game of Thrones series. And still, in popular culture, we can't forget the PlayStation. Ólafur Jóhann Ólafsson was responsible for its introduction.

But we're better off to think of Iceland as the land of the ice and snow.

As Jimmy Page and Robert Plant described it:

We come from the land of the ice and snow. From the midnight sun, where the hot springs flow. The hammer of the gods. We'll drive our ships to new lands, to fight the horde, and sing and cry, 'Valhalla, I am coming!'

Yes, Immigrant Song, famously written after the Zep toured into Reykjavik. Shop assistants in Reykjavik wear the lyrics on tee-shirts to this day.

I was not an immigrant in Iceland. It is where I'm from, but I've moved so many times I feel like an immigrant everywhere now. At least I do not feel *of* the place. More like an outside observer.

I can only remember a few events from my time in Iceland. We lived on a smallholding with a selection of sheep and horses. If it sounds in any way glamorous, it was not. My Pabbi worked the land and managed the animals. The horses were the typical Icelandic type, which sometimes people mistake for ponies. They taught me to ride from an early age and have memories of being on a horse, helping Pabbi bring in the sheep.

I am sure that's what has toughened me to the elements too, Iceland was cold, and very snowy. When the winds blew it could be icy, yet the overall climate was well-tempered. Mamma used to put me outside when I was a little elskan, in all weathers. I have since heard that this was considered cruel by some people, but the culture in Iceland is to do this and ensure the baby gets fresh air.

Our place was about three hours outside of Reykjavík on the F35, sandwiched between two glaciers. There was always a view out towards ice both to the east and to the west, although Pabbi said that the eastern ice was melting quickly.

It meant that in my early years I learned from the land. How to read the skies, of animals and their ways and their tracks. We had a small local school, but I was told that I would need, at some point, to go to a big city for my education.

In the evening, indoors, we would sing songs, and I learned to play the piano, except I could not reach down to the pedals on the old upright piano that we had.

I discovered that my other source of learning was the television. The Americans had an Air Force base at Keflavik, and they'd installed a huge aerial that transmitted American television to the whole of Iceland. I think it was to make the Americans feel at home when they transferred to Iceland, but it also meant that most of Iceland learned English from the broadcasts. We also learned about a lot of American products which we could not get in Iceland, but that the Americans had flown in on their transport planes.

I could play many of the jingles from the television on the piano. At one time, as children, we even formed a small band who practiced together in one of the bedrooms of the farm-house. I think it was a subtle way that Mamma ensure we had music lessons.

I had not accounted for Pabbi's other job. As well as his business as a smallholder, unknown to me he was paid to watch the sky. One of our farm sheds was off-limits to me. When I had friends around to play, we were told never to go into the Ullarverslun - the wool store. I was told I was allergic and that it would make me ill.

The threat of illness was enough to keep me away until one day when we were playing some kind of hide-and-seek game. Hekla - my best friend - had run towards the Ullarverslun and made as if she was going to hide somewhere near it. We were past the window weather and into the warm summer months with bright sunshine.

There was a sudden crack, and a piece of timber fell from the store. It turned out Hekla was trying to climb over the top of the door to a flat area of roof, where she could both hide and catch some sunlight.

Instead, she fell through the roof and into the building. It wasn't much of a drop, maybe two metres in total, and she knew to lower herself through the gap so she'd only need to drop about a metre. No problem for a nine-year-old.

Then she came back to the door and opened it. I was expecting to see wool piled up from floor to ceiling. I'd never really thought about it being any different.

Sure, we had sheep. Proper Icelandic sheep which did get woolly in the winter months. They were sheared by Pabbi and Kristján, who used to come up from the town to help. I'd never really thought about where the wool went, except that it was in the wool store.

So, it was a surprise to finally see inside the store. It looked electrical. There were several boxes with lights flashing, a desk and a computer terminal.

There was also what looked like a huge satellite dish, pointing upwards, although there was a roof above it.

Hekla was as surprised as I was.

"Is your dad a spy?" she asked.

"No," I said, "He's an astronomer - a man who looks at the stars."

Even at this young age, I was adept at ad-libbing and the American television we picked up had given me even more ideas.

"We'd better tell Pabbi," I said, "Don't worry, I know how to explain this - let me do the talking."

Hekla was very frightened in case Pabbi was angry. She asked if it would be all right if she left early that day. I knew that she was not allowed to walk across the fields alone and that she would have to wait for her Mamma to pick her up in the car.

We went back to the house, and I found Pabbi repainting a water trough. He could tell that something was wrong and asked what it was.

I told him we'd accidentally broken the roof of the Ullarverslun, and he looked concerned.

"Are you both okay?" he asked, "No bangs and scrapes?"

We both nodded, and Pappi looked less annoyed than we had expected.

"I was worried about that roof," he said, "It needs fixing - I hope now you'll remember to stay away from there."

He looked at both Hekla and me and could see that we were both breathing and didn't look more scratched than normal.

"Let me tell Mamma about this," he said.

And then he carried on with his painting.

Well, Hekla and I ran back outdoors, "I wasn't expecting that," said Hekla, "My dad would have been furious if I'd smashed one of his sheds. Even if it needed fixing."

I pretended that Pabbi was cool, but really I wondered if he'd been nice because of Hekla being around to play.

That night-time, it was time for bed and Pabbi's turn to tuck me in. He asked me a question, "Today, when Hekla fell through the shed, did either of you notice what was inside?" he asked.

"We did," I said to Pabbi, "It looked like a telescope or something,"

"Yes, they have asked me to look after it for some men who live a long way away." He replied.

"They asked me to keep it a secret, actually,"

"Why's that Pabbi?" I asked.

"Well, they give us some money for the farm," he replied, "They just ask me to look through the telescope every so often." Then he kissed me on the forehead and left the room.

I wondered what it all meant, but I didn't have long to find out. A few days later Hekla's mother came around and was chatting to Mamma. They were in the kitchen. Hekla's mother said, "Thank you," to Mamma for being so nice the day that Hekla had fallen through the roof. She explained that Hekla had been worried about being told off. Mamma was very curious by this. She looked like she was hiding it but pretended to know what had happened. I could tell she was fibbing.

Then, at tea-time, Mamma and Pabbi talked about it some more. Pabbi looked worried that Hekla's mum knew about the wool-store.

"I'll have to report it, and then it will only be a matter of days," said Pabbi.

A few days later, some men in a big red car arrived at the farm. They said they were from the insurance company and would talk to Pabbi alone.

After they had left, Pabbi said he had a family announcement.

"We've been told by the men who visited today that we are such excellent farmers that they want us to show some other people how to do it."

Mamma looked sad, but I thought we had just won a prize.

"Yes, he said, we are invited to a new land to show people how to farm sheep."

"Where Pabbi, where?" I asked, hoping it would be America and that then we could get some of the items advertised on television.

"We are going to Russia," he said, "To Arkhangelsk- It is very like Iceland."

"Then why are we going?" I asked, "if it is just like here?"

"You will learn a new language," Pabbi said, "And you won't be confused by the climate."

"Will I still be able to watch American television?" I remember asking.

"No, but you will have a good selection of Russian television instead."

"Will people understand when I speak Icelandic?" I asked.

"No, but they will understand English, or at least some of them will."

I can remember being shocked by this, but also excited at the chance to go to Keflavik airport to catch a big plane to Russia. We were going to fly to Moscow and then catch a train for the last part of the journey.

"How far is it, ástin mín " Mamma asked Pabbi.

"From Moscow, it's about 1,200 kilometres. It's on the White Sea."

Mamma started crying. I think she was sad to be leaving Iceland.

Leaving Iceland

Things moved quickly. The men who had visited in the red car came back.

I had to get a passport and have pictures taken.

Hekla came around to say goodbye. She said she wondered if it is because we had looked in the wool store that it meant I was going away.

I said we were going to a new country to teach people how to look after sheep. This impressed Hekla, but she also asked if they had American television.

The time came, and I had to say goodbye to the dogs and the horses. I was especially sad to say goodbye to my favourite horse, the wonderful Einar. The dogs seemed to sense that there was something happening, and we threw them more treats than usual. Our dogs were working dogs and they lived outside in kennels. The idea that they would get treats was especially unusual to them, because they had probably only ever received them when they were puppies.

Then a taxi arrived, and we climbed aboard. It was a big mini-bus and had space in the back for our luggage. I realised that we were leaving a huge amount behind and that we would need to start anew when we reached Archangel.

The plane ride was a thrill for me, and I was preoccupied with the airport, the fancy shops, unusual food and even some American goodies on offer. When we took off, I could see Keflavik below, then Reykjavik, and then we flew right over the glaciers. I looked at the gap between them and tried to work out where our farm was, but I couldn't see it.

We were flying with Islandair, and the plane had to stop over in Amsterdam. We were allowed to disembark, and I could look around the airport. It was huge and had shops and even a casino. We ate some pizza upstairs in a cafe before we continued with our flight. I asked Pabba how far it was, and he said the whole flight was 17 hours.

While we were at the airport, I listened out for other people speaking Icelandic, but I didn't hear anyone, apart from in the lines for our plane. Some spoke Norwegian and even Swedish and I could understand them both. I could not understand someone speaking Danish at all. But what I also noticed was just how many people spoke English. It differed from the American English on the television, although I decided I could understand that the best of all the languages being spoken.

We had different seats for the second part of the flight, although Mamma and Pabbi still let me have the window seat. I could see the patchwork of Europe spreading out in front of the plane until we were above the clouds. We seemed to be above the clouds for a long time but then, as we came through them, I could make out the first of what I realised was Russia.

Then some announcements in a new language (which I subsequently realised was Russian). We were in the flight path to Sheremetyevo International Airport.

We landed, and I remember the first sights. When we approached Keflavik airport, there was something that looked futuristic about its architecture. To me, it looked big too. But Sheremetyevo AS Pushkin was huge. Plate glass, it looked as if a spacecraft had landed. Sweeping curves of glass. This Russia was even more impressive than the America as I'd seen it on television.

We were soon out of the plane, and in an airport that seemed vaster than Schipol in Amsterdam. And Schipol had its own train station built into the airport as well!

Pabbi said we had to go to a special delegations' lounge where we would be met by some men. We followed the signs and soon arrived at a golden waiting room. On the way to the area I had noticed that there were several other VIP lounges too and each of them was even more golden than the last. I decided I would only fly from this airport if I could sit in the golden areas first.

We found the area, and everyone sat around a low table. The men were drinking something which I think might have been vodka. Pabbi and Mamma were asked if they would like drinks too, and they offered me some Coca-Cola. At least I could still get American things in Russia.

It turned out that the men were giving us some tickets for the train and also a stay in a hotel in central Moscow.

We would spend a day in Moscow before travelling to Archangel. I asked how long the train ride would be.

It shocked me to hear that it was 21 hours. The men showed me a picture of the train. It looked like something from America. It was streamlined, and bullet shaped. It looked as if it could travel very fast.

"Not only that," said Pabbi, "These tickets are for first class. We can travel this next piece in comfort." I looked over to Mamma. She looked as if she had been crying.

The men said they would get tickets to Moscow for us on the subway, but they thought it would be better to give us the cash instead. We could then get a taxi from outside directly to the hotel. It would be better than carrying our suitcases around the streets of Moscow.

Pabbi asked how much the taxi should be. The men told him, and he smiled. The taxis in Moscow were good value after the costs of taxis in Iceland.

Then we went to the place where the bags are unloaded. Another man was waiting there with our bags. They had unloaded them and put them into a trolley for us.

I decided that Pabbi must be thought of as important in Moscow to get this kind of treatment, with the golden lounge and then with the luggage. It startled me when the Russian announcements in the baggage hall also included one in Icelandic. I realised it was for our plane.

Then to the very centre of Moscow. What a city! It was so messy after Reykjavik. The traffic was unbelievable. It was also very polluted with car, and lorry fumes rising while we sat in still traffic. Some of the trucks seemed to have huge exhaust pipes that pointed out sideways at just the height of the windows in our taxi. A few cars with blue lights seem to dash past us, but they couldn't all be police.

In English, the taxi driver explained that the cars belonged to 'the Mafia' who could buy blue light passes.

The taxi driver said he had a brother in Chicago and that he was originally from Pakistan, which is where he had learned his English. He sounded different from the Americans I'd heard on television.

The hotel we were going to was a Radisson, which is a Swedish firm. We were expecting it to be like a lot of Swedish things with maybe some pine wood on display. It was a bit of a family joke and I suppose was part of the friendly tension between Iceland, Norway and Sweden.

How wrong we all were! The hotel turned out to be one of Stalin's skyscrapers in the centre of Moscow. It was more like a palace and had a river view.

The entrance lobby was all marble columns and had a floor like a mirror of marble patterns. There were chandeliers hanging from the ceiling.

We checked in and were then accompanied to our floor where we had two rooms with an adjoining door. I had my room on the top floor of a palace in the centre of Moscow!

We were told that we had the room booked for overnight and because our train was late in the day, we had it booked until the next evening!

The lady at the check-in also told us (in English) about the hotel's boats which ran along the river and would give us a chance to see the city without getting tired. I don't think she knew how far we walked in an average farm-day!

A man took our bags to the rooms, and then we were ready to look around. Mamma looked tired, but I wanted to see this city. Pabbi suggested that we should all have a rest and then go to the river and catch a boat.

We went to our rooms, but I noticed that Pabbi and Mamma had a visitor for around 15 minutes. I think they were checking on our progress.

I watched some television, which had about a hundred channels including American and British, which I could understand and Russian, which I couldn't understand and seemed to be boring.

Then we left for the boat trip, all along the river under a glass canopy. Moscow was well lit from the boats and I thought we were making faster progress than we did in the taxi. Wherever I could see traffic, there seemed to be a jam.

The next day, we started with a good breakfast, of anything you could think of, and then decided to walk to Red Square and The Kremlin and on to St Basil's church. The previous evening we'd worked out that it was a short straight line to get to all of those sights, although the boat had wound its way there because of all the bends in the river.

It still took us about an hour to complete the walk, but it was very interesting to see the modern Russia at work, plus the scores of tourists in the Red Square.

Too soon it was time to collect our bags from the hotel and make our way to the train station, with another taxi. We could have walked it quicker than the taxi, although we'd have had to carry the big suitcases with us.

Then we arrived at the train station. It was a different feeling here. A much messier form of Russia and very limited signs in anything we could understand. We asked about the train to Arkhangelsk and were pointed towards a particular platform. We were going first class, remember.

Then came the shock. The train on the platform was an old one. Not a bullet train like in the picture, but an old set of silver-coloured carriages and a separate diesel engine. What's more, the journey wasn't 21 hours. It was now shown as 23 hours and with around 40 stops.

"Guð minn" said Mamma. I wasn't used to hearing her swear. She looked towards Pabbi and asked, "Are you sure this is the right train?" He looked at the tickets, the numbers on them and said, "Yes, I'm sure."

We edged along the train to find our compartment, hoping that things would get better.

They didn't. This was the standard train first-class compartment, roughly equivalent to 2nd class on a mainline train elsewhere.

"At least it is clean," I can remember Mamma saying, as she looked at the chairs and table.

It was a plain-looking carriage and we would be in it for a whole day, travelling to Arkhangelsk.

First Class explanation

The train ride was when Pabbi told me what was really happening. All three of us were seated at the table in the compartment of the train. Pabbi explained that we were being relocated by the Russian FSB. Pabbi had once been a pilot in Russia but had been asked to move to Iceland by his bosses.

He had suffered from stress as a consequence of flying military jets along the boundaries of other countries. The instructions were always to fly as close and low to the ground as possible, to escape radar detection. This was extremely tough flying and even in the latest Sukhoi SU-35s he had found it difficult to keep to the contours. At any moment he could trip an alarm and be subjected to anti-aircraft fire as well as setting off a diplomatic incident.

One day, his buddy Nikolay in the same flight had done just that and triggered a jet scramble from a Finnish F-18 Hornet, which he should have been able to outmanoeuvre. The Finnish plane had fired a warning shot across the front of the Russian, but he'd panicked and ejected from the flight. He'd landed in Finland and been repatriated.

Nikolay's plane had crashed into a field and created much wreckage but no injuries or fatalities. Nikolay had been a mental wreck after that and was threatened with court-martial for losing an expensive plane.

Pabbi said he realised that he was also burned out at the same time as Nikolay and sought to get out of the flying. He said he had done over 100 stressful sorties by this time.

The authorities had offered him the farm as an incentive for him to move and Pabbi had been pleased to accept. He had always dreamt of life as a farmer and this life away from everything seemed like his best option.

Pabbi had been dating Mamma at this time, and she had an Icelandic background, so they would select Iceland as the new location.

This was ideal for Pabbi, who knew he could then propose to Mamma and would have some property to his name. The chance for Mamma to get back to Iceland was additional incentive. That's why they had chosen the last name Örnólfs; it was Mamma's last name before she had moved to Russia with a fisherman, from whom she was now divorced.

So, do you have a Russian Name?" I asked Pabbi.

Pabbi looked at Mamma and said, yes, "Its Arnol'd. Arnol'd Miasnikow"

"Okay, so you will have to tell me about the wool store," I asked

"It was part of the deal," said Pabbi. "I was an ex-fighter pilot, so I knew a lot about aviation."

"The authorities wanted me to set up a listening station in the middle of Iceland. It was part of the deal for me to transfer out of the Air Force."

"I was to listen to the UN radio chatter and to monitor the planes circuiting through the area. Keflavik was still a big American base when we started out."

"So Hekla was right? - You were a spy?" I asked Pabbi.

"That's a strong word for what I was doing, " said Pabbi, "It was more like a plane spotter."

"But one that did it in secret?" I asked, still a little surprised by this whole thing.

"There's still more," said Pabbi, "There would have been trouble for me in Iceland, if I'd been picked up by the police. Your little friend might have accidentally said some things to her mother and that could have caused ripples which would alert the authorities."

"So, the Russians agreed to move us all out?"

"Mamma knows all of this, but - yes - they did offer," answered Pabbi, "But I wanted to make sure that you and Mamma would be all right too."

"Mamma already speaks Russian, and has lived here, so that isn't such a problem. But for you, dear Aggi, I wanted the best education and no chances lost."

"Because of my record in the Air Force and my time spent abroad doing the listening work, I'm regarded as something of a Russian hero back in Moscow. That is why I am being treated so well. That is why we all are being treated well.

The authorities have agreed to rehouse us all in very nice accommodation in Arkhangelsk, to offer me a farm-based job if I wish, but most importantly, to put you into the Academy in Arkhangelsk. That's the highest education establishment available and normally requires passing a special entrance examination. They say that the Academy is also holistic. It looks at the whole person mind, body and soul. Mamma and I are very proud that you will be able to go to this Academy."

I was taken aback. In the course of a couple of days, I'd said goodbye to my best friend, to my favourite horse, to my home, and I was now travelling across North West Russia in a train to a new home and life in an Academy.

"I can see this is a lot to take in," said Mamma, "We have thought long and hard from way before this happened about what we would do if such a situation occurred."

"We couldn't talk about it to you, in case you mentioned it to someone, see what happened when your best friend found out by accident - and we don't - in any way - blame her for any of this."

"It can be like a new start for us, your parents, and for you the beginning of a great adventure," said Pabbi.

Preparation

Пан или пропа́л.

To become a master or to be gone.

Russian Proverb

(up or out)

Agnessa Dobrayadoch

That was when Pabbi showed me my new Passport. It was Russian.

I wanted to see my picture. "Agnessa Dobrayadoch", it said.

"Is that me? " I asked.

"Yes Aggi, my dear, it is," said Pabbi.

Mamma nodded," We've all got new names," she said.

"So, are we the Dobrayadochs?" I asked, somewhat confused.

"That's right," said Pabbi, "The goodmans - Dobraya is good. Doch is Man"

"Like Björk Guðmundsdóttir," I said, "I'll be Goodman's daughter."

Agnessa is the Russian for Agnes. So, you keep your first name, We can still call you 'Aggi'.

"What about you?" I asked, "We had had to take this new last name so we can't be mistaken for the Russian people that we were when we left," explained Mamma.

So that's how I got my second name, Agnessa Dobrayadoch. At least it sounded Russian.

We travelled across a huge expanse of Russia, but I realised from a map that it was still only a tiny part of the vast country.

We travelled through forests, cleared for the train line and an accompanying road. Every so often, maybe every 50-100 kilometres, there was another small town and a train station. We always stopped, and I realised why the journey would take so long.

Then the train line started to follow a river and I could look out of both sides of the carriage to see the way the river changed sides as we crossed small bridges. The road was following a similar route but didn't seem to carry much traffic.

Occasionally I'd see a walled city, or a brightly painted church, like a miniature version of the one at St Basil's back in Moscow. Compared with Iceland, the land was very flat, with views across many miles. The river we crossed also seemed very brown, not like the glacier clear waters around our farmstead.

Most of the buildings by the railway track side seemed very 'used'. They were industrial looking, coated with dust and looked as if they had a hard life.

Occasionally I could see large advertisements alongside the road or on hoardings by the side of the rail tracks. They seemed to advertise everything either literally (like a picture of an oil can) or with women holding it (car tyres, pizzas, soap powder, more oil cans). The women didn't seem to have much idea about what they should be wearing either.

I decided to grade adverts on the train to pass the time. I had a little notebook.

A good one was for some kind of food, which seemed to come in a selection of baskets.

A brash one was for a gold Rolex, which was about the size of the moon.

A repeating one was of a woman reading a newspaper. She looked like she was from the 1950s and I could work out that the advert was for Pravda.

A readable one was for Coca-Cola, usually as we approached the next town.

I saw several for what I thought were cigarettes too, but I later learned that these were an anti-smoking campaign that copied cigarette branding. Two cowboys in Marlborough hats with the slogan "Bob, I've got emphysema" or two 1950s film stars with the slogan "Mind if I smoke? - Care if I die?".

The Apartment

When the taxi arrived at our new home, I was quite shocked because of the size of the apartment block. I'd been used to living on a farm with several buildings, and the livestock. Here in Russia I'd been told we would be in an apartment. Most apartments I'd seen were in American TV shows, and quite spacious.

I realised quickly that housing in Russia is quite different from Europe or the U.S.

The first thing I realised was that we would be living up in the air. The twentieth floor, actually, and I was told that the apartment was larger than a typical one in Moscow, because we were out in Arkhangelsk, where there was more space.

We met a woman downstairs, and she showed us to the apartment. We caught an elevator to our floor, but I think we were all wondering what would happen if it went out of service. The woman was fairly quiet but spoke quite good English.

She told us that normal apartments were about 30 square metres, but we were moving to a 45 square metre two-bedroom apartment with a balcony. By Russian standards, this was well above average.

She showed us along the corridor and explained about the extra door in the corridor which was locked at night. It wasn't like a normal door, more like a metal gate. She explained it was added security and ensured that only the right people would be in the corridors.

She showed us the camera on the wall, which was linked to the entry phone system. "Extra security," she said.

It was so different from on the farm where we'd leave most of the doors unlocked and could tell if we had visitors right from when they came in through the main gate.

Pabbi must have been well thought of. When we walked into the apartment, I was also very surprised. I had expected it to be somehow "homely", but it was very modern and sleek. It didn't look as if anyone had lived there before. There was a washing machine which still had the stickers on it from the shop. There was a very large window in the lounge area, which looked out towards the water, although it was a couple of blocks to the shoreline.

If this apartment was in Reykjavik, it would have been very expensive. The kind of place that bankers lived.

I looked at Mamma and for the first time in ages I saw her smile. Pabbi looked relieved, too. I don't know if it is just because we had arrived, or whether they were also worrying about where we would live.

Now, compared with our kitchen on the farm, the kitchen here was small, but it had all the essential items.

A hob, oven, microwave and even a dishwasher. They were all condensed into a small space, but somehow it didn't matter because they looked somehow 'cool'.

Then we looked at the two bedrooms. They were both almost the same size, although one had better windows, that went from floor to ceiling and let in lots of light. It looked as if the glass opened and there was access to the same balcony that went around to the lounge too.

I guessed that's where my parents would go. The other room was a similar size, but the smaller window looked out across the city and I could see the sea. It had a built-in storage cupboard. Big enough that I could stand up inside of it.

Then the bathroom had a large bath and a quite fancy looking shower. Along one wall ran a huge mirror and some lights that were hidden behind it and came on when we flipped a switch. It was like something from Hollywood.

The bathroom didn't have the toilet in it. Instead, there was another small room which had the toilet. It seemed unusual, but the woman said it was considered a privilege to have a separate toilet in the apartment.

We also didn't have the usual kind of lights. We had spotlights in the ceiling and shining down in each area. I guess this was another modern touch.

The woman said that the block was only recently built and that this apartment was brand new. She explained that it was one of the better apartments in Arkhangelsk.

I looked in the fridge. Someone had already stocked it. We had cheeses, vegetables, fruit and drinks. The woman walked over and took a bottle from the fridge.

"A small drink to celebrate," she said and poured three glasses of sekt. Mamma, Pabbi and the woman chinked their glasses together. I could tell that things had become more relaxed.

The Academy

It turned out that my arrival at The Academy was like any first day starting out. A new school and a new term. All normal. What I wasn't expecting was that there would be so much English spoken. I was taken into see the Principal. Professor Kuznetsov. He introduced himself and explained that the Academy taught a broad range of disciplines. Well beyond the normal range for a school or college. He called it the Dominion Academy a few times.

He explained that the Dominion helped keep the world in proper order. They were known for delivering justice into unjust situations, showing mercy toward human beings, and helping those in lower ranks stay organised and perform their work well.

I'll be honest. I could see a problem with this. How could I tell what was the right thing to do? Kuznetsov explained that the rest of the holistic instruction would help make this clear. He spoke mainly in English, but dropped into Russian for a few of the key terms. He said

I'd soon pick up Russian language alongside my Icelandic and English.

Once the brain had been woken to languages, especially in the young, then adding a new language should be a matter of patience.

надеюсь, что это так - I hope so.

So now I was subjected to the regime of the Academy. I was told to think of the other pupils as brothers and sisters. The Academy was outside of the town, and for the first few weeks I caught the bus from outside of the apartment. It stopped at the end of the drive leading to the Academy and usually a few pupils got off and we walked in together.

One of my friends there, Mila, told me that most people only came on the bus for a few weeks, but then moved into the Academy. They had dormitories there and usually the parents could get a special grant via the Academy for the student to stay on campus.

I could qualify under various schemes, including being an international or out-of-town student. Mila told me that in most cases from 2 to 4 students share a room, but if I liked I could apply with her and we could try to get a 2-person room. In a typical room there would be writing desks, chairs, closets, bookshelves, beds and nightstands. The Academy would have shared kitchens, gyms, recreation rooms, canteens, and laundromats. There are also locker rooms and bicycle sheds available. A security service operates on the premises.

I knew I was a little young for this, but I'd been used to doing my own cooking and laundry back at the farm in Iceland, so none of it held any fear for me. I would miss my parents, but secretly I thought it would be a much quicker way to learn the language and become integrated with the others.

I was soon mixed in with the others, had some friends and we'd help one another out with the schoolwork, which seemed to consist of a lot of teaching about military exploits of Russia and criticising the Americans. I couldn't help thinking the way America was described was very different from how I'd seen before.

Dormitory with insults

We agreed at home that I could start at the dormitory from the next term. Mamma and Pabbi were sad to see me go, but I would be back every weekend and during the breaks from studies. It was also only a bus ride away and Pabbi said he'd been given a full grant for my accommodation.

I was right as well. It helped speed up my language skills and also helped me make friends. Even after a couple of weeks, Mamma said she noticed how much more I was speaking Russian.

I didn't realise it but I was picking up the northern Russian dialect. We used to make the 'ch' sound like a 'ts', for example. I hadn't realised that there was a southern and a central dialect, with Moscow speaking the central dialect and most learned and literary types speaking the southern variant. It wasn't like some places where there were different words, just different pronunciations.

Something else about the lessons. They started early and went on for a long time. The morning was filled with learning to the head, but often the afternoon would include sport. I realised also that my time on the farm had made me very fit and that I also had good endurance.

The field sports were unusual. I had to learn archery, cross-country skiing (which was easy - I'd skied since I was tiny) and various types of rock and mountain climbing.

The instructor used to call me to the front quite regularly to demonstrate a new technique to the others. A couple of them called me *devushka fermer* or *derevenskaya devushka*, both of which meant 'farm girl', but I didn't mind. It meant I was known around the place quite quickly. Mila was a good friend to me with this though; she was Russian through and through and knew all the best insults to whip back at anyone.

Сволочь (*svolotsch'*) — The cat just dragged in this old curse word from the 14th century, and it just so happens to describe "what the cat dragged in"

Я бы вас послал, да вижу вы оттуда! (*Ya by vas paslal, da vizhu vy ottuda!*) — "I would send you there, but I see you came from there already!" Where is "there," exactly? A place only an idiot would visit.

Козёл (*kozyol*) — Calling a man a "goat" like this in Russian is a really bad form of insult and comes from old prison slang that referred to a snitch or informant.

Иди в баню! (*Idi v'banyu!*) — If you want to tell someone to get lost as dismissively as you'd swat a fly away with your hand, tell them to "go to the bathhouse."

There are a lot more, but I'm too polite to explain them.

There was one other girl in the Academy, a couple of years older than me, who understood Icelandic. Her name was Sofie, she was Norwegian, from Sunndalsøra and she spoke Norwegian, which is easy enough to understand when from Iceland.

The Academy soon split its students into different streams as they identified the strengths and weaknesses of everyone. I was put in the same group as Mila and Sofie. And that's when I began to notice a change in emphasis.

Love

"Not that she wanted to have sex with him, necessarily.

Only that she was happy to acknowledge, on this late-summer evening, that he was a man and she a woman, and if he found her attractive, that was all right with her."

— Anne Berest

Love's young dream.

Yes, the change in emphasis was because the top tier of the Academy was being fenced off for other duties. It was a subtle process, with various scheduled times that we could drop back into the more normal classes.

This Academy life spun through the years. I felt very established in the Academy. I even referred to it as the Dominion Academy. I knew we were, for all intents, being prepared to become Soviet intelligence officers.

Back in the town, my parents were quietly proud. They knew I was selected for special duties, and I think they were aware of what these were. Pabbi once saluted me, using his best, crisp Air Force salute, and I knew that he knew more than we would ever talk about. Mamma would always say how much she missed me, how I was turning into a fine young woman and attempting to give me lots of practical advice.

They had both adapted to the life and fortunately their one-time Russian language skills had returned. They appeared to be known as 'The Farmers' although Pabbi had actually gone back into a ground role in the Air Force at a local base. Mamma seemed to be happy enough, although I thought I could see she missed the farm and the animals. She had been offered a job at the Arkhangelsk Agricultural College, to talk about running a farm, and had taken it, although the environment of the college screamed 'run-down tower-block' more than farming college.

Then I had a chance to try out some of my newly gained skills. In a class above us there was a boy named Pavel. He was like most of the boys in the higher classes. They had a manner about them which was to behave larger than life. It was a kind of machismo which seemed to be the same for many of the Russian boys and men. In Reykjavik we used to call them hnakki - A *"hnakki"* literally means "neck" and describes men, possibly from the suburbs, that are so tanned that they're orange, have highlighted or dyed hair, possibly shaved on the back and sides, go to the gym a lot and listen to bad techno music. You mostly find them at the gym, at a mall, as radio station hosts or cruising down Laugavegur in a converted car with something like Basshunter blaring from the windows.

Pavel, wasn't like that. Sofie (from her Norwegian) said he was more of a *lattelepjandi lopatrefill*. We evolved to that term, by discussing Oslo boys that hung around The Thief on Tjuvholmen and then compared them with city dwellers in Reykjavik. The term literally means "a latte-sipping woollen scarf". It's used about mostly men to describe someone who is arty, left-wing, environmentalist and who lives in 101 Reykjavik. A derogatory term applied by more conservative Icelanders who live outside of Reykjavik, and a term also popular with the *hnakkis*. Other versions include *"Lattelepjandi listamenn,"*(latte-sipping artists)   and

"Lattelepjandi miðbæjarrotta" (latte-sipping city centre rats).

Well, it didn't matter to me, Pavel was my first true love and we were seen sitting around like moody teenagers everywhere *Å leve på luft og kjærlighet* (living on air and love) as Sofie would say .

It turned out that Pavel's father worked at the *МАЛЫЕ КОРЕЛЫ* - Small Karelia, which was a museum just on the outskirts of Arkhangelsk. It was an open-air museum which featured a collection of wooden buildings reminiscent of the olden days. In the right weather it could look very picturesque and had a big car-park for tourists.

Pavel said he'd got some tickets from his dad and could take me along. I went to see it in the snowy weather, and I was surprised to see how much it reminded me of Iceland and the farm. Pavel said we should stop off at his father's office there - I don't know quite what he did - but I think it was on the administrative side. We dropped around and I was getting all ready to say thank you.

Pavel's dad seemed to know too much about me. Pavel had obviously talked! Anyway, his father made conversation by saying that he hoped we liked the place. He thought it would be even better when there were a few wild animals roaming around. He told me there were plans to have a few goats in the place, which could roam around freely.

I mentioned that we'd kept sheep on our farm, and he laughed, "I don't think your Father and Mother - A pilot and a college lecturer, would want to keep goats now!"

I said, "Don't be surprised, we all miss the farm. Even me, when I walked into the museum it reminded me of the farm and where we kept the horses and the sheep."

I was also thinking Pavel was probably obsessed with me, judging by how much he'd told his parents. This might need to be the end of my time with a *Lattelepjandi lopatrefill.*

I took the information away and as it was Saturday; I was planning to go home after the day out. Pavel and I left the museum, and he accompanied me right back to my apartment block.

I thanked Pavel for the day out and he squeezed and kissed me a bit too much. I wriggled free as the elevator arrived. Now I had interesting news for my parents. I'd need to skirt around the Pavel boyfriend part though; I don't think I'd mentioned him to them.

So I told Mamma about the museum, explained that I knew one of the people running it through a classmate, and told her the news that they were thinking about adding some livestock as a tourist attraction.

Mamma didn't initially sound that interested, but I mentioned it again over the Golubtsy, when we were eating dinner. Yes, we'd gone properly Russian at home and were eating dolma, but instead of a grape leaf – we did like the Russians and made it with cabbage leaves. Cabbage leaves stuffed with minced beef and rice. I do not need to say, that the best sauce is sour cream, right?

Pabbi looked interested in the news about the museum and said to Mamma she should look if she wanted. He knew she still missed the animals and that the repetitive lecturing to teenagers wasn't as enjoyable as her time with the land. He said he knew that a lecturer sounded higher than a land worker job, but if she was keen, then she should consider it. He said he'd also be able to spend some time there. Pabbi had received a promotion since his return and was quite a senior rank and well remunerated on the base.

Well, it went to plan. Mamma went along to the Museum, met Pavel's dad and soon had a job to obtain the goats and start them on the land at the museum. Mamma had also asked about horses and Pavel's father was interested but had said Mamma should get the goats working properly first.

So, I guess that's my first use of influence to get something; I think it showed my ruthless side too, because Pavel and I split soon after the Day Out.

I did feel slightly sorry for Pavel, when I saw him out with the hnakkis. He still looked like an outsider and I was pleased for him when he met Galinka and could go back to hanging around living on air and love.

Of course, I was getting plenty of practical advice from the Academy, not least from other students, as well as slightly artificial classes covering varied life skills. Some of these were in English too, which a few of the others struggled with, but I never had a problem thanks to Iceland's television.

The criteria were strict. We need to speak Russian. At least one other language, which was preferably English. We needed a grasp of the Western culture, maybe by having lived for some time in a western country. It was hilarious when we had a lesson on western fast food, for example.

Then we needed to be especially fit, fast and strong. We needed good practical skills and an academic ability.

They were also keen to see how well we could hunt, I remember sessions on cross-country skis with a bow and arrow, like some kind of Hunger Games Katniss Everdeen although the full implications of those sessions weren't to occur to me for several years.

Then our schooling was taken up a notch. We were expected to understand a range of training that was reserved for FSB agents.

We needed to understand espionage, subversion and subterfuge.

Our topics included: "Psychological Methods", "Psychologically Influencing Foreigners", "Disinformation in Intelligence Materials".

They gave us computers and access to electronic manuals that covered much of this material. I thought most of it was outdated, with an apparent heritage in the 1960s to 1980s.

I was told that no less than Vladimir Putin had insisted that this tradecraft be provided to his new spies at Russia's domestic and foreign intelligence academies.

We had to practice some techniques on one another, and through this Sofie was eventually removed from our work stream- they said she didn't have a grasp for the technical stuff - but I think it was because she had a drippy cadet boyfriend messing with her studies. We were instructed to look into the documents to find lots of how-to guides, including information on "how to recruit and psychologically manipulate agents on Western soil," "how to root out enemy disinformation schemes, "how to infiltrate international scientific gatherings to recruit agents" and "how to outflank suspected agent provocateurs."

The methods had hardly changed from the true Cold War and had simply been modified to accommodate newer technologies as they came on stream. It accounts for how Russia can manipulate social media right the way through into the 2020s.

K

In my upper years at the Dominion Academy, I was schooled in KGB skills.

We were not called the KGB by then; the KGB had gone through a couple of name changes. First was the Federal Counterintelligence Service (FSK) of Russia, and then in April 1995, Russian president Boris Yeltsin had signed a law mandating a reorganisation of the FSK, which resulted in the creation of the FSB.

All the renamings didn't affect most of our papers and examples though. They were still stamped KGB and, I suppose, looked like they could have come out of the Cold War.

By 2003, the FSB's responsibilities had widened to incorporate the previously independent Border Guard Service and a major part of the abolished Federal Agency of Government Communication and Information (FAPSI).

I guess this was all political machinations behind the scenes, but didn't have much effect on the Academy, which would issue new organisation charts occasionally, but still carried on giving us old KGB Handbooks to read.

So, I was technically studying in a military academy. Under Russian federal law, the FSB is a military service just like the armed forces, the MVD, the FSO, the SVR, the FSKN, Main Directorate for Drugs Control and EMERCOM's civil defense, but its commissioned officers rarely wear military uniforms.

We were even given military ranks. Initially, I was a Kadet. I even had some epaulettes with a K to wear on special occasions. Parade Insignia looked pretty cool. Bright Red with gold stripes (of course) and a letter K.

Dominion

The upper years of the Academy were increasingly referred to as Dominion and became more focused towards the FSB training. We'd had a strong grounding in all the usual subjects. We'd all taken our *Diplom O Nepolnom Vysshem Obrazovanii* (Diploma of Incomplete Higher Education) a couple of years early. I said I thought the 'incomplete' Diploma sounded awful, but everyone said it was great to get this so young.

Then we were to study for the next level, where we would receive our Basic Higher Education. A *Bakalavr's* degree is equivalent to the Bachelors degree in the US or Western Europe.

Instead of the usual five years of studying, we were told that because we were on a compressed syllabus, we should expect to gain this after two years. And although The State Educational Standards regulate nearly 80% of curriculum content, the Academy had a special dispensation to change the syllabus.

I soon understood why. We were being given special training for our future roles as state operatives.

As an example, one of the classes covered "intelligence operational environment".

It described the climate for agents and operatives in a given country or other setting.

We were told that, as Marxism-Leninism teaches, in order to determine the direction and forms of any activity, all the conditions for that activity must be studied.

The environment for us as agents was shaped by the political atmosphere in the country; the administrative and police regimes; geography and demography; the means of transportation; people's everyday life; the system for foreigners' residence; the means of communication and the rules and traditions for socialising, the climate and so on.

Such an environment would affect the choice of the agent's forms and methods of intelligence work.

We were told that, despite still having KGB handbooks, the intelligence climate changes constantly, influenced by politics, the economy, law, with even geography and culture having long-term effects.

The FSB also looked at what social classes there are in the country; the government's attitude toward development and the socialist countries; the presence of progressive or reactionary forces; the presence of progressive elements in the government, civic and business circles; the local population's attitude toward the government; the existence of a peace movement; and the degree to which other capitalist countries affect it.

It sounded all-embracing and not something that one person was going to be able to change.

Then we wren told that a range of factors influenced the government and everyday life including political parties, individual political figures, major monopolists of the economy; the status of science and technology; the stage of economic development.

And in a more modern vein, we should look at the various media and propaganda outlets, especially in light of the changing social impact of social media. It looked at media funding as well as the comparative population's standard of living.

So, we were looking at the scope of intelligence activities in target countries through the prism of the FSB's own communist belief system. This seemed ironic in the modern and increasingly corrupt Russia as the gangster classes were moving into the positions of influence.

The FSB could study and identify a capitalist system. The major monopolists or a conservative government hostile to the Soviet Union and/or socialism; maybe a population influenced by capitalist-controlled media distrustful of communists will all conspire to make the work of agents much harder.

I thought some of this was outdated. It was like watching a TV show in black-and-white. It accidentally emphasised the work of the new order thugs taking power in the Federation.

Another course covered "The Intelligence Officer's Agent and Operative Dictionary," Over decades of interacting with the FSB and receiving defectors from the Soviet Union, Western intelligence agencies learned some unique terms the KGB had used to describe itself and its activities — the *rezidentura* or station in a foreign country; *konspiratsiya*, which really means "tradecraft" more than it means "conspiracy"; *razrabotka*, the "developmental" which is the art of luring recruits with a whole range of incentives and coercions, and so on.

This handbook is riddled with Marxist-Leninist ideology about class warfare and "progressive ideas" and a skewed understanding of the West.

For example, curiously, the term *oblava* or "raid" is characterised as a "specifically capitalist police activity," which is performed "especially at moments of political difficulties and during war at train stations, marketplaces, hotels, cafes, nightclubs and other public gathering places and are accompanied by the checking of documents".

It was like someone had played a couple of old movies and TV series to alien invaders and they had taken them to build their model of what everything looked like.

The FSB manual makes a distinction between an agent and a confidential contact — and the intelligence officer who is the full-time, trained employee who runs them.

I could see my destiny being pinned towards being the intelligence officer but operating with some laughably inaccurate manuals and briefings.

These sessions were easy for me, because I had so much of real life to balance the theory I was being told. I couldn't keep interrupting the instructors, so I kept my mouth shut, conscious that they were telling everyone else the wrong stories. I realised I'd need to remember these inaccuracies in order to pass the exams too.

Speaking of exams, there were some aspects that reflected the bureaucracy of Russia. Like having at least 15 types of agents - all neatly classified - and which I'd need to remember like a form of the times table.

There were the well-known agents of influence and double agents; the illegals and the tails and the informers.

Then there were the "agent identifiers" whose sole purpose is to identify people living under cover or hiding their identity under false passports. There were the "route agents" whose job is simply to follow a target on a trip abroad.

We were also supposed to learn American codes too, like "DP" (displaced person) or "G2" (the intelligence units of the US army).

And the all-important "cocktail" which is "a form of diplomatic reception".

Some terms have Western equivalents, like "safe house" and others seem specifically Soviet.

There was the KSP, *Kontrol'naya sledovaya polosa*, a 5-meter wide strip of land along the border kept regularly plowed so that the footprints of anyone attempting to escape from the Soviet Union became visible.

There are the "legals," which are the officially known intelligence officers in the *rezidentura* and the "illegals," the spies who burrow into foreign societies, sometimes spending years creating their identities, awaiting the signal to be activated.

Then there was the requirement for information gathering, so called "Information Work in Intelligence," The FSB was clear as to what motivates information work: "to reveal the enemy's secret plans and measures in a timely manner, primarily the imperialists of the United States, against the countries of the socialist alliance."

The information to be gathered includes documents on political, military, economic and scientific issues and also sketches, maps, diagrams, photos, models of technology, clandestine recordings and recordings of operatives' verbal reports.

But most of all, the FSB was interested only in secret information that would reveal enemies' secret plans and intentions. It wasn't interested in the mere recording of events, citations from the press or reports from people who didn't have access to classified information.

A lot of this dealt with physical materials, the kind of stuff one sees in the old spy movies on TV. It didn't seem to account for the move towards the Internet and data sharing. Nor, in those days did it seem to particularly interested in economically damaging information.

That all changed as Putin and the oligarchs came into power and decided that the Russian Federation could be carved up like a cake.

Another aspect was just how old some case studies were that we were given. Maybe more recent events were more sensitive, but I don't think so. They gave us case studies from the 1960s or in one case 1952, which meant we had to learn all about the prevailing climate of the time and the sometimes obscure players to understand the subterfuge that was played.

Then we had to learn about gathering Operational Backgrounders, known as sets. The "set" is a one-time operational activity involving the clandestine gathering of basic information and character references about persons or groups of interest to the FSB, and about the activity and features of the enemy's important facilities. Sometimes the set is made for the purpose of vetting information about facilities and persons.

The FSB gets these profiles to help carry out various operations, although often officers do not use them, citing them as unreliable. But then, the officers are often unreliable and don't complete the due diligence on the information supplied.

This course was interesting for the first-person narrative and variety of examples from a particular officer's experience.

When he was just starting out, he was casual and careless about preparing the profiles but then found himself in trouble when having to do them on the fly.

Despite an extensive, two-month study of public places such as museums and cafes, learning traffic rules and customs; reading local newspapers; and even striking up conversations with strangers, the agent found himself ill-prepared when he went to a foreign country.

We were given exhaustive lists of activities needed to prepare the operative who will draw up such background reports.

- study the assignment and clarify its tasks
- use official sources of information
- make a preliminary study of the target's area
- work out and document the cover legend
- preliminarily study the sources of information
- create a plan for talking to sources
- create a plan of action

When gathering information for the target's profile, there are the obvious factors such as where he went to school, whether he is married and happy in his family life and where he works but also his past residences, his close relatives, his political views, civic activities, attitude toward work, style of socialising, ways of meeting foreigners, financial status and sources of income, moral profile, recreational activities, degree of discipline, and so on.

As a cover for such detailed snooping, the FSB agent suggests pretending to be from the phone company, an insurance company, a notary/real estate office, a public opinion pollster, or a member of a society seeking supporters and donations.

I'm less convinced about the effectiveness of the last ideas, because I know when in Iceland we used to get the mobile phone companies or pollsters come around or stop us in the street, we'd just say 'No' to everything - mainly because they were usually trying to sell something.

Then there was the course on the somewhat ambitious "Mobilisation of Capitalist State Police Services in Fighting Organised Crime and Its Effect on Foreign Intelligence Activities," .

This analytical survey looks at the growth of organised crime in the West and the related increase in police activity in the capitalist countries from the perspective of its effect on the FSB's intelligence work.

Intriguingly, it doesn't mention the equivalent increased in Mafia-like activity in Moscow, nor the huge infrastructure created to launder money and run illicit operations in Russia. It is similarly quiet about the ways that they have redistributed money from the large energy and power organisations (to name but two).

Being in the right 'wrong' club in Moscow hasn't done certain oligarchs any harm.

The course still referred to older historical events such as terrorist attacks such as on Pope John Paul II and the assassination attempt on Reagan as part of "organised crime."

Modern techniques to skew politics in varied countries including the Motherland are all missing from the course and handbook. I guess too many people could go to prison.

The course does recount the features of organised crime groups and their methods (using fake documents, transporting illegal contraband and persons, renting safe houses, etc.), which are similar to the FSB's own methods.

I thought the level of detail wasn't so different from watching an American TV show like Sopranos though - I wonder what the authors were doing writing this stuff, and I wasn't sure it would really help the next generation of agents.

The training lists the actions taken by the capitalist police forces against organised crime, along with a description of the campaign against international crime groups. A separate section describes the (so called) new technology which police were using to battle organised crime.

Police now had better methods to identify people using their photographs and fingerprints, voice prints, footprints, DNA and forensics and making use of then-new methods of hand-writing and text analysis – not to mention lie detectors.

There was some practical advice. Criminals looking for safe-houses — like the FSB — look for apartments whose windows don't face on to the windows of other apartments, which have a telephone and an elevator and an underground parking lot.

Police look for tenants who have paid in cash for several months in advance; who used fake names; who never received mail at the addresses and had mailboxes that were always empty.

None of those techniques was exactly mind-blowing, but I suppose they just needed to work.

The course went on to describe various drug cartels around the world and the top cities for drug sales and their need for buyers, sellers, loaders, transporters, etc. Drugs are often concealed in cosmetic cases; in feminine hygiene items; perfume bottles; canned food; packaging inside medication bottles; inner belts; false bottoms in shoes or suitcases, etc. Drug dealers often swallowed plastic bags as well.

Once again, most of this could just as easily be seen by watching a good movie from the right genre. Later movies explain the techniques of injection moulding the drugs to the shape of electrical goods packaging, as an example.

The course tutor complained about how the capitalist law-enforcers' stepped-up campaign against terrorism is targeting not criminals, but revolutionary and liberation movements, partisan and rebel groups who are rightfully, in the Soviet mind, fighting imperialist regimes.

The training went on to say that crime was built into the bourgeois social system itself, because there is social inequality, discrimination against minorities and other factors that push people into crime.

Ironically, the equivalent corruption in Russian society doesn't get mentioned.

Murder, smuggling, and drugs are, at the end of the day, were, the presenter said, methods of expressing dissatisfaction with the bourgeois social system.

The Soviets were critical of UN efforts to combat terrorism as they felt the definitions were vague and the means of prevention problematic.

The FSB was concerned about automated systems for population registration involving telephone numbers, rent payments, payment for gas and electric services, car registration, hotel registration, registry of radio and telephone equipment and so on which were already being done electronically, enabling authorities to amass large data bases and quickly compare them.

At German customs, it was observed, an IBM machine enabled border guards to type in a name and get three responses: "not in list," "detain" or "put under surveillance."

I wondered if the FSB was simply jealous of these more advanced countermeasures?

The next course was one I'd forever regard with scepticism. "Using Delegations and Tourism for Intelligence Purposes,"

Soviet intelligence was required to maintain "high vigilance, timely detection and interception of hostile plots and intentions of the imperialist states, above all the USA and their partners in the aggressive blocs aimed at the USSR, states friendly to us, and progressive forces."

Tourist trips abroad and other kinds of exchanges with foreigners offered an opportunity for Soviet intelligence to gather information. FSB divisions can use Soviet tourist organisations to:

- study and cultivate foreigners, above all Americans in the USSR, for the purpose of drawing them into collaboration as either agents or confidential contacts, to use them abroad in the interests of political and scientific and technical intelligence and to penetrate the enemy's intelligence services;
- to obtain intelligence political, military, scientific, technical, counterintelligence information on the USA and other imperialist countries;

- to conduct active measures and promote disinformation against the enemy;
- to bring foreigners of interest to the USSR to the USSR;
- to perform special intelligence tasks from illegal positions.

The irony here is that the FSB didn't seem to get the memo that this was an outdated tactic. Famously, even on a recent deadly mission to the UK, two Russian agents cited a cultural trip to Salisbury cathedral to see...and then quoted a word-perfect rendition of the Google description of the Cathedral.

Of course, the Cultural exchanges went both ways, with Russians abroad and tourists into Russia.

Despite the increasing prevalence, Russian brides didn't get a mention during this course. We were all waiting for it to be mentioned, but I think the presenter was embarrassed.

I suppose the nearest we got to Russian Brides, was the so-called "Dangle" technique to expose something of great interest as a hook.

In the FSB teachings, the Dangle could be a much longer-term thing, sometimes extending to many years.

A complicated example described an agent who first worked for the KGB, but then was found to be double-crossing them. The story sound more like a long and rather tired joke being told in a pub.

It involves "Albert" a furrier and wealthy Cossack who fled to Turkey, then back to Germany where he had a romance with the daughter of a German Air Force general, and opportunity via an Englishman obtaining various items like paint, window frames, door handles and carpentry tools, at discount prices to supply a construction company repairing post-war East Berlin.
Albert then switches from construction to start a business selling carpets in Germany which runs for ten years before he asked by the KGB to do anything. When he is, he is already tailed by the Germans and finally picked up by the Russians.

It smacks of a comedy that was largely uncontrolled and without purpose yet is being trotted out as a worked example in the training. No wonder "Albert" disappeared.

By now, you'll be getting the impression that this training wasn't very helpful. Well, in one way it was, it helped show many of the flaws in thinking of the average agent operative.

I'll briefly mention another technique we were shown, that of 'False-Flag Recruitment,' Because of the worsening climate for intelligence operations, the FSB had to refine its false-flag recruitments. Once again it was far too complicated to be successful, with people tripping over their own and everyone else's shoelaces.

The simple idea is to put someone in, under another country's flag, to be the advisor or assistant to someone important. The FSB way is to have more than one person doing this and then complicated hand-offs and monitoring.

Easily this can lead to some double agent moments. The most likely thing is that the agent entering into these arrangements will later be compromised and end up being either blackmailed or caught and shot, often by the very same FSB who placed him in the first place.

If I don't sound too keen on any of these schemes, it is because I think they came from an earlier age and are just unsuitable for modern thinking.

I never dreamt I would be enrolled in any of them.

Officer

Not everything assumes a name. Some things lead beyond words.

Aleksandr Isayevich Solzhenitsyn

Krasimira Radka

By now I'd been Agnes Dobrayadoch for around eight years. So, what would happen next? Yes - another new passport.

I was through the first wave of the Academy now, and they had passed me with flying colours. My mother and Father were proud because I was given a new rank. Yes, I'd be a Lieutenant now, which was a proper field officer grade. OF-1. There was a ceremony for all of this, and my father gave me another one of his proper salutes. Mamma asked me to look after myself.

The ceremony was also the time when I was told about my first official posting. They wanted to send me abroad, but to somewhere that I could learn about military hardware. This was getting to be a long way from sheep, horses, piano playing and singing.

The Russians gave me another new passport. This one was Bulgarian. They said I would go to Bulgaria, to another Military Academy, to learn about weapons. It was The Vasil Levski National Military University and was right in the middle of Bulgaria.

The first time I went there I'd say it was closer to Bucharest in Romania than it was to Sofia in Bulgaria and it was also over 200 twisty kilometres from Plovdiv, the main airport.

I'd had to fly from Arkhangelsk to Moscow and then change planes to one to Plovdiv International, in Bulgaria. Then an army truck picked me up to take me on the last part of the journey, which was some 3,600 kilometres in all, from the cold of Arkhangelsk to the heat of middle Bulgaria. Sitting in the back of the truck, Bulgaria looked poor. There were farmers scratching a living, but they seemed to be using horses and carts to get around. Several of the towns we passed through still had giant statues of one-time Communist party leaders.

I arrived at Vasil Levski under the name Krasimira Radka, a Bulgarian national who had spent her whole life in Russia. This time, they didn't give me a proper back-story, so I made one up about living on a small farm in Russia. I just transposed all of my time in Iceland, which meant it was easy to have good anecdotes. I must have learned that in the Academy.

"Here we go again," I thought, as I realised that Bulgarian language may look similar to Russian, but it is completely different. I could read most signs and notices and understand about 80%, but I didn't have the right grammar to start talking to anyone. Luckily there were three of us transferred to Vasil Levski and so I had a couple of other Russian accomplices while we got to know our way around. The other two had not been given backstories either, and all three of us had new names, which were difficult to remember, when we knew each other from the Academy, with our original Russian names.

I decided that this was also a part of the training, to be placed in a foreign country with an alias and to then get along.

Most of the others at the Bulgarian Academy were also Bulgarian, although there were a few other nationalities mixed in. The true Bulgarians made some fun about us, saying that we were pretend-Bulgarians. They seemed to know about the Russians placing people in the Academy. They had a nickname for us - *Kifla* - which meant loaves but was their slang for selfie models. It implied that we were there to get selfies of ourselves standing by Bulgarian scenes.

We decided it was best not to have a slang for the Bulgarians, because it would only escalate. Andrei Raikov and Aneta Yanev were my accomplices during this time. We were all Russian, but when we chatted, we discovered that we'd all been somewhere else before the Russian Federation. Andrei had been in Finland and Aneta had been in Sweden. We began to see the picture developing.

Now this Bulgarian Academy was much more about Boys and their Toys than the Archangel Academy. My impression of Bulgaria was of an old-fashioned version of Russia. They spoke in an old-fashioned Slavic style and there were greater remnants of the Communist era left in the streets. But they knew how to set up a modern military academy!

We had everything, firearms, rifles, anti-tank, anti-aircraft, actual tanks. Both Russian and American. I was told that Bulgaria had skilfully played the NATO game and been given hardware by just about every country. No wonder it was such a good place to train. There were fields to play war games and laughably, if the weather was bad, there were also indoor shooting ranges.

I think I learned just about every type of weapon and also got a reputation as an excellent shot, and gun handler, which I reckon was because of my prior time on the farm.

The instructors all said my field skills were almost instinctive and several of the other class-mates grudgingly admitted that this *Kifla* was actually pretty good. One day Andrei, Aneta and I took our camera phones to the class and posed in front of a few tanks and other weapons for a few selfies. It only took a moment and there was a scramble from the rest of the class to be in the pictures. Even the instructor!

And that's when we seemed to get accepted into the rest of the gang. They still laughed at our Bulgarian - why do some words even get spelled the same but have different meanings? - And they accepted our flimsy stories about our past.

The year passed quickly, and I was soon on my way back to Arkhangelsk. By then, I would miss some of my classmates and the mild weather and I knew that when I got back home, they would probably give me yet another identity before releasing me for work.

PART TWO

Operative

*"Wear a black bra under your white blouse,
like two notes on a sheet of music."*

— Caroline de Maigret

Katarina Voronin

Well, I was right. I returned to Arkhangelsk to yet another promotion. I somehow jumped from one star to - wait for it - four stars on my epaulettes. They had made me up to Captain. It was a little unbelievable, but they explained that when I was a field officer on a mission, the grade was needed to ensure that other people did as they were asked.

I'd never really thought about the degree that I'd be dealing with the silent Russian bureaucracy until this moment, so anything that could help would be useful. On my dress uniform, the stars were arranged in a kind of arrow formation and now I had so much gold that the red stripe had almost turned into a line.

In all modesty though, I realised that the actual grades I'd gone through were OF-D, OF-1 and now OF-2.

When I returned, and we had the Defence of the Fatherland Day ceremony, I realised that I'd jumped much higher than some of my compatriots, some of whom still had their red epaulettes with the letter 'K'. They had to salute me now, which we all thought was hilarious.

Needless to say, Pabbi and Mamma were still as proud as anything of me, although Pabbi didn't salute me this time but instead hugged me and said I should be careful. Mamma looked at me with a tear in her eye as if she couldn't believe that I'd made it to this grade.

To top it all, I was awarded a PhD from the NMU in Bulgaria. The National Military University had looked at my work and it had been deemed good enough for the Ph.D. I was told by my instructors back in the Archangel Academy that one of the aspects of a good officer was that they had both rank and qualification. In practice, the Ph.D was window-dressing for my role.

Now my passport was once again Russian. I was called Katarina Voronin, and the passport came with its own back-story. It looked as if I'd already travelled to several countries, judging by the stamps in it.

I was told that I'd be sent on some missions to various countries to interfere with their smooth running. At first glance, this looked as if it was quite evil. But I'd been through the training and belief system of the Russian State. A first and most important implication is the belief among Russian soldiers that their country is already at war.

Some in the West want to draw a clear distinction between war and peace. The current Kremlin leadership does not see this divide. The message it has portrayed over the past several years is that Russia has been engaged in a defensive "war" against the West/United States, which remains intent upon preventing Russia from regaining its superpower status.

Using economic, information, diplomatic, and other means, the Russian soldiers believe that their country has already been "attacked" by the West/United States. Having repeatedly been taught that Russia is engaged in a defensive struggle against U.S./Western aggression, they honestly believe that theirs is a just struggle and that truth and righteousness are on the Russian side.

The prevalent mood in Soviet society after World War II could be summed up as "do everything possible to avoid another war." That generation had experienced the full horror of modern conflict, and even after the USSR attained superpower status, Soviet society understood that war should be avoided at all costs.

Nowadays, this sentiment may no longer be prevalent, particularly among the younger generation, who have been taught that war is a viable option.

Believing that their country is now under threat from the United States, young Russians are increasingly prepared to take up arms to fight against the "enemy."

I was told that my missions would be secret and that I would be denied if I was caught. Of course, the military gave me a good pay cheque every month because I was a Russian field officer, but I could not admit to the rank if I was detained. Only if I was working with other Russians and needed a command structure.

As Katarina Voronin, I did dozens of missions. Sometimes I needed a weapon, other times not. It was mainly work of a security nature. The thinking seemed to be that the men from the Academy would handle the offensive work and leave the defensive and security work to the women.

My first missions were mainly of a security nature. As an example, the Russian State was using money supplied by oligarchs to influence trade deals. I was along to ensure there was no tricky business during the summits. In the jargon I was a 'gun girl' sent into a 'pay-to-play' deal. What this meant was that some high-ranking official, maybe from the United States, was offered money - a lot of money - to help foster an advantageous trade deal for Russia.

The setup was straightforward enough. The politician or western influencer would set up a Foundation with a seemingly innocuous title. Either just their name or some kind of children's or health charity. Then the influencer would deposit a large donation. Maybe a million dollars, or more, into the Foundation.

An example was a Royal who "donated" $12 million to a Foundation in return for a meeting with a very senior politician. It later resulted in a $157 million weapons deal for an African monarchy. Pay to play.

In another example, a different senior politician accepted a $1 million check as a "birthday present" from an Arab state. The generous "gift" was followed by a 1,400 percent increase in arms sales to that Arab state, in a deal signed off on by the politician-run State Department. Oh yes, you'd recognise the name too.

I had to attend these meetings, in plain clothes carrying concealed weapons. It was to insure against trickery, double-cross, or maybe a scam from some kind of media hack trying to capture something untoward on camera.

I came to realise that the real ruling class in America are the largely Russian oligarchs. Putin's Puppet may be a moniker for the President, but it is surprisingly accurate too.

And I should mention the well-known case too, of a company called "Uranium One" which was sold to Russian government-controlled interests, giving Russia effective control of one-fifth of all uranium production capacity in the United States.

I was in the room during the negotiations, running protection for the Russian negotiator, one of whom had a sleazy penchant for women protectors. Since uranium is considered a strategic asset, with implications for the production of nuclear weapons, the deal had to be approved by a committee composed of representatives from a number of US government agencies.

Among the agencies that eventually signed off the deal was the State Department.

The Committee on Foreign Investment in the United States (CFIUS) comprises, among others, the secretaries of the Treasury, Defence, Homeland Security, Commerce and Energy.

As Russian interests gradually took control of Uranium One, millions of dollars were donated to a well-known Foundation between 2009 and 2013 from individuals directly connected to the deal including the Chairman of Uranium One.

I had to attend around a dozen sessions, spread all over the world, including on a huge Russian yacht in the Mediterranean. The sleazy negotiator had insisted that the female crew members wear sailor outfits for that one. I didn't, claiming that I needed my clothes to conceal the weapons.

Mysteriously these contributions from the Chairman of Uranium One were not publicly disclosed. Some of those papers disclosed by Julian Assange in the Podesto Papers, appear to make reference to this set-up, as does the New York Times from the era.

There were plenty of other sessions as a part of a security detail. I wasn't dressed up in a black business suit, nor did I have a curly wire headset and dark glasses, like some typical TV bodyguard. Sometimes the macho guys would think I was part of the laid-on entertainment, but I had various moves to handle that, the most extreme of which involved an ice bucket and elevated my status within the protection community.

Being Russian, that quickly got changed to an ice pick in the rumours.

I told everyone that my signature item of clothing was a pistol. And because I'd been trained at the Academy, I was increasingly referred to by my callsign Archangel-1.

Triple Threat

Now that's when things got complicated. I mentioned that my passport had other stamps in it. What I didn't realise is that Russia was operating three separate Katarina Voronins. We all had similar looks, so were getting consistently identified by any eyewitnesses. The problem was that the other two Katarina Voronins were involved in more hideous crimes.

I was mainly running protection, whereas they were out on assassinations and some forms of terrorism.

It was when I was pulled in by the British as the result of a small assignment to London, that I realised this. The questioner was fairly low-level and probably gave away more than he should have done. It was the first alert to me that Voronin was being used as a blanket cover-name for different people.

I was accused of a bombing in Amsterdam. Some kind of market square had been blown up, with civilian casualties. I was even shown pictures. I realised immediately that I was not even in Europe at the time this occurred. I had been detailed to go to San Jose in California and was running a security operation in the

San Jose Fairmont on the date and time of the explosion. It didn't take long to get proof of this, although I was concerned that it could interfere with another mission.

In San Jose, Russia was attempting to buy a source code for an anti-virus package, stolen from a well-known American software house. Fortunately, I could keep most of what was happening secret from SI6 during their questioning of me. It was interesting to see how quickly they let me go when they realised there was no case to answer on the Netherlands situation. If that had been Russian interrogation, they'd have left me on the hook for a whole lot longer in case I blabbed about something else.

But what I also gained from the SI6 questioner, was that they had an inconsistency in their tracking of Katarina Voronin. She was alleged to have been in Istanbul at the same time as Amsterdam. I realised at once that it was different people, but I'm not sure that the Brits ever cottoned on to it.

I also wondered if the other Katarinas had ever been in a similar situation and realised that there was more than one of us.

Better than Kifla

I didn't mind being called Archangel. For a start, it was better than *Kifla*, which I'd been called in Bulgaria. And I was getting so used to the constant name changes now, although I sometimes didn't look up when someone called for 'Katarina'.

Michael as an Archangel was Arkhangelsk's official Saint. He becomes featured in many of the major religions and is described as leading armies against Satan's forces in the Book of Revelation, where during the war in heaven he defeats Satan. Catholic sanctuaries to Michael appeared in the 4th century, when he was first seen as a healing angel, and then over time as a protector and the leader of the army against the forces of evil.

Most of the depictions, including those on the flag of Arkhangelsk, showed the Archangel defeating Satan, sometimes shown as a person and other times as a black shadow.

And that's sometimes how I thought that America was portrayed to the Russians. Forget the homely television programs I watched in Iceland. Friends, Malcolm in the Middle, 3rd Rock from the Sun. Instead, think of America like that black shadow on the flag.

The United States has been portrayed unremittingly in the Russian media as the primary source of much of the world's instability.

According to Kremlin-sponsored pundits, the United States deliberately sows unrest (often under the guise of liberal democracy promotion) to maintain its global hegemony. There's been several movies about this very act and it often features in the back-stories of American TV heroes.

At the end of the Cold War, the United States assumed the role of the "indispensable nation," disregarding the global security structures built after World War II. It was an early manifestation of America First, set to play out again in the 21st Century.

According to Russian commentators, because the United States controls the global money supply, Washington has been able to convert its economic advantage into sheer military power.

The Kremlin leadership often points out the wide discrepancy between how much the United States spends on the military compared to the rest of the world.

A key theme within much of the Russian information space is the belief that given their long history of repelling foreign invaders, Russia has experience, wisdom, and truth on their side.

The Russian media have portrayed U.S. operations in Iraq, Afghanistan, Libya, Syria, and elsewhere largely as failures, where the United States has only exacerbated problems in these countries.

Every botched American operation, every errant missile strike, every case of torture or criminality perpetrated by U.S. military members, and every scandal or leak that reflects poorly on U.S. Armed Forces receives the widest possible exposure within the Russian media. Putin and The Kremlin's narrative highlights both the lack of a comprehensive military strategy and what they consider as the hypocrisy of promoting American democracy via military power.

The American military is portrayed as being over concerned with safety and political correctness, while being soft and dependent upon a huge logistical tail.

The American soldier is depicted as unwilling to fight if he or she is not supplied with all the comforts of home, right down to the GI MacBurger.

At the official level, Russia remains a very traditional, conservative country, whose population regards gender equality and gay rights as both weak and decadent. We women trainees from the Academy had to take a lot of shit on the way through. It was satisfying to have four stars on my epaulettes and to look into the faces of some of those original *muzhestvennost'* boys.

The same sentiments led to the Russians coining a derogatory slang term for American soldiers, *"пиндосы"* [pindosy], using it to mock and belittle Americans in uniform. Pindosy became associated with stupid and ill-bred, yet cunning and dangerous people (and it was also a bit reminiscent of several Russian curse words). I'll stick to being called the far less offensive *Kifla*.

The superiority of Russian weapon systems is also a popular topic within the Russian media. Russian media are constantly claiming that Russian modern, conventional weapon systems "have no analogy in the West."

I'll reserve judgement there. I know when I was in Bulgaria, the US-made pistols and other weapons certainly felt more precise than some of the jangling Russian ironmongery they gave me. The AK-47 was the exception to this. Maybe it was made from old tractors, but it was entirely dependable. Of course, US-made rifles shot straight, although were not a match for some precision UN-supplied Swiss weapons.

The same braggadocio about supremacy exists in the nuclear realm. Over the past few years, the Russian media have repeatedly reminded their audience of the country's ability to transform the United States into a parking lot or as the head of Rossiya Segodnya news agency Dmitry Kiselyov put it, 'radioactive dust.'

Based upon Chernobyl, I'm less sure. We in Russia may be able to make the whole world into a parking lot. I'm less convinced we could do so selectively or without a lot of paperwork.

I don't usually wear my uniform, but I see a lot of young Russians now wearing military uniforms and prepared to challenge U.S. claims of dominance. Up to the highest levels, Russian military personnel may have fallen victim to believing their own propaganda as to the superiority of their military power.

All of this sabre rattling by the Russian army is great bait for US presidents. They wait to be goaded and to be able to show some position of strength.

The U.S. military has already begun to recalibrate and adjust to an increased threat from the Russian military and the Kremlin's associated information operations.

This increased focus on measures to thwart possible Russian aggression needs to be balanced by both an awareness of escalatory dangers and a willingness to cooperate where security interests align.

But where Americans might refer in Newspeak terms to 'democracy promotion' or 'concern for human rights,' a Russian would see naked aggression or geopolitical manoeuvring.

U.S. military personnel should understand that their Russian counterparts question U.S. claims of global dominance and will not be intimidated by threats of 'shock and awe.' Nor by the comedic posturing of an idiot nominally put in charge.

Given the Kremlin's indirect control over the major Russian media, they could be directed to adopt a more balanced and objective approach toward today's 'enemy.'

Nevertheless, despite economic challenges, there are currently no signs that the Kremlin leadership has modified its strategic objectives of weakening the United States and NATO. The American leadership is making much of this easy for Russia. Quite contrary to the prevailing climate, the oddly erratic current US-leadership is also challenging the NATO alliance.

Now that's the world that Katarina Voronin (and her two shadows) has to negotiate.

Assignments

*And I wonder when I'll be home again
and the morning answers "Never"
And the evening sighs,
and the steely Russian skies go on
forever*

Al Stewart

Krasnaya devitsa

After the time I was hauled in front of SI6, I was sent off on various other missions around Europe, maybe a dozen to twenty per year. I knew, now, that there were other copies of me running around, and I wondered if it would be possible to make contact.

I had to listen out on the varied news feeds for signs of what an agent like me would do. I also tried the social media sites, but after one incident they almost dried-up completely. A wave of cadets from one of the central Moscow Military Academies had all reached their passing out time. They foolishly celebrated by hiring a dozen big black Hum-Vees and driving them around Moscow in formation, while playing loud music. They also took both selfies and video footage of the occasion and then, with the stupidest of ideas, added a music track and posted it to YouTube. Very handy to help the west identify this group of budding agents.

The hierarchy went ballistic about this and pulled in the culprits. I'm not sure if any of them have been posted yet, or whether they are all still scrubbing floors in the Academy.

Because of this and a few other indiscretions, information gleaned from social media sites used by Russian military personnel has largely dried up.

There are still several other sources that can be exploited to gauge what military personnel are thinking. Besides the sites sponsored by the Russian Ministry of Defence (e.g., *Zvezda* TV and *Krasnaya Zvezda* newspaper), there are military-themed programs on major Russian media, as well as websites, blogs, and publications that reflect current Russian military thinking.

The Komsomolskaya Pravda Radio program, *Voennoye Review* (Military Review), provides a good example of current Russian military attitudes.

This hour-long program airs nationwide, Monday through Friday, and is hosted by two retired Russian army colonels, Viktor Baranets and Mikhail Tymoshenko (As cadets, we called it the Vik and Mik show)

It usually comprises a short introduction on a military-related topic with the rest of the program devoted to answering questions from the call-in audience. It's an example of 'only in Russia' really.

Occasionally, they will host senior military personnel who will also answer questions from a phone-in audience. As they record this program live, it often captures the raw sentiments of both the hosts and the audience.

Unlike most official Russian sources, the colonels Baranets and Tymoshenko have no problem expressing their open disdain and scorn toward the United States and its military.

Not only do they constantly repeat the Kremlin's assertion that Washington is intent upon preventing Russia from recovering its superpower status, but, in nearly every episode, they also find grounds to disparage how the United States conducts military operations.

There is likely a generation factor among Russian military personnel and how they view the American military. The older generation who were influenced by Soviet propaganda may be more inclined to embrace the current Kremlin rhetoric. Even though some of these more senior military personnel may see through the current Kremlin propaganda, to speak out could have negative career consequences.

And then younger military members have been exposed to the same anti-American, patriotic onslaught of past decade, but they may be more proficient in relying upon other, less tendentious media sources.

None of this filled me with hope, nor did it bode well for the next layer of administration to arrive in the FSB. Young guns with flippant attitudes, brain conditioned by the old guard. I decided that we Voronins were an endangered species.

Vzyatki (bribes)

The mission that tipped the scales for me was another protection one. This time it was the Russian Prime Minister who was involved in a meeting with a US administration representative. Russia was setting up sanctions and wanted the US to play along. A particular US businessman (guess who?) was in opposition because of a large deal he was about to fulfil.

Anyway, after the angry meeting, the Prime minister put up on his Facebook page that, "Any hopes of improving Russian relations with the new US administration are dead, that the current administration demonstrated complete impotence by transferring executive power to Congress 'in the most humiliating manner', and most notably, that the US just declared a full-scale trade war on Russia."

The signing of new sanctions against Russia into law by the US president leads to several consequences. First, any hope of improving our relations with the new US administration is over. Second, the US just declared a full-scale trade war on Russia. Third, the Administration showed it is utterly powerless, and in the most humiliating manner transferred executive powers to Congress. This shifts the alignment of forces in US political circles.

What does this mean for the U.S.? The American establishment completely outplayed the President. The President is not happy with the new sanctions, but he could not avoid signing the new law. The purpose of the new sanctions was to put the President in his place. Their ultimate goal is to remove the President from power. An incompetent player must be eliminated or at least positioned advantageously.

At the same time, the interests of American businesses were almost ignored. Politics rose above the pragmatic approach. Anti-Russian hysteria has turned into a key part of not only foreign (as has been the case many times) but also domestic US policy.

What does this mean for Russia? Russia will continue to work on the development of the economy and social sphere, deal with import substitution, solve the most important state tasks, counting primarily on themselves. Russia has learned to do this in recent years.

Within almost closed financial markets, foreign creditors and investors will be afraid to invest in Russia due to worries of sanctions against third parties and countries. In some ways, it could benefit Russia, although sanctions - in general - are meaningless.

Separately, Russia's foreign minister indicates that Russia retains the right to impose new countermeasures, adding the US sanctions are short-sighted, and risk harming global stability. He concludes that and attempts to pressure Russia will not make it change course.

The Kremlin also chose not to escalate the situation further. "This changes nothing. There is nothing new here," Vladimir Putin's press secretary, Dmitry Peskov, told the media in Moscow. "Counter-measures have already been taken."

From my protection perspective, I could see that the wheels were in motion to use soft power to manipulate the situation. The Russian click-farms were primed. There would be a massive manipulation of the American public over a sustained period.

No-one needs to know that this is happening and by its very stealth it could prove immensely effective. The Americans in the negotiation took another view. They simply wanted to lash out. Sanctions, Oil Pricing, Currency, Threats. It was in a downward spiral, and the pilot had lost control of the plane.

Alya Sokolov

Oh yes, the countermeasures were taken by the Putin administration. They were busy setting up click-farms around Russia and one was coming to Arkhangelsk. A click-farm was a large group of workers hired to click on paid advertising links, like, share, comment, subscribe, follow, or leave reviews for any social media page or account. It is click fraud that helps companies and individuals gain online influence.

Russia latched on to this for manipulating elections and stirring politics, long before it became popular with other socially engineered aspects of the Internet.

Click-farms are an example of astroturfing, which is a term used to describe online activity where people generate the impression that something is real, while it is fake. It is about generating likes, comments, views, etcetera to manufacture an impression of popularity.

People may use it to sell carpet cleaners or to put the next politician in power.

The click-farm in Arkhangelsk was in a building that looked almost identical to the Agricultural college where Mamma had worked, before she moved to the open-air museum.

For just a few dollars, people can purchase thousands of clicks, for example in the form of 'likes'. These clicks, this simulated traffic, is difficult to filter as fake because the visitor behaviour of the farms appears the same as that of an actual legitimate visitor.

In influence strategy, there's the popularity principle. "The more contacts you have and make, the more valuable you become, because more people think you are popular and hence want to connect with you'.

In other words, more engagement means more visibility.

I saw this as a decay of values. I was supposed to run security for people managing this click-farm, which was, itself, trying to make certain items popular at the expense of others.

The sales pitch went that buying followers or likes does not break any laws, but the practice is generally discouraged by social media companies. Social media platforms try to detect the work of click-farms, but have difficulty doing so.

In general, buying fake likes or followers is legal, but social media companies are constantly working on detecting the fake activities, and there is a chance the online marketing loses its viability if you rely on fake activity in boosting your visibility. Not so to a Russian.

Whether click-farms are legal is a different story. There are no government regulations that render them illegal but click-farms do breach a number of laws.

For example, Thai police discovered a massive click-farm in Bangkok and arrested the three Chinese owners. The perpetrators used about 500 smartphones and 350,000 SIM cards to sell views and likes for the Chinese messaging app WeChat. Three men were charged with working without a permit and importing phones without paying taxes. The fraud is punishable under law in China, and the choice to operate in Bangkok may have to do with China allowing only one phone linked to a WeChat account in to prevent fraud.

When I was running a security assignment, I went inside a click-farm. It looked like miserable work, sitting at screens in dingy rooms facing a blank wall, with windows covered by bars, and sometimes working through the night.

Click-farms operate in the dark - literally and figuratively and the working places are usually dark rooms without any daylight or windows for fresh air.

Since click-farms want to be active 24 hours a day, most click-farmers work in a three-shift system. But that system is not always followed, and most farmers work around 12 hours a day. This means that click-farmers spend long hours in dark places behind a screen.

Each click-farm generates thousands of fake accounts with fake emails, and for the names of these accounts they use a random name generator.

For just a few dollars, people can buy thousands of clicks. The reason people want to buy these clicks is because in our current media environment, social media are important spaces for creating trends, for being visible and gaining audiences. Besides that, social media influences what is visible in 'traditional' media as well, which further encourages the use of click-farms to generate visibility for oneself or one's cause.

In Putin's Russia, these click-farms were a way to buy approval. A way to tilt the game without other bloodshed.

After all the training in the Academy and spread over other countries, I could see my role being changed by the recent technology and the influence strategies of robot telephones.

So I quit.

I'd been training, or active in the FSB for half of my life. I'd run dozens of successful missions, with no blow-back. They tried to dissuade me but could see that my mind was made up. They told me about Katarina Voronin and her multiple roles and that I would therefore need another new identity.

I had to pretend to not know about Katarina.

I soon became Alya Sokolov, a freelance agent, complete with full passports and other documentation, provided by the very grateful Academy, along with an immediate retainer income, which was pitched at the same level as my enhanced military salary. They said they'd also give me the permanent agent name of Archangel, and that in return for their release of me, they would prefer to stay in touch.

I knew what this meant. Live my own life but be an agent capable of reactivation. I realised they had all of us agents on a conveyor belt. I'd just reached the next stage.

I told my parents that I was financially secure. Mamma was mightily relieved and said she hoped I'd return home to the apartment. Pabbi could see that I'd grown past it and was now wanting a free life, away from the parents. He understood. He hugged me and did one more of his best salutes.

We both knew that it would probably be the last one from him, as I became a civilian again.

Free will

Болтуна язык до добра не доведёт.

The tongue will bring the chatterer no good.

Russian Proverb

Freelance

I'd had good pay from the FSB and they also provided me with an ongoing retention fee. I soon realised that I'd need some additional income if I was to live outside of Russia. It meant I didn't need to work particularly long hours, so I kept my fee rate card set high.

I was still offered work and I think my multiple languages, cultures and hands-on use of so many weapons meant I was always in demand. I used my new name, Alya Sokolov, but became known by my code-name of Archangel. I didn't promote the latter, but it just seemed to follow me around.

I thought it helpful because it added to my status and had a superhero ring to it as well. It was kinda cool. I learned from other freelancers that it was best to get paid in hard currencies too.

I needed to base myself somewhere and initially thought of London, where I'd been asked to operate on several occasions. Then I was contacted by one of my girl friends from Archangel, who happened to live in Paris. Her name was Galina Nabrovsky, and we'd been an item in Archangel. She'd just returned to Europe from the USA. An ice skater; she did the freelance security work alongside it. Being a skater, she was also super-fit. She suggested that we should get an apartment together in Paris. It was in the 6th Arrondissement and close to Saint-Germain-des-Prés and Mabillon on the Metro. We were hidden in the bohemian part of Paris and could walk to Châtelet in a few minutes to get a metro to any part of Paris.

We both knew the situation as we moved in together and could look out for one another. Galina was already part of the LGBT scene in Paris and her friends were often a little wild when they came to visit. I didn't know so many people in Paris to begin with, and had to learn the language, although my Slavic-sounding Russian and my English attracted its own followers.

The amusement of our frequent visitors was that both of us seemed to travel extensively. We were often on assignments, and in Galina's case she explained it away as being competitions or trials for her skating. I didn't have any good excuses for my travel and thought at one stage of saying I was a photographer. I ran into an immediate problem with this because it was a practical skill that others wanted to use. Instead I re-awoke my singing and guitar playing and said I was also a musician.

That gave me the reason to travel, although people in Paris were also pressuring me to sing for them.

I knew I'd be cornered one day and quietly acquired a guitar to practice some songs. I mainly knew Russian and Icelandic folk songs and at home in Arkhangelsk I'd played these on a Balalaika. That's right, a three stringed instrument where two of the strings are tuned the same. It would take me some time to get competent with the guitar.

I started out playing *Krassnyi Sarafan* (The red Sarafan), *Kalakoltschik* (The little bell) and *Maja Galobuscka* (My little dove). Galina said I should learn to play Kalinka too, but she kindly got me a Beatles Made Easy song book from Shakespeare and Company on the rue Dupuytren. It also gave me the excuse to sing in English instead of Russian. And to be honest, I didn't have to play so fast as with some of those Balalaika tunes.

For the assignments, we both shared a handler. His name was Theo, and he was Belgian and said he was from Brussels, but we were never really sure. He could speak French and English but seemed to blank out if we spoke to one another in Russian. Most of his missions for us were security-related. Nothing particularly dangerous, and I think he underestimated our capabilities. Still, the money was good, and it was also cash, so we didn't complain too much.

One day, a massive parcel arrived for Galina, which we opened together in the kitchen. She hadn't expected it, and when we did finally open it, we both took a step back.

"It's a 511," said Galina. "A Swiss Arms 511 sniper rifle."

"Er - DID you order it?" I asked, rather stupidly.

"No - you can't exactly buy these on Amazon," she answered.

"Someone is sending this to me for a job," she said.

We looked at it some more. Many kilos of black metal, packed small into a shipping box, but unfolding to make a deadly weapon capable of firing a huge bullet up to three kilometres.

The instructions in the box were in German. It explained that this was the 600 mm barrel version and weighed around 13 kilos. The magazine could hold 5 shots and there were two mags in the container, along with a box of .50 bullets, which looked more like shells.

'Präzise, kraftvoll ist die SAN 511 für leicht gepanzerte Ziele, bis zu 3.000 m, einsetzbar!' said the marketing spiel.- 'Precise, powerful, the SAN 511 can be used for lightly armoured targets, up to 3,000 m!'

We looked at one another. Galina was fit and powerful, but I wondered if she could even carry the weight of the fully assembled weapon, let alone use it.

"There must be someone they really dislike," said Galina, looking at the unexpected delivery.

"Have you used one before?" I asked, thinking about the practicalities.

"Yes, I've used an OM50," said Galina, "They were like the predecessors of these. It doesn't look so very different."

"Yes, what were they called? The Nemesis!" I remembered.

"It's one thing to have the rifle delivered here, but quite another to use it," said Galina, "I'd need to get out on some land and trial it, calibrate it, that sort of thing. It's tougher to do that in the heart of Paris than it was in the fields around Archangel."

I looked at Galina. I realised she wasn't as proficient with weapons as me. I spoke before I could check myself, "I'll come along and help, if you like," I said.

I have never seen Galina look so relieved.

"Would you? Mon cher'" she smiled, "I'll have to bring the car around to the apartment."

We looked at the packaging. Contained within, there was a large-sized box to carry the dissembled weapon. We'd have to carry it downstairs and into the car without attracting attention.

The box screamed Dangerous Black Gun Box from every angle. We'd need to revise it somehow.

"I know," I said, "We can flaunt it as something to do with my act."

The next afternoon, we were out at Rue de la Roquette, in Brico Corner, buying spray paint.

"Pink?" asked Galina. I nodded, "And maybe something else eye catching?"

"Purple? Asked Galina.

I nodded again. We'd make the case into a part of a stage act.

"We still haven't heard from anyone about this, " said Galina.

"He'll be along," I said, referring to Theo.

That's when Galina's phone rang.

"Hi," she answered, she nodded toward me and mouthed, "Theo"

"...Yes, I have,"

"...I'll need more information,"

"...When?"

"...Where?"

"...Ok, at seven,"

She put the phone down.

"Theo's coming to the cafe tonight, seven o'clock. He says he'll explain everything. Can you come along?" she looked at me.

"Sure, I'll come," I was thinking about what I was getting into, but also that I wasn't sure Galina could handle it on her own.

There was also the factor that Theo was a slightly creepy and usually sounded intoxicated.

We made our way to Café de Flore to be there for 7 pm. It was as busy as usual. A mix of locals and tourists on some kind of literary pilgrimage. We took two chairs and a small table outside on the pavement. We both wore sunglasses to help us people watch in case Theo was late.

"deux cafés s'il vous pla"t et une bouteille d'eau," asked Galina.

The waiter smiled and was away. Then a voice to the waiter..."Préparez ces trois cafés, s'il vous pla"t," It was Theo - he'd ordered himself a coffee too and was bringing over a chair to join us. He kissed us on both cheeks, but I thought he held both of us just a little too long. I could tell he'd been drinking.

"So, you received the item?" asked Theo.

"Yes, thank you, but we'll need to be told the purpose," said Galina.

"This is a simple one really, "said Theo, "Your role is to stop a car on the edge of the Seine. It needs to stop at a precise point, so your role is to, " he lowered his voice, " shoot out the engine with the provided weapon."

"Okay," said Galina, "But from what distance?"

"Across the river on the other bank. You'll be high enough to see the car in its convoy and yet close enough to make the bullet count. It only needs to go into the engine block. Whatever damage it does will be enough to create the confusion we want."

"Where am I shooting from?" asked Galina,=.

"It's a college; they are always people going in and out. You'll be in a lecturer's office with a river facing window. The shot will be less than 1000 metres."

He pulled out a map from his pocket, "You can look this up properly on Google, but it's around here," he pointed to an area on the map.

"Why it's so close to your apartment you could almost walk to it," he said, "but oh, you'll have that heavy piece of luggage."

"What's the point of shooting at the car?" asked Galina. "Is something else going to happen?"

"No," said Theo, "It's enough, we just need to show that the people in the car are under threat of attack."

"No one gets hurt?" asked Galina.

"No, no one gets hurt," answered Theo, "This is a precision shot to create an incident. That's all."

Galina looked at me. "I'll need support," she bargained, "I'd like Alya to help me," she looked at Theo.

"The fees were set for this assignment, but I'll see what I can do, I know this means a lot to the client,"

"Good," said Galina, "Let me know the outcome. Then I'll confirm that I'm in."

He smiled, "A pleasure, as always," he said as he stood to leave.

He tucked a 50 Euro note under his cup. Enough for all of our coffees.

Galina looked back to me. "Sorry about that," she said, "But I wanted to see him squirm a bit, I should have asked you first."

I'm in," I said, "Let's see if I can get paid as well,"

We walked back to the apartment. Theo was right, it would take less than 20 minutes to walk to the building where the rifle was to be used.

We took the weapon's carry box out onto the balcony of the apartment. It seemed heavy even without the rifle in it. We laid the area with newspaper and pieces of cardboard and sprayed the very manly-looking gun-box into a pretty pink colour, with a couple of purple patterns on each side. Then I applied a few cut out stickers which we'd bought in the Brico' to the sides. Little flying unicorns and clouds on a pink background. Very pretty.

"Okay, we'll let that dry, then we have a perfect 'hidden in plain sight' situation."

We'd decided to leave Paris the next day, to go north around 100km on the A1 to Forêt de Compiègne. It was also the nearest large woodland that we could find, where we could test the rifle without being disturbed. The other nearby forests of Haute Vallée de Chevreuse Regional Natural Park and Gâtinais Français Natural Regional Park were crisscrossed with so many roads and were so close into Paris that locals and tourists alike would venture to them.

We'd also worked out that if the test was successful, we could make a day of it, continue on to Reims, pick up some champagne and then head back on the A4 into Paris.

We both said we felt like we were in a Frederick Forsyth novel and were waiting for a heavily disguised Bruce

Willis to turn up. We decided against taking a watermelon.

The next day, we started early for Forêt de Compiègne. We soon found an area away from people and parked Galina's unassuming little Renault. We carried the big pink box to a field ditch. Then we had to build the weapon. I left it to Galina, who had it assembled in less than ten minutes. It looked suitably lethal once assembled.

Then we rigged up the rifle on its supports. Now to find a target. I'd brought some binoculars and spotted a tree in the distance. There was an overhanging branch which looked as if it would break when hit by a high-velocity shell.

I told Galina, and she took sight. There was a gentle breeze and so she adjusted the sights for drift. One squeeze of the trigger, a pause whilst the bullet travelled and then blam, we could see the branch judder from the impact. I looked through my spotter binoculars and could see that Galina had missed the branch but hit an adjacent area of tree. It had made a huge hole, where the shell's force had wiped through the tree's body.

"Wow," I said to Galina," That was so close, I think you've only got about 30cm of drift over 1000 metres."

"Okay, she said, "The second bullet is in the chamber. One more go," She appeared to concentrate and ever so gently squeezed the trigger. We waited for the bullet to reach the target.

Bam. This time the tree branch didn't just sway, it more or less exploded. We could see bark and leaves pattering to the ground. The branch had been cleanly cut in two.

"This is some rifle," said Galina, "It is a step up from the OM5-s"

"That was some serious shooting, Galina!" I replied. She'd done an amazing job with her second shot. I was less worried now about her ability to pull off the mission.

We were very aware of any passing people in the forest and decided we'd better pack up quickly now, before anyone spotted us or wondered about the distant tree.

Inside the car, Galina looked happy, but I could see she was still concerned.

"What is it?" I asked.

"Theo," she answered, "Can we really trust him? I don't mean about the money; I mean about whether anything is going to happen to the occupants of the car or the convoy when we attack it?"

"We've got little choice," I said, "But he knows that if he double crosses us or misleads us then he'll find himself at the wrong end our anger."

"Yes," nodded Galina, "Let's go find that champagne."

Next we had to decide on the get-in and get-out. We'd thought we'd be able to take the box to the room early and leave it under a pile of discarded cloth. Before we did so, we were going to load up the weapon with DNA. We did this by old-school tradecraft. We got one of those sticky rollers for getting hair off clothes and then ran it along a couple of metro carriages. Blech. We got more DNA than we would ever need. Galina got some surgical gloves. After we'd put the roller over the weapon, neither of us wanted to touch it again.

Then Theo called. A change of plan. We were not going to use the college and the room. He said he had found somewhere better. A hotel - we could take the rifle in as part of the luggage. We were both worried at these last-minute changes. He said it would help him with logistics.

It came to the day. Theo made contact. He told us about the timings and the car to expect. It was to be at eleven o'clock in the morning. It was part of a convoy which was to move east along La Rive Droite. From television, we worked out it was part of a G8 working party convoy. We thought it would be filled with special advisors rather than the top people. The revised room that Theo had told us was a hotel room on the Quai Voltaire. Easier, although the hotel would have security cameras.

Galina's LBGT Friends helped us here. In a nearby Theatre's tiny changing room, we were soon transformed into a couple of cross-dressed slutty men, which could have formed a comedy duo. Either that or *Une nouvelle amie* - at least the French had an understanding for such behaviour.

It was a sensible precaution. Instead of adopting disguises, the hotel staff would remember us as two cross dressers. The descriptions given would be laughable.

We checked in, carried our bags and the rifle to our top floor room, and Galina set it up. It was barely 500 metres to our target, across the Seine. The cars would move along Quai Francoise Mitterand, accompanied helpfully by some leading motorcycles.

I helped Galina set up a table and pull the rifle back so that nothing showed from the outside. The silencer on the end of the rifle made the whole setup look even more menacing.

"Shall I order room service?" I said to Galina.

"Ta Gueule!" she answered; I could tell she was not amused.

Eleven o'clock approached.

We could see the car making its way along the riverbank. There was a whole procession of blue lights. I spotted for Galina, with a pair of binoculars. I could see the car. It had a little flag on the front.

"Got it," said Galina, as she prepared the weapon. I could hear her breathing. Then Blam, a noise so loud it startled us both. She'd fired on the car. The bullet took a moment to cross the river and then a metallic shudder. The whole car was knocked sideways by the round. Neither of us had expected that. We'd thought it would make a clean hole in the front of the car.

The commotion of squealing brakes, sirens and even some further handgun fire made its way across the river. We knew we needed to get out and slipped into the elevator. Downstairs the hotel staff were looking out of the front of the hotel.

"What is it?" I asked.

"Don't know, a car crash or something. It looks bad."

"We'd better go the other way," I said.

We walked right from the hotel, along the left bank and away from the commotion. We turned right on Rue Bonaparte and were soon back at our own apartment. We'd shed a few clothing items on the way, into our backpacks. By the time we arrived back at the apartment, we looked almost normal, certainly not oddly dressed in a way that would attract attention.

Galina tuned in the television to 24-hour news. There was a coverage of the event. There had been an explosion in the leading car of the convoy. It had lost control and crashed into the sidewalk. No-one was injured, but there was to be an investigation because it had security ramifications for the upcoming Summit.

From our apartment, we could hear the helicopters gathering around the scene.

We guessed this was the desired outcome. They would move the Summit to another city now. The news was not mentioning the rifle shot. We reckoned that would come out the next day, when they discovered the weapon.

Theo rang, "Hey girls," he said, patronisingly, "Good work, that was a short Summit," he said.

"What was it about?" asked Galina.

"Arms control," said Theo, "They'll need some extra pages after that, I think."

"What about when they find the rifle?" asked Galina.

"What rifle?" asked Theo, "I sent in a delivery man to collect the package, just after you left the building. He said it was very pink."

"So, you've moved the weapon?"

"Yes, it's gone, as have your two small luggage bags. You were never there, aside from what they have on the cameras - and I think that might disappear tonight," he said.

We looked at one another Theo had used a big team for this operation. It must have been well-sponsored although he would never tell us.

"Okay - I'll see you at the cafe, with the cash," he said, "Ciao Ciao."

Instead of a sense of relief, we were both concerned about the twists and turns of this last piece of work from Theo and the way that he was information hiding much of it from us.

We talked long into the night but eventually decided that this would need to be the end. We'd both had some fun, but now Theo knew where we lived, we were concerned that he could turn us in as part of operations. We couldn't work out who he operated for, an whether there was any sense of duty or conviction driving him.

We'd, literally, turned into hired guns. "Gun girls," as we suspected Theo would describe us.

Next day we met Theo at the cafe. It was early, but he was drinking Pastis, so we followed him and ordered two Absinth. We could all drink aniseed flavors although ours were just that hint more rebellious.

"Hi Ladies," he said," Here' are the envelopes. I divided it for you both." He handed the envelopes across underneath a copy of Le Figaro. We noticed the front page featured the incident from yesterday.

"I'm going away for a while," he said, "It's become difficult for me around here. Don't expect to hear from me for a while."

With that, he stood, tipped back the last of his Pastis, bowed towards us slightly formally and left,

It spooked us, and we looked around the cafe, in case there were any signs of movement or surveillance. We knew that Theo was good at his job, so we doubted he would have been followed.

It cemented our decision from the prior evening. We would split up. We both looked at one another.

"It's been good," said Galina - she was speaking Russian. *"ochen' khorosho - luchsheye - moya lyubov'* ", I replied.

We knew the best split was immediate and without explanations about our plans. We'd swapped a cover email address for the future but knew this was most likely it.

The next morning, I woke up. Galina had already gone.

I hurried to the Gare du Nord. Eurostar to London. Same name, but different country.

Hot

You will not grasp her with your mind
Or cover with a common label,
For Russia is one of a kind –
Believe in her, if you are able…

Fyodor Tyutchev - 1866

Coin

London. I was living in East London. It was slightly cheaper than out west, and hilariously hipster, but with a more European twist than the west side, which was stuffed with Russian money and gold-plated apartment blocks.

I decided to lie low and not do any work for a long time. I had my income from the FSB and I'd also amassed plenty of extra cash from the various assignments.

I was living just off Brick Lane, so had Shoreditch, Spitalfields and the towering chimney of an ex brewery turned gallery on my doorstep. There was a steady wash of tourists and Londoners through the area and I often heard Russian, and even Bulgarian and Icelandic being spoken.

To my great surprise, I even discovered that there was a farm about five minutes from where I lived. It wasn't anything like the size of the one we'd had back in Iceland, but it still kept sheep, goats and donkeys, so I could get my occasional fix of city farm tranquillity.

I needed it after the scary news report about Theo. He'd been found in the Seine. The report didn't go into much detail, but made it look as if he'd jumped from one of the bridges.

I didn't buy the story and I was sure that Galina wouldn't either. I decided not to contact her though. The secret email was for a real emergency use, not just because we'd heard something from our last assignment.

I speculated that Theo had been too elaborate with his plans for that rifle job. He'd had to get too many people involved. The cancelled college room, the hotel, obtaining the weapon, the weapon drop-off, the pickup, the room cleaning. He was leaving quite a trail. Even meeting us in Café de Flore twice, which we'd both thought wasn't tradecraft.

If I had to bet, it would be the college room that was the weak point. Fixing it with someone low-level, hiring a room and then them getting greedy. Theo cancels and the college room owner trades the information to make some money. I'll mark that as unfinished business. Theo might have been creepy, had a bit of an alcohol thing, but didn't deserve to be betrayed.

I'd been in London for around three months. I was in the process of restarting my music thing and had been practicing singing and guitar with a few people I'd met. I decided it was better to be purposeful rather than scenic.

That's when I was contacted about an assignment. This was from the FSB, but I was quite suspicious. I decided that the longer one was out of the game, the more unappealing the offers. This time it was babysitting a couple of operatives in London.

The Moscow handler was as obscure about the mission as Theo had been. I was to go to two different locations in London and to extract van drivers, who were to be taken away to another location by taxi. The taxi was also one of ours and I'd be in it until I collected the van driver. I was told I would need to run some light protection for the van driver and that the area that I'd be operating in would be under a major disturbance. The assignment was to do the same kind of manoeuvre twice, within a few days of one another.

I knew it would be hard to turn this job down. After all, the FSB were paying me a good retainer which was allowing me to live in London. In addition, they would pay me a good contract rate for each job. They knew I was good and even referred to me as Captain Voronin, which was itself a flattering flashback.

I agreed, and soon found myself in the middle of a bomb plot. I don't know why, but a couple of non-lethal bombs had been let off around London. I think they were at UK Security Services buildings. I had to extract the van driver who had delivered the bombs to the locations.

That's when the plan seemed shaky. I talked to the first driver - in Russian - but he couldn't understand me. I realised he was someone local that had been hired and I had to go on talking to him in English. The taxi driver was another problem. He didn't know London. Anyone who has lived there knows that is impossible for a black cab driver. They spend years doing 'The Knowledge' so they really know the streets. This one couldn't even get us back to around Hyde Park Corner without referring to his phone's sat nav.

The same thing happened with the second van driver and I realised that if this was FSB, then they were running the rest of the mission on a low budget. What was worse, was that they let my name slip into currency and the next thing I hear is that they have pulled in someone with my name, from the Russian Embassy. I still don't know whether this was one of the duplicate Katarina Voronin's which Russia seemed keen to deploy.

I think the local handler was skimming the fees for the work. My contract had been agreed directly with FSB in Moscow- who didn't tell much but at least were honest with the payment. The local guy seemed to run his own books. No great maths brain to work out he was pocketing some of the assignment fee.

His mistakes risked getting me into deep trouble, because there were all kinds of additional allegations against Voronin, all across the time that I was living in Paris. One of them included the bombing of a Dutch marketplace, which seemed indiscriminate, and not even something that the FSB would arrange.

It turned out to be linked with some kind of cyber currency laundering scheme, which the Russian government and bank were trying to chase down. I was simply caught up in the middle of it. It made me think twice about taking this kind of bluebird mission in the future.

And even as Alya Sokolov, I still hadn't met any of the other Katarina Voronins.

Amelia Brophy

I flipped my identity again after that situation. I asked FSB to provide me with two further identities as a consequence of the mess from that last operation.

They agreed, and I was given an Irish identity as Amelia Brophy and another English one as Christina Nott.

I decided to put Christina's identity away and to only use Amelia for the next couple of years. If I was kept out of the limelight during this time, then things should stabilise.

I hadn't allowed for the changes in Russia. The oligarchs were taking increasing control of the administration and Putin's friends were getting into high places in most of the administration. Putin was privately saying that he'd fix it so he could stay in power for many years.

So it didn't surprise me too much when an organised crime lord made contact with me. He was Russian and had cousins in the FSB and a son who was working his way through the Kremlin's Academy in Moscow.

I was cornered and had to do what they wanted. It was some kind of industrial scale money laundering and they wanted me to help manage the loose ends. It turned out that an American Colonel Manners and bunch of London-based Brits were digging around inside the processes.

I was tasked with some runner operations within this situation which I could only see leading to a big show-down between the Russians and some Arab based interests. The Russians owned the pipelines, and the Arabs provided much of the oil. What could possibly go wrong? Well, plenty it turned out, what with careless botched assassins waving guns in London and even a restaurant bomb, which blew a big hole in a street in Knightsbridge.

I had to figure out a way to escape from this mayhem. It was clear to me that the disciplines instilled back in Archangel were not being followed by these Russian gangsters. If anyone could wave a golden gun, then it would be these bling-laden people.

So I made my escape from the gangsters, and just kept driving north. Ironically, when I reached Manchester, I decided I could do worse than to take a flight back to Kevlavik. Yes, I would lie low in Iceland for a while. I couldn't use the Amelia Brophy passport there though, for fear of being traced. I'd have to go into Iceland as Christina Nott.

PART THREE

It's all about the music

I come completely from the mountains

(Ég kem alveg af fjöllum)

Icelandic saying

Christina Nott

It was many years since I'd been in Reykjavik, and yet the vibe around Laugavegur was still the same. Amusingly, there were also still Hnakki driving noisy cars around nowadays playing Aviccii and SHM instead of Basshunter.

And there was something really comfortable about being able to talk in Icelandic, although I noticed some language drift as new phrases had replaced the old. Fortunately, my hipster London speak could override most of it and everyone wanted to get some modern English idioms into their chat.

This is really the time when I decided to do what Galina had done so well in the Paris and the USA. She'd create a proper second realistic career. No, I didn't want to become an ice skater, but I thought I could reignite my music.

I knew I was too old for the full-on pop scene, but it shouldn't deter me from a more niche position. I used to know one of the members of a well-known band who was now on the local Reykjavik Council. I went along to a council meeting to meet him and he remembered me from the farm and my piano playing. I think as children we had formed a mini quartet with two others. He played the trumpet and sang, although in those days it was mostly Icelandic folk tunes.

I told him about my plans, and he looked me up and down.

"Well, you've got the packaging," he said, matter of factly. I blushed at this unexpected compliment.

Then we both laughed. "Don't worry," he said, "I got married a couple of years ago."

"Then we'd both better worry," I said regaining my composure.

"Look, I can put you in touch with some people in the business, but it's cut-throat."

"No," I said, "It can't be as cut-throat as where I've just come from."

"Can you sing? - Maybe play an instrument still?" he asked.

"Yes to both, I can sing, play guitar and piano, oh and Balalaika, " I answered.

"Huh?" he said to the last one.

"Yes, you'd be surprised how fast it can become."

That got me started on the path towards what became my singer/songwriter phase. I could write songs about things that had happened without giving too much away.

EST (Electro-shock-therapy), was about a relationship. *"You've always been high-voltage; You know how to rock the room"*

Then there was French Kiss-off, which was about the break-up with Galina, *"No letter on the table; No lipstick mirrored why. No bitter final reasoning; Couldn't tell what made her fly."*.

And the one overt one about the line of business, *"Not saying it's the Barbie full of pins, not sayin' it's your screams. Not sayin' that revolver shouldn't be; But some of ya, Some of ya, Some of ya stuff - ain't normal"*

There was even a song about being a Hitman.

To be honest, I was told to dial it back a bit after these early songs. They wanted me to be more disco and less punk. I realised that we can't all be Björk Guðmundsdóttir from Iceland and I had to make plans to return to London if I was to make a go of the music angle.

This became something of a lost time for me though. I did get to London, become involved in the music scene, with follow up invitations to recording studios in Manhattan and then Amsterdam.

One of my security assignments had led me into contact with a group of Brits who seemed to be running a media enterprise. I decided to make contact with them, under my Christina name, to see if they could help get me further along.

Sure enough, they had no recollection of my involvement in a previous assignment, but they did have music contacts via someone called Clare, media contacts via Jake and a strong technical capability though Bigsy.

Clare took me out to a London pub one day and tried to warn me about the business. She said that their company - called The Triangle - could try to get me some gigs or a recording contract, but that I should be very careful that I didn't get conned or ripped off by someone along the way.

She gave me a copy of Elmore Leonard's book "Be Cool" and said that it was a fair representation of the business.

Clare seemed to be pretty straight-talking and we became good friends. They did get me some gigs, but I came to realise there was an awful lot more to their enterprise than at face value. I could not tell them about my special skills, although I did feel, from time to time, that they could really have used them.

I soon realised that 'Be Cool' was right though. Elmore Leonard's L.A. music scene was incredibly tough. Most people lied and were trying to get money from your purse. The Russian hitman in Elmore Leonard's portrayal was a little suspect though. I don't think he would have talked so much.

But Elmore got it right about the music business racket. Through Clare, I did get a couple of club tunes out as an EP, which was played around the dance scene, but then I was offered a recording contract in Amsterdam.

Clare's advice was, "It's good money but there's probably a scam in it somewhere. And don't agree to take any packages anywhere."

I flew from London to Amsterdam, slightly wary, not least in case it was a trap by someone from the past. It wasn't. They wanted me to sing on an album. It turned out to be a Factory-Pop gig, where they wanted other artists to copy the real artists, so that the music could be played royalty-free. It's died out since streaming but used to be a big business in the Netherlands. That was the scam. Ripping-off real artists.

Of course, I didn't realise this until I was in Amsterdam, and so I spent a couple of weeks going into a studio behind Damrak, where I was hit upon by stoner-musicians while I copied vocals from well-known artists. The tunes were then going to be played as the backing to car-commercials or in lobbies and coffee-bars as background music.

I stuck with it though, because I learned a lot about the recording process and could see a few of the real professionals in action, who could get a vocal down on one or two takes.

I stayed in a small room close to Damrak for the duration of this, collected my money and went back to my London flat.

I told Clare and the others about this. I think they were upset for me, and at one point I think they were going to dip into their company's funds to pay me some more money. I stopped them from doing this, but I couldn't tell them where I was getting my extra income from.

Today

Well, that brings me almost up to the moment. I've had to leave London again now. I helped Clare and the others on one of their side-projects. It involved me performing at a gig where all kinds of mayhem was unfolding.

I think I was identified there by an American Colonel. Chuck Manners, I think, was his name. A real hard player who we'd watched from the FSB for years. He knew me as Amelia Brophy, but it won't take him long to follow the trail back to Katarina Voronin.

So now I've had to change identity and country yet again, to shake off the last identification. It means I'm indebted to the FSB again.

It suits them to be able to deploy me occasionally now. They've given me my new passport and papers. They still refer to me as Captain, but it's gone back to Captain Dobrayadoch. I hope they are burning the trail to the more recent name, although I still get referenced inside FSB as Archangel.

You won't be getting any more music from me, just a few written-down song lyrics and the album produced by the gang and called "Singularity'. Ironic titling, maybe?

I won't be saying my next name here. I've a whole planet to explore, although I think somehow, I'll be somewhere that means I can still receive my pay cheque from the FSB.

Signing out, Archangel. x x x

RAVEN

Book 2 of the Archangel Trilogy

Ed Adams

a firstelement production

Raven

First published in Great Britain in 2020 by firstelement
Copyright © 2020 Ed Adams
Directed by thesixtwenty

10 9 8 7 6 5 4 3 2

The Owens Edition

A CIP catalogue record for this book is available from the British Library.

ISBN 13 : 978-1-8380146-7-4

eBook ISBN : 978-1-8380146-8-1

Printed and bound in Great Britain by Ingram Spark

rashbre
an imprint of firstelement.co.uk
rashbre@mac.com

Mailing list: https://mailchi.mp/9f0b30712620/ed_adams

THANKS

A big thank you for the tolerance and bemused support from all of those around me. To those who know when it is time to say, " step away from the keyboard!" and to those who don't.

To thesixtwenty.co.uk for direction.

To the NaNoWriMo gang for the continued inspiration and encouragement.

To John, for many hours of intense scrutiny, whilst I was delicately scoffing asparagus.

To the symbol seers and adepts everywhere.

To my compadres across the years, in Austin, Texas

And, of course, thanks to the extensive support via the random scribbles of rashbre via http://rashbre2.blogspot.com and its cast of amazing and varied readers whether human, twittery, smoky, cool kats, photographic, dramatic, musical, anagrammed, globalized or simply maxed-out.

Not forgetting the cast of characters involved in producing this; they all have virtual lives of their own.

And of course, to you, dear reader, for at least 'giving it a go'.

Books by Ed Adams include:

Triangle Trilogy		About
1	The Triangle	Dirty money? Here's how to clean it
2	The Square	Weapons of Mass Destruction – don't let them get on your nerves
3	The Circle	The desert is no place to get lost
	The Ox Stunner	The Triangle Trilogy – thick enough to stun an ox
		(all feature Jake, Bigsy, Clare, Chuck Manners)
Archangel Trilogy		
1	Archangel	Sometimes I am necessary
2	Raven	An eye that sees all between darkness and light
3	Card Game	Throwing oil on a troubled market
	The Archangel Trilogy	the above three in one heavy book.
		(all feature Jake, Bigsy, Clare, Chuck Manners)
Stand-Alone Novels		
1	Coin	Get rich quick with Cybercash – just don't tell GCHQ
2	Pulse	Want more? Just stay away from the edge
3	Edge	Power can't be left to trust
	Now the Science	the above three in one heavy book.

About Ed Adams Novels:

Triangle Trilogy		About
	Triangle	Money laundering within an international setting.
	Square	A viral nerve agent being shipped by terrorists and WMDs
	Circle	In the Arizona deserts, with the Navajo; about missiles stolen from storage.
	Ox Stunner	the above three in one heavy book.
		(all feature Jake, Bigsy, Clare, Chuck Manners)
Archangel Trilogy		
	Archangel	Biographical adventures of Russian trained Archangel, who, as Christina Nott, threads her way through other Triangle novels.
	Raven	Big business gone bad and being a freemason won't absolve you
	Card Game	Raven Pt 2 – Russian oligarchs attempt to take control
	The Archangel Trilogy	the above three in one heavy book.
		(all feature Jake, Bigsy, Clare, Chuck Manners)
Stand-Alone Novels		
	Coin	cyber cash manipulation by the Russian state.
	Pulse	Sci-Fi dystopian blood management with nano-bots
	Edge	World end climate collapse and sham discovered during magnetite mining from Jupiter's moon Ganymede
	Now the Science	the above three in one heavy book.

Raven

RAVEN
Table of Contents

PART ONE

The Eye of Providence is a symbol,
having its origin in Christian iconography,
showing an eye often surrounded by
rays of light or a glory
and usually
enclosed
by

a
triangle.

It represents
the concept of
divine providence.

The setup

Among all you angels is a champion angel
Among all you devils there's a free soul
Up from the disenfranchised the engine cries
Up from the circle there's a hole

Benjamin Knox Miller / Jeffrey Carl Prystowsky /
Jocelyn Jager Adams

Providence at a top table in London

It was a busy reception. Drinks, canapés, a few celebrities, including some A-listers. Piano and guitar songs from a well-known pop-idol. An inspirational speech from a member of the Chiefs rugby team.

Off to the side was a compact room. In different times they would have filled it with cigar smoke. Nowadays just the dark-suited men.

"We're going to need Brant, " said one.

The others nodded.

"Make it look like a ship of fools, " said a second voice.

"Yes, it is my little indulgence, " said the first voice, " We can rotate the staffing after we have positioned the deals."

"Who can we use to position it?" asked the second voice.

"Someone who hasn't sipped at Mimir's Well. Someone we can control. A puppet."

"I have the very person, a clean skin, " said a third voice.

"Well, let's invite him into the club." Said the first voice, as if concluding the discussion.

Rammed

The small bar was crowded, yet they'd found a table.

Corporate away day and everyone had come to the same place, some spilling onto the Croisette.

"We'll be moving on?" asked Rizzo.

Lieke nodded, " Yes, this place is rammed with the sales boys, breathe in the testosterone."

There was a crash behind them as two suited men grappled with arm-wrestling, for some kind of bet. In another corner there was a loud quiz betting machine with around a dozen people crowded around it.

A few loud shouts across the noise - orders for drinks. And two intense people in front of them talking about trading algorithms.

"Ladies, " said a voice, " May I join you?" A smiling suited repster was walking towards them.

"We were just leaving, " smiled Rizzo back. Rizzo - Elena Ricci, was from the Milan office. This junket to the south of France was an eye-opener in more ways than one. It was supposed to be to entertain and educate clients, but by mid-evening had turned into a corporate drinking fest.

Lieke stood and put on her leather jacket. She nodded towards the door of the bar. Rizzo picked up her bag and joined Lieke. The charm of the suit in front of her hadn't worked, but she noticed he was also calling to a couple of his mates who were in the process of taking over the table they had vacated.

Lieke shuddered outside the bar. "We work for that organisation, yet the main sales force are like predatory animals, " she said.

Rizzo nodded agreement, " Yes, do you think we'll become like that if we stay with the company long enough?"

"I hope not, " answered Lieke, " It's a scary thought."

"Although they always say that without those people we'd not get paid because we'd have no clients, " answered Rizzo. She was looking along the road for a taxi and at just that moment one appeared.

"Shall we go back?" she asked Rizzo.

"Yes, " replied Rizzo, " It'll be quieter at the hotel."

They gave their instructions to the taxi driver. Lieke spoke French to the driver, although she wondered if his grasp of the language was less than hers.

The driver sat on a wooden massage seat cover and took the long way back to the hotel, along the Promenade missing the nearest turn-around and driving significantly further before changing direction.

'No cards', it said inside the taxi, 'Cash only'

They arrived back at the Carlton, a few minutes away.

"Quatorze euros, " said the taxi driver.

Lieke handed over a twenty euro note.

"No change, " said the driver, in English.

Rizzo was onto him. She called over the doorkeeper from the Carlton.

"He's got no change and wants to charge us an extra six, " she said in English.

The liveried doorman bent down towards the driver's window. The driver looked under the passenger seat and magically found his leather bag with loose change.

He counted out three two-euro coins.

Lieke took the money and climbed out.

"Godverdomme, " she said in her native Dutch, " wat een plek, geramde bars en overvallers. Klootzakken."

Rizzo didn't understand but laughed. "I agree, she said, " With all of that."

Carlton

"One more?" asked Rizzo.

"Yes, it's still early, " said Lieke.

The ambiance inside the Carlton was altogether different from the rammed bar they had left. They spied a table and sat down. Cool prestige emanated from the bar and its clientele.

"I can understand why Grace Kelly used to come here, " said Rizzo.

"Hi Lieke, " said a voice behind them. They turned to look.

Lieke immediately stood and smiled, " Hey Nelson, I didn't expect to see you here."

They kissed one another on the cheeks, in the Dutch way. He looked to Rizzo, " I don't think we've met?"

"Hi, " said Rizzo, " Elena Ricci, from the Milan office. I think we've met by phone and email!"

"Hi Elena, it's great to put a face to a name! And thank you - from me personally - for those complicated predicaments you've saved me from in the past!"

"Do you mind if I join you? I've been deserted by the gang. They all wanted to go to some rowdy bar along the Croisette."

"Please do, it'll be good to hear what's happening in London. How's the old bosses Liz and Ron getting on?" asked Lieke.

"Uh, they're doing fine, since they moved on, they've just set up a new shell - The Summerhouse. I think they are filling it with artworks and some kind of trainer project, " answered Nelson.

"Trainer project?" asked Lieke.

"Training, yeah, you know the kind of thing. Expensive and many types, if I remember correctly, " replied Nelson, " I'd forgotten that you knew them."

The waiter appeared, " Gin and tonic, " said Lieke.

"G-Kelly, " asked Rizzo.

"You know what, " said Lieke, " Make that G&T a Bombay Ultimate."

"Er - I'll have a San Pellegrino, " said Nelson.

"Saving yourself?" asked Lieke.

"Kind of, " said Nelson, " I was with a client earlier and we drank too many Manhattans. It's a real killer."

"That and the mad prices in here, no wonder it's quiet. I could fly to Monaco by helicopter for the price of a round of drinks, " said Rizzo.

"That's why I swapped from a G&T to a cocktail, " said Lieke, " Might as well get the money's worth!"

"Don't worry, we'll charge them to my room, " said Nelson, " Time to get something back."

He grimaced and then leaned forward, " You haven't heard then?"

"No, what's happened!"

"What will happen more like."

"There's a few planning sessions running here alongside the main event. It turns out that part of the company is to be hived off to another one."

"I'm in the piece that is moving."

"We are no longer Raven; we'll be Brant Holdings."

"Brant?" asked Lieke, " I've never heard of them?"

"Exactly, " said Nelson, " It's a file and forget manoeuvre."

"What? They are shifting people out of the way?" asked Rizzo, " That's surely not legal, workers' right and all that."

"No, they have brought in one of those specialist firms to hack through the structure."

The drinks arrived.

"Wow, these look good, " said Lieke, " Er even your big bottle of San Pellegrino looks good with that glass, " she nodded towards a glass chilled with ice. See, they have given you two glasses, so that one can be chilled and then you can tip the ice into the other one!"

They chinked glasses and said, " Cheers!"

"Which piece is going then?" asked Lieke, " Not the whole London operation, surely?"

"No, they are being very selective. I think they are keeping the corporate trading division but losing the retail arm. It's supposed to be to do with profitability."

"We haven't heard about this in Amsterdam, " said Lieke.

"Nor us in Milan, " said Rizzo.

"To be honest, I smell a rat in all of this, " said Nelson, " There's something about this that doesn't add up. The money men have been crawling all over the situation, I think they are up to something bigger."

"So, what will you do?" asked Lieke.

"I've little choice but to move. I might just rack up some expenses here first though, " Nelson chuckled, " But seriously, I think there is something dodgy about what they are doing. Meetings on golf courses in Ireland, that type of thing."

"So, you think the company is up to no good? More than usual?" asked Lieke.

"Yes, but I don't know where to find out what's been happening."

They sipped their drinks.

"I know someone, " said Lieke, " She is living in Amsterdam, but I think she's originally from somewhere else. She seems to have a bit of a reputation as a corporate problem solver. And I think she knows people in London too. I think this is right up her street."

"Hold on though, won't she want to get paid for delving into a company?"

"Not necessarily, " said Lieke, " I think she finds prizes inside the companies. More a kind of Risk and Reward deal. I'm a good friend of hers, shall I ask her about it?"

"Well, it's all supposed to be a company secret at the moment, " said Nelson., " And I don't want to jeopardise my transfer fee."

"Christina can be very discreet, " said Lieke, " Let me talk to her about it in the vaguest of terms."

London

My mother was a Chinese trapeze artist
In pre-war Paris
Smuggling bombs for the underground.
And she met my father
At a fete in Aix-en-Provence.
He was disguised as a Russian cadet
in the employ of the Axis.

And there in the half-light
Of the provincial midnight
To a lone concertina
They drank in cantinas
And toasted to Edith Piaf
And the fall of the Reich.

Colin Meloy

Boxpark

Christina was in London when Elena called from Cannes.

"Hi, I was just on my way to the Spitalfields Boxpark, " she said, " Time for some renewal."

Elena smiled, " I didn't even know you were in London, "

"And I didn't know you were in Cannes. What are you doing there? A boy? Vacation? Or is it work?"

"Yes, it's work, loud and shouty, " answered Elena, " Het is zo verdomd saai - het zijn allemaal cretins."

"I always thought that about your co-workers, at least the ones that I got to meet, " answered Christina, switching back to English.

"Well, it looks as if there's something else happening to the company now, some kind of weird deal. Raven is going to sell off part of itself to another organisation called Brant Holdings.

"Some of my friends are being transferred away. It's being planned from London as far as I can tell. I was wondering if you'd take a little look. My friend Nelson thinks there is more to it than meets the eye."

"Interesting., " said Christina, " Why would he say that?"

"Put it this way, " Raven always has a reputation for sailing close to the wind, we reckon it might be trying to cover something up this time."

"Let me think about it, " said Christina, " If I say yes, do you want me to work alone, or can I bring in some friends?"

"I was hoping you'd ask that, " said Elena.

Fortunes

The Boxpark was bustling when Christina arrived. She knew her way around at what was considered to be the world's first pop-up shopping mall, built on containers stacked on top of one another.

She had arranged to meet some people at one of the bars, but before this was wondering about whether to browse a few of the small shops.

Then, she saw something that caught her eye. A fortune teller. She didn't believe in any of it but thought it would be good to try someone for ideas about what she'd just heard from Elena.

The inside of the container was a small room, heavily decorated with soft furnishings and a few pieces of ju-ju art. Across the way sat the fortune teller. She looked up as Christina approached. Christina realised that the teller was a man in drag.

"Hi, " she said, " I'm interested in a reading, " she smiled across at the teller, who she could see was slightly confused by her sleek appearance.

"Hello, " said the teller, affecting a mysterious Madame's voice.

"Look, " said Christina, " We can be friends if you like. Please drop the tourist act though."

"Okay, he said, " Can I dispense with the crystal ball too, I can see you don't need one?"

"No ball-shit here, please, " said Christina.

"You're the real deal, you are beyond the powers of a scryer" he said, " I can tell you bring certain powers to me today, as strong as you bring the gods from the north."

"You are pretty good yourself, just dial it down a little, you don't have to impress me, " said Christina, although she was already wondering about how he got to gods from the north.

He sounded relieved, " Okay, I wasn't expecting anyone for about half an hour."

"Okay, that's not the best of fortune teller explanations, " smiled Christina, " So what do you prefer as a personal pronoun?"

At this the teller recovered slightly, " You know something, I hardly ever get asked, but as you have, let me say I don't really mind. When I'm looking feminine, the 'she' is good, when I'm masculine, then 'he' works for me, but when I'm in here, I can handle 'they' as well."

Christina laughed, " I'm from Iceland, where we have masculine, feminine and neuter. You can normally tell which is the right one to use."

"So, you are saying I'm an exception?" asked the fortune teller.

"I expect you are an exception to many rules, " laughed Christina, " So you'll have to tell me your name, I'm Christina."

"I'm Roberta, " answered the fortune teller, " I like you."

"That's good. Let me cross your palm with some silver."

"A credit card is also good, " replied Roberta.

"Okay, then, let me tell you want I'm interested in first. I just need some ideas."

"Go on, " said Roberta, " I think you've done this kind of thing before."

"My mother was a Chinese trapeze artist, " answered Christina.

"Ha ha, " said Roberta, " In pre-war Paris, Smuggling bombs for the underground."

"Very good, " said Christina, " You know them too, "

"The Decemberists? I sometimes sing one of their songs in my stage act- on the uke, but not that one. But you know something, I can tell, someone in your line has been a Russian cadet in your past."

Christina felt as if something small had just walked across her back. How could this guy possibly know she had been a Russian Cadet in Arkhangelsk?

"Now you are starting to intrigue me, " she said.

"My friend phoned me, she wants me to look into a company called Raven."

"Raven, " said Roberta, " You know that is a powerful symbol."

"Many references to ravens exist in world lore and literature. Because of its black plumage, croaking call and diet of carrion, the raven is often associated with loss and ill omen.

"Yet a raven's symbolism is complex. As a talking bird, the raven also represents prophecy and insight. Ravens in stories often connect the material world with the world of spirits.

"What? Like psychopomps?" asked Christina.

"Christina, who are you?" asked Roberta looking surprised, " to know of psychopomps?

"Those are the guides through the various transitions of life. Like from Greek *pompos* (conductor or guide) and *psyche* (breath, life, soul, or mind). Stories of psychopomps are widespread throughout the mythological tales, religious texts, sacred narratives, and real-life stories of people around the world."

"My strange education, I suppose, I was brought up living in different countries."

"Well, some of the most well-known psychopomps include the Greek god Hermes, the Egyptian jackal-headed god Anubis, the Archangel Michael, and the female Valkyries of Teutonic legend. A wide variety of angels, animals, birds, and other helpful beings have also been known to act as guides to the afterlife. And Archangels too, in general."

"Well, let's just say I have a special relationship with Archangel Michael. But don't go all seance-y on me. I'm much more interested in Ravens and anything about something called Brant."

"Brant - like brannt or verbrannt, " said Roberta, " Burning or burnt"

"Go back to ravens, " said Christina.

"I will, " said Roberta, " but first you remind me of something important."

"Das Narrenshiff. The Ship of Fools. I believe the first to use the phrase 'Ship of Fools' was Sebastian Brant, back in the 1400s. Ship of Fools: a ship—an entire fleet at first—sets off from Basel, bound for the Paradise of Fools. In it, Brant conceives Saint Grobian, whom he imagines to be the patron saint of vulgar and coarse people."

Roberta continued, " You know the story? It goes right back to Plato. The ship of fools is an allegory, originating from Plato's Republic, about a ship with a dysfunctional crew.

"The allegory is intended to represent the problems of governance prevailing in a political system not based on expert knowledge, such as democracies."

"This is interesting, " said Christina, there was still a chill in her back.

Roberta continued, " Well, there's the shipowner, larger and stronger than everyone in the ship, but somewhat deaf and rather short-sighted, with a knowledge of sailing to match his eyesight.

He leaned forward and softened his voice, " The sailors are quarrelling among themselves over captaincy of the ship, each one thinking he ought to be captain, though he has never learnt that skill, nor can he point to the person who taught him or a time when he was learning it. On top of which they say it can't be taught. In fact, they're prepared to cut to pieces anyone who says it can. The shipowner himself is always surrounded by them.

"They beg him and do everything they can to make him hand over the tiller to them.

"Then they immobilise their worthy shipowner with drugs or drink or by some other means, and take control of the ship, helping themselves to what it is carrying.

"Drinking and feasting, they sail in the way you'd expect people like that to sail.

"As for how the captain will steer the ship - regardless of whether anyone wants him to - they do not regard this as an additional skill or study which can be acquired over and above the art of being a ship's captain. "

Roberta paused, then asked, " If this is the situation on board, don't you think the person who is genuinely equipped to be captain will be called a stargazer, a chatterer, of no use to them, by those who sail in ships with this kind of crew?

"Fascinating, " said Christina, " But I think I should pay you now. You said someone else arrives here around now."

"No, not really, " said Roberta, " I always say something like that to my guests, to make them think I am in demand. If I have a difficult customer, I also know that they can go after half an hour. See, I'm giving you my trade secrets now."

"Like running an air conditioner behind me to make me feel the chills?" asked Christina.

"Okay, you got me, " said Roberta, " But I said already that I liked you. What are you, Russian born? I don't think so. But you've travelled a lot.

"Back to the raven. If you've a Russian background, you'll associate the raven with death or more specifically with an aftermath of a bloody or significant battle. Ravens often appear in pairs and play the role of harbingers of tragic news, usually announcing death of a hero or a group of heroes.

"But in other indigenous cultures, like the Native American Indians and even as far as the Inuits and Iceland the raven is the Creator of the world, but it is also considered a trickster god.

"What, like Loki?"

"Like Loki in the Viking stories, not the Marvel movies. By the time Tom Hiddleston took over, it had been somewhat corrupted."

"But let's take the Russian view for a moment, in Russian Pacific north-west Tlingit culture, there are two distinct raven characters which can be identified, although they are not always clearly differentiated.

"One is the creator raven, responsible for bringing the world into being and who is sometimes considered to be the individual who brought light to the darkness. The other is the childish raven, always selfish, sly, conniving, and hungry.

"When the Great Spirit created all things, he kept them separate and stored in cedar boxes. The Great Spirit gifted these boxes to the animals who existed before humans.

"When the animals opened the boxes all the things that comprise the world came into being. The boxes held such things as mountains, fire, water, wind and seeds for all the plants.

"If you hear the Navajo native Americans tell this story, they will tell it a different way, with a fox that caught the sun in its mouth, but it is all stories with the same ideas.

"So, one such box held by the animals was given to Seagull and contained all the light of the world. Seagull coveted his box and refused to open it, clutching it under his wing. All the people asked Raven to persuade Seagull to open it and release the light. Despite begging, demanding, flattering and trying to trick him into opening the box, Seagull still refused.

"Finally Raven became angry and frustrated and stuck a thorn in Seagull's foot. Raven pushed the thorn in deeper until the pain caused Seagull to drop the box. Then out of the box came the sun, moon and stars that brought light to the world and allowed the first day to begin."

"Wow, " said Christina, " Thank you, and how did you know all of that?"

"Honestly? I act as well as doing this. I was in a show at Theatre 503 about the Ship of Fools and another one about Native American people, it's amazing how much I can work in from my other roles."

Christina smiled again; she'd got plenty of stimulating ideas to take into the assignment suggested by Elena.

"Here's my card, " she said, " You can probably predict how much I will pay."

Roberta smiled, " Here's my flyer for my next show, it's in the Vaults, by Waterloo. I'll be doing a cabaret sketch show. Dress wild. Sorry - I mean dress even wilder."

"I'll try to be there, " smiled Christina.

Put us in the corner 'cause we're into ideas

Christina left Roberta's fortune telling shop in the Box Park. She would have to hurry across to where she said she'd meet the others.

"Hi, Christina, " called a voice.

Christina turned around, " We're over here."

She hurried over to a table. There, in a corner, sat Clare and Bigsy.

Clare was looking a little preoccupied on a phone call.

"It'll only be a minute, " she mouthed.

Bigsy stood and shook Christina's hand.

"Hi Bigsy, how's it going?" asked Christina.

"It's going good, " said Bigsy, " I've finished the studio, you know, you're welcome to try it any time."

"Thanks, Bigsy, but I still need a low profile, " answered Christina, " I was just called up by my friend from Amsterdam, actually, "

Bigsy had a sizeable burger in front of him, " Have a French fry, " he offered, " They are delish."

"I'm good, " said Christina. Clare pressed her phone off, and leapt up to hug Christina, " How are you - I thought you were camped out in Amsterdam nowadays?" asked Clare.

"I've made a return to London, " answered Christina, " And there's an assignment in it as well - for The Triangle, if you like."

"It's a case of straight fees and then a risk and reward tail to it."

Clare looked intrigued, " But I thought you'd checked out from the Life?"

"Checked out, checked back in, " said Christina, " Wait until you hear about my little puzzle."

Christina recounted the story of Raven and how they were hiving off a part of the company into Brant Holdings. That the new part was being filled with the unwanted people from the old organisation - just like in the old story of the Ship of Fools.

"That's okay, " said Clare, " But what's the angle on it?"

"Why are they doing it?" added Bigsy.

"It can't just be for money, can it?" asked Clare.

"No, there's got to be a higher stake. Maybe state manipulation, " agreed Christina.

"Now I've got a tricky question for you, " said Clare, looking at Christina.

"I know you changed your name and went into almost exile after your last exploit with us. You said it was something to do with Chuck Manners. Well, Chuck is back on the scene. He is with Jake right now. He's over from America and asked to see Jake. What would happen if he met you?" Clare looked at Christina.

"Do you know, I've really got no idea, " said Christina, " I've changed my name, stopped producing any kind of music to throw people from the trail and was hoping that there wouldn't be anyone following me."

"Well, Chuck has had to do that a few times, " said Bigsy, " Remember when he had to lie low after that van explosion in London? - You remember - the one outside the Bank of England?"

Christina nodded, " Yes, I'm just not sure how he would react to my reappearance now."

"Well, let's be honest, there's more to you than we ever realised, " said Clare, " I think you've got a few secrets tucked away somewhere?"

Christina nodded, " For another time maybe."

Getting a grip

Christina called Elena again.

"Hi Elena, I've been following up on your situation."

"Christina, that's great. It looks as if we are being divested in the next stage. The Brussels office will remain but we, from the Amsterdam office, are to go to Brant."

"Do you know the timescales?" asked Christina.

"It's best to ask Nelson about all of that, " said Elena, " He seems better connected to the big picture than we are in the Dutch office. Also, he's based in London, so you should find it easy enough to see him.

"He says there's a reward now for figuring this out. It's in shares though. A lot of Raven shares which would transfer across to you. He's involved with a consortium of agitated shareholders."

"Okay, I'll go visit him, but you'd better tell him I'll be along, " said Christina.

"Sure thing, " said Elena.

A few days later Christina received an email from Nelson. He asked to meet Christina at the Head Office of Raven, in London. Christina confirmed the arrangement and then contacted Clare to provide some additional cover during the meeting.

Raven

Christina, Clare and Bigsy all arrived in separate cabs at the offices Nelson had specified. The offices of Raven were not what they had expected. They expected a tall, plate glass building, but arrived at what looked like a stone building from the early 20th century.

"This doesn't look much like a Corporate Headquarters, " said Clare, " I hope we have come to the right place."

"It is probably like a lot of august organisations in central London, they keep their older buildings for show and then build big operations centres in places like Canary Wharf, " suggested Bigsy.

"The old Lloyds Bank board room used to be close to the Bank of England, then the building got turned into a fancy pub, nowadays it is gym, " said Clare, " and along the road from it, there's that old bank vault which has been made into a cocktail bar."

"Yes, and there's that oil company in St James, that looks like it is in quite a small building, but that's because they have all their operations centres around the outskirts of London, " added Bigsy.

They entered the Raven building, through heavy doors and were greeted with a neat looking reception desk, off to one side of the main lobby. A couple of low-key security people stood around the entrance area. Bigsy could see a few black leather sofas along the edge of what was an ornate entrance hall.

Clare was looking at the diagonal black-and-white tiled flooring, " It's Masonic, " she whispered, " Their head office is an old Masonic Hall - look up"

She pointed to the vaulted ceiling. It was breathtakingly decorated with stars and constellations, " That will be the stars at a particular point in time, " she said, " like when this building was built or when the Grand Lodge of England formed - it's to remind Masons that everyone lives under the same sky."

"How do you know so much about this?" asked Bigsy.

"My father was a mason until he gave it up, and he used to take us to an open-air museum, where they had rebuilt a whole temple. The guys that ran it used to tell us the stories, " she replied.

"But I thought it was all secret?" asked Bigsy.

"Except the bits that are not secret, " said Clare and winked.

"So will Nelson give us a dodgy handshake?" asked Bigsy, " You know, all fingers and thumbs?"

"I don't know about that, " said Clare, " you have to count along the knuckles to know which degree of mason you're dealing with in their handshake. But remember the Masons are a bit weird about women. They had to set up separate societies for women members. The main lodges are still men only."

"And look, there's a sunburst in the centre of the ceiling. You can tell where the Master sits, in the east, by a rising star above his chair and then a setting sun in the west above the Senior Warden's chair."

"What about the 'G' in the middle there?" Asked Bigsy, is that for God or something?

"Not quite, " said Clare, " I think it stands for Great Architect, I suppose, a Supreme Being believed in by all Freemasons. My father said the later versions of the Masons pinched a lot from Christianity to drop into their symbols. It is like the clean-up of Pagan ways conducted by the Church by marking everything with crosses.

"Yes, " said Bigsy, " I remember, like the original meaning of hot cross buns was the wheel of life, in Pagan times – grand scale re-purposing"

"I've seen that serpent eating its own tail somewhere else, " said Christina pointing to a circular depiction, " Ouroboros - alchemy - I think it is a symbol for infinity."

"Yes, the circle of life, " said Clare, miming holding out a lion cub, like the Disney movie.

"But what about the seven stars inside of it?" asked Bigsy,

"I think there's a giveaway on the walls, answered Christina, " Look: grammar, rhetoric, logic, arithmetic, geometry, music and astronomy."

Christina noticed some brochures on the reception counter.

"Look, " she said, " This leaflet is all about the hall!"

She picked it up and read about the hall decoration,

"Look, it says here that The Master's symbol is the square, said to be the controlling force. The Junior Warden represents the sun, marking it at its highest point and seated on the south side. The plumb rule is his symbol of justness and upright behaviour.

" The Senior Warden, represented by the moon after sunset, sits opposite the Master in the west, from where he attends to the closing of the lodge. His symbol is the level showing equality.

"The candlesticks also represent the roles played by the three men using the three main orders of architecture: Ionic, Doric and Corinthian. The Master's is of the Ionic order denoting wisdom; the Senior Warden's is of the Doric order denoting strength, and that by the Junior Warden of the Corinthian order denotes beauty."

"Okay, well I think we can safely say that we are in the zone now, " said Bigsy, " Except that it might not allow you two ladies to go much further."

At that moment Nelson appeared. They had expected him to come from somewhere inside of the building, but he arrived at the same front door that they had walked through.

"Nelson?" asked Christina.

"That's right, " he answered, " You must be the friend of Elena - Christina isn't it? she spoke very highly of you."

Hi, and we are two colleagues of Christina, " said Bigsy, self-consciously shaking hands with Nelson.

"I'm Bigsy and this is Clare, " Clare smiled at Nelson.

"This is one mighty impressive place you've got for a headquarters, " said Bigsy.

"Yes, I wanted to show it to you, I'm normally based in the Corporate Operations building in Canary Wharf, " said Nelson, " But let's have a brief look around here and then we can go grab a coffee or something outside."

He looked around and all three of them realised that this might not be the best place to talk.

"So, what actually happened here, then?" asked Bigsy.

"Sure, " said Nelson, " I know - I'll ask the receptionist to find us one of the guides."

They spent the next half hour walking around to the various rooms, while the guide from Raven gave them a brief corporate history.

At the end, Bigsy asked Nelson, " So okay, Are you one?"

Clare and Christina looked over at Nelson.

"There's a little clause about no bondsmen, which doesn't seem to have been revoked around here, " said Nelson.

"Bondsmen, what the slave trade?" asked Bigsy.

"Yes, " said Nelson, " You'll probably have deduced I'm of Caribbean descent!"

"Of course, " said Bigsy, " What was I thinking!"

"No, you are right to question it all nowadays, " said Nelson, " The Masons project outwardly that they have no race or creed issues. That they are open to anyone. That all you need to do is be a man and believe in a Higher Being. That the Masons are not secretive and don't do favours for one another."

"That's a mighty good piece of PR, " said Clare, " My father said there were all kinds of secrets and initiations. He did it for a while, but said he got tired of the whole thing. It wasn't compatible with his line of work either, which involved driving. Most of the members seemed to drink a little too frequently to routinely hold a steering wheel."

"Speaking of which, shall we go across to the pub, then?" suggested Bigsy, " It'll be easier to talk there."

"That was my thinking too, " said Nelson, " Maybe not the Freemason's Arm's though - which is just around the corner."

"How about that Irish place, " suggested Clare, " Philomena's? They do food too, I think."

"Good idea, " said Nelson, " Although I should point out it is right by the side of Freemason's Hall, "

"Are we in the Masonic part of London, by any chance?" asked Christina.

"You could say that, " answered Nelson.

Philomena's

Christina was relieved to see the Philomena's was an Irish style bar. There was sport showing on the televisions, but it looked as if it was old football matches being replayed.

They sat together, Bigsy brought over a tray of drinks, which included a couple of Guinness. Nelson called up a friend to join them, " He's called Javel Blackwood - he's an analyst whizz."

"It's a bit like a school classroom in here, " said Bigsy, " and if we are going to talk about, " he lowered his voice, " ahem freemasons, then I think we might need to go somewhere different."

Clare looked around. The next table had four slightly drunk looking businessmen seated at it. Across the way was another group of five, suited and booted talking loudly about some kind of deal they were trying to win.

They kept referring to "the client" but Clare thought she had worked out who it was, by their references to St. James and 'petro-chem'. The youngest looking of them looked freshly kitted out and his bags were all neatly displaying their firm's name.

"I'd be somewhat horrified to hear the consultants talking about my organisation like that, " she said, " especially as we can see who they are, too."

"It's the way things work now, " said Nelson, " Bring in the hired guns to provide sanctions in line with whatever the man or woman at the top wants."

Clare could also see that they would be overheard in this pub.

"We need to move again, " she said.

Christina nodded, " I agree, and - don't all look around - but I think that guy with the green over jacket followed us in here. We'll see if he follows us to the next place."

Bigsy finished his beer. A particularly fine glass of Guinness. He looked at the person that Christina had identified. Forty-ish, weathered skin, quietly sipping a cola, and sitting at the bar.

"Let's go then, " he announced.

"What about Nelson's friend?" asked Christina.

"Javel? - I'll text him with the change of plan. Where are we going?"

"Indian, " said Bigsy, " We'll find somewhere."

The others followed him, and they all set off toward Long Acre and towards the bustle of Covent Garden.

A few minutes later they had found a place in Floral Street.

"Perfect, we'll get a table and Nelson can tell us all about what has been happening to Raven."

Nelson was busily texting to Javel.

"And don't look now, but our friend has followed us here, " said Clare. Christina also looked up.

"Do you want him gone?" she asked.

"No let's observe, " said Clare, " It might be useful to know some more."

Sfogliatelle

They looked at the menu. Bigsy had done well, and they now had a compressive selection of Indian food to select from.

"Poppadoms, " announced Bigsy, " While we wait for Javel."

At that moment Nelson stood up.

"Hey Javel, you found us then!"

Javel smiled, round-faced, close cut dark hair, a small beard under the chin and a vibrant green shirt underneath a suit jacket. The merest hint of a beaded necklace.

"Hey Nelson, Hello friends, Nelson has been leading me a merry dance around London."

"How did you get here?" asked Clare.

"Aw, all right then, Nelson was leading the taxi-driver a merry dance."

"You over from CW?" asked Nelson.

"Yes, what are you doing so close to Head Office?" asked Javel.

"I wanted to tell these people something about what has been happening over at Raven."

"Ah yes, Raven spins off Brant, Board Members in line for huge bonuses!" said Javel, "I can predict the headlines now."

"Okay Javel, I think you can explain about Raven's business exploits better than me."

Javel began, " Okay, let's start at the beginning. Raven was founded in 1920 and is one of the world's largest providers of products and services to the energy industry.

"Raven employs over 60,000 people in over 80 countries. It claims to maximise value through the lifetime of the energy reservoir. Then it has spun off a whole raft of other interests. Once it is operating at near scale in a country, it invests and develops the infrastructure too.

"A few example countries outside of the USA or UK where Raven operates are Venezuela, Saudi Arabia, Canada, Iran, Iraq, Kuwait, the UAE, Libya and Nigeria.

"Most of them are unstable. Venezuela has two competing Presidents; President Maduro, who had been sworn in to a second six-year term in office and acting president Mr Guaidó trying to get the military to switch their allegiance to him.

Javel continued, " Saudi Arabia is mostly thought of as a totalitarian absolute monarchy with Islamist lines, where the King is both the head of state and government. US airbases to give the US reach into the middle east."

"Yes, and I get it that Iran, Iraq, Libya are all in turmoil and with heavy US presence, both seen and unseen, " said Jake.

Javel continued, " Kuwait - Like a key block in a board game - a desert stuck in the corner between Saudi and Iraq. The US treats it as a partner now, after the conflicts of Desert Shield and Desert Storm. It has sold Kuwait a large number of 'defensive' missiles and airborne defences too."

Javel paused and looked around, " You get the picture, without me carrying on. Raven operates in all of these territories. And it is no secret that there's been revolving doors between big business and government. "

"It's another case of the 'Stupid White Men' who run big business, said Nelson, " Except they are not so stupid, "

Javel continued, " I can't prove anything, but I think there's been some kind of lobbying running."

"The Americans fight a war somewhere and blow up a place. Then it is time for a large infrastructure corporation to come in and repair it."

Nelson agreed, " That's been Raven's business model for ages. Okay, it builds hospitals and shopping malls too, but most of its non-energy income is from what I guess you'd call war reparations."

Javel added darkly, " It's not unlike the crows that descended on battlefields in medieval times, only the picking here are millions of dollars.

"With supplying the fuel, helping build military bases, supplying the war machine, conducting the clean-up and extending the infrastructure, one could call it a virtuous business cycle" added Javel, " The share price has done well out of it, as have the main board.

"In the US, the Pentagon's Defense Policy Board has connections with highly paid consultants for companies hoping to profit from conflicts."

"It's all a matter of cashflow. How many days can the US run a bombardment and how much revenue generation will it create as a consequence?" said Javel.

"That's sick, isn't it?" asked Clare.

"Well it's definitely immoral, profiteering from a war, " answered Nelson.

"So, you are saying that Raven has interests in this form of business?" asked Christina, " No wonder you wanted to talk about it away from the Head Office."

Javel said, " Well, let's just look back for a moment at a few encounters.

He started, " There's Libya. The second Libyan Civil War, which has seen the US deploy hundreds of airstrikes against the Islamic State. The cheque might be in the post on that one.

After a pause, Javel added, " Then there's Yemen. A War on Terror target and part of the ISIS Campaign. The US put a naval blockade in as well as supporting Saudi Arabia to bomb large chunks of the territory. And let's not forget that Yemen is one of the poorest countries on the planet, beset with famine and cholera. That all kicked off in 2015 and is still running."

"Yes, I see that footage of the poor people and wonder how they can afford to run such wars., " said Clare.

Javel continued, " How about Syria? It's part of Operation Inherent Resolve, the Syrian Civil War, the War on Terror and the International ISIS campaign, so it has around 20 forces involved now. The US alone is estimated to have run over 11,000 airstrikes into Syria. That all started in 2014."

"I suppose giving it a mission name like that helps to legitimise it?" asked Clare.

Javel nodded, " Take Iraq - another example? It is another part of Operation Inherent Resolve, the Iraqi Civil War, the spill over of the Syrian Civil War, the War on Terror and the International ISIS campaign. Another dozen or more countries involved, including troops from Australia, New Zealand and Canada. This one tallies over 13,000 airstrikes into the zone."

Nelson chipped in, " The same thing with Operation Ocean Shield, which was the Indian Ocean pirate ship reduction, also put down to the War on Terror."

Javel continued, " So like Clare says, the US will adopt an attitudinal position branded with a campaign, like 'Ocean Shield, Desert Storm, Inherent Resolve, The War on Terror' and then drop troops and armament to smash up the landscape. After the designated number of days, it'll declare victory and bring in the cavalry to tidy things up."

"…Were you ever beaten up at school?" asked Bigsy, " and then had the bully's henchmen tidy you up again afterwards?"

"That's a kind of Mafia trick, " said Christina, " Sfogliatelle; where they rough someone up, then shove a lovely pastry in their mouth. It's like a warning."

"Where'd you learn that stuff?" asked Bigsy. Christina looked at Clare.

"Oh, in my travels, " said Christina.

"I always knew you were bad-ass, " said Bigsy.

"More than you might realise, " answered Christina, smiling.

"Are you two flirting?" asked Nelson.

"No, " answered Christina still smiling.

Bigsy could feel his face redden.

"So, what have we got then?" asked Clare, " A tricksy organisation which seems to be profiteering on the back of US-declared wars?"

"Yes, " agreed Nelson, " And of course it isn't the only one. There are many friends of people in high places who dip their noses in the trough from time to time."

"But do you think something new is about to happens? Based upon the company spin-off?"

Nelson leaned forward, " Well, think about it. Raven is, at heart, an energy company. They exploit energy globally. Find it, extract it, refine it, ship it, trade it."

Javel also leaned it, " And now we are joining the dots. Oil has always been a primitive leading cause of war - and Raven has seen its share of them. Political effects generated by the oil industry makes oil a driver towards war. At least a quarter and maybe as much as one-half of wars since 1973 have been connected to oil-related causes."

Nelson added, " No other commodity has had such an impact on international security and in a country like the US the influence of oil on conflict is often poorly understood."

Javel nodded, " America will usually find other public debate to deflect from their economic interest. In the 1991 and 2003 Iraq wars, both sides focused excessively on the question of whether the United States was fighting for possession of oil reserves; neither sought a broader understanding of how oil shaped the preconditions for war."

"Remember how the Americans were told by President Bush and his administration that the U.S. was going to war with Iraq because of the imminent threat of Saddam's weapons of mass destruction and ties to terrorism?

"Oh yes, they never found any WMDs, " said Bigsy.

"Exactly, " said Javel, " Look I'm sorry if I sound too polarised about this, but I'm really trying to stick to facts."

Javel continued, " Then another justification for invasion was the purported link between Saddam Hussein's government and terrorist organizations, in particular Al-Qaeda.

"I'm not saying that Saddam wasn't a tyrant, but the cause was branded so wide as to allow all kinds of other American actions.

"In that sense, the Bush Administration cast the Iraq war as part of the broader War on Terrorism. Remember, in 2013, FBI Director Robert Mueller testified to Congress that 'seven countries designated as State Sponsors of Terrorism—Iran, Iraq, Syria, Sudan, Libya, Cuba, and North Korea—remain active in the US and continue to support terrorist groups that have targeted Americans.'

"Well, that brought out the overarching branding of 'War on Terror' - used in several subsequent and ongoing conflicts, and the oil situation goes as an unnoticed third or fourth agenda topic.

"A bit like 'God on our side arguments,' " said Bigsy.

"Hmm. Yes and no, the religious zealots have stayed out of a lot of this. It has been a more secular set of claims that drive the US branding of campaigns. Remember USA is multi-cultured, so a religious backdrop would only get factional."

"So, as with the argument that Iraq was developing biological and nuclear weapons, evidence linking Saddam Hussein and Al-Qaeda was discredited by multiple U.S. intelligence agencies soon after the invasion of Iraq."

"It is well-known that critics of the Bush administration say in the build-up to war with Iraq, policy-makers were cherry-picking intelligence from CIA and other intelligence agencies, publicising only the information that would bolster the case for war and ignoring contrary evidence."

"Yes, it was a big deal here in the UK too, with Blair portrayed as a poodle to Bush. Massive protests and a disputed report. A scientist involved in the report committed suicide, " said Bigsy.

It wasn't really in the interest of politicians to do otherwise than to spin it all. Sure, they couldn't help stem the footage of oilfields on fire, but there was still spin about fighting for the freedom of the people and similar stories.

"But why would this current situation require a divestment?" asked Clare, " Surely Raven must be impenetrable by now?"

"Yes, that's what we thought, " answered Javel, " They have enough people in high places to be unassailable."

"That's unless there's a new situation about to go down," said Javel, " New lobbying, maybe a new country about to be put in the searchlights?"

"How will we find out?" asked Bigsy.

"Dib, dib, dib, " said Clare.

"What, you think there's a Masonic twist in this?" asked Bigsy.

"Hello!" said Clare sarcastically, " Top Masons run a company which trades into conflict zones. Maybe has some links to the UK government? It might be spmething else, but the evidence is starting to stack up. It does raise the question about how we'd ever get a look though."

Christina stood.

"I'll just be a minute, " she said as she walked towards the ladies' room.

"So how long have you two known one another?" asked Clare, looking at both Nelson and Javel.

"Pretty much since I worked for Raven, " said Nelson. "I ran into Javel in the first week. We were at a company offsite and I didn't know so many people. I'd just gone back to the bar and Javel was standing there with a laptop. I made some quip about working too hard and he came back with a remark about needing it finished so that the share price would go up.

"I believed him, of course, not that he was just answering an email from his daughter."

"We've been buddies since that time in Brussels, " replied Javel, " And strange as it may seem, we work in the same building yet normally only see one another in the canteen or when we are at an off-site."

"Not at all, " said Clare, " I believe you - It's the modern way, what with virtualised meetings and ATCs all the time."

"Yes, " agreed Bigsy, at least with an Audio Tele Conference I can be doing something else while I listen to the over-lengthy messages from the big chiefs."

There was a crash.

They all looked around. It was Christina, she had just stumbled on the bag of the man who she thought had been following them.

"I'm so sorry, " she was saying, the man looked embarrassed as he stood to wipe wine from his shirt.

"It's okay, " he said, " It was my fault to leave the bag there."

"I think I tripped on its carry strap, " said Christina, " I always have to watch out if I'm carrying a bag like that."

A waiter had appeared and was ushering Christina back to her seat. Another waiter was checking that the man was okay.

"Oops, Sfogliatelle " said Christina, as she sat down. Clare looked her. She had done something.

"At this rate we will need to move to yet another bar!" said Bigsy.

"Then we would need to reclassify the evening as a pub crawl, " answered Clare, " I'm sorry guys, " she said looking towards Nelson and Javel, " We can't take Christina anywhere!"

The Triangle

"heart, mind and desire"

Christina Hyde

They had left the Indian Restaurant.

"How will we keep in contact?" asked Nelson.

"Don't worry about that, " said Clare, " I'll be in contact over the next couple of days. We need to do some digging first. You and Lieke were right, there's something very fishy about all of this."

They split up, and Nelson and Javel grabbed a cab.

"Let's walk, " said Christina, the others nodded.

"So, what do we think?" asked Clare, " It looks like a business model to get work on the back of war damages."

"Yes, but that doesn't explain why they would want to hive off to Brant Holdings though, " said Bigsy.

Christina looked around, " The guy. The one following us, He's gone now. I saw him get in a cab after the others."

"Is he following them?" Asked Bigsy.

"Could be, but if he is then its Nelson who is being tailed. I wonder why?" said Christina.

"Perhaps this will help us to find out?" she held out a phone.

"No way!" said Clare, " You didn't steal that from him!"

"Borrow, " said Christina, " Borrow. We'll return it later."

"To where though?"

"Maybe to his home address. On the way into the ladies' room I borrowed his wallet. I've taken photographs of its content, which included his driving licence. It will be quite disturbing to him when we send the phone through the post. Don't worry I put his wallet back in his jacket."

"What about *where_is_my_phone.com*?" asked Bigsy, looking worried.

"I think we can lose the phone fast, once we have copied its memory, " said Christina.

"How will we get past the pin number?" asked Bigsy.

"Well, the excellent news is that he's left it as four digits, " said Christina, " And it's an iPhone, so we can't use 4 digits the same."

"Okay, " said Bigsy. "Give me a moment. Excluding repeats, the most common pins are: 1234 1212 1004 2000 6969 1122 1313 4321 2001 1010." Normally I'd include 1111, 2222 etc. but on an iPhone that won't work."

"He looked more like a minimum movement kind of guy to me, " said Christina, " Clandestine, so he needs to work the phone when it is still in his pocket."

"1212 or 1414, " she announced, " I know it is not on your list, Bigsy, but it is an easy one to feel for using the edge of the phone."

They all watched as she typed in "1414." To their amazement, it worked.

"We're in, " she said as she flicked across to the security settings and removed a couple.

"Er, where did you learn all of this?" asked Bigsy, slightly startled to see Christina so proficient at phone hacking.

"Basic skills training, " answered Christina.

"What, at music school?" answered Bigsy.

"Not exactly, " said Christina, " I should tell Bigsy?" she looked towards Clare.

"Yes, " said Clare, " I know Bigsy will be discreet."

Okay, said Christina, " Bigsy, I don't want to freak you out, but I'm not quite what you thought I was."

"What, a lovely pop-star that I know?" answered Bigsy.

"There's more, " answered Christina, " I'm also a trained agent."

"What? Microsoft software engineer? Carphone Warehouse agent?" asked Bigsy.

"No, you are being silly. I'm an agent for a foreign government - or I was, anyway."

"What Holland, or -wait - America?" asked Bigsy.

"Not quite, " said Christina, " I have worked for the Russian government."

Bigsy looked at Clare to see if she was grinning. He could not work out her expression.

"I was trained in Russia and have then worked in many countries. Nowadays I'm resting."

Bigsy looked incredulous. "Em, this is quite a lot to take in. Does Clare know this already? What about Jake?"

Clare answered, " Christina told me about this some time ago. She swore me to secrecy, although I've really wanted to tell both of you about this."

"You'd be such an asset to us in the Triangle, " said Bigsy, excited that they were with a Russian agent.

"But wait, are you rearranging all of our election results and manipulating events through twitter and social media?" he asked.

"No, " said Christina, " Although I have visited a click-farm."

"Really, " said Bigsy, " I've always wanted to see how they worked…Are they hot inside, with all of that technology?"

"Let's leave it that I've been trained by the FSB to do a lot of stuff, and I still know how to do it."

"FSB? Is that like the KGB?" asked Bigsy.

"Bigsy, it is the KGB - Don't you remember they were renamed?" said Clare.

"Wow, Christina Nott, KGB Agent, " said Bigsy.

"Not quite…Christina Hyde, FSB Agent, " replied Christina.

"I see - we used to make jokes about you being Nott Christina, and now you are Hyde-ing?" smiled Bigsy.

Then as if as an afterthought, " Whoa, so Christina - did you get married - hence the Hyde?"

"No Bigsy, I'm still single, if you are asking. My name change is in the interests of my profession."

Clare laughed.

Clone a phone

They looked back to the phone.

Maybe this would yield something?

"We should get this back to my place, " said Bigsy, " That way we can clone it and download a copy of all the data."

Christina persisted to check around the phone. She tapped phone album. There were several pictures of them all sitting in the restaurant. He had propped the phone up on the table to take these. Christina had come over during the photo sessions. It was why it had been so easy to lift the phone.

Next she tried the email. It was almost empty. There were a couple of emails to another anonymous google mail user id. It was just a number series.

"Old-school number code, " said Christina, " and not Russian."

They took a taxi back to Bigsy's place. He had moved to an apartment block in East London, close to Canary Wharf.

"It's easy for me to get to where my clients are, from here, " he explained, " Most of them are one or two stops away, or even walking. I've figured out the subterranean world of Canary Wharf and can usually walk in a straight line to wherever I need to be."

"It's a lovely place, " said Christina, looking around the flat, " How many bedrooms? It looks pretty spacious."

"Yes, two beds, although I've kitted the second one out as a kind of office, " said Bigsy, " Take a look."

He showed them in, although it surprised neither Clare nor Christina to see it was full of technology and bookshelves.

"Neat!" said Clare, who was used to Bigsy's sense of order. "And will some of that stuff let us copy that iPhone?"

Bigsy retrieved the phone from his pocket. Christina noticed it was also in a little pouch.

"What's that? A shield?" asked Christina.

"Yes, " said Bigsy. I was concerned about it being able to track us on this journey, so I shielded it. I'll do the same when we connect it up. I got the shield from a Madonna gig. They were stopping us from making recordings or taking photos."

He went to a wardrobe with sliding doors. He looked to the floor and riffled through some flat objects.

"This one, " he said, as he finally picked a laptop from the pile, " I know, some people have shoe collections. Oh, I nearly forgot. Would you ladies like a drink?"

"We'll help ourselves while you set up the wizardry, " said Clare, leading Christina back into the kitchen area.

Bigsy busied himself with wires and connections, before also returning to the kitchen.

"I'm copying everything from the phone to the laptop, " he said, " The iPhone thinks the laptop is another iPhone, and it is doing what normally happens when you buy a new phone and want to make a copy of your old one to it."

"Excellent, " said Clare, " So we can still read it from the laptop?"

"Yes, or we could even make another identical phone, " said Bigsy.

"When we've finished, we should put it back in the pouch, but ultimately post it back to its owner. If we do that anonymously, he might even think it was an accident or that he lost it."

"Agreed, " said Bigsy, " How about adding an anonymous message, like "found in the street."

"No, said Christina, " We should just let him wonder."

Bigsy checked the progress of his copying.

"It's finished, " he said, " Successful."

"Okay, are you all right to dispose of the phone?" asked Clare.

"Yes, you bet, " said Bigsy, " Let's see what we've got."

Burner

Together they huddled around the screen. Bigsy had done well, and they seemed to have everything faithfully copied from the phone. There was not a lot of information.

"What can we tell?" asked Clare.

"It looks like a one-purpose phone...A burner, " said Bigsy, " Like the kind that drug dealers use."

"Except this is being used for something else?" asked Christina.

"Yes, and that's probably why there is only one number stored on it. Probably a control, " said Bigsy.

"What are the language settings?" asked Christina, " And have they ever been changed?"

"Ah yes, interesting, it is set to English - American English though, and look, it has been set to Russian at some point."

"Photos?" asked Christina.

"Only the ones in the Indian Restaurant, " said Bigsy.

"Try the camera, " asked Christina.

"Ah yes, there's something else there. A couple of snaps of a document, " said Bigsy, " It's in Russian."

"Let me look, " asked Christina.

"She paused and then translated, " It's about oil…

"Russian Arctic: So far this year, Russia has discovered nearly 1.5 billion barrels of oil equivalent (Bboe) thanks to the Dinkov and Nyarmeyskoye finds on the Yamal peninsula shelf in the Kara Sea. In natural gas terms, that's 17 trillion cubic feet (Tcf).

"When it comes to Arctic oil, Russia's state-run firm is having a tougher time. To get its Arctic projects off the ground, the state-run company will need $40 billion in tax cuts from the government.

"According to The Moscow Times, the state-run oil company has secured a deal with Indian financiers to invest in a 15 to 20-percent stake, but that would only happen if the state-run company was granted a $40-billion tax break over the next 30 years.

The problem for investors is that while the Vostok Oil project reserves are worth around $15 billion, climate change is causing oil and gas infrastructure to sink into the ground, making the project even more costly. So, Russia may be leading discoveries so far this year, but extraction is another issue entirely.

Christina paused, then she said, "Here's the second page; it talks about Celarus…

"US companies just put Celarus on the oil and gas map for the first time. It is a huge discovery. In fact, it is a string of 14 discoveries so far. Celarus had already hit 6 billion barrels of oil equivalent in the Stabroek Block. The potential for Celarus is huge, with some estimating Celarus's future production at 750,000 within the next five years - which would put it on to a similar footing to Guyana."

Christina added, "So this nets down to Russia discovering oil, but it is hard work to extract it and Celarus discovering plenty through US companies."

"I'm not sure why that would be on the phone though?" asked Bigsy.

"It's an article from a newspaper, photographed. Just a lazy way to get the clipping, " said Christina.

"What it points to, is that there's some interest in all of this, probably from Russia."

"Yes, and it points to our friend in the Indian restaurant being Russian, too, " said Clare.

Freemasons

A man in the corner approached me for a match
I knew right away he was not ordinary
He said, are you lookin' for somethin' easy to catch
Said, I got no money, he said, that ain't necessary

Jacques Levy / Bob Dylan

Meet the Freemasons

"So, do any of us know any Freemasons?' asked Bigsy, " I only know Fred and Barney."

Christina and Clare looked at one another.

Christina chipped in, " I think I might know someone, but it would get complicated for me."

"Well, who then?" asked Clare, looking intrigued.

"An old flame, " said Christina, " from the Arkhangelsk days. We were together for a while."

"Complicated?" asked Clare,

" Well he split from me, so it shouldn't be, " said Christina, " And it was all school-style crushes back in those days. The thing is, his father was the Senior Warden in one of the Masonic Lodges in Arkhangelsk. It was called the Lodge of Jekaterina. Antanov was keen on the Masons too, although then was still very young to be involved."

"How will you contact Antanov?" asked Bigsy, " I mean, he could be anywhere, "

"I think I can contact him via the FSB, " said Christina, " Although it could wake them up to me again. They will probably want something in return."

"Can you just dial up the Russians, then?" asked Bigsy.

"You bet, they still pay me so you can imagine they will want to keep an eye on me. To be truthful, it's the Americans that I've been careful to hide from, so your buddy Chuck Manners is a problem for me."

"Chuck? He's been in a similar position himself, needing to go to ground. Unless you've done something directly to him, I would think you'd be all right, " said Bigsy.

Handler

Christina thought long about her next move. She could ask Fyodor Kuznetsov, her handler, to contact her. It would restart her direct dialogue with the FSB, which was something she had tried not to instigate.

Kuznetsov's code name was Blackbird, which Christina didn't think was all that smart. Blackbird was just a little too close to 'blacksmith', which was the English translation of Kuznetsov.

Still, he had left her alone, and the money continued to roll in, so being asked for something in return for access to her Masonic friend was the right trade.

Christina rang the number for Kuznetsov. A London-based car dealership answered. "I'm interested in taking on of your vehicles for a test-drive, " she continued, " A hatch back."

There was a pause on the line and then a recorded voice asked for her reference code and the nature of her enquiry.

She gave a number, and after a moment was connected to a voice.

"And how may I help you today?'

"I'm seeking a colleague, " she began.

There followed a protocol to verify security, and then Christina waited.

"Eventually a voice said, " Hello, Christina? - Or should I call you Archangel?"

"Fyodor, " she replied, " It's been a while."

"Four years, actually, you have done a wonderful job of becoming invisible."

"Is everything okay?" he asked, " It is so unusual for you to make the initial contact."

"Everything is fine. I'm back in London now."

"What, no more Amsterdam?" he sounded surprised.

"Not now, and I've been keeping a low profile. I wanted to contact one of my friends from the Academy," continued Christina, " Antanov Chekeryn."

"Ah yes, he was in your group. From St Petersburg, I recall, his father was also a high-ranking member of the FSB. Well-connected around St Petersburg."

"What is the reason for your link?" asked Fyodor.

"I heard he was looking for me, " Christina lied, " We used to be more than just friends back in the Academy."

"Yes, he has moved back to Europe, " said Fyodor, " He was in South America for several years. I will attempt to contact him. If I am successful, how shall I arrange that you speak to one another?"

"Phone is fine, " said Christina, " Two Russians chatting by phone, nothing unusual."

"Okay, we have a number for you here."

"I'll give you my latest one, I'm not sure your system will have been able to keep up."

She recited the number to Fyodor, who recited it back.

"Okay, leave it with me, " he said, " You'll know in a week-*uspokoysya, beregi sebya, detka*"

"You stay safe too, " answered Christina.

Connections

Christina sat with Antanov Chekeryn.

They both ordered vodkas.

"za zda-ró-vye, " they said as they chinked glasses, " to your health."

"Za nashe khorosheye zdorov'ye i zdorov'ye nashikh kolleg v Arkhangel'ske, " said Antonov, *"For our good health and the health of our colleagues in Arkhangelsk,"*

"You are looking great, " he said. This western lifestyle suits you. Do you live in London now?"

"Yes, thank you, you look good yourself. I've moved around on various assignments for the FSB, life is never dull after you've been to Arkhangelsk, is it!?"

"No, I've also travelled widely. They sent me to South America. I was in Chile, then Ecuador, and then Brazil. I think they called me a disruptor. Brazil was far more expensive than the other two countries and Ecuador was the least expensive. It was strange in Brazil. There was a lot of German spoken. I think some transfers there were from Europeans after World War II. Nowadays I'm in Brussels, I've got a job in the EU. Then Blackbird called me and said I needed to come to London to meet Archangel. Said it was important."

"Yes, well thank you for coming over, and at such brief notice; I think this situation might intrigue you, " she grinned towards Antanov.

"Let me ask you, did you keep any links running with the Masons during your time in South America?" asked Christina, " I remember your father was into it."

"Yes, I did, actually, Chile, Ecuador and Brazil all had a Masonic presence - as the son of a Russian Senior Warden, they treated me like a special guest. I was initially quite surprised, but it looks as if the French were involved in the establishment of the Order over there.

"To be honest, it made my life so much simpler, being able to go to the meetings and find out what was happening from the well-connected people who attended. It's what my father did in *Sankt-Peterburg* to find out what was happening. Coincidentally, I've just joined the Grand Orient de Belgique. It's odd for such a small country that they seem to have about four different types of Freemasonry - it is like the EU all over again.

"And one for the women, no doubt?" asked Christina.

"Yes, they've a Women's Grand Lodge too, " nodded Antanov.

Antanov moved closer to Christina. He looked into her eyes.

She smiled back, " It's so good to be with a Russian man again, " she said.

"I was thinking just the same about being with a sexy Icelander, " he whispered, " Maybe we still have unfinished business?"

"Business. That's not the word I would use" said Christina.

She leaned towards him, and they kissed. Ever so briefly, but enough to set a tone.

"Power plays; they say the Masons isn't clandestine, but it is, and factional too, you'll see obedience cropping up in the descriptions of the Women's Lodges, " continued Antanov.

"You remember in Arkhangelsk there were two different Masonic houses? It was the same in Brazil. There was the Grand Orient of Lavrado Valley and the Grand Orient of Benedictino Valley, the former inclined to Roman Catholicism, the latter opposed to it.

"By 1872 the two parties had united but the following year they divided again. Catholics and Lutherans, one could say.

"After various arguments, by 1914 the Grand Orient exercised authority over 390 constituent Lodges, while England, Germany, and Italy were also represented.

"Wow, " so it wasn't difficult to stay connected, then?" asked Christina.

"Not really, although some of our Russian Order was subservient to the Germans and used the Adonhiramite Rite in our meetings. It was strange, we'd have their degrees and yet use French names."

"I can tell you are still fully up with all of this, " said Christina.

"Yes, I'm no Past Master, in fact I'm rather Select, " he said, " …that was a Masonic joke."

Christina shrugged, " Boys and their toys, if you ask me."

"I'd forgotten your forthrightness!" he smiled, " So what is it you want me to do with the British Freemasons, then?"

"Infiltrate, please, we need to find out what is happening. Something is wrong."

"I guess I'll need more than that. Does it mean I must spend some time here in London?" asked Antanov.

"Yes please, " said Christina, " I might even have some room for you at mine."

"Well, there's an offer I can't refuse, " replied Antanov.

He picked up his glass, " *Vot chtoby proytis' po goryashchim mostam!*"

"Yes, " said Christina, " Here's to walking over burning bridges."

Eight Mechanisms

The next morning, Clare visited Christina's apartment.

"Hey Christina, we thought you'd better come around to our office and brief everyone together. With your friend Antanov."

Christina invited Clare into the flat. Seated at the breakfast bar was Antanov. Clare admired Christina's choice. He looked suitably toned in his grey tee-shirt, with a pair of trainer bottoms, which could well have been Christina's.

"Hello, he said, " I'm very pleased to meet you. Christina has told me some things about you."

Clare listened to his accent; it sounded mid-European rather than Russian. Slightly upper-class. It fitted very well with London.

"I'm delighted to meet you too. Any friend of Christina's is a friend of mine. And she'd probably told you I go weak at the knees when I meet her friends' friends."

"Easy, tiger, " said Christina. Clare noticed immediately that Christina seemed particularly cheerful this morning. Christina passed a black coffee across the kitchen surface to Clare.

Clare noticed that Christina was behaving just slightly more Russian this morning. Subtle, but noticeable.

"Okay thank you, Christina. When you are both ready, I'd like you to come over to our office in Hoxton. We call it The Triangle Works, but it's really a tiny old foundry which we adapted to make a pretty good base for what we do."

"It sounds great, " said Antanov, " I can be ready in about 15 minutes." He jumped up and left the kitchen.

Clare looked at Christina. Christina grinned back. There was nothing else to confirm.

"So where did you meet him?" asked Clare.

"Back in the day, " smiled Christina, " ...We were an item. Still best friends."

"I somehow worked that out, " smiled Clare.

Antanov reappeared, " Okay, ready, " he said. He was wearing a black leather jacket, still the grey tee-shirt but now had a pair of dark jeans. They walked to the elevator and down to the street where they could catch a cab to the office.

"Can I just check? Chuck Manners won't be at the office?" asked Christina.

"No, he is in London at the moment, met Jake yesterday, and they'll be keeping in contact, but there's no reason for him to be at our offices today."

They arrived, and Clare showed them into a meeting room. Jake appeared and was delighted to see Christina and greeted Antanov.

They shook hands and Jake said, " So you'll be telling us about Russian conflict strategies? - This could all be so useful to our understanding of what is happening."

Antonov was at one end of the table. "Sure, I'll take you though some of the basics. This is stuff that we present in FSB, but I'm sure the US presents almost identical thinking to the CIA."

"Christina's told me about this in the context of Raven - which as we all know has its fingers into everything related to energy, but oil in particular. That's what we'd call the big lever.

"It's a big lever because in Russia we take a view that oil fuels international conflict through eight distinct mechanisms. We know that is how the US sees it too, and that they are active to agitate these situations. Let's list them:

"1. Resource wars, in which states try to acquire oil reserves by force;

"2. Petro-aggression, whereby oil insulates aggressive leaders such as Saddam Hussein or Ayatollah Ruhollah Khomeini from domestic opposition, and therefore makes them more willing to engage in risky foreign policy adventurism;"

"I think you are saying that some messaging is manipulating the genuine reason?" asked Clare.

"That's right, " answered Antanov, " Let's see now, "

"3 Externalization of civil wars in oil-producing states ("petrostates");

"4 Financing for insurgencies—for instance, Iran funnelling oil money to Hezbollah;

"5 Conflicts triggered by the prospect of oil-market domination, such as the United States' war with Iraq over Kuwait in 1991;

"And then the making up of branded campaigns?" asked Jake.

"Precisely, and there has been no shortage of these from the Americans, " said Antanov.

"6 Clashes over control of oil transit routes, such as shipping lanes and pipelines;

"7 Oil-related grievances, whereby the presence of foreign workers in petrostates helps extremist groups such as al-Qaida recruit locals; and

"8 Oil-related obstacles to multilateral cooperation, such as when an importer's attempt to curry favour with a petrostate prevents multilateral cooperation on security issues. These mechanisms can contribute to conflict individually or in combination.

"That's why we always see conflict zones on TV shown with burning oil wells?" said Bigsy.

Antanov nodded, " I feel like I'm talking from an FSB manual when I say this, but these linkages between oil and international conflict are growing increasingly important in light of three transitions under way in global energy markets. The Americans are also troubled by each of these factors.

"The first is the shift in patterns of global oil production away from traditional suppliers in the Middle East and toward both suppliers of unconventional oil reserves in North America (like shale) and new suppliers of conventional oil, especially in Africa. As many as sixteen developing countries will become oil exporters in the near future, creating a swathe of new international security concerns. America and Russia are both concerned about this.

"Second, the low oil prices of the 1990s have given way to higher and more volatile prices, increasing the magnitude of the consequences one can expect from oil-conflict linkages.

"Third, the relative decline of U.S. hegemony may reduce the provision of public goods such as security of shipping lanes and pipelines. Although these transitions alter some of the ways in which the oil industry contributes to international conflict, none eliminates linkages between the two or allows the United States to disengage from global markets.

"Doesn't this all make for new sources of conflict?" asked Jake.

"That's right and some of them are unexpected sources of conflict, " Antanov nodded towards Jake and then continued, " It is important that policymakers think systematically about oil-security linkages when monitoring emerging security threats as the global oil industry transforms itself.

"As more countries export oil in the near future, new international dynamics will materialize, especially in Africa.

"Furthermore, if oil prices stay high, incentives for resource grabs will grow. Resource wars are most likely to occur in unpopulated territories or naval zones, as oil can be extracted from these areas without the need to manage a populated, potentially hostile territory.

"But what about the various blips over oil prices in the last few years?" asked Clare, " Like knock-on effects from the COVID-19 global pandemic?"

Antanov continued, " Yes, there are some wild fluctuations, but still an underlying sense of sensible pricing. There's almost too many variables, for some trading algorithms, but underneath it all there's a common-sense price point, which still allows the extraction and production to make a sensible profit."

"Thus, policymakers should be most concerned about disputed territories in the East China and South China Seas and naval borders in the Caspian Sea. There are already competing sovereignty claims to territory in those regions, and considerable uncertainty about the size of the energy resources located there, creating conditions ripe for miscalculation and mutual suspicion. There is already talk of testing weather-manipulating hardware from this region.

"What?" asked Bigsy, " How can anyone do that?"

"Both China and Russia have been experimenting with this technology and long had ways to make it work, " said Antanov, " For example, the Chinese have long had cloud chamber machines. In order for water vapour in the air to form clouds and eventually rain, it requires a nucleating particle.

"Typically, this is a tiny particle of dust which en masse produces the clouds we see in the sky. By artificially "seeding" the Tibetan Plateau with silver iodide particles the Chinese government is inducing the formation of clouds where there weren't any before. Once the clouds become unstable, this leads to artificially induced rainfall.

Each rain machine (chamber) is expected to create a 3-mile long strip of billowing clouds. When multiplied by the thousands of chambers China is installing along the Tibetan Plateau, it is estimated that China will be artificially controlling the weather over an area similar to the size of Alaska."

"But bring us back to the oil, " asked Jake.

"Well, I am in a way. Imagine weather manipulation of the sea-based oilfields.   Policymakers should be especially concerned about security threats that arise from unexpected sources, such as allies' energy needs or benign actions that prompt hostile responses from rivals.

"It is only by appreciating these ways in which oil contributes to war can help policymakers design grand strategy, allocate military resources, and shape domestic energy policy.

"Many policy analysts focus narrowly on "energy security" as defined only by reliable access to fuel supplies, while missing the broader relationships between energy and security. Only by thinking systematically about the oil-conflict relationship can they craft intelligent foreign policy."

Box of Daylight

Step into the daylight and let it go

-Taylor Swift

Look around Raven

"Look. I've laid it out, but I can't see how these linkages tie together. Raven could be doing something, and clearly has an interest in energy, but why would it split itself into smaller organisations? It's not exactly a Bell Telecommunications monopoly situation." said Antanov.

"No, but there is something not right about this whole thing, " said Christina. The others nodded.

"So, you want me to dig around in Raven, but to look at their influence strategies?"

Antanov looked around the table, " And this is all because of a chance meeting between a Raven employee and a friend of Christina? It looks like a slender linkage."

"Well, there's clearly some other interest from Russia. We were followed when we discussed this with Nelson, " said Bigsy.

"The man carried a burner phone which only had a couple of entries. One about emerging oil-fields and the other was a Russian cell-phone."

"We didn't ring the number for fear of being traced."

"Well, I know a quick way of finding the number's origin, " said Jake.

"Unfortunately, it involves someone that I hear Christina isn't so keen to meet?"

"What, Chuck?" Asked Clare.

"Seriously?" said Bigsy, " I don't think Chuck would be put out to meet Christina. In fact, I think he'd be rather intrigued."

"It's not so much Chuck as the set of people behind him, " said Christina, " I think they would like to meet me and find out about a few things from my past."

"I think the same could be said of Chuck, " answered Clare, " I think we have a standoff!"

"What, like in Red Dead Redemption on PS4?" asked Bigsy, " That Mexican gambling scene, where a character says, 'There must be a name for this…' to which the Lee Van Cleef type called Landon Ricketts replies 'An impasse, sir. An impasse.' "

They all looked around the table. None of them knew what Bigsy was talking about.

"How about if I test Chuck on it?" asked Jake, looking for a way forward, " If Chuck says it's cool, then I'll believe him. After all, we've helped him out enough times."

"He told me yesterday that he was keeping Washington DC hours whilst he was over here, so I guess it'll be another couple of hours before I can call him at his hotel."

Chuck awoke to the sound of his phone. It wasn't the alarm. Someone from London was calling him.

"Jake?" he queried as he picked up the phone.

"Hi Chuck, thanks for yesterday and all. There's been some developments. Someone has re-appeared. Someone you might feel a need to turn in. She's a trusted ally of us though and we wanted to see whether we could persuade you to work with her in our team?"

"Her?" said Chuck, shaking his head from side to side, " You know I'm on Washington time?"

"Yes, I factored that in."

"Maybe not the late breakfast, though, " answered Chuck.

"Her, She, its Voronin, isn't it, " said Chuck, " I remember you worked with her when she was that singer, what was her name - Christina, er Christina Nott?"

"Katarina Voronin is how I remember her and that she was one slick operator, " said Chuck.

"I don't know the name Voronin, she's always been Christina to us, " answered Jake.

"Yes, well we found out that Voronin was a clever alias used by her along with at least two other women. They all looked similar, and it meant they could be in different places at the same time, which was helpful for alibis. A coupled of the Voronins were terrorists and assassins. I think the third one was more linked with security and covert operations. Finding out the head honcho in crime syndicates, that type of thing."

"Anyway, I'm sure that the CIA pulled the Voronins at least a couple of years ago. I think it will be case closed now, so nothing to see - let alone report."

"So, are you saying that you'd work alongside Christina without feeling the need to shop her to the US Agencies?" asked Jake.

"I don't think I could be much plainer. I know her as Voronin. The two Voronins have been apprehended. The case is closed, " answered Chuck.

"Anyway, I'd love to meet this person, she is a legend."

Politics in big fat cars

Bernard Driscoll was in his car being chauffeured to the next meeting. It was hard not to feel important when the powerful Jaguar was escorted by a couple of dark Range Rovers and two motorcycle outriders.

Despite a few unfortunate gaffes in his past, his luck was on the ascendency now. He was in some of the most influential Cabinet meetings and rubbed shoulders with the Prime Minister. If they wanted someone to set the scene on an important agenda topic, then he would be called to handle the early slots on BBC Radio Four. Why he had even been invited to take part in that hard-talking interview series on BBC World Service.

Driscoll thought back. It was since that chance meeting at the defence show. He had met a woman there who had introduced him to a supplier to Royal Kingdoms. That supplier had introduced him to a special men's meeting in East London and they had invited him to join their regular meetings.

He'd been wary of going to the men's meeting to begin with, but the supplier had urged him that 'it's not like that, " so he'd taken the plunge. It was in a pub in

London, reputedly close to the site of the Devil Tavern, which had been the place where Masons met in the 1700s.

Driscoll had been surprised to enter the pub and to see many men of around his age who were drinking and animatedly talking together. He thought he recognised a few from around Parliament, plus a couple of police chiefs talking loudly together.

"The great and the good, " he thought as he turned towards the person standing beside him at the bar.

"First time?" asked the person, " It's all a bit much isn't it? I'm William Whitehead, by the way, I practice law across the street there." He gestured out of the window of the pub and Driscoll could see the Royal Courts of Justice just across the street from the pub.

"And you are?" he asked.

"Ah yes, Driscoll, Bernard Driscoll, MP actually."

"There's quite a few of you here, this evening, I wonder if you go around in packs?" quipped William, " Look - let me introduce you to some others - don't worry, I'll steer away from the Parliamentarians."

He showed Driscoll into a small group of suited men, " Hello chaps, here's a fresh one, Bernard Driscoll from the Cabinet Office."

Driscoll monetarily wondered how William had worked out he was a Cabinet Minister, but then assumed his fame preceded him.

The group shuffled around to make an additional space for Charles to join in, and he soon found himself engrossed in a conversation about helping countries after warfare.

He left those distant thoughts and wondered instead at how time had moved on, as he watched the evening London traffic as he rounded Parliament Square. He would be driven inside the Parliament complex and then could make his own way through the tunnel back to his office in the newer construction of Portcullis House.

Yes, he had been quite a hero when he'd managed to get that arms deal concluded which involved many new British jobs to complete the munitions to be shipped to a middle eastern country.

Then he'd been able to facilitate the reparations project for the land area partially destroyed in an American bombing, also in the middle east.

And his track record was further enhanced as he persuaded the development of a new oil pipeline across the desert in Algeria and onwards towards Morocco.

The British engineering support that could be provided to the Iberian Peninsula was second to none.

Of course, he knew he'd need help to pull off these feats, but that's where his new friends and contacts were proving invaluable. He now knew just about everybody, it seemed. Why even his move to Portcullis House from Parliament was a stroke of good fortune from the Masons. He's only been talking in there one day about the school dinner smell that he had in his office and then, the very same week he was told that he was moving across the way.

Something that he'd noticed but was a pure coincidence, was that several of the big contracts for oil pipelines, the munitions and that city reparations had all gone to subsidiaries of Raven.

But he had no interest in the firm, didn't own shares in them and wasn't on their boards. No need to declare anything at all in the members interests' pages.

He just arrived at Parliament's drop-off point. A police officer opened the door for him. "Good evening, Mr Driscoll, "

…Yes, this was the life.

Amanda Miller

Amanda's phone rang. She was sitting in her office in SI6, south of the River in Vauxhall Place.

"Amanda?" came a voice, " It's Chuck, Chuck Manners."

"Chuck Manners? I thought you were dead. After that bomb in London - outside of Bank of England? I should have guessed?"

"Yes, I'm back working with Jake, Clare and Bigsy, " he said, " I hope that's enough information to verify that it is really me?"

"Okay, I was just getting ready to ask you some security questions. You are still the same!" she smiled to herself. Chuck seemed to be in a hurry - as usual.

"What's the situation then?" she asked.

"A UK company running interference into the middle east."

"Oh yes, and who would that be?"

"I can't quite say at the moment."

"How widespread?"

"Oh, this is pretty wide and involves some leading politicians."

"Well, I take it you don't want to storm anywhere on UK soil at the moment, so what do you want?"

"I just want a phone number traced, " answered Chuck, sheepishly, " I know what you are thinking. It's not one of my more outlandish requests."

"Sure, " said Amanda, " And in return?"

"D'you know what?" said Chuck, " I'd like to take you to dinner."

Amanda was not expecting this. Chuck had usually seemed so preoccupied with his missions.

"I accept, you give me the number and I'll bring along the contacts details."

"How about Sheekey's?" asked Chuck.

"I'm impressed, you know your London restaurants, "

"They do a fine oyster too, " said Chuck.

J Sheekey

They met just outside the restaurant at precisely seven pm. Chuck greeted Amanda, they kissed on both cheeks.

"That kissing thing is so European, but it's catching on in parts of America now, too, " said Chuck.

"We might as well make the evening have a little frisson, " said Amanda, " It's been an age since I last saw you. I assume you have traversed the globe a couple of times in the interim?"

"Less than you might think, " said Chuck, " Remember I had to do a disappearing act after that London bomb."

They were shown to their table. "An outside one, if you'd prefer?"

They looked at one another, " Yes that would be great, " answered Amanda, " Look there's heaters too."

"Even blankets - this is better than the Marines, " smiled Chuck.

"They say that Ian Fleming wrote the James Bond books not while sipping martinis, but over oysters and a black velvet – that's Guinness and Champagne - or two in Covent Garden, at J. Sheekey." Said Amanda, " True or not, this ought to be the place for it."

Chuck looked around. Inside he could make out the leather banquettes and wood-panelled walls covered in framed photos., quite a few of which featured well-known faces.

"Well, I don't know about you, but I'm in the mood for seafood, " said Chuck.

"Well, I'm in the mood too, " flirted Amanda.

They ordered a dozen oysters and then fish for two. A sommelier appeared and Chuck discussed wines with him before ordering a Meursault - Les Tillets - Pierre Labet.

"I know it is a bit fancy, but you Brits, you seem to have no end to the lengths of your wine lists, " said Chuck.

"I feel very flattered by all of this, " said Amanda, " I guess this number and name must be very important to you."

"Not quite as important as this chance to be with you, " said Chuck, slightly clumsily.

Amanda laughed and so did Chuck who said, " Well, that is, if I had a better scriptwriter"

They enjoyed the meal and the ambience and made light chatter. They both kept a studied professionalism about what they could discuss but felt easy in one another's company. Chuck reached his hand across to touch Amanda's.

"This is a wonderful evening, " he said, " And you know how to relax me."

Amanda smiled; she was deciding but had almost made up her mind. The bill arrived.

Chuck took Amanda's hand and they left the restaurant.

"Can we make this last a little longer?" he asked.

"I'd love to, " said Amanda.

Chuck hailed a cab and they climbed in.

Mondrian

Amanda awoke, she had to remind herself where she was. It was a room overlooking the Thames in a modern hotel called The Mondrian. It had been the offices of a sea container shipping firm and had received one of the most stylish makeovers in London. It was just along the river from The London Eye.

She looked around. Chuck was outside, sitting in a chair on the balcony.

"I didn't want to wake you, " he said, " My plans to stay on Washington time went haywire yesterday."

"I think I might know something about that, " smiled Amanda, " So, Chuck, you seem to be away from the life here? Is that so?"

"Not really, " he replied, " I think I've reached - what's that hackneyed phase - 'Mastery' so I can do my role but still relax for the rest of the time."

"Well, thank you for a wonderful evening yesterday, "

"And thank you for being a lovely guide to this busy city,"

They kissed lightly.

"I suppose I should look at that contact that you gave me yesterday, " said Chuck, he flipped open the small piece of paper.

<<Oskar Hermann, Stuttgarter Straße 8A, Böblingen D-71032 Germany>>

"German, " he said, " Interesting."

Stuttgart

"Let everything happen to you
Beauty and terror
Just keep going
No feeling is final."

Rainer Maria Rilke

Triangle Works

Jake's phone rang. It was Chuck.

"Any luck?" asked Jake

"Oh yes, in more ways than one, " answered Chuck.

Jake mentally edited his next reply, " Excellent, so who is the lucky recipient of our tail's phone calls? And hold on I'm putting you onto speaker so that Bigsy and Clare can hear too."

"It makes little sense, " said Chuck, " It is someone in Germany, in a place called Böblingen."

"Böblingen?" said Bigsy, " I know Böblingen. It's next to where we had to pick up that car. You remember, Clare, when we picked up the new car from the Mercedes factory?"

"I remember, it's close to Stuttgart...Sindelfingen, that's where the factory was, but we stayed overnight at that hotel in Böblingen."

"Oh yes, I'd forgotten that you two went to pick up the blue car, factory fresh, " said Jake.

"It was a very interesting trip. Fly out, go to the factory, get a factory tour, then get delivered a brand-new car by literally the men in white coats."

"Yes, and then we went to that restaurant…" said Clare.

"Oh yes, the asparagus one. Spargel, " remembered Bigsy, " Spargel with everything. Spargel Suppe, Spargel Salat, Spargel as vegetable and then Spargel for pudding. That was an unusual experience."

"Remember that British guy at the next table? He was being entertained there by a computer company. I thought he would explode at the thought of asparagus with everything. Like a revenge of the Spam song."

"Oh yes, I think they placated him with steak and a lot of red wine in the end. Although they were very proud of their white asparagus and said they celebrated it through the whole of May, " said Clare.

"We made up for it by diverting through Champagne country on the way back. No luggage so we had plenty of boot space."

"Much as I enjoy hearing your reminiscences, we need to know what to do now that we've found the only person who the tail seemed to know., " said Jake.

"I think we need to contact this person, " said Clare, " Maybe we should do another Bigsy and Clare expedition, like the time we found Darren Collins in Zurich?"

Bigsy nodded, " Yes I'm fine about going out to Stuttgart, we can hop a flight from Heathrow."

"You know what, " said Clare, " I think this time it might be better if I go with Christina."

"How so?" asked Jake.

"Well, think about it. The guy following us was probably Russian. We could find out that Oskar has Russian connections too, it would be better for Christina to be able to follow what was happening."

Chuck's voice crackled on the Polycom, " Clare has a point - Christina also knows how to handle herself if things get difficult. Excellent, we have a plan."

The three in the office looked at one another. Clare would need to call Christina. Chuck seemed to be okay about her and Christina also seemed good with the idea of Chuck being involved. They would have two state operatives, one from Russia and the other from the USA, working together on a Triangle case.

"This can't get much more bizarre, " mused Jake.

"Trust me, it can!" replied Bigsy.

Clare called Christina. "Hey Christina - It looks as if we are on. We'll be visiting this strange contact in Germany. We fly to Stuttgart and then cab it to Böblingen. The address is very central."

Christina replied, " That's fine. Although this is one of the slenderest leads I've ever followed. A single number in a burner and then an address supplied by SI6, via a friendly US contact. I should have alarm bells ringing everywhere. But you know what? Let's do it."

Böblingen

They arrived at a roundabout in central Böblingen. There was a bakery on one corner and a couple of hotels on the others. The junction seems to be at the top of a hill.

"Now we need to find 8A, " said Clare, " It looks as if it is this way."

They walked along the street. It was soon apparent that the numbers were erratic. 8A was an apartment building along a side street. They looked at the entrance hall. There was a large post box with maybe 40 compartments.

"Oh my god, " said Clare, " I wasn't expecting this."

Christina was less phased by the apartment's size, having spent many years living in much larger blocks around Arkhangelsk.

"We'll just look through the names on the entry phone, " she said, " What are we looking for? Ah yes, Oskar Hermann…" She looked across the various bell pushes and at the individual boxes where mail could be left.

"Well, look, " she eventually said, "Here he is, flat number 14, see there's some mail for him."

She picked up the mail and looked through it.

"Interesting, it doesn't look like an agent lives here. This is all too routine, a couple of bills, and a magazine about golf."

She showed the papers to Clare.

"Now the question is, do we ring his door? To see if he is inside?"

"I'd say yes, said Christina. It is the most straightforward way. We can tell him the story we've made up."

"Ok, then, we'll ring the bell"

"Ja? Wer ist da?" came the reply.

"Hi, we are here to meet Oskar."

"Moment mal, "

They could hear someone being called.

"Could you stand outside the door, so that I can see you, please?"

They walked outside of the entrance and stood looking up in the air, towards the balconies of the apartments.

"Okay, just one minute. I will come downstairs, " said the voice, " We can go across the road."

Christina and Clare looked at one another and then towards the elevator.

"There's a set of stairs to the left, " said Christina, " Just in case- you know."

They could hear the elevator start up. Go up to a floor. Doors opening, return to ground level.

The doors opened.

"Oh my god!" said Christina, " Pavel!"

"Hello, Agnessa Dobrayadoch!" he walked towards her and briefly hugged her.

"Hold on, I'm confused, " said Clare, " My name's Clare, who are you?"

"Hello, Clare, my name is Oskar Hermann, Agnessa and I go back a long way!"

"Let's walk around the corner to Café Frech. We can explain all."

Café Frech

They walked the fifty metres or so to the nearby coffee shop. Café Frech was bustling and clearly popular with the local clientele.

They each ordered a coffee. Clare looked around at the wide selection of cakes and other treats being delicately enjoyed by the patrons.

"I think this is one of the best coffee shops and bakeries in Germany, " said Oskar.

"Okay, explain, " said Clare, looking at both Christina and Oskar.

"I had no idea, " said Christina, " None whatsoever."

"Well, it is complicated, " said Oskar.

"Agnessa and I both attended the same Academy."

"Why are you calling her Agnessa?" asked Clare, " She's Christina?"

"Yes, I am, " confirmed Christina, " But I was once Agnessa Dobrayadoch. For around eight years actually. I was in Russia at the time."

"But I thought you were from Holland?" asked Clare.

"No, I'm Icelandic, from near to Reykjavik."

Clare looked wild-eyed, " This doesn't make any sense."

"Well, you know that I had to change my name recently from Nott to Hyde? This was another example."

"We end up with quite a few aliases in our business, " said Oskar.

"Yes, it's the same with Pavel- He appears now to be called 'Oskar'."

"So, what were you doing in Russia?" asked Clare, " Some kind of spy thing? - It has to be that."

"Yes, you could say that. But Pavel and I were also 'loves young dream' together at that time."

"You know, that's why Blackbird called me to come along here, " said Oskar, " He said he'd checked the Arkhangelsk records and found that you and I were an 'item'."

"Well, we were pretty close, your father even helped my Mamma get that job at the Museum, " agreed Christina.

"Yes, and the very next week you broke up with me - I was devastated, " said Oskar.

"But not too devastated to become very friendly with Galinka a few weeks later. I can remember you two hanging around living on air and love, " smiled Christina. She leaned over and gently kissed Oskar.

The coffee arrived, " Drei portionen Kaffee, " said the server.

"Danke sehr, " said Oskar and smiled to her.

"Okay, so which names should we use?" said Clare, " Christina and Oskar or Agnessa and Pavel?"

"We should use our current names, " said Christina. Oskar nodded.

"I've only been Oskar for a few days, " he said, " You seemed to be able to disturb the ant's hill when you spoke to Blackbird!"

"How so?" asked Christina.

"Well, it looks as if that person whose phone you stole was another Russian agent. A tail. Mid-ranking - *sredniy* - I don't think he was that good, if you managed to steal both his wallet and his phone."

Christina sailed, " You forget how good I am!"

"I agree, and that was the other factor. Blackbird was worried that his tail of an important company insider was being disrupted by what turned out to be one of his own operatives. That's why he called me. I was in Frankfurt, embedded. I have a family now. I married Galinka, you know."

Christina smiled, " Congratulations, I'd not have known."

Clare said, " Yes, but why did the tail in London have your phone number in his burner phone?"

"That's just it, " said Oskar, " He didn't. I was told to become Oskar Hermann by Blackbird on Tuesday. To drop everything and to come along from Frankfurt to Stuttgart and then to stay in the Böblingen flat until Agnessa, sorry, Christina made contact."

"Blackbird's thinking was that Christina would be more receptive to what was happening if she could see someone she could trust."

"So, what is happening?" asked Clare.

"Look, I need to know how much to trust you, " said Oskar, looking towards Christina.

"Christina, will you vouch for Clare?"

"Of course, I trust Clare completely. We are also good friends."

"Okay, then I'll tell you more." He looked around the Cafe, as if taking stock.

"I think we can safely say we are not being followed here, " said Christina, " I looked on the way in for tails or plants."

"Okay, then I'll tell you what I know, " replied Oskar.

Oskar's tale.

Oskar began, " We have to remember the context. Celarus sits on the doorstep of Russia. It has been a dictatorship for years and the Americans have quietly shored it up, preferring a buffer zone between Europe and Russia.

"I can't quite visualise Celarus, " said Clare, " What area is it in?"

"Imagine the western borders of Russia, where it joins into Europe. It's along part of that, a corridor partly created by the *Reka Sozh* - River Sozh."

"Yes, the river name sounds like *сожжъ* - *sozhzh'* - which is a Russian word for 'the burned parts of a forest prepared for ploughing', " said Christina.

Oskar continued, " At first glance, the whole situation might seem surprising. Celarus is naturally presumed as a traditional ally of the Russian Federation, which also leads to its limited engagement with the European Union.

"Yet in reality, bilateral relations between Moscow and Celarus for many years now have resembled a game of tug-of-war, in which each side seeks to maximise their own benefits.

"For Russians, we would measure such benefits in political influence, while for Celarusians – in currency. As long as Moscow pays part of the sustenance costs of the Celarusian regime, the political flexibility for the latter remains limited, including the cooperation with EU states.

"I see; under Russia's influence, then?" asked Clare.

"Yes, and that applied to diversification of oil and gas supplies, " continued Oskar, " For years, the Celarusian economy was heavily subsidised by the Russian Federation and duty-free oil shipments were one of the fundamental instruments in that regard. This form of subsidy was gradually reduced because of the tax reforms in Russia, leading to the replacement of crude oil export duty fees with a mineral extraction tax.

"Cynics might say that no oligarch has managed to get over the top of Celarus, presumably because of Tomas Kutnavenko's ruling dictatorship. The Celarusian authorities put significant effort into silencing alternative sources of information not under their control.

"Most Celarusians do not have access to independent media and as a result, public opinion in the country is determined by the state-run media, which is mainly pro-Russian and anti-Western.

"Another example of social media influence, driven from Russia?" asked Clare.

"Yes, and with consequences. The most active opposition activists and journalists are often fined or sentenced to jail. Participation in an unauthorised demonstration may result in police detention or a fine, " continued Oskar, " That's when President Tomas Kutnavenko invited the foreign investors to have a poke around to find further oil."

"In return, the US Secretary of State, Mike Pompeo, provided a short-term deal underwriting the Celarus requirement for oil - like a bridging loan to cover any shortfall, " Oscar took another sip of coffee.

"This was a big win for the USA; they got to go prospecting and could also provide oil, in effect disadvantaging Russia. Celarus was also a way into the EU-pipelines for America, so altogether advantageous, if you didn't mind dealing with a dictator-state.

Christina chipped in, " I suppose for Kutnavenko, he got to have a few American planes in his country, as the merest hint not to be messed with."

Oskar said, " Yes, on one hand, Russia was determined to set up new supply framework and proceed with the signing of in-depth integration agreement with Celarus . On the other, Celarusians now had alternative supply source, which could outprice Russian crude."

Christina added, " That was almost CIA level disruption to the economics of the region."

Oskar continued, " Yes, but then, surprise. One of the American companies discovered a new oilfield. It's significant, a real game changer for Celarus. They can dispense with the US supply once they start bringing it on stream."

Oskar paused and looked at Christina and Clare.

Christina looked surprised. How could this Cadet have learned so much? Then she realised, he would probably think the same of her.

"So, what was the basis of the operation in London?" asked Christina, " They must have told you?"

Poor Nelson

Oskar looked around the busy cafe again.

"You've heard?" he said, " about Nelson Redmund?"

Christina and Clare shook their heads.

Oskar continued, " They found his body. By a canal in Central London. They said it looked like a random crime. A robbery that went wrong."

"Nothing random about it, " said Clare, " Nelson seemed pretty grounded and savvy."

Christina and Oskar looked at one another. Clare could see they were weighing up the method.

"Yes, too much co-incidence in all of this, " said Christina, " Nelson was also our original lead into this."

"What about his buddy, Javel?" said Clare, " Do you think he would know any more?"

"I think we'll need to find out what the Russians know, via Blackbird, " said Christina, " There must be an angle on this, after all, they were tailing Nelson and bothered to send Oskar to meet us."

Oskar nodded, " I agree, I'm getting a strong feeling that this is dangerous now."

Ask the Russians

*'Sometimes it is necessary to be lonely
in order to prove that you are right.'*

Vladimir Putin

A place by the lake

"Are you staying in town?" asked Oskar.

"Yes, we've a place down by the lake. It's a small hotel where we've a couple of rooms. I think we could walk there from here."

"Okay, give me until tomorrow. I'll see what I can find out, " said Oskar.

They parted from the cafe and Christina and Clare walked together down the hill, past several other shops.

"What did you make of that?" said Christina to Clare.

"Some things I didn't know, " giggled Clare, " About you and him. Christina with a boy in every town. Antanov, Oskar…"

"Stop it, " said Christina, " I can't help it if they all fall at my feet. You know something:

Время для бизнеса, час для веселья - Vremya dlya biznesa, chas dlya vesel'ya. - time is for business, the hour is for fun, as the Russian saying goes."

They had reached to end of the hill and were standing near a busy road junction. Ahead they could see the lake.

"Over there, to the right, that's where our hotel is., " said Clare.

"But what did you think about the whole situation?" asked Christina again.

"Complicated and messy. I can see the Russians would want to get involved if they thought that Celarus would become a threat. Another American aircraft carrier."

"Except its land locked, " said Christina.

"Okay a military base then, " said Clare.

"Yes, America wins big time - they get to put in military, to exploit the resources via their own companies and to wrest some oil control from the Russians, " said Christina.

"Won't that divide your loyalties though?" asked Clare.

"Ask me again tomorrow after we hear what Oskar has to say."

...

The next morning, they were back in Café Frech.

"It's no good, I'm going to have some breakfast here, " said Clare.

"It's great, " said Oskar, " They do a breakfast basket, with the typical German breakfast items in it. I recommend it."

They ordered three Frühstuckkörble and then turned to Oskar.

"So, what did you find out?" asked Christina.

"Well, first Blackbird didn't seem to know so much, but I think that was his training to not tell us anything. I decided it was best to say you were in danger, Christina, just to make him open his mouth more. I told him that after Nelson we suspected that you were next on the hit list."

"I also discovered that Nelson's death was not anything to do with us - Blackbird had been as surprised as us to find out when he was killed."

"That helped loosen Blackbird's tongue; he said he thought the plan was related to the divestment. It turns out that the person following you that evening was from Russian Intelligence. His name *Марк Лисон* - Mark Leeson, was as burnable as his phone. Blackbird said he was a temporary asset set to work as a tail."

Christina remembered her training from the Academy. The Russians had a long list of agent types, mainly because some of them were for a single purpose. She could remember being annoyed at how long it took to remember them all.

Clare said, " Leeson? Wasn't that the name of Rogue Trader? I see the FSB have a sense of humour."

"Yes, well I asked Blackbird directly what the agent's code name was. He took a while to answer, but finally came back with "Olivier.""

Christina laughed, " Now that's what I call a quick snack!"

Clare looked confused, " What's so funny about his name?"

Oskar was laughing too, " Olivier - Russian Salad - Take boiled potatoes, boiled eggs, ham, meat cut into cubes, green peas, mayo - This is not haute cuisine; rather, a quick snack when you don't want to treat your guests to a "real salad." That's why it's so popular during New Year celebrations. It's easy to cook, and not as tasty as you think."

"Do you think that were having a laugh when they handed out the code names?" asked Christina, " Say Oskar, what's your code name?"

Oskar smiled as he said, " Sable - very high class! And what about you, Christina, what's your codename?"

Christina smiles, " Archangel, " she said, " Arkhangelsk."

Oskar's expression changed, " No way, " he said, " I'm in the presence of the next Tsarina of the FSB, or at least a supergod legend. Everyone has heard of your exploits. Some even know your names - Katarina Voronin, for example."

"Don't believe everything you are told, " said Christina.

Clare looked at the two of them, engaged in spy-banter, " So do I get a name too?" she asked.

"Not unless you want to join the FSB, " said Christina, but let's think for a minute…*Clare, Клэр, бордо, кровь жизни, krov' zhizni, krov', boltun…" - How about "Magpie?"*

Oskar laughed, " I can see how you got to it. Clare, Claret, Lifeblood, *Krov' zhizni* - Crow, Magpie - all through the Russian. - But you know that Magpie is considered a chattery bird in Russian?"

Clare laughed, " Hmm I'm not sure how to take that, but I'll go with Magpie for the moment, anyway."

They chinked their coffee cups together, " To Sables, Magpies and Archangels" said Oskar.

Okay, said Oskar, " back to the Russian salad. So, Olivier was tasked to follow Nelson. It was clearly something to do with Raven and the evolving situation in Celarus."

"That's why the Russians would be interested. They'd be rattled by the corporate moves of America."

"Well, we also know that Raven was getting ready for a divestment, to set up another company called Brant Holdings, " said Christina, " But I don't think Nelson knew much about this. He was asking us to do some digging."

"Yes, so the Russians followed Nelson around, mainly to see who he was speaking to, " said Clare.

"But then Nelson mysteriously dies, because of a suspected robbery. The coincidences are starting to stack up, " said Christina.

"I asked Blackbird if we could trace Olivier, " said Oskar, " He was hesitant, but gave me this address. Blackbird said he was worried that this whole thing was spiralling out of control."

He showed Clare and Christina a piece of paper. It was an address on Olympian Way, in the Greenwich Peninsula.

"Wow, " said Clare, " That's close to the Dome, let me check it on my phone, " She tapped away, " Yes, it's as I thought, the address seems to be an office block in the main O2 conurbation, facing across the river towards Victoria Docks."

"It looks as if they've given an accommodation address instead of where he lives, " said Oskar.

"It's still useful, " said Christina, " Who knows what we'll find there!"

"It should be our next port of call, " said Christina, looking to Clare, " Oskar, I guess you'll be staying here in Germany?"

"Well, technically, my assignment was over when I made contact, " said Oskar, " and Galina and the kids will be expecting me back in Frankfurt. It might take some explaining that I've been with two beautiful ladies, one of whom was an ex 'true love of mine.'"

Christina laughed, " Oh yes, when you were the great moody poet with a scarf. - A *lattelepjandi listamenn*!"

"You forget I don't speak Icelandic, " he said.

"Makes no odds, we are still first loves, " said Christina as she walked up to him and kissed him on both cheeks.

Clare then felt awkward, she was running out of farewell moves.

"Goodbye, Oskar, " And thank you, " she said.

He rose, hugged her and said, "Farewell, my little magpie."

Christina and Clare walked out of the cafe, aware that they were both drawing stares from the adjacent tables.

"Heathrow? I think Antanov might be feeling a little lonely" said Christina.

"Heathrow." Confirmed Clare.

Echterdingen

They sat in Echterdingen airport awaiting their plane. Christina was reading a magazine, and Clare was listening to music on her headphones. Someone approached.

"Christina?" he said, " Is it Christina Nott?"

Christina looked up. She recognised the face, but not from where.

"Amsterdam, " he said, " I'm Ian - I played guitar on some of your tracks. When we were making those copy tracks."

"Ian!" said Christina, " I remember, you had that hand-built raw-wood Telecaster. The one I borrowed. I even made a track with it - 'Telecaster blues (I only borrowed it)' "

"Yes, we were just doing a gig here in Tübingen - my band are over in the cafe - I spotted you and just wanted to say 'Hi' - you must get it all the time!"

"Not really, " said Christina, she waved across to the band, sitting in the cafe. They waved back and the female blew kisses to Christina.

"Can I? -Er - this sounds kind of lame - can I get a selfie with you?" asked Ian.

"Of course, you can - how about with Clare as well?" suggested Christina.

Ian set up his smartphone. They all crowded in. A flash and the picture was taken.

The airport announcement called for the flight to Heathrow.

"Great to see you; enjoy Amsterdam!" said Christina.

London, the Triangle offices.

Jake, Bigsy and Clare were sitting around a table.

Christina and Antanov walked in.

"Christina, I wasn't expecting you today, " said Jake, " And hello again Antanov, it's good to see you both, actually."

"Let's see if we can devise a plan, " said Bigsy.

Clare began, " Well, we know that Raven is splitting off Brant Holdings. That it has rattled the Russians. That a whistle-blower - Nelson - has been suspiciously killed. That the Russians tailed Nelson and have a base somewhere near to the Dome, on the Greenwich Peninsular."

"We also know that the tail for Nelson was a low-level Russian, not a killer, so I'm guessing that Nelson met his fate at someone else's hands, " added Christina.

Clare replied, "They must be hiding something. I'd have thought that Raven's sale of Qube to create Brant was a typical post-Brexit move? Shifting yet more British companies into Europe?"

Jake nodded his agreement, " 'Selling England by the Pound,' as a prog-rock group might say. It has been going on ever since Thatcher's Britain. One of the early ones was Vickers plc which sold Rolls-Royce Motors to Volkswagen Group, for £480m. I guess that opened the floodgates."

"That was under Tony Blair," added Bigsy, "Not Thatcher."

"Oh all right, Thatcher's privatisations – like of British Telecom opened the floodgates and then it took a while to catch on and for the lawyers to work out how to make it all seem legitimate selling a company so that the previous management could make a bundle," said Jake.

Bigsy could see that Jake was getting irritated, but Jake continued anyway, "Now it's difficult to tell who owns what in the high street, through a succession of packaging of sell-offs. It doesn't ma. There's Boots the Chemist sold to US company Walgreens as well as the well-known UK bookshop Waterstones now owned by Russians."

"The treasured NHS has American IT all over it and services from Southern Cross, which is in turn owned by Blackstone, the huge American Corporation."

"Step on a train and its likely to be run by Deutsche Bahn, SNCF, Keolis of France, Abellio from the Netherlands. Heck, even the Essex commuter train C2C is Italian."

Bigsy nodded agreement, "Apple UK is taxed through Ireland, MoD research spun off the high-tech Qinetiq which was then bought by Carlyle (with ex PM John

Major on board) and the clever people at ARM semiconductor went to Softbank in Japan."

"I remember when Kraft bought Cadburys, and that the Royal Mail is German," interrupted Clare, "It says it on their vans."

"And most of our energy in the UK comes from German Eon, French EDF and Spanish Iberdrola," added Jake.

"Like BA," said Bigsy, "That's Spanish isn't it?"

"And it has been in all the papers about British Steel and that Chinese Company - Jinye, isn't it?" asked Clare.

"Ironic that," said Jake, "First they flood our steel markets, then they buy us up."

"Well Raven is lining up a similar move, hoping to go underneath Parliament's scrutiny, but maybe needs a tame minister to help it along."

"And that Raven is well connected, heck, its head office is kitted out like a Masonic Lodge, " added Jake.

"We've also got American involvement via Chuck and even SI6 interest, because he used one of his contacts there to get us the address in Germany, " added Clare.

"And Antanov, is well-connected in the Masons to help us find out more."

Antanov smiled, " We shall see how our 'interests' converge or diverge? - Russia, The Masons, Raven. But good news, I've been busy while Christina was away. I've been invited to a Masonic meeting. They say it is officially a 'Ladies' Night', when the wives and partners of Masons can also attend."

"So, no real business will be transacted then?" asked Bigsy.

"Correct, but it is a great way to meet people and, in my case, to find out about joining. And to top it all, it is at the Raven offices. Their Head Office in London."

"And another advantage. I can take along a lady."

Everyone around the table looked towards Christina.

"Oh, I see, Okay, yes then, " she said.

Ladies' Night

Now, if I was an actor or a dancer that was glamorous
Then, you know, an amorous life would soon be mine
But now the tinsel light of star break
Is all that's left to applaud my heart break
And eleven o'clock I watch the network news

Goodnight ladies, ladies goodnight
It's time to say goodbye
Let me tell you, now, goodnight ladies, ladies goodnight
It's time to say goodbye

Lou Reed

Infiltrate

They were back at Christina's flat.

"Okay Antanov, so what do I need to know about this Ladies' Night at the Masons?" asked Christina.

"It'll be glitzy, and quite formally structured. Although a few lodges that accept women as members, the traditional lodges still maintain a men-only membership.

"It is more of an evening gowns and frock kind of night, the fancier, the better. It's the perfect time to bring out the jewellery as well. If you want to really impress, wear a small brooch with a rose on it. It is a signal of power.

"I hope you are thinking of 'Eyes wide shut' by now?"

Christina smiled, " Well, I wasn't and I'm assuming we don't get the kinky bits either?"

"No, it's pretty staid, except for the conversation. Evening gloves are about as kinky as it gets. They are part of the tradition. They should worn until grace is said, after which, they can be taken off.

"Once we arrive, we will be presented to the Worshipful Master and his Lady. Make sure you have something nice to say to the Lady, to create a good impression. Because I'm a son of a high-ranking Mason, it should also mean we get to sit at a good table.

"And I can talk to anyone about anything?" asked Christina,

Antanov replied, " Yes, use your instincts for that part, it doesn't matter if you ask a few probing questions about Masonic things, either. Most women are fascinated to know what their men-folk are up to with their strange leather aprons and their chisels."

"At the start of the meal, everyone is to stand behind their chair and wait for the Director of Ceremonies to bang the gavel or ring a bell. After the signal, the Chaplain will say grace. Usually there's a few ushers to remind you of these things.

"My quick description is to think of a traditional wedding reception with service à la russe."

"Got it, " said Christina.

"The Rose Song is a regular part of Ladies' Night. Here, roses are presented to the Master's Lady, after which toasts will be made. See why the rose brooch is important. And by wearing it you are showing a power and daring.

"I doubt whether a single other woman would do so. I'm going to find you a particularly powerful rose symbol, with a cross, triangle and an ankh. The Lady will notice it.

"After this, the men often have a song prepared for their ladies. There will also be presents, and speeches will be made. The rest of the night can be used for further fellowship.

"Okay, " said Christina, " So what kind of gown? I can go traditional style Diane von Fürstenberg or wild-child Wunderkind?" She flicked on to her smartphone.

"Here, I saved these pictures as examples?"

Antanov took a look, " Oh. My. God. He said at the first picture - That's Wunderkind. You will blow their minds if you show up like that. Too edgy by halves. I love it."

Then he looked at the Fürstenberg, " That's the right kind of slinkiness. You can still own the room in that one, without causing a riot."

Christina laughed, " I had a feeling you'd pick that one. The blue one says it should be worn with sandals though, but I was hoping for Louboutin."

Handshakes

They arrived back at the now-familiar entrance to the Raven Head Office. They had come by taxi and there were several other glamorous looking types also arriving. Outside, the security seemed to have been beefed up and men in dark suits with small radio packs were marshalling those entering. There was a funnel that led to a short red carpet. Everyone seemed to have brought their invitations along.

"Antanov? We do have some tickets somewhere?" asked Christina.

"It's fine, " he said, " I have the right handshake, " He winked towards Christina.

"Hello, you have your ticket?" asked one of the security people. Antanov took the security man slightly to one side and said something quietly to him.

"Oh, Sir, please come this way, we have a special entrance for special guests."

Antanov gestured to Christina who slipped out of the line. They followed the security man to a different door.

"Here, he said, " Special guests' entrance, "

They pushed at the door and instantly were inside a spacious lobby. There were golden columns and a photographer already snapping their pictures, "

"Hello, " greeted a woman in a dark gown, " Wow that blue gown is stunning, " she said to Christina, " Could I have a photo with you - you don't mind?" she shot a look to Antanov, who nodded approval.

"Here, now take some of this champagne. Look I'd like to present you both with these small brooches to wear; it helps identify you in the room - as special guests."

Christina looked at the brooch. It had a small picture of a spring of acacia on it.

"And this means?" she asked. She noticed that Antanov had a different symbol, his was a more traditional compass and set square, in gold but outlined in red.

"Yours is a symbol of Immortality of the soul and innocence, " he began, " Mine is more or less a symbol of rank and how long I've been a Mason. They are both pretty serious. You should wear the acacia brooch underneath the rose brooch that I gave you."

They paused to pin their brooches. They entered the main room from the side lobby and already there was an atmosphere of excitement. It seemed very different from the Head Office visit day with Nelson.

Christina could see that Antanov was instantly at ease with the proceedings, approaching various people to say hello and introducing Christina. He introduced her as his partner, which she did not mind, realising that the label was for simplicity of explanation. She remembered back to the Academy and thought about the briefings there on 'cocktail parties'. This was not anything like the session they described.

Eventually, it was time to sit down for dinner. Christina remembered about waiting until the Worshipful Master and his Lady had sat, the Director of Ceremonies had banged the gavel and a Chaplain had said grace.

She decided it was wise to say nothing of these events, even if she did think them arcane.

Then, as if on a signal, conversation broke out. Several men started to chat to her and Antanov appeared to be talking to a stunning blonde woman across the table from him. Christina looked either side of the blonde but couldn't decide who she had come along with. The scene had the appearance of a much younger woman with an ageing businessman, however she cut it.

One of the men proposed a small off the cuff toast to the lovely ladies present, and Christina thought she caught the blonde saying *"za zda-ró-vye"* - which intrigued her. Perhaps the woman was actually Russian - surely not the cliché of a Russian bride?

"…for a living then?" droned one of the men.

"Oh, I work in public relations, " said Christina, " It's for a very small firm, we help small businesses get started, " she replied, somewhat on autopilot, " oh and you?" she said feigning interest.

"I'm in one of those companies that specialise in mergers and acquisitions, actually, " he said, " We work mainly around the city, you may have heard of us? ISMC?

International Strategic Management Consultants? We help bigger clients through the merger or divestment processes."

"Oh, that's very interesting, " said Christina, " I guess you get to see how many companies operate?"

"Yes, we are often in their board rooms, or their strategy meetings, all over Europe. My name is Gerhardt, by the way, Gerhardt Schmidt - from Germany."

"Oh, I was in Germany earlier in the week, near Stuttgart, actually, "

"I'm from Wiesbaden, which is close to Frankfurt. That's where we have our main office."

"In Germany? You have such an English or American-sounding name for the company?"

"Yes, branding, I think, to get the kind of coverage we want, es ist besser to have a London-sounding centre - still - even after Brexit!"

He laughed.

"So is your partner here?" asked Christina, looking around the table.

"Yes, she is, that is Nina, across the way, she is the one with the blonde Haar."

Christina thought for moment. Nina, a useful Russian name that does not sound out of place in most of Europe.

Another man had caught her eye, " I like your brooches, " he said, eyeing the acacia and the rose, for what Christina considered just slightly too long.

"Yes, I thought they were pretty to wear this evening, " said Christina, " and the acacia one was given to me on the way into the event."

"Ahah," said the man, " We are in the presence of honoured guests!"

   "And yes, that's my partner, " Christina gestured to Antanov and saw the man take an eyeful of Antanov's regalia.

"Oh, I see, we have an honoured guest from another lodge here present this evening."

"Yes, Antanov is now in the Belgian Lodge, but before that was in the Brazilian Lodge. His father was an officer too."

The man seemed impressed by this, Christina thought to herself that the von Fürstenberg gown was working.

"So, I hear there is something happening with Raven? They get more successful but are planning to sell something?" ventured Christina.

"Really?" asked the man, " I wouldn't know about that. There's always rumours sweeping around."

"I know, I expect I've got it wrong, " said Christina, " This salmon is delicious - it tastes so fresh - it bursts in my mouth."

"Yes, it says in the menu that this is Icelandic salmon, something of a rare treat, " said Gerhardt.

Christina bit her tongue, she knew better than to answer that particular point. She could see Antanov getting more deeply involved in his conversation with the blonde and another dark-haired woman who reminded Christina of Angelina Jolie, in a modest black dress, high to the neckline. Then she realised that 'Angelina' was the partner of a 55-year old balding businessman.

There was something unusual about these men's choice of partners. Christina decided that they were either all punching above their weight, or that the Ladies' Night was a thin excuse to bring someone else along.

She would have to wait until later to ask Antanov about this. She looked around the room, there was still a good smattering of 'reasonable match' husband and wife combos. Perhaps she had just landed on an usual table?

The evening continued. Several other men came along to chat with Christina, she could not work out whether they were simply being friendly, or whether there was something else at play.

She did not try any more direct questioning, although she found it useful to mention ISMC a couple of times, which got a reaction from whoever she was talking to.

Apparently, ISMC was known as a cost-cutter, as one man put it 'a butcher' who would strip out unwanted headcount. Christina could see how this would play to the Brant agenda. She was curious that here no-one was aware of any form of divestment, though. She wondered if it was a corporate secret, although in this area of free speech it seems that they would talk openly about other company secrets.

She found out that the Chairman had been replaced in an office coup. That the finance for the last five years was being inspected by HMRC. That someone had been sacked from energy trading for setting up a small cartel among the traders from other organisations and manipulating the forward price.

Christina decide that this was the stuff of big business, that nothing exceptionally bad seemed to be on the list, but there were undertones of corrupt practice.

She thought this was more likely to be a Raven thing rather than anything involving the Freemasons, who seemed harmless enough with their special leather aprons and impossibly long climb to the top of the organisation. 33 degrees to get to the top? It was worse than the Russian Army.

Then something happened.

A man who knew Gerhardt came to sit at their table. He was quite loud and seemed to know Gerhardt from a few trips abroad.

"Hello Bernard, " said Gerhardt warmly, " How was the Grand Prix?"

"Which one?" asked Bernard, "Hockenheimring or Monza?"

"Ah yes, " I'd forgotten you went to both circuits this year. I suppose we'll see you again at Abu Dhabi. - I hear the Yas Marina circuit has had no expense spared!"

Christina was intrigued by this. Bernard did not look like the kind of man who would be able to go swanning round the world to Formula 1 races. She always thought of the type of Russians that did this. Tanned, gold cufflinked shirts, gold bangles and women. This man was wearing a Seiko watch. Mail-order inexpensive practicality.

She also noticed the "we'll" in the phrasing. This was one of the old-corruptibles. An industrial tourist. Leveraged travel at a consultant's expense. In someone's pocket.

Now she had to guess what he did for a living.

She didn't have long to wait. Another man came along, " Bernard, how the devil are you? How's things in The House? Gerhardt, are you talking to Mr Driscoll about work things? - Naughty naughty. And let me introduce my friend Marion Charlotte."

Christina noticed a fairly ethereal looking woman walk over. She smiled at Bernard and said, " Yes Charles tells me you are an MP."

Christina could see that Driscoll was smitten by the soft charm of Marion and watched with fascination to see how it would play out. Driscoll's eyes were on stalks like a comedy cartoon character.

"I'm delighted to meet you, Ms Charlotte. This is a very special occasion isn't it? and Hello Charles, good to see you, " said Driscoll, " To answer your original question - Gerhardt is talking about Formula 1 racing. So, no harm done there.

"Sir Charles, a pleasant co-incidence to run into you here this evening!"

"If you could excuse me, gentlemen, I know something about Formula One racing drivers, but had better move before my ears start to burn!" Marion smiled to them all and lingered on the smile to the still popper-eyed Driscoll.

Then she breezed on to meet another small group at the next table.

"Fascinating, " said Driscoll.

"Oh yes, she and one of the Formula One drivers were an item for a while. I think she could give you the insiders' track on the sport."

"Oh, it would be great to meet her for longer, " said Driscoll.

"Leave it with me old chap, " said Sir Charles, " You never know! Standing here it seems damn lucky that I was invited at the last minute, I think our firm are helping out to run the event and so they asked me if I could make an appearance"

Christina worked it out. Bernard Driscoll was some kind of minister in the House of Commons. And now these two fellows were working the old one-two with him. One to snare him and then to pass him along to a senior partner - "Sir Charles".

A senior partner who would add Marion Charlotte as a sweetener. And Driscoll didn't seem to have a clue that he was being played.

Christina remembered her Academy training - the western influence strategies. Cultural webs. Johnson and Scholes. Charles Handy. The so called 'cocktail parties'.

Oh yes, mark the senior players at an event such as this. Create a signalling system, for when there's an opportunity. Be prepared to stand down if the object realises what is happening. Inject the ideas at multiple levels, so that they will coalesce when the organisation gets back together.

Christina stood. Everyone looked towards her.

"Excuse me, gentlemen, " she said.

She was making her way to the washroom, but it was also partly to check on the organisation of this event.

She found the main signage. In very small letters underneath Ladies' Night, were the words 'sponsored by ISMC.' Okay, so they could probably have an input to the arrangements. Or maybe they had run the whole event to take the 'pain' away from Raven.

She was checking her makeup when the blonde woman appeared, " Hello, " she said, " We're on the same table, do you know Jennifer Sussex too?"

"Jennifer?" queried Christina, " Oh yes, Jennifer, I call her Jenny!" lied Christina.

"I thought so, " said the blonde, " My name is Natalie, " she held out a hand. They shook hands.

"It's good to get a few minutes break, but Jennifer will be around if we stay here too long, " she said, " that man I'm with is exhausting, he talks about golf all the time and wants to keep showing me hand grip positions."

"I've heard it called a lot of things, " said Christina, " but never that."

"Well, it's good money at these Raven events, so I can't complain, " said the blonde; she shook her hair, twisted on her heels and was gone.

Christina returned; Gerhardt was sitting alone. It was turning into one of those wedding dinners.

"Hello again, Gerhardt, " she said, " What happened to your two friends? - The one you called Sir Charles and the MP?"

"Oh, Sir Charles Frobisher and Bernard Driscoll; they walked over to one of the side rooms to discuss something. I have a horrible feeling it was work!" he laughed.

The old one-two thought Christina. One to catch them, the second to tie them up.

The Corruption of Bernard Driscoll

The next day, after the Ladies' Night, Christina and Antanov were trying to make sense of what they had discovered. They were around at the Triangle offices and sat together with Clare, Bigsy and Jake.

"What have we got?" asked Jake.

"Well, it's all rather strange, " answered Christina, " We need to work out how much of what we discovered was driven by Raven, how much by the Masons and how much via a firm, employed by Raven. They are called ISMC and are a German-based M&A consultancy."

"Mergers and acquisitions, what about divestments?" asked Clare.

"I think it amounts to the same thing, it's a case of buying and selling, " said Antanov, " From what we can make out, Raven have hired this consultancy. In turn, they are driving the agenda along, using various influence strategies. The Masons appears to be one of these approaches and they are using it to pick off some of the players needed to make whatever Raven is doing work."

"You are not defending the Freemasons in any way? We respect your loyalty to them but would prefer to know, " said Jake, knowing he was broaching a difficult subject.

"No, absolutely not, " said Antanov, " I'm as keen as all of you to find out what on earth is going on and to understand how the Freemasons are being misused, "

Antanov continued, " For example, let's say a company needs influence in government. Normally this would be through lobbying, but a more subtle attack could be by using some tamed and slightly corrupted MPs to drive the agenda along.

Christina picked up, " So now, we discover that Bernard Driscoll, who is the Member for Ilford Central and also a member of the Cabinet as Minister for External Relations and Chancellor of the Duchy of Windsor, is also a Formula 1 enthusiast.

"No big deal, except if he is able to go to a whole range of the races, in exotic locations, Germany, Italy and United Arab Emirates. These seem to be visits arranged by ISMC."

Antanov continued, " And we also noticed that there were some additional attractive partners at the Ladies' Night event. I'm not sure that Freemasons would countenance such behaviour, but one of the women mentioned to Christina that Raven paid well."

"Yes, and I did seem to be getting quite a lot of attention from roving single men, " said Christina.

"Antanov, tsk-tsk, " Clare waggled a finger toward him.

"I could see that Christina was ably looking after herself, and I was sitting next to her, " replied Antanov, " I had the impression that people thought our table had been stocked with some spare ladies."

Jake recapped, " So we seem to have some kind of corruption, operating at a top level, via the mechanism of a Masonic meeting, but one hosted by Raven and sponsored by ISMC."

"Did you get any additional contacts?" whilst you were at the event?" asked Bigsy, " People who we could trace or track down for their public history?"

"We did, " said Christina, " I talked to a contact at ISMC - a Gerhardt Schmidt, from their Frankfurt office. He also pulled over his boss, Sir Charles Frobisher. I get the impression that Sir Charles was a special deployment at this event. Schmidt seemed to be more like a low-level sales type, there to snare the big animals."

"So, we think that Driscoll is being manipulated?" asked Clare.

"Most certainly, " said Christina, " but we don't know by whom, nor why."

Masonic friends

"I'm going to make some calls, " said Antanov, " See if anyone knows anything."

"This is where the Rose comes in useful."

"I noticed that rose had a small golden cross in the background, " said Christina, " I thought I saw others were examining it. As a woman you get used to strange men staring at one's chest."

Clare nodded. Christina produced the small brooch from her purse along with the golden acacia twig.

"They are lovely, " said Clare,

"But no doubt there's some symbolism?" asked Bigsy.

"I like the touch of gold, " added Jake, pointing to the small golden cross subtly behind the rose. And a Triangle?

"Yes, " said Antanov. "I decided to give Christina a symbol, which would cause the others present to treat her well."

"The symbol is Rosicrucian, it's a Templar Cross, but in case this it doesn't look overtly religious. That triangle is another powerful symbol. The cross from which it is inspired pre-dates Christianity by about 1400 years.

"Hmm, the cross; I always wondered about the Christians using a Roman torture instrument as a sign of faith, in any case, " said Bigsy.

"Very cool, " said Clare, " but I've only heard of the Rosicrucians in that book by Umberto Eco - the one they made into a murder mystery. James Bond as the main investigator in a Benedictine monastery filled with too many monkish murder suspects. Agatha Christie in Church."

"Yes, that's like a primer in Hermetic Alchemy, " said Antanov, " but I think even Eco himself was conflicted when he wrote the story."

"Hermetic Alchemy?" said Bigsy, " That's a bit of a rich one for this time in the morning."

"Let's start with the rose, " said Antanov. Most Freemasons are on the lookout for symbols, so Christina showing up with an acacia - sign of innocence, but then a rose - powerful alchemy and a Triangle - which normally contains the Supreme Being's ever watchful eye. It'd blow their minds."

"And I thought it was the von Fürstenberg!" said Christina.

"Mmm. Nice, " said Clare approvingly.

"Well the rose, " said Antanov, " It has three tiers of petals. The first tier, of three petals, represents the three basic alchemical elements: salt, mercury, and sulphur.

 "The tier of seven petals represents the seven Classical planets

"The tier of twelve represents the astrological zodiac. Each of the twenty-two petals bears one of the twenty-two letters in the Hebrew alphabet and also represents the twenty-two paths on the Tree of Life.

"It's shaky pseudo-science then, " said Bigsy. "I thought petals followed a Fibonacci series. And anyway, most roses have a five-petal centre?"

"Come to think of it the planets number is a bit off too. Some artful thinking here?"

"Bigsy, when was the last time you've given a bouquet to a love of your life? - Give the man a break, " said Jake laughing.

"Okay, I agree, the whole premise may have some flaws, but plenty of people will follow its direction in any case, " said Antanov, "And it meant Christina was flaunting an attitude to those Freemasons."

"And then we get to the Rosicrucians themselves. Rosicrucianism is a spiritual and cultural movement which arose in Europe in the early 17th century after the publication of several texts which purported to announce the existence of a hitherto unknown esoteric order to the world and made seeking its knowledge attractive to many.

"Christina turning up at the Lodge signalling herself as an Adept of the Rosicrucian order will have blown some of their first-degree minds. Being clad in that blue gown adds another dimension too. There's a thing called the Blue Lodge, which only the top Masons can attend. There isn't even one in the UK anywhere, so it has a kind of mythical status. Think about it, 'A woman from the Blue Lodge, an adept Rosicrucian' - it's off the symbolic scale.'

"The Rosicrucian manifestos heralded a 'universal reformation of mankind', through a science allegedly kept secret for decades until the intellectual climate might receive it.

"Some sort of fake news included though, " said Bigsy.

Antanov continues, " Hmm, yes, controversies arose on whether they were a hoax, whether the 'Order of the Rosy Cross' existed as described in the manifestos, and whether the whole thing was a metaphor disguising a movement that really existed, but in a different form.

"The mysterious doctrine of the order is 'built on esoteric truths of the ancient past', which 'concealed from the average man, provide insight into nature, the physical universe, and the spiritual realm'."

"Wow; it almost sound primordial, " Said Bigsy.

"Yes, it is supposed to, " answered Antanov, " That's part of its power - and you can see how it could be sealed hermetically inside a monastery, like in that Alberto Eco story."

"Or exploited cynically, by some opportunistic financiers?" added Clare.

"Antanov, I'm so glad you didn't tell me all of this before. It's a lot to comprehend, " said Christina.

"I would have, but we didn't really have lot of time and then that ebullient woman adding the sprig of acacia meant symbolism overload. You were really signposted like Alpha to Omega. Innocent to Adept."

"So, is that why I had so many men come over to say hello?" asked Christina.

"Er, I think that might have been because we were on the same table as Nathalie and her blonde friend, Nina" said Antanov.

"Oh yes, the ones arranged by Jennifer Sussex - I just remembered her name - Nathalie told me it when we were in the washroom."

"Useful, " said Jake, " There's another line to follow. We might be able to work out how often these events take place."

"So, is this moving us along?" asked Clare.

"I think so, " said Jake, " Look, we now know who sponsored the session, at least one of the people being influenced. We know who is doing the lobbying and the means being used. Plus, we've external leads to follow up. The office by the Dome and some sort of contact with Bernard Driscoll."

"You know who could help with that last point? - Amanda Miller." Said Bigsy, " And I think that is how Chuck got the address in Germany that we followed."

Mystery address at the dome

Bigsy and Christina took the Jubilee Line to Canada Water. They emerged from the long escalator to a courtyard that led in a semicircle towards the Dome.

"Many's the time I've been here to see music acts, " said Bigsy, " Although sometimes they can be little dots in the distance."

"Sometimes the gigs are in the smaller venue, " said Christina, switching into muso mode for a few seconds.

"Oh yes, I suppose you know all about venues and their capacity from 'living the dream', " said Bigsy, " We'll need to turn to the right here, "

They branched off towards some colourful plate glass buildings which seemed to be arranged along the bank of the Thames.

"Now remember, we are here for an interview, " said Bigsy.

They looked again at the address and checked the floor. It was to be the 6th floor of the building.

Their meeting was entirely fictitious, but they thought it might get them through the first stage of the building security.

They entered through the revolving doors. Christina quickly scoped the layout. Reception to the left, turnstiles central, no separate access for the lifts. Excellent."

"Hello, we are here to visit Recognition Consultants, we are from Bluefish Recruitment. We have a meeting with the head of HR."

"Okay that's Janie Parker, just one moment."

He dialled a number. "Voicemail, " he muttered.

"Okay, I think Ms Parker said if she was not available then to go to speak to one of her staff."

"Let me try again, " He dialled again, " Oh, Hello, I've two people here to see Janie Parker, they are from Bluefish Recruitment…Okay…I'll check…Yes…Right…Ring you again…Okay…Yes…Okay."

"They will see you in a moment. Here, let me make the badges. They will get you in and out today only. Please hand them back to one of the security people when you leave. Please look at the Blue square on the wall. Thank you. And now you, Sir, Thank you."

They completed the rest of their details and were each handed a lanyard.

"Please put this around your neck and keep the badge visible. The orange denotes visitor."

"You can go on through now, to the Sixth floor. Tap it in the elevator. Someone will meet you at the doors."

"Excellent, " said Christina to Bigsy. "We are in."

They were met at the Sixth floor.

"Hello, I'm Petra, Janie isn't available at the moment, but I can probably help you."

She showed them through to a glass sided meeting room.

"Look, I haven't booked this one, so we might get kicked out at half past. People just book these rooms and then don't turn up to use them."

"Coffee, or water?"

"A coffee would be lovely, " said Christina.

"I'm good, " said Bigsy.

"Okay, it'll be machine - you don't mind? - I'll just go outside to fetch some."

"I'll come with you, " said Christina.

They left Bigsy alone in the office. He wandered out through the door. In front was a wall of filing cupboards, there was an occasional gap which served the function of door access to the clusters of pods. He noticed they were packed pretty tight, much like call-centre. Everyone he could see had a headset, with a microphone. This was a call-centre. He noticed a couple of supervisor booths in the corner of the office. Slightly higher flooring and a glass side, like the meeting room, so that the supervisor could look out.

He noticed Christina and Petra returning.

"Now what can I help you with today?" asked Petra.

"Well, that's just it, " said Christina, " Ms Parker invited us in for a talk about requirements, I think she said you were hiring?"

"Em, this is quite embarrassing, " said Petra, "But I'm not sure I know what this is about."

"That's okay, " said Christina, " We flew in from Amsterdam this morning, but we have meetings with a couple of other clients as well, *Hey Dave, je controleert je afspraken voor later, nietwaar?*"

Bigsy looked confused and said, " Yes, later today we've more appointments."

Christina was calling him by his real first name - very formal.

"I'm afraid this might all be a visit in vain, today, " said Petra.

"Okay, no worries, although perhaps you'd give us the tuppenny tour of the floor on the way out, for future reference."

"Why certainly, " said Petra.

"As you can see, we are an American organisation, Consultancy, but we field a lot of direct enquiries from here in this call-centre. They can be direct from clients or passed on via our field representatives."

"It sounds like it is multi-lingual too, " said Christina, " That's probably why you contacted us. We couldn't use the name babel fish, but Bluefish consultants deals with many languages too."

"I can see the little flags now, this must be the Scandinavian section, there's Norway, Sweden and -er - Denmark?"

"That's right, " said Petra, clearly a little confused by flags and the languages being spoken.

Bigsy held out his phone and quietly took a couple of pictures. He noticed the number of American accents talking as well as the multiple languages. The large screens in the room were running US television too, no sound but subtitles. Each set of cubicles has a cluster of TVs showing a mix of Fox, CBS, NBC, BBC America, Bloomberg and CNN.

He also looked at the desk clutter, there he noticed a lanyard and a badge. Blue circle, white shield, red compass, white eagle's head. It could only be one thing.

CIA.

Now they were back at the lifts.

"Here we are, " said Petra, " Back at the elevators, don't forget its G for ground not 1, " she showed them through the doors, they waited a few seconds and then the lifts appeared.

"Well, I'm real sorry for your trouble today, " said Petra.

"Not at all, " said Christina, " And thank you for the refreshment."

They climbed into the lift.

Christina pressed G. Bigsy then pressed 5.

They looked at one another as the lift started to descend.

"I'm going to take one more swift look, " he said, " Please take my jacket."

They arrived at 5 and then he pressed 6 again. The was going to go to the ground before starting its ascent.

At the Sixth floor he came out of the lift. Instead of turning left, he took the doors to the right. He wondered whether his lanyard badge would open the door to the floor. It did and he walked in. It looked like a mirror image of the area he'd visited earlier.

He walked through the cubicle areas to one which looked more lightly populated. Then he walked along the rows of seats to one with a jacket on the back of the chair. He put it on and was walking out.

"Hey, who are you - that's Jim's jacket, " called an American voice.

"Oh, this is so embarrassing, I can tell now that this isn't my jacket. I've lost mine and was about to go to a meeting. All these cubicles look the same. Is this the north side of the building?

"Take a look out of the window, Bud, what can you see? - No River eh? No, you are southside. You need to cut through those double doors and across to the other side. You'd better put Jim's jacket back though. Don't worry, we've all got lost at some time or other in this place."

The questioner smiled towards Bigsy as he very carefully placed the jacket over the seat.

"Thanks for your help, " said Bigsy as he made his way back to the double doors.

Christina was waiting downstairs when Bigsy arrived.

"What happened? She asked, " I got lost, " said Bigsy. They both beeped their way past the turnstile and then handed their lanyards and badge in to a security guard.

Outside, the sun was shining, they walked back towards the tube.

"Well?" asked Christina.

"Definitely American, " said Bigsy, " Some kind of monitoring operation, judging by the screens on the desks. I got this."

He fished into his trouser pocket.

He pulled out a badge, 'Anne-Marie Bristow', it said, CIA Field Agent, " I had to grab it from a desk as I walked past. I nearly got caught." Said Bigsy, " Curious, though, I was expecting it to be a Russian setup."

"Yes, that's what they are doing. The Americans are laying a false trail to the Russians for what they have been doing around Raven, " said Christina, " It would also explain why Blackbird knows nothing about this. I'll probably need to report this in - or get Antanov to."

"I suppose they can monitor finance systems from here, quite well."

"They have a clear look at the London flightpath to Heathrow too, this could be an excellent location for a listening post, " said Christina. She was thinking back to her father's listening station built into the wool store when they lived in Iceland.

Chuck

Mud can make you prisoner,
and the plains can bake you dry
Snow can burn your eyes,
but only people make you cry
Home is made for comin' from,
for dreams of goin' to
Which with any luck will never come true
I was born under a wandrin' star
I was born under a wandrin' star

Alan Jay Lerner / Frederick Loewe

'Bin a long time

They were in the Triangle's offices, sat around a table.

"So now we really do need Chuck, to help us get to the bottom of what is happening over in Canada Water, " said Clare

"That is okay then, " said Jake, " Chuck is due to be here today. He'll finally meet Christina too, and we can reset things onto an even keel."

"And then we can ask Chuck what he knows about CIA in East London, " said Clare.

At that moment, Chuck entered the office. He was on his cell phone. He hung up and turned to the group.

"Hello, I'm Chuck," he said warmly, " but I don't think I've met you before?"

"I'm Christina, " said Christina, " Very pleased to meet you. I have heard so much about you." She stood as if to shake his hand.

"Hi Christina, Katarina Voronin, and various other names. Your reputation precedes you. I'm fascinated to meet you." said Chuck, " And I guess this office and work with "The Triangle" should be considered neutral? – See I can follow Jake's instructions!"

"Agreed, " said Christina, " I hear you can be pretty lethal too, with a SAM or two. I think there's probably enough to do here without worrying about one another."

Chuck held out his hand and Christina delicately shook it.

"Accord, " said Jake.

"Glastnost and Perestroika, " said Chuck.

"Prozrachnost' restrukturizatsii i mira, " said Christina, " Transparency, Restructuring and Peace."

Clare laughed, " We'll all drink to that."

"So, what have you discovered?" asked Chuck, " Something about an American Station in Canada Water?"

"Yes, we think we stumbled on a listening station, but the strange thing was that the American agents there were pretending to be Russian."

"We'll, they were pretending to be Russian to the outside world, but inside there were Americans and some hired help that was operating as multiple nationalities."

"Okay, I'll have a dig around, but what would this have to do with Raven?"

"We are not certain, although it seems that a German outfit might be implicated: ISMC, "

"And more, we think Bernard Driscoll, you know, the MP and Minister, might be being used as an unwitting influencer in all of this."

"Hold on, ISMC isn't German, we've had dealings, " said Chuck, " It is based in London."

"It makes sense, said Christina, the guy I was talking too, Gerhardt Schmidt, might have been bragging about his own importance. He was from Germany and said that was where the company was based."

"Unreliable source, I'm afraid, I think there are some UK top brass fronting up ISMC, " said Chuck.

"Sir Charles Frobisher, by any chance?" asked Christina.

"No idea, " said Chuck, " I don't really follow who is who in the corporate side of things. I'm more of a 'hands-on' kind of guy."

"Well, let's see what we can find out, is there someone you can ask?" asked Clare.

"Not directly, I should go through my channels, but don't you see what that would do? If our CIA is running an operation to tip a country towards America, they won't appreciate my little questions getting in the way."

"It must be the same for you, Christina? If Russia is getting twitchy about what Raven is trying to do then a Russian agent probing around in the mix is going to cause ructions. I think we are reaching a stalemate."

Christina was looking thoughtful, " What about if we use another power to intervene in this? One option would be the mysterious forces of the Freemasons, but another would be the Brits. After all, most of this is happening on their soil right now. Raven, Masons, ISMC, Frobisher, Driscoll. All being used to tip the scales."

"Yes, and remember what Nelson's friend Jeval said, It seems to be about oil rights in Celarus. Who would ever suspect the UK of manipulation in such a situation?"

"Can we contact SI6? Amanda Miller? We had quite some dealings with her back in the case of the toxins and the London bomb outside of the Bank of England."

"Ahem, I might just have a good contact with Amanda at the moment, " spluttered Chuck, looking unusually bashful.

"Chuck?" asked Clare, " Nooo? Are you and Amanda - er -friendly?"

"In a manner of speaking, we had an enjoyable dinner last week in J Sheekey's, as it happens. Well, I was in town and called her up. That phone number identity that Jake requested."

"J Sheekey's is an awfully big 'thank you' for a phone number Chuck, " said Clare.

"Let's say I wanted to see Amanda…Look can we move on, "

Christina and Clare looked at one another, they could see that Chuck was quietly squirming.

"Okay, so let's figure this out, how do we best describe this to Amanda?" asked Christina.

Clare continued, " Well, we know that Amanda doesn't think much of Driscoll. She seems to think he's full of self-importance and puffery, has little respect for others and pretends to always know what is best for everyone. As I describe this, I realise that she is right."

"So that would make some interesting incentive for her to get involved in this?" asked Bigsy.

"You bet, " said Clare.

"The weirdest dynamic is that we are right in the middle of a political situation though. Celarus aided and abetted by the Americans to get out from under Russia. This could cut up rough for Christina and Antanov, "

"Trust us, we've both had jams like this before, " said Christina, " and situations where we were asked to act but we didn't even know the moves being made."

"Okay then, we'll ask Amanda for help. She can check up on Driscoll and may even be able to find out some more about that American station on the Thames."

"Who is going to ask her?" They all looked towards Chuck.

"Er, I guess that's going to be me then."

"Good luck, " said Clare.

Fake News

Amanda received the call from Chuck. She couldn't help wondering if it had been planned, although Chuck protested most strongly that this had all come along since she'd found him that phone number in Germany.

It was an elaborate example of follow the dots.

Chuck had told her two pieces of news. About Driscoll and about the American Station in Canada Water.

He had not needed to tell her about the second item, so she guessed he must have been feeling particularly sheepish about how things had played out. Anyway, she would treat the American Station with some caution as she started to investigate. Of course, she already knew about it, but the American station was really annoying her.

She knew the Americans had moved their operations to the South side of the river, when they set up shop in Nine Elms. And just because they had a friendly sounding ambassador with a name like 'Woody' didn't mean that Yael, Elizabeth and Susan wouldn't get up to something.

She supposed the Americans were following their Grosvenor Square playbook. For years the gilded aluminium bald eagle on the roof of the Chancery building had made it a landmark, but also pulled eyes away from the myriad of smaller satellite buildings quietly going about America's work.

Ever since the Americans sold the original building with its underground labyrinth to the Qataris, it was to become the finest spy hotel in London., right in the middle of the diplomatic area. Property developer Trump had said the Americans had got a bad deal, but he'd done nothing to intervene.

Instead, the Americans now had a moated building with some pleasant gardens away from the normal protest areas of London, yes still within listening device distance of the Houses of Parliament and the Cabinet Offices. Maybe not at the peppercorn rent from the Duke of Westminster, but who is counting?

Amanda had long understood the Americans wanting another listening station to cover East London too. It was not so far from the financial sector in Canary Wharf, literally one stop on the strategic Jubilee line. And it could also probe into the emerging area of New Chinatown, being developed along by the Victoria Docks and the City Airport.

Amanda had put in a similar request for SI6 premises along that stretch of river but had been told to wait until the Chinese developments were further along. It was like kicking her plans into the long grass. But what bugged her was that somehow the Americans had got away with doing what she had planned - and in her own home city.

As for Bernard Driscoll, she remembered her dealings with this blustering politician. Bullying, lying, feeble minded, yet his reassuring haughtiness seemed to convince the public that he knew what he was doing when he clearly had no idea. He always seemed to be shored up by some of the tabloid press.

What was worse was that he seemed to convince himself. Amanda wondered whether he was also being operated by someone else.

A few days ago, he had been in the Commons to give what came billed as an "urgent statement on defence measures following our change of status".

He wouldn't directly confront issues either - we would have to guess whether he was talking about post-Brexit, an oil situation or a possible financial meltdown.

No end of probing by interviewers would deflect his path either. It was recognised among the media that this was not Driscoll being clever, but that he was mentally challenged and rather thick-skinned.

A standard speech by him usually included one of his greatest hits' statements: "We haven't got everything right" he would concede as an afterthought – a bit of humility never goes amiss – but by and large he couldn't think of a thing he would have done differently.

Whole streams of questions could be fired at him, but because of his status as the Minister for External Affairs, he could parry most of them with puffery.

His Ministry was well provisioned by the Official Secrets Act, meaning we may find out about his position in 30 years' time, but Driscoll was at his most Uriah Heep in his other answers.

Even on hard facts like statistics, he would wriggle and bend the truth. Numbers of troops, status of preparedness, strategic alliances.

With his way with arithmetic, where every finger and thumb could have been counted separately let alone shoes and boots, such that we could have as many boots on the ground in any territory that he deemed significant. Fake News spun here.

He'd been investigated on Panorama too, for a couple of situations where the UK had sold armaments and munitions to unusual foreign powers. It always seemed curious that his name would be in there somewhere greasing the wheels of commerce. No, he could not take credit for any of these situations.

Bernard's ears always pricked up at the suggestion of any admission of wrongdoing. He had been in politics long enough not to implicate himself in anything that might have legal liability when a public inquiry is an inevitability.

He could wheel out scientists or experts, just as well as Tony Blair did. He was always working to the scientist or military advisor specification. That the hitherto unknown advisory group SMIG Scientific Military Intelligence Group had been all over his plans. It didn't tally with anything heard previously. Amanda had cross checked the SMIG files but found them embarrassingly empty; apparently the Group had been retro fitted onto another one that discussed tracked vehicle rights of access to sites of scientific interest. Another false underpinning.

No journalist had bothered to dig that far, and Driscoll had got it all blocked with redactions, Secrets Act and Top Secrets classifications. All of which could be quickly dismantled to help the scientists be lined up for a show trial if and when the dust finally settled.

Amanda knew she would need to approach Driscoll but was ready, once again, for his veneer of civility masking condescension and contempt.

She knew, that whatever she said to him, he wasn't going to apologise for anything. Why should he? If he was going down, he would be making sure to take as many of his colleagues with him and particularly any already identified as potential fall-guys.

Yes, Driscoll, with his surrounding bubble of corporate advisors would think himself invincible.

Excuse

Amanda had called Bernard Driscoll's office and set the agenda for a meeting. She had said that it had come to light that a new 'fake sheik' was doing the rounds and that he needed to be aware of the implications.

Driscoll had responded well to this, particularly because Amanda made it seem as if another Minister had already been caught out. Amanda knew he would want to feed on the gossip from such a situation and look for any angles where he could bury a potential rival.

She was waiting in Driscoll's outer office in Portcullis House. She had been there thirty minutes. She remembered that Driscoll liked to convey an impression of importance by being busy.

Sure, enough at 31 minutes after the booked time, she was let in to see him.

She opened the door to his office. He appeared to be on the telephone.

"Yes…Yes…Possibly…That's settled then, " he hung up.

"Ah Amanda, how good of you to come over, " he treacled with a schoolmaster tone.

She remembered that he also delighted in getting people to come to him, rather than to go out. Unless it was to somewhere thoroughly agreeable.

"Hello Bernard, I thought we should catch up, I've some potentially disturbing news for you, especially given your role in export of defence equipment."

Driscoll sat upon the defence export marketplace, which positioned the UK as the world's second biggest defence exporter over the last decade, selling about $122bn (£98bn) of equipment of which 63% of its defence exports were sold to the Middle East.

"You'll have noticed that someone is using a series of written parliamentary questions to uncover the statistics of the sales, " said Amanda.

"That the person is part of a TV production team looking into allegations of bribery and corruption and that sufficient action has not been taken to ensure that the UK's defence sales are held to the highest standards, " she continued.

"Piffle, " said Driscoll, " Balderdash and piffle."

Amanda noticed the new vocabulary which became prevalent in the current Parliament. Very public-school framed.

She continued, " They say they do not believe that the UK government should permit weapons sales to regimes such as Saudi Arabia which use them against civilians, but if they do so, then they must at the very least ensure that UK taxpayers' money is not spent on bribing foreign officials who are part of corrupt regimes."

Driscoll started one of his speeches, " For the UK to fail to uphold standards on corruption and transparency erodes both our good reputation abroad and our ability to be a positive influence around the world."

"Our interactions with other countries should prioritise human rights and the public good, which does not involve bribing dubious regimes to buy weapons from us which they will then use in contravention of international law."

"Look Amanda, this is old news. The Ministry of Defence has already rebutted these allegations. They said that they took allegations of fraud, theft, corruption and bribery seriously and worked hard to detect and deter it. I think they went on to say that there were robust processes in place to raise awareness of the need for vigilance and MoD actively encourage individuals to report any of these acts. To be like whistle-blowers."

Amanda continued, " Well, we both know that the MoD routinely carries out checks on potential contractors prior to contract award, including on criminal activity, such as convictions for tax evasion, bribery or fraud, and a review of a company's audited accounts. "

"Yes, " said Driscoll, " Then the Cabinet Office coordinates procurement of public sector contracts and says it has made the process more open and transparent, becoming the first G7 country to commit to standards that will ensure every part of the process is visible to the public."

"I think we can say that the UK Government is committed to be the most transparent government in the world."

Amanda thought to herself, " He'll be using that line in interviews next."

Amanda said, " So it would take a Deep State conspiracy to provision arms to somewhere less desirable then, and there's no hint of bribery or corruption."

"None whatsoever, " said Driscoll, " I hope that puts your mind at rest."

"I guess I'm paid to worry about these things, " said Amanda, " And to warn Ministers when I see trouble looming."

"Not this time, " said Driscoll, " I think you've wasted your trip from Vauxhall Cross. You can tell your experts there that they are barking up the wrong tree. Was there anything else, or are we finished?"

Amanda noticed a programme for Formula One tossed onto Driscoll's desk.

"No, that's all I think, at least I feel better now I've raised the flag about this."

"Well, goodbye, then, Ms Miller. Audrey will show you out."

A suited woman appeared, and ushered Amanda from the room. "That's a lovely brooch, " she said to Audrey, noticing the small golden emblem on Audrey's lapel. Amanda noticed it seemed to be like sprig of some kind of tree.

"Thank you- it is pretty, my husband gave it to me, " Audrey replied, " Do you know your way from here?"

"Oh yes," said Amanda, "Many's the time I've walked this corridor!"

Amanda calls Chuck

Amanda was back close to her office in Vauxhall. She was on the bank of the River Thames, sitting on a bench. She called Chuck.

"Hi Amanda, I guess you can talk now?"

"Hi Chuck, yes, I'm away from my desk', " she said.

"Got it, so did you find out anything?"

"Not so much. Driscoll is even more infuriating than I remembered him. He wasn't in the least bit interested in my warning about a corruption investigation. He said it was all old news and that he had it all covered. Something I noticed, though, was that his assistant is an interesting form of gatekeeper. I noticed that she had a small brooch, which I think was Masonic. She said it was a present from her husband, so that might be a lead in itself.

"You think Driscoll's assistant has a link to the Freemasons?"

"Could be, and as a woman she'd be beyond suspicion."

"What was their chemistry like?"

"Brisk, I'd say, business-like. I doubt whether Driscoll would ever recognise that he was being played."

"And nothing leading about new developments?"

"No, I wonder whether Driscoll is clever enough to cover it up, or whether he simply doesn't know at the moment."

"Okay, thank you Amanda, I do appreciate this; would you like to stay involved?"

"I would if you think it leads to something, or maybe if I can assist again, otherwise I've plenty of other situations that we are handling right now. I've got to go to Cheltenham tomorrow about one of the situations."

"Okay, but I hope you'll keep some time in your calendar for me?" asked Chuck.

"I think I might be able to manage that, " said Amanda, smiling.

Acacia

Chuck was back in the Triangle offices with Christina, Jake and Clare.

"I thought I'd bring you up to date, following Amanda's visits to Driscoll. There was nothing obvious that she could find. Driscoll is slippery at the best of times and on the thought of an implied corruption he was reaching for the scapegoats."

Amanda told me about Driscoll's assistant too. She was wearing a golden brooch like a sprig from a bush or tree. I always thought that was a Chinese lucky symbol, but Amanda wondered if it was Masonic."

"Leaves" queried Christina, " Are you sure it wasn't an acacia bush? Let me show you."

She dived into her purse and found the Freemason brooch from Raven.

"Can I photograph it?" asked Chuck, who snapped it to his phone and then tapped in something else.

"I've sent it to Amanda, " he said, " Let's see if she identifies it."

As he said that, there was a ping on his phone.

"Wow, she must like you a lot!" said Christina.

Chuck replied, " Yes - It's the same as the one that Amanda saw. Driscoll has a Freemason assistant. Well, a woman who knows a Freemason, at least."

PART TWO

When we all fall asleep, where do we go?

White shirt now red, my bloody nose
Sleepin', you're on your tippy toes
Creepin' around like no one knows
Think you're so criminal
Bruises on both my knees for you
Don't say thank you or please
I do what I want when I'm wanting to
My soul? So cynical

Billie Eilish Pirate Baird O'Connell

Iraq news report

IRAQ [INR-01278AP] Based upon recent media reports: A vehicle convoy of 12 Raven trucks (civilian contractors) and a security element consisting of five Humvees departed from LSA Python en route to Forward Operating Base McKlusky. The Humvees belonged to the Transportation Company of the 207th Battalion of the Corps Support Group.

During the mission, inaccurate map data caused the convoy commander to make a wrong turn and led the convoy into an ambush with small arms fire, rocket-propelled grenades and hand grenades. Unfortunately, three civilians employed by the Raven subsidiary Qube were killed during the attack. Three other Qube civilian employees and one Soldier were also wounded.

Immediately following the attack, the Corps Support Group based at LSA Python conducted an investigation into the incident.

The investigation determined military personnel responded properly to events on the ground and did not abandon the convoy as it came under attack. Although the convoy commander conducted thorough pre-combat inspections and checks in accordance with standard operating procedures, the investigation report recommended that convoy rehearsals be more comprehensive in the future.

During the course of the ambush with small arms fire, RPGs and hand grenades, gun trucks continued to lay suppressive fire and several of the Qube drivers were wounded and their vehicles disabled. At one point during the ambush, the convoy commander ordered his vehicle to move forward and assist the Qube personnel in the lead convoy vehicles that were disabled and under fire. This was likely the gun truck pictured in a video provided to the media by a Raven employee who was injured during the ambush.

Multi-National Force-Iraq officials said although they have not seen the video in its entirety, it appears that the gun truck moving forward in the video was not fleeing the kill zone but instead was moving to contact the disabled Qube trucks in front of it (outside the camera angle). This gun truck stopped at those Qube trucks and laid down fire; eventually it proceeded out of the kill zone to the rally point established by the lead gun truck, calling in close air support, a quick reaction force and medical evacuations en route and later preparing a landing zone for the inbound medevac helicopter.

The other gun trucks (in the rear of the convoy) remained in the area directly behind and continued to return suppressive fire. A combination of those escort military gun trucks and Qube vehicles moved up the line of Qube vehicles rescuing drivers in two vehicles. Attack aviation helicopters responded to the attack, and the quick reaction force arrived within approximately 30 minutes to repel the insurgents. Two individuals were medically evacuated from the scene.

MNF-I officials said the actions of the Transportation Company saved numerous lives during this attack, and at no time did U.S. military personnel abandon the convoy. The Transportation Company bravely returned fire and protected the convoy while waiting for reinforcements and attending to casualties. U.S. military personnel, as well as Qube truck drivers, demonstrated valor and level-headedness during the attack. Their actions were honorable and should not be depicted otherwise. The investigation recognized the noble actions of one Soldier and one civilian and recommended they be submitted for awards commensurate with their actions.

Despite the valiant actions of the Transportation Company, three Qube civilian employees lost their lives. MNF-I officials said civilian contractors are a vital part of Coalition efforts to develop a peaceful and democratic Iraq, and the MNF-I deeply regret their loss.

Burghers

Amanda looked at the report. It would normally be routine, but on this occasion, she noticed it because it mentioned Raven and their subsidiary Qube, caught up in a firefight in Iraq.

She selected the report text and pasted it across into her notepad. There were no security markings. She guessed this was because the report was trying to clear the US Army from an accusation of not protecting a civilian convoy on its way to a forward position.

She would have to tell Chuck of this situation, it looked pertinent to the situation with Driscoll and Raven.

"Meet in Victoria Tower Gardens" she texted. "By the Burghers."

"Ha ha, " came a reply from Chuck, " Give me one hour, please, "

She checked her watch. She could easily walk there in an hour, but she had no idea where Chuck was travelling from.

After half an hour she decided to set off and realised that she would be in the Victoria Gardens in about ten minutes. Another ten to reach the statue so she would have ten minutes to look at one of Rodin's masterpieces.

Amanda knew that 'Les Bourgeois de Calais' commemorates an event during the Hundred Years' War, when Calais was under siege by the English for about eleven months. Calais commissioned Rodin to create the sculpture.

King Edward offered to spare the people of the city if six of its leaders would surrender themselves to him, presumably to be executed. Edward demanded that they walk out wearing nooses around their necks and carrying the keys to the city and castle.

One of the wealthiest of the town leaders, Eustache de Saint Pierre, volunteered first, and five other burghers joined with him. The six Burghers of Calais.

Saint Pierre led this envoy of volunteers to the city gates. It was this moment, and this poignant mix of defeat, heroic self-sacrifice, and willingness to face imminent death that Rodin captured in his sculpture, scaled somewhat larger than life.

The burghers expected to be executed, but their lives were spared by the intervention of England's queen, Philippa of Hainault, who persuaded her husband to exercise mercy by claiming that their deaths would be a bad omen for her unborn child.

"But was it real, or political theatre?" asked Chuck, smiling as he approached. They kissed, and Amanda felt like a naughty schoolgirl on a secret assignation, rather than the head of a major UK secrets unit.

"We ought really to be more careful, " she said, " With you a foreign agent and all."

"But have you declared me to the people inside?" asked Chuck.

"You know, I ought to, but I just haven't got around to it yet. I wasn't sure if we were 'a thing'.

"Wasn't sure! wasn't sure?" smiled Chuck, " Well I think I know…however awkward this gets in the manuals and HR departments!"

"So, what did you find out?"

Amanda showed Chuck her note from her phone's notepad.

"This is very useful, " said Chuck, " We can use this event creatively to shake the tree, "

"That's what I wondered, " said Amanda, " Although it might call for a combined operation."

"Let me take this to the guys in the Triangle, it's not got any confidentiality markings, has it? - Can we air share it, please?

"Certainly, and it is obvious they wanted this to get out onto the wires, " answered Amanda, she pressed some keys on her phone and the image transferred to Chuck's phone.

"Excellent, and how about tomorrow evening, I could report back to you from a lovely relaxed setting?"

"Mondrian?" asked Amanda, " How could I refuse!"

Time for Stetsons?

Chuck arrived at the Triangle offices.

"What? Three days in a row? We are indeed honoured!" quipped Bigsy.

"I've something of interest, " said Chuck, " A report of a skirmish. In Iraq, it included Raven and Qube contractors. Sadly some casualties."

Chuck beamed the memo to their wall projector. It was sideways.

"Wiggle your phone to turn it around, " suggested Bigsy.

"I'm all over this technology, " said Chuck, instead clicking a couple of controls on the screen. The image rotated and they all started to read it. Bigsy snapped it onto his phone as well.

"I was thinking of a visit, " said Chuck, " to Raven's main Headquarters."

"Been there, " said Bigsy.

"No, not their Head Office, their main HQ in the USA."

"Where's that?" asked Clare.

"In Austin, Texas, " said Chuck.

"Austin!" said Clare, " I've been there - actually Christina and I were there together for SWSX a couple of years ago. Christina had a gig in Maggie Mae's; it was rammed."

"Yes, that whole Sixth Street music scene is pretty lively, " agreed Christina. Just lucky we both had Stetsons and boots for that particular evening."

"And the street was full of people, bobbing from club to club. Sixth Street nights, eh!"

"Well, this seems to be a Headquarters building in an altogether more corporate campus part of Austin."

"So how are we going to play this?" asked Bigsy.

"I think we'll use some investigative journalism. What happened on that mission? What's the link to Raven, to Qube? I feel this one might be good for any journalists we might have amongst us?"

Everyone looked towards Jake. Journalism had been his main employment right up to the start of The Triangle and it had got him into the mischief that led to them being able to fund the Triangle.

"Okay, count me in, " said Jake, " Will you go too?" asked Jake, looking towards Chuck.

"Tricky, " said Chuck. "I think I'd set off all kinds of alerts at Homeland Security when we entered the USA. If I'm going back innocuously then it's okay, but when I'm on a mission, not such a good idea."

"Okay, who then? I think you may need to be able to handle yourselves in a scrape. I'd recommend Christina as the most likely, " said Chuck.

Christina looked up, " Sure, although - ahem - I've still got Antanov staying with me now. I said he could stay while he was in London."

"Okay, but I think this will be a short trip, in any case, " said Chuck. "Visit Raven, ask questions, return."

"That's the thing, " said Jake, " Normally we'd do this kind of short sharp thing by conference call."

"Not if we are taking photographs as well, " said Christina, " You forget, I was also photographer in Paris."

They looked at Christina. "I had to give it up, people kept wanting me to take pictures for them."

"Great, " said Chuck., " We have a plan., " Christina and Jake to visit Raven, for an independent voice of truth investigative journal in the UK. Jake to run interviews, Christina to take photographs and both of them to snoop around."

"Okay, we'll need a magazine title or something, " said Jake, " Not one of Bigsy's made up web pages, but a real one. Ideally something that brings in guest journalists, sometimes anonymously. - I'm thinking Spectator."

"Ew, " said Clare, " That's tricky to impersonate and I think they'd be quite annoyed if they found out."

"Yes, but they love the USA and are all for close ties. They even have an American edition; Let's remind ourselves that Boris Johnson wrote for them as well as a few Cabinet Ministers."

"We can modify what we say, that we are freelance but planning our article for publication in the Spectator."

"That works, " said Jake, " and gives us some wriggle room. Now we need to get the interview."

"Assumptive close, " said Clare, " We imply that its already been agreed and we are just tidying up the loose end arrangements."

"Let's find their Board, " said Bigsy looking through the internet, " Here we are, how high do we want to go?"

He flicked the list of Corporate Officers onto the screen.

"Skip over the CEO and Head of Global Business Lines; we'd need someone like HR Officer for a realistic interview. They might also want to bring along a General Counsel, " Said Jake.

"Okay, " said Clare, " I've got a couple of names here: Mark McKown and Mary Spalding, Let's see what I can make happen. I'll go into the quiet room, if that's okay with everyone."

Clare lifted her laptop and set off for another office, one that Bigsy had soundproofed, but which they had discovered was also ideal for making phone calls.

"If anyone can get us the meeting, then it'll be Clare, " said Bigsy, " Her PR skills and contacts are second to none."

Texas

I learned to drive on those East Texas red clay backroads
And I mean to tell you my friend
They weren't no easy roads
You had to watch out for all the curves
Down by Kelsey Creek
And detour through the Lindsay's pasture
When the water ran too deep

Michelle Shocked

I'll need to get a bigger camera

"It is done, " said Clare, triumphantly. "Raven's PR actually said they were hoping that someone would bite at that newswire listing. There were accusations about the US military running scared at that ambush, but DoD, Raven and Qube all want to refute that story. They say that the Press Release was an attempt to do so, but they would welcome any more in-depth investigations to re-position the story.

"Their PR is going to get us a senior member of their HR team, plus, as we suspected someone from Legal Counsel and one of the Qube employees involved in the ambush. They asked, Christina, whether you'd prefer the employee to be in their desert gear, rather than a suit, for the photographs. They also said they would try to arrange for a Qube truck to be available for the day, for some photographs.

"Clare, that's outstanding, " said Chuck, delighted with what he was hearing.

Clare continued, " They also saw the need for speed on this story, before it melts away into the background. I went along with this and so I've arranged the shoot and interview for Friday."

"Friday this week! We'd better get moving." said Jake.

"I'll also need a bigger camera, " said Christina. "One that looks more impressive to the client."

"Let's hire some gear then, " said Bigsy, " We can go comprehensive that way and it will look well-used."

"Good idea, " said Christina, " Portrait lenses, something wide angle to capture the truck. Some LED lights. A wheeled case to transport it all."

Frozen Margaritas machine

Christina was sitting next to Jake on the plane, they had been pleasantly chatting and watching movies. Then the movies suddenly came to a halt.

"They always do that, " said Jake, " Now I'll have to watch the whole film again."

"Was it any good?" asked Christina, " This Jane Austen adaptation seemed fairly good. Emma's rich girl hobby is manipulative match-making, but she's not particularly good at it, nor at her own attempts at romance."

"Your one seems to have a lot of flashing violence on the screen?"

"Yeah, it's one of the Marvel characters, who has a bust up with the Joker and then blows up a chemical plant, I'm pretty sure there's more sassy mayhem to follow, " said Jake, " But I'll have to download it."

They both looked around the plane. The air stewards were in the early stages of preparing for a landing.

"So, tell me about your time in Austin, then?" asked Jake.

Christina began, " People hear the word Texas and they visualise a longhorn skull bleached by the sun, cactus and miles of sand; maybe some oil wells with those nodding donkeys. In Austin, that could not be further from the truth. They say in Austin that its only problem is that it's surrounded by Texas."

"Austin is famed for its nightlife and is regularly dubbed "the drunkest city in the US". Austin is to Texas as Berlin is to Germany, which is to say it proudly, provocatively, perversely bears little resemblance to the rest of the state.

"Even its airport has kitted-out six performance stages where bands – hip hop, indie country, rock – play through arrivals and departures alike.

"Austinites are everything the rest of Texas despises; politically liberal, socially diverse, obsessed with the latest artful food fads, kooky vintage fashion, upcycled jewellery, nude swimming, community values and shopping local.

"Aha, like parts of London then, not so far from our office!" said Jake, " Except the swimming. Too cold."

Christina continued, " Pretty awesome, huh? You will need to say it while there -'Awesome!'

"I think I can do Awesome, " said Jake, " I've been doing UK lifestyle magazines for years."

"And Austin still does that elaborate Southern politeness that means even the simplest request – for a menu or directions or a hotel bill – must be book ended with a sincere "How are you today?" at the start and a heartfelt

"Have a nice day" to finish, " she continued, " It's the norm across the Deep South, but in Austin it just amps the sense that everybody is on holiday."

Christina smiled, " Jake, you'll have to imagine you are being a willing extra in one of those annoying, aspirational phone TV ads."

"You know the sort; achingly cool shiny happy people drinking craft beer and browsing antique stalls, complete with a scratchy fretted soundtrack of an earnest girl on an acoustic guitar singing about sunshine, swimming in the lake and everyday happiness."

"Right on, " said Jake, " I can do that." He reached into his seat pocked and produced his William Painter sunglasses, which he slid on his nose and hooked over his ears.

"That, in a nutshell, is Austin, " Jake could see Christina was smiling at the thought.

"So how did you come to be in Austin in the first place?" asked Jake.

"It's all about the music - as they say - I've always played musical instruments since I was tiny, my feet couldn't reach the pedals on our old upright pianos. It means that I have an instinct about what to play most of the time. It fits right in with the Austin vibe, " answered Christina,

"For example, when I was young, I could usually pick out the tunes from the TV adverts and replay them. We had a small farm, and my mother used to encourage my playing and she was really quite subtle about it."

Christina looked like she was remembering a distant past, " When I was really young, we formed a band and used to play in the room with the piano. Other local kids came around and it was one of them that when much older - gave me a break to get into music."

"It meant that when I started taking the music seriously, I could play, sing, learn new tunes quickly and I was also used to playing with other folk. You know - letting them have their piece of the tune and being able to copy their playing style."

"So when I was touring with my first CD's worth of tunes, I could show up in somewhere like Austin and adapt to the musical climate."

"I was really excited to be in Austin the first time. There were so many accomplished musicians there, and I could tell that they were also instinctive rather than manufactured. Even someone like Stefani Germanotta (that's Lady Gaga) was able to both be glitzy and yet sizzle out a country and western vibe version of her electropop Born this Way.

Stefani and I were staying at the same hotel and I met her quietly sitting in the bar with one of the Pussycat Dolls - Kimberly Wyatt. They called me over and said they had recognised me from a poster - they knew how tough it was to get started in the business, which is what Clare had also told me.

"It turns out that Stefani had also been made to practice piano from an early age - in the Upper West Side - then she went to Creative Arts Camp, so we had some similarities, although she seemed to have about 50 creative projects on the go at any time.

I could hardly tell her about my side assignments with the Russian FSB or the *Glavnoye razvedyvatel'noye upravleniye* - you know, the GRU."

"You never fail to surprise, Christina, "

"The next time I was here, it was with Clare; I'd got some gigs around Austin for SWSX and Clare was handling the PR side of things. We'd arrived with a couple of boxes of CDs too and would give some away and sell others at the gigs."

"That was the time we stayed at a Marriott, which was opposite a Mexican Café and Cantina. They had a kind of Margarita machine there and Clare and I went along to find out how it worked."

Jake pulled a face, "Margarita machine sounds dangerous?"

Christina continued, " We were chatting away and I became conscious that both of us were earnestly putting the world to rights. You know that feeling when the room seems to shrink away from you? It comes a while after that little 'crack!' inside your skull. The one that reminds you to stop - like your brain saying, 'No.'

"It was too easy to point to the machine and get served two more slushy Margaritas. They tasted divine, but *Vá* did they provide a headache the next day. Clare, the ever professional, had put us off going to that bar until after all of my performances."

Christina paused for a moment, and then continued, " I can remember the next morning going out for a walk to clear our heads. Stetsons, tied-high check shirts, jeans, cowboy boots, shades. We were living a dream. We'd linked arms and were walking back along towards 6th street. It looked so different with everything closed and no-one around. The harsh sunlight showed the dust and reminded us that Austin has risen from the desert. It was still impressive how quickly the town had been reset overnight from the prior day's revelling.

"No, so I didn't get to see the corporate side, except I'd notice a few suited types in the crowds swirling around the night-time scene. I think there were several big corporations based in the area and I guess Sixth Street was the place to show visitors a good time."

An aircraft announcement cut into their conversation.

"Sounds like we are about to arrive, " said Jake.

Austin, Texas

They had booked into the Marriot and Christina had already looked outside for any signs of a Mexican restaurant with Margaritas.

"I think it is the same hotel, but I can't be sure." she said.

"It's late enough, " said Jake, " We need to be fresh for tomorrow. Let us recap our objectives."

"Okay, " said Christina,

"Interview them about the truck convoy. Photograph them and one of the trucks, Snoop around and steal things."

"Er, that last part - steal things? - You added that."

"Well only steal things if we think they are relevant, " said Christina, " And keep an eye open for anyone following us."

They both looked around. The entire lobby of the hotel was deserted.

"They are all out having fun on Sixth Street, " explained Christina.

Raven Headquarters

Christina and Jake were in the lobby of the hotel.

"08:30 for the pickup, " said Jake, " Clare arranged all of this."

"That's great, " said Christina, " Although, did you say that Raven were picking us up?"

"Yes, " said Jake, " Be careful then, said Christina, " As an agent I'd usually get my own car to their place."

"Why so?" asked Jake.

"A couple of reasons; first they can't listen in on our conversations and second they wouldn't know where we are staying. Its Espionage 101, " smiled Christina.

"Christina Nott, femme fatale, " whispered Jake.

"It's Hyde, " said Christina, " Remember?"

"Oops, " said Jake, " I'd make a rubbish spy."

A black Lincoln town car was pulling into the hotel entrance.

"I think this will be us, " said Christina, wheeling her Pelican Protector towards the door of the hotel.

"That's a lot of kit, " said Jake.

"Need to look the part, " said Christina.

"Spectator?" asked the driver, " That's right, " said Jake, thinking that he was not from the Spectator and this was an entirely freelance operation. Clare must surely have got it wrong in her PR explanation.

"It's about 20 minutes, " said the driver, " The building and campus is over by Walnut Creek. Assuming the MoPac is clear, that is, "

They climbed into the back of the coolly air-conditioned car. Even the short walk from the lobby to the vehicle had reminded them of how warm it could get in Texas.

And then they were on their way.

"Great view of the Capitol, " said Jake, looking out of the window, " We're heading straight for it, "

As if he'd heard, the driver took a left and then headed towards the Expressway. They were soon on a fast road, cutting through a flat area punctuated with corporate glass buildings.

Then an exit and a few minutes driving through fields, interspersed with more plate glass and a few convenience stores.

Then a private driveway. They had arrived at Raven, a tall blue building, in a campus with several other smaller buildings. The site looked immense.

"We are going to Building 903, " said the driver. I'll drop you there and then there will be someone to meet you."

Jake looked at his original email from Clare.

They checked into the reception. Both Jake and Christina had photographs taken and were issued with passes.

"Can we get lanyards? Please?" asked Christina.

"Oh, why yes, of course, ma'am." The guard pulled a couple of light blue lanyards from his supply behind the desk.

"They have a little clip, here, let me show you. And someone will be here to collect you momentarily, you have a nice day now."

A few minutes later someone appeared, " Hello I'm Scott Eastin. You must be Ms Hyde and Mr Lambers, Welcome to Raven Headquarters. I am here to collect you and to show you to our Corporate Briefing Centre. There you will meet Mark McKown and Mary Spalding. It is only a short walk; you'll both be okay to follow me - or does anyone require special assistance?"

"That's fine, thank you, " said Jake, " We'll follow."

Scott walked them through some double doors and across a fairly plush looking break-out areas, then through a second set of double doors and they found themselves with an extensive view out across the gardens of Raven and a couple of water fountains and a small lake.

"Wow, you know how to make an impact, " said Jake, " This is very idyllic, "

"I guess we all get to take it for granted when we work here so much, " answered Scott.

"Say, I know we started early, if you had to skip breakfast, we've some prepared around the corner there."

He showed them to a buffet area, like any in a hotel, and Jake noticed that the food was anything from a large steak, through Texas style scrambled eggs, omelettes, tomatoes, bacon and a pile of waffles.

"Bigsy would like it here, " said Christina and Jake nodded.

" I guess some coffee would be great and maybe one of those bagels, " said Christina, " Me too, I think, " said Jake.

They grabbed a couple of the plates, the informal mugs and scooped up a modest breakfast each.

"Ah, I'm glad to see you've made yourselves at home, " said a voice, " Hello, I'm Mark McKown - welcome to the Corporate Briefing Centre."

"You must be Jake, and Christina, why hello."

And at that moment their second host appeared, along with another man. "Hello, you are all doing the introductions already! I'm Mary Spalding and this is Kevin Dubner."

They all shook hands and introduced themselves.

"Kevin was involved directly in that ambush in Iraq, I think he will be able to tell you about it. Look, I can see you have managed to grab some fixin's from our chef. We'll give Kevin a chance to grab a plate o' that steak and then we'll be off to one of the meeting rooms."

Christina and Jake realised that they were in a well-rehearsed process in the Corporate briefing centre. They would need to listen carefully for nuance in the words that were about to be spoken.

"We pride ourselves on our plain and simple southern hospitality here, " said Mark, " and it usually makes the chit chat move along real fine."

Jake was trying to work out whether the Southern-ness of the speech was being specially applied for his and Christina's benefit.

"Let's go over yonder to the meeting rooms, " said Mark.

The room was small, with a table and eight chairs, and seemed darker after the huge plate glass looking to the sunlight in the entrance area. It included a screen for presenting pictures and what looked like video recording facilities.

"Will the recording be on?" asked Christina, " We need to know for any copyright reasons."

"Oh, don't worry about that, " said Mary, " It's purely for archival purposes."

"Now let me tell you, we were madder than a wet hen about the original coverage of the ambush, " said Mark, " It implied that the US Army didn't help us. Even with the video footage."

"Let's hear it from Kevin, " said Jake, " After all he was there - and we've read that report quite thoroughly."

Kevin began, " Yes, it is like it shows in the report. We did get lost. A few of us were checking on our phones and had even told the convoy leader he'd taken a wrong turning.

"They said that it could have been our own phone chatter that alerted the insurgents."

"Then the first vehicle ran over the first IED. It took the track off the vehicle which rendered it static. It was when the guys tried to clamber out that the gunfire broke out."

"It sounded like machine gun fire, and we could see a red Toyota flatbed with a machine gun on the back. It looked like an NSTV Toyota Tacoma, with a belt-fed machine gun, such as a M240 or M249, fitted to a roll bar behind the cabin. It even looked as if the gun had a Raptor night sight fitted to it. And I could see the aerials and brackets for what looked like C4ISR - sorry I mean Command,

Control, Communications, Computers, Intelligence, Surveillance and Reconnaissance mounts and wiring.

"Kevin, Could I stop you there for a moment?" asked Jake, " Your description is very precise. Have you been in the US Army, by any chance."

"Yes sir, I did my tour in Iraq. I guess the military training doesn't wear off."

"Sorry, can I ask a question too?" Interrupted Christina, " I notice you said NSTV - what does that mean?"

"Oh, Non-Standard Tactical Vehicle, ma'am - We use that term for modified commercial vehicles that could be used on special operations. The Tacomas were a standard USSOCOM configuration. A high-end one with raptor sights and C4ISR would be something of an exotic animal, but I am certain that was what we saw.

"It's also on the video that Victor took. It's the red 4-door pickup coated in sand, with what looks like a pile of junk in the back. I thought it also sounded petrol driven, which makes me think it was from Afghanistan. The Afghanistan ones had petrol instead of diesel engines because they were quieter."

"And what were you driving?"

"Well, I was a passenger, but we were in M939 trucks. You know, the standard US Army transport of choice in the desert. Our convoy was a mix of short and long wheelbase vehicles, and although they looked like army trucks, they all carried civilian markings too. They did not carry guns though. It is against the RoE to carry weapons on civilian trucks."

"The AFSOC - sorry Air Force Special Operations Command that was with us had made sure that the HUMVEES were tooled up. They were all up-armoured and carried enhanced weapons.

"You see a Hummer H4 in a commercial car park at the shopping mall and think of them as heavy duty. In the Army, we think of Hummers as light four-wheel drives, at least until they've been up-armoured. So much were they thought of as light that they've been mainly superseded by the JLTV now - oh that's the Joint Light Tactical Vehicle.

"You can see from this situation that a single Toyota with a rapid-fire machine gun doing death blossom could successfully ambush 12 trucks, and 5 Humvees.

"Death blossom?" asked Jake,

"Oh yeah, the tendency of Iraqi forces, in response to receiving a little fire from the enemy, to do the "death blossom" spraying fire indiscriminately in all directions. I think it comes from a Star Wars movie in which a single starfighter can single-handedly wipe out an entire armada, " answered Kevin.

"All, I think that Kevin has given more than enough information for your article, " interrupted Mark, " I think that, together with something from the original press release and some photographs should give you ample coverage."

Mary nodded, " Yes thank you Kevin, you have been most helpful."

"We'll take some photographs now, " said Christina, " I suggest a couple indoors here, portrait style, and then a couple outside with the truck."

Christina unpacked some equipment from the large case and set it up. "I'll take a couple of quick test shots to get the lighting right, " she said, " and then a couple more of you, Kevin."

Jake said, " We are not sure of a format yet- so we'll probably want pictures to cover every eventuality - that's both portrait and landscape format so our editors have options when they lay it out in the publication."

Christina worked away on some photographs for several minutes. Then she announced, " That's good, I'm done. Can we go outside now?"

"Sure, " said Mark, " I think Mary will accompany this part of the visit. We don't want you getting lost in here, do we?"

"Yes, and maybe a couple of office shots on the way to the truck?" said Christina.

"I'll see what we can do, " said Mary.

They all walked back to the main entrance. Mark said his goodbyes and wished them all a mighty fine day. Mary accompanied them to the swing door area.

"We've, a utility vehicle coming to collect us for the short ride to the transportation depot, " she said, " Christina, I hope that won't be too difficult for you with that case?"

"Not at all, " said Christina, " I'm used to it."

They clambered aboard the minibus that arrived, and the driver told them it would be around a five-minute ride to the transportation depot.

Jake noticed that they were weaving their way around the Raven campus and, after a few minutes arrived at a fenced-off compound.

Compound

They climbed from the bus, and Kevin said, " They said they have prepared the vehicle for us, I guess that means they have cleaned it."

"It is not one of the actual trucks used in Iraq, but it is the same type, " said Kevin, " Look, I don't think you'll want to get that Texas tag in any of the photographs."

"Thanks Kevin and well spotted, " said Christina.

"I'd like a couple of moody shots from alongside the cab, I think we can hide the tag if we do that, " Christina made ready a reflector and the camera, " See I'm using the reflector like we do with models, to bring out the detail!" smiled Christina.

"So, I'm a model now!" laughed Kevin, " Don't tell the guys!"

 "That was excellent, " said Christina, " I think you've nailed it, look here's my card." She passed a Bluefish card to Kevin.

"Bluefish?" He queried, " Yes, I'm on hire to the magazine for this story, " said Christina.

"Oh, I get it - like a lot of us contractors, " said Kevin.

"That's fine, " interrupted Mary, " I think you've enough for the story now. I'll call the Town Car to take you back to your hotel. And thank y'all for visiting Raven like this. It is a long way to come for the story, "

"Yes, but we want to get it right, " said Jake, " And thank you, Mary and Kevin, for being so helpful."

On cue, the Lincoln Town Car appeared inside the compound. Jake and Christina said their farewells and were on their way.

What did we learn?

Christina and Jake kept quiet on the journey back to central Austin. They arrived in the Marriot and Christina said to Jake, " Twenty minutes, back here? Then we can talk."

Twenty minutes later they met again. Christina had moved the big case into her room. They had both showered and changed from the clothes they had worn around the transportation compound.

"First thing we need to do is change hotels, " said Christina, " There's a Four Seasons across the way. I just don't feel happy that Raven know where we are staying. I want us to do the re-booking, not leave it to this hotel."

"Sounds like a plan, said Jake, " if somewhat paranoid."

"Only the paranoid survive" said Christina, quoting Andy Grove, the ex-CEO of Intel. "See, we learned some things from the west when we were going through training!"

"We seemed to pick up several things, I'm not sure that Kevin was supposed to say some of them, " said Jake.

Christina agreed, " The biggest was the Toyota truck tricked out like a US Special Ops vehicle. That whole scenario seemed highly dubious."

"I thought that Kevin was highly dubious, too, " said Jake, " Like someone trying too hard. All that detail about Non-Standard Tactical Vehicles - The Tacoma as a USSOCOM configuration with raptor sights and C4ISR. Nothing like planting the evidence."

Christina continued, "I'll buy the stuff about M939s being used in the convoy. Although that truck, they showed us for the photo wasn't a 939 or anywhere near to it.

"Trust me, that's an M977 eight-wheel drive, 10-ton diesel truck. A HEMTT in battle-field jargon. Heavy Expanded Mobility Tactical Truck (HEMTT).

"I'm no specialist on this stuff, but anyone would know the difference, especially if you've been in a front-line operation position. You really want to know how well protected you'll be when you take a ride, " Christina thought back to the times she was bounced about around the fields of Bulgaria in miscellaneous trucks while she studied at the Vasil Levsky National Military University.

Christina added, " I'm amazed that Kevin didn't say anything, whilst he stood next to a truck which usually carries containers. It makes me not quite trust the rest of his pitch to us, like we should take it all in because we are hearing it from a veteran who has been in harm's way.

Jake said, " Yes but the other thing about that truck was the civilian markings. Yes, it had Texan number plates, but did you see where it had the civilian designations. It also had company of origin markings. It didn't say Raven, nor Qube. No, it said Brant."

"Yes, I even managed to get a photo of that, " said Christina.

"So, are we moving out, or what?" said Jake.

Touchdown

There was a screech as the wheels touched down.

"Back in Heathrow, and we didn't even get to Sixth Street," said Christina.

"It'll do my reputation no-good with Clare, " said Jake.

"Too much at stake, " said Christina, " We needed to quietly disappear that evening."

Christina called Antanov, to check whether he could meet her at the Triangle offices. Jake similarly called Chuck. This would be an interesting mission debrief.

They took the Heathrow Express back to Paddington and then hopped onto the tube around to Liverpool Street.

They decided it was simpler to cab the last part to save dragging the large camera case along the street.

They arrived in the offices to see everyone present; Jake, Bigsy, Chuck, Antanov and Clare. Clare asked, " Did you get my message?"

They looked at each other. They had switched their phones back on at Heathrow but been in Tube tunnels from Paddington until the cab ride right at the end.

"Sorry Clare, no we haven't" said Jake, " What is it?"

"It's all off, Raven have asked us to pull the story, No explanation, just an apology."

"Interesting, " said Christina, " Wait until you hear the story anyway, "

"Well, as we were never intending to publish it, I think we can call it a result!" said Jake.

"I seem to remember once before you had a story pulled - about Darren Collins actually, and that got us into a lot of hot water, " said Bigsy.

"Okay, well this one will take some beating, " said Jake.

"We are not even sure if the person we met as a civilian from the Iraq confrontation is really genuine, " said Christina.

"Here's how it played out. They were nice as pie to us, gave us access to Kevin Dubner from the Iraq mission.

He told us about the ambush. His story was generally consistent with the news report"

"Except for one thing, " said Jake, " The Iraqi intercept of the convoy. It seemed to have been done in a Special Ops Toyota, kitted out with all the latest tech."

"It makes no sense, " said Clare, " Why would America Special Ops attack an American convoy?"

"Well, Kevin gave us other information too. Chapter and verse of detail - too much detail in some cases. Remember those Russians with the Novichok at Salisbury? It was a bit like that, reciting Cathedral detail that could have come from a script."

"Then we went to take some photos outside in the vehicle compound. He'd given us all of that detail but was then quite happy to stand next to an entirely wrong kind of truck for the photographs."

"We decided that Raven were putting up a story and then deflecting us to the wrong trail. If we had published something, it would have been a new definitive account, which was good for them, but with a few accidental errors embedded in it which could have destroyed credibility. I think that is why they pulled it."

"Oh yes, and the last thing, the truck that we photographed. In its desert camo colours. It was a civilian badged truck from…Brant."

Primal Barrier

Pearly gates look more like a picket fence
Once you get inside 'em
Got friends but can't invite them

All the good girls go to hell
'Cause even God herself has enemies
And once the water starts to rise
And Heaven's out of sight
She'll want the Devil on her team

Billie Eilish

Antanov Analysis

"To a Russian mind this is altogether more straightforward, " said Antanov, " Let's consider."

"Correct, " said Christina, " To begin with, remember what Antanov explained a few days ago about oil conflicts."

"Oh yes, " said Clare, " The eight mechanisms, "

"We only need to throw one or two into the mix, " said Antanov, " oil-related grievances, whereby the presence of foreign workers in petrostates helps extremist groups such as al-Qaida recruit locals; and oil-related obstacles to multilateral cooperation, such as when an importer's attempt to curry favour with a petrostate prevents multilateral cooperation on security issues."

"So, think about it, " said Christina, " We've got America attempting to salvage the Iraqi situation and then insurgents running interference across it. Bingo. America will need to stay in Iraq and even shore up its presence against the petro-aggressors."

"I make that 2, 7 and 8 from my original list, all by sending in one Toyota Tacoma with a machine gun on the back. Admittedly it's a US Special Ops Toyota, but no-one needs to know, " said Antanov.

"Chuck, do you have any thoughts?" asked Christina.

"Em, not really, it is entirely plausible. To be honest it's the sort of thing I've been asked to do in the past, " said Chuck, "Although I'll always deny it."

Christina added, "Then we can add in the loyal flavour of Raven's subsidiaries supporting all of the Iraqi infrastructure reconstruction. It casts Raven as 'good guys' suffering in a conflict zone."

"You've thought this through, " said Jake, " While I was watching another Marvel movie on the plane."

"Not really, " said Christina, " Antanov and I are just distilling some of the thinking from our training. Maybe it was old KGB manuals, but some of the manoeuvres still seem to work."

Warp-speed farewell

They were back at Christina's flat.

"Christina, it's been good, " said Antanov.

Christina looked towards him, " It really has."

"This is the 'I'm going now' speech?" asked Christina.

"Yes, that'd be the one, " said Antonov, " I don't know what to say - except 'Thank you'!"

"You've been more than hospitable, " said Antanov, " But I can see you still live at warp-speed. You've been to Germany and to Austin while I've been staying here, as well as to the fancy Masonic event - For me - just the Masonic event is already a highlight."

"I know, " said Christina, " I feel privileged to have had so many lives too. Like a cat. Iceland, Russia, Bulgaria, New York, Vancouver, London, Milan, Paris, Amsterdam and back here again."

"You are already past nine lives, " said Antanov,

"And past nine loves, " said Christina adding, " If you only count the men, "

They both laughed, in a higher pitched voice Christina added, " But I'm working on the score for women."

Antanov said, " Look, shall I move out tomorrow? When you are at the office? If you need anything more on the Masons, you now know how to contact me."

Christina nodded and closed to embrace Antanov.

"Remember I positioned you into that last shindig as a Rosicrucian adept. You had that discreet rose with the cross, but it pushes you towards the Golden Dawn of theurgic spiritual development. Put another way, it's heavy shit. Consider it a woman's shortcut to the top of the pyramid."

Christina looked thoughtful, " Strangely enough, I met a fortune teller named Roberta the day before I made contact with you. He said that I should steer clear of the crystal balls, although he deduced, I had exceptional scrying powers. I'd never heard of scrying - it's like divination through staring into objects, but it does tie in with some of my Icelandic gods."

"You are moving outside of the Rosicrucian thought now; it will blow the minds of rank-and-file Freemasons."

"Yes, but as an edge creature one gets to notice the low-level fluctuations in the stability of edges, " said Christina.

"You have passed beyond me and there is little I can add, Oh Archangel, my dearest " said Antanov smiling, " Let me kiss you and then I will be gone."

Accessories

Bernard had been intrigued to receive the invitation from Sir Charles Frobisher. A private dinner and a chance to meet with a couple of Formula One racing heroes. Sir Charles had hinted that Bernard Driscoll might even be on the same table as one of them and to wait to hear from an enchanting A-lister who would be his +1 for the evening.

Now was the day of the dinner and Bernard was still reeling from being contacted by Marion Charlotte who she informed was to be his +1.

He'd had to google Marion to make sure. He remembered that this stunning A-lister looked a lot like Audrey Tautou in her Priceless era. She would certainly turn heads at the dinner, and he knew she was rumoured to have had assignations with various Formula One drivers.

Sir Charles had been careful to point out that this was a very private function and that there would not be any press present. Indeed, he described it as a quiet meeting of the Brotherhood, with some delightful accessories.

Bernard wasn't sure about this last part. It seemed to him that the event was skating close to the President's Club in terms of its presentation style.

He remembered that the 360 guests at the President's Club annual dinners – all men – included leading figures in business, entertainment and politics. They would pay for a dinner and participate in auctions of such prizes as meetings with influential people. The proceeds would go to charities, including children's charities, and other organisations.

It all sounded innocuous enough, but then the *Financial Times* sent two undercover reporters to join the 130 scantily clad "hostesses" specially hired for the event by the Artista agency. It reported that several of the guests had harassed or assaulted the hostesses in the course of the evening.

Bernard was sure he did not want to get into anything like that, although the thought of attending this event with an A-lister on his arm was too good to let pass.

The dinner was set to be held at The Dorchester, which Bernard viewed warily as an echo from the President's Club days.

Marion had suggested they meet in China Tang before the main event. It was a cocktail bar conveniently attached to the hotel and Bernard was happy to follow this plan.

Marion was stunning and Bernard could feel the endorphins of pleasure sweeping through his body as he approached her.

"Bernard! So glad you are accompanying me this evening, you will be able to tell me all about how things work in Parliament!"

"Only if you'll tell me about some of your racing driver friends!" he replied.

"That's a little saucy, for an opening line, " twinkled Marion, " First, let's have a cocktail, maybe trade a little gossip and then we can go through to the main event."

Soon, she took his arm and they climbed the stairs out of the bar in Tang's and walked around to the main hotel entrance.

"You are here for the special event?" enquired the doorman, " You'll need to follow my colleague over there."

He pointed towards a very primly turned out female host.

"This way please, oh. and could you have your invitations ready? There are a few formalities on the way in, for security reasons."

They arrived at the understated security area. There was an electronic arch, artfully decked out in flowers. They walked through in single file and on the other side Marion was given a tiny bouquet of exquisite miniature flowers.

"Something pretty for your table, " said the security person.

Marion took the flowers and the two of them walked towards the main doors. They entered a ballroom which had been laid out with many large circular tables. At the front entrance was a plan which showed where they would sit.

 Bernard read off the list of names. He was to sit on a table with two racing legends. A current Formula One driver for Ferrari, and a British racing legend from the Hall of Fame.

Next to him, he noticed, was his contact from ISMC, Gerhardt Schmidt. He wondered if Schmidt would be bringing Nina, his blonde partner as well. The listing unchivalrously just said +1. He noticed that his partner Marion Charlotte was spelled out in full.

He could feel Marion moving on his arm. It gave him chills. She whispered in his ear, " I think we have a good table, and look, there's that film actress, the one in that movie sweeping all the awards. I think she is on the next table. " More chills.

Bernard thought all of his cards had come up at once as he sat at his place around the table.

"Hi Bernard, " said a familiar voice, it was Gerhardt. He squeezed Bernard on the shoulder and said, " This is quite an occasion! That's twice recently that I've seen you at something in London. Have you met my partner? Here's the lovely Marina, and Hello, you must be Marion Charlotte. I have heard so much about you!"

Bernard said his greetings to Marina and mentally noted that she had similar length blonde hair to Nina, who he had met at the last event.

At that moment a small choir struck up. They were singing something mournful and pretty. Bernard did not recognise it.

"It's Leonard Cohen, " said Marion, " 'Anthem', I think, I believe it is about political and social justice- beautiful, how they are singing it, " she gestured towards the singers.

"Well Hello EEEEEveryyyyy-one," blasted out a compere. Bernard was vaguely aware that this man on the television. Irish, he thought, possibly gay. He was giving it some this evening.

They listened to the introductions, which then passed over to Sir Charles Frobisher who gave a short earnest speech and mentioned that there would be an inspirational rock-climber and a rock band during the rest of the evening.

"Thank God it is not someone from X-Factor, " murmured Marion, " At least they've got someone who has earned their way here."

Bernard wasn't very up to date with his musical choices. He'd liked the Beatles, and his hall-mates had played some of those progressive bands like The Genesis and The Pink Floyd. The music scene to him nowadays was a mystery.

They were well into their main course before Gerhardt cut into the conversation again.

"I hope you are enjoying the evening; Sir Charles would probably appreciate it if you said a small thank you to him in private. I believe he is seeing people in a small suite. You won't need to worry about Marion though, she will realise what you are doing, and I'll keep her amused whilst you are away."

Bernard stiffened. This didn't sound like a suggestion. More like an order, and it was one that he realised he'd better follow up.

He whispered to Marion, " I'll be going to see Sir Charles soon, to say thank you."

"Yes dear, you probably should, " she whispered back in his ear. Driscoll could feel the autonomous sensory meridian response as a tingling sensation in his scalp and down the back of the neck, in response to her gentle whisper. What was in that main course? Or was it purely his response to Marion?

He stood to find the room with Sir Charles Frobisher. No sooner had he done so than one of the attentive waiting staff guided him to one side, checked what he wanted and then escorted him to Frobisher's room.

Cohiba

"Come in, dear boy, come in, " Said Sir Charles affably, to Bernard Driscoll.

"This room somehow reminds me of The Peck, " said Sir Charles, making a reference to one of the quadrangles of Christ Church at Oxford University.

In a phrase, Sir Charles had distanced himself from the red-bricked Driscoll.

"Come sit down here, have a cigar, " said Frobisher, pulling Driscoll further into the web.

"Can we smoke in here?" asked Bernard,

"Well, I can't think why they'd keep a humidor in here, unless we can jolly well use it, " said Frobisher.

"Here, have a Cohiba, " he gestured towards the cabinet. They each selected a cigar.

Frobisher cut the end from his and offered to Driscoll, " Shall I?"

"Thank you, " Then Frobisher produced a butane lighter, "We could light them from the cedar wood spills, but I think this way is just as effective and doesn't mar the taste."

They were both lit up.

"I want to thank you, for tonight's experience, " said Driscoll, " It is really something rather special, "

"Not at all, my good man, "said Sir Charles, " It must make a break for you being so highly bound up in all of that state work."

"It is, and the delightful company too."

"Oh, has Gerhardt been up to something I don't know about?" asked Sir Charles.

"My Plus One for the evening is Marion Charlotte, " replied Driscoll.

"How divine, " said Sir Charles, " Although, I should warn you, coming to see me like this, she will probably have flown away. You'll need to cherish what little time you did spend with her."

Bernard suddenly chilled. He was having an ASMR flashback to her whispering in his ear.

"Of course, that needn't be the end of it, "said Sir Charles.

"You seem to be well-established now as a member of the Brotherhood, " he continued.

"Em, I'm not supposed to be involved with those kinds of organisations, " replied Driscoll.

"No, and neither should you be," answered Sir Charles, "That's why we try so hard to protect the members. No point in being a secret organisation if we can't have secrets!"

"But I can remember not so many years ago when Theresa May came down heavy on Freemasons and similar organisations."

"Ah yes, Theresa May went to the Police Federation conference and ripped into it. The Federation had to decide whether it would adopt a package of 36 reforms, with May, who was then home secretary, threatening that if it failed to do so, it would be taken over by the government and forced to. Ironically, her government got overruled by Parliament, so that was the end of it."

Sir Charles continued, " Of course, Parliament has its own lodges too, one for ex-MPs and another for the Press lobby.

Sir Charles looked towards Driscoll, " You'll have heard of New Welcome Lodge, which was set up to recruit MPs, peers and parliamentary staff?"

He continued, " There's also Gallery Lodge, established for members of the political press corps known as the lobby.

"Both remain active, although the United Grand Lodge of England says that no MPs or lobby journalists are members of those lodges.

"And it doesn't stop MPs from being Freemasons.

He paused to take a puff of cigar.

"These Cubans know how to make a fine cigar, " he said.

"So, let me tell you about something that I think you'll find interesting and let me introduce you to someone else."

He plucked a slim phone from his pocket, " James, can you drop in on us now, please?"

He pushed the phone back in his pocket.

"Captain James Wylie is a bit of a specialist on matters related to Iraq. He was out there serving Queen and Country, including time in Basra, before we handed everything back to the Iraqis."

"That was almost like a siege?" queried Driscoll.

"Oh, it was a siege, all right, " said a voice, James strode into the room, shook both their hands and sat down on a chair facing Driscoll and Frobisher.

"Hello Charles, Hello Mr Driscoll, I'm James Wylie. Charles invited me to paint the picture for you.

Frobisher offered him a cigar, which he declined. "I gave up smoking in Iraq. Too much hassle. There were never enough smokes around. The US soldiers used to get theirs at TCPs - that's Traffic Control Points. They'd see an Iraqi car with smokers in it, flag it down and then ask for a cigarette. The Iraqis - not wanting trouble - used to give a whole pack - sometimes a carton. It made those checkpoints unreliable.

James continued, " They were supposed to be looking for car bombs, not packets of Marlboro. Then there was the red cherry of a lit cigarette at night, which would compromise your position. Snipers, spotters, you know."

Driscoll could sense that this man must have had PTSD after his return. It seemed that dragging up memories was going to pay its price.

James continued, " The Basra airport base was constantly hit, upwards of dozens of times a day, by mortar and rocket fire. Yet, despite the weight of fire, there was relatively little disruption to operations, as considerable effort had been put into Force Protection measures.

"These included passive measures on the base, such as physical hardening of structures, and active measures, such as fighting patrols conducted by RAF Regiment squadrons in the Base's ground defence area, beyond the perimeter.

"We used external contractors to bolster parts of the infrastructure. For the passive measures, that sort of thing.

"We could better do our job of aggressive patrolling activity. It denied the militias the opportunity to use the airport's ground defence area for launching anything other than a small number of rockets.

Driscoll asked, " Didn't that just push back their aggressive position?"

"It did. It forced the militias to use firing points that were further away, which meant that larger rockets, with correspondingly larger warheads were used.

"More than 300 rockets hit the airport in the two months between June and August. Sniper attacks were also a deadly and common occurrence for British service personnel as well as IED attacks on patrols that were going out of the bases.

"At times, even when it was blazingly hot, we'd walk around the camp in full battle rattle to avoid snipers and other kinds of attacks."

James paused as if thinking.

"The IED attacks and organised ambushes also hit convoys from the airport that were transporting food, fuel, ammunition and other equipment. Convoys were primarily used for this task because helicopters were at high risk from being shot down.

Bernard asked, " I know that that was traumatic, but it was still quite a few years ago, wasn't it?"

Charles nodded, " Yes, but even now, the Americans are still hesitant about how to handle Iraq. For example, even in 2020, there was that MQ-9 Reaper drone of the U.S. Air Force which launched several missiles targeting General Soleimani, striking his convoy as it departed the airport, engulfing two cars in flames and killing 10 people. That was ordered by Trump."

Sir Charles cut in, " Some could say it was a President posturing for acceptance. The US President asserted that Soleimani had been planning further attacks on American diplomats and military personnel and had approved the attack on the American embassy in Baghdad.

"According to Saudi-based Arab News, the drone that struck Soleimani's convoy had been launched from Al Udeid Air Base in Qatar.

James picked up, " Yes, a statement by the Air Force of Iran's Islamic Revolution Guards Corps stated that Ali Al Salem Air Base in Kuwait participated, among other bases in the region, in the operation that was executed near Baghdad airport.

James continued, " Then Kuwait summoned the Iranian ambassador to Kuwait over the statement and expressed Kuwait's resentment and categorical denial at such statement.

Sir Charles added, " These skirmishes led to something of an impasse. It wasn't repositioned by the Press, but the day after the strike, the US had to send in the 1st Airborne Brigade Combat Team, 82nd Airborne Division, deployed to the Middle East. So more boots on the ground and more infrastructure support required."

James continued, " Yes, and so it went on, Iraqi state news reported that the day after the drone strike there had been another airstrike against a convoy of medical units of the Iraqi Popular Mobilisation Forces near Camp Taji in Taji, north of Baghdad."

Sir Charles added, " But we were into Fake News by this time. An Iraqi Army source told Reuters the attack killed six people and critically wounded three. The PMF later said there was no senior commander in the convoy, and the Imam Ali Brigades denied reports of the death of its leader."

"The PMF also denied that any medical convoy was targeted at Taji. There was no information about who conducted the attack. A spokesperson for Operation Inherent Resolve said the coalition did not do it, while Iraq's Joint Operations Command denied reports of any such attack, saying it was a false rumour that spread quickly due to the prior airport strike."

James continued, " To be honest, it's impossible to know who to believe. We sometimes used to watch the Ali Baba television stations and they would show American planes flying along the perimeters blowing up comms or munitions. Then we'd check and no-one would know about the operation."

Sir Charles added, " We are getting more examples of these kinds of things. There is going to be increased pressure to corral the effects. It is extremely likely that the UK would be called in. That is unless it can head this off at the pass."

Sir Charles looked at Bernard Driscoll, " Think about it. The UK can either send politically sensitive troops into these areas, or they can head off the problem, paving the way for infrastructure reconstruction and secure stability through the judicious sale of munitions.

"A quiet influence behind the scene is all that is required to make this run along nicely. That's where we think you could be instrumental in stopping the violence and helping the trade position simultaneously.

James nodded, " There's got to be diplomatic ways to contain this."

Sir Charles continued, " Bernard, there's less overt glory in this path, but every opportunity to benefit greatly and without personal sacrifice. And to top it all, you'd be one of several people of influence to make this happen."

"I'll need to think about this, " said Bernard. After he had finished thinking about Marion's whisper in his ear from earlier.

The American Station

"It is still bugging me, " said Amanda.

"What is? " asked Chuck.

They were sitting on the balcony of Chuck's hotel in central London.

The skyline was on fire as the sun tiptoed towards the west. They had both ordered a cocktail - A Peachy Canchanchara and a Golden South Sea Pearldiver - from the bar downstairs that was several times named the best cocktail bar in the world. Just after it won the last prize, it mysteriously changed its name from Dandelyan to the Lyan-ess.

"…That the Americans would set up a listening station along the Thames. Almost exactly on my spot, " said Amanda, " …And that you have such an outrageous expenses budget, "

"We should dig some more, " said Chuck, " But we'll need to be careful not to trip any wires. Let's make it a priority tomorrow."

...

Amanda was already on the phone when Chuck awoke. He waited patiently for her to finish.

She started, " I've called through to GCHQ. To Grace Fielding. We go back. Turns out that GCHQ know all about the listening station - more - laughably than the CIA."

"How can that be?" asked Chuck.

"I wondered that myself. It turns out that in the Land of the Free everything is fair game for outsourcing. That's what the CIA have done. They've outsourced the station."

"Incredible!" said Chuck, " But then, I suppose, come to think of it that's only what they do with people like me."

"Big difference. You go doing things that are Black Ops. They need the deniability. A listening station is, well, at the core of things."

"I bet it doesn't cost any less to run, either, " said Chuck, " You still need to hire the same number of people and to secure it."

"Well it seems that a friendly contractor has managed to convince the DoD and the CIA that they are capable. It's a company called Qube."

"I know Qube - they are part of Raven, aren't they?" asked Chuck.

"Very good, " said Amanda, " And according to Grace they do their job quite well. They are comparable to Blackstone Defense Services or some of the units that Halliburton runs."

"That's pretty broad spectrum, " said Chuck, " Everything from a so-called woman-owned small business to a mega-corporation."

"Well it goes to show who the US will do business with nowadays…" said Amanda, " And there's always pages of jobs advertised by both of them, in Counter Intelligence, right up to Top Secret."

"It's a little bit crazy, really, isn't it?" said Chuck, " Nothing like those old spy novels."

"I agree, " said Amanda, " But we've got to live with progress I suppose. Look, I need to get back into the office, there's a few other things on my plate right now. I could almost walk to Vauxhall Cross from here!"

"But you'll take a cab, I assume?" suggested Chuck, " I'm not going anywhere tonight, but tomorrow I'll need to check in with the Triangle gang."

Tap on the window

It was already past sunset. Clare and Bigsy were still in the Triangle offices. Clare was searching internet records and Bigsy was trying to piece together a trail from phone links.

An adjacent streetlight was shining in through the window at the back of the office and both Clare and Bigsy had their desk lights on. Bigsy had also rigged up some computer lights to come on around the edges of the office and to give some illusion of sunlight.

There was a commotion outside. A scraping sound. Then a tap on a window.

Clare looked up. It was too heavy to have been the yard cat that played around the area and occasionally spooked her by staring straight into the office.

A second tap and then a crash.

The window. It sounded as if something had hit it quite hard. Bigsy was running towards Clare. He tugged her by the hand.

"Come on Clare, we need to go into the back office, " as they ran, they heard a clunk as if something had dropped in from the window. Then a bang and a hissing sound.

"What the F…!" said Bigsy, " Stay back Clare, I don't think either of us need to be brave about this!" Another crash and suddenly they could hear the fire alarm.

"Don't open that door, " said Bigsy, " We'll have to go out through the back."

With that, he pulled at Clare's arm and then quietly slipped the lock on the back door to their offices. He opened it slowly, not wanting to make a sound.

"Quietly, " he said to Clare.

They slipped outside. Clare could hear her pulse banging in her head.

The back yard was silent and well-lit by a different streetlamp.

"We'll wait here for ten minutes, " said Bigsy, reaching for his phone from his pocket.

He dialled 999. After a quiet conversation with someone he spoke more loudly to Clare.

"I was calling the police, but the Emergency Services said they had already been alerted. Apparently, our building is on fire and the alarm has tripped to Jake.

"Fire engine is on its way. The police will turn up now I've requested them. I think we will be safe to go outside into the street.

"They gingerly opened the back gate and peered outside. No people, but Bigsy could see smoke and a small orange glow from the broken window.

"It's on fire all right, " he said to Clare, " but whoever did it has made a run for it."

Clare looked like she was in shock to Bigsy.

"Here, let's sit down on the pavement and wait for the emergency services."

As he spoke, a fire tender appeared. It was flashing its blue lights but not making any sounds. It seemed to take up the whole street."

"It's there, " said Bigsy pointing, and then realised that the professional firefighter would know what a fire looked like. Clare laughed and Bigsy thought some good had come out of his stupid statement.

One of the firefighters came along to them, " Are you the owners?" he asked,

"Yes, we work here - we were working inside when it happened. Something through that window, " Bigsy pointed.

"Okay, was anyone else inside?"

"No just us, we got out through the back."

"Okay, we'll be here for a while and I'm afraid we might make some mess of your property. We will try to save whatever we can. Are there any canisters, paint cans or other types of flammables inside?"

"No, it's just a regular office, with papers and computers, very normal, " said Clare.

"Okay, so my men won't come across anything unexpected inside then?" asked the firefighter.

Bigsy realised that the firefighter had a body camera and that he'd recorded everything. Bigsy remembered that he had put some small cameras around the outside of the office and that some of them might have recorded something from the event. He decided to stay quiet about this until he could take a look himself. He was glad that he had rigged the cameras to record to the Cloud instead of to a hard drive in the office.

Now it was the turn of the police. Another blue flashing light but no sound. Bigsy wondered why the need for stealth but he realised that there could be people around and they may not wish to disturb them. Certainly, he'd expected a small crowd to gather but so far there were only a couple of bystanders.

Clare, " You'd better take some footage of this, " said Bigsy, thinking that it might take Clare's mind off the shock.

Clare fiddled in her jeans and found her smartphone. "I'll take a few shots, but it is all quite upsetting, " she said.

A police officer was talking to the fireman and now made his way over to Bigsy.

"Here we go again, " thought Bigsy, as he prepared to answer the policeman's questions.

PART THREE

Secret Agent

Fire in the disco
Fire in the Taco Bell
Fire in the disco
Fire in the gates of hell

Electric Six - Danger! High Voltage

Diversion

Chuck's taxi approached the area of the Triangle Offices.

"Sorry Mate, There's some road diversion around here. They're always doing that. You don't know from one day to the next. Look, I can do a 'U' turn here, then we can cut up Shipton Street if you like and try to get into the area from the other end?"

"That's okay, " said Chuck, " You can drop me here"

"You know where you are? You'll have to go up past the roadblock and then take a left?"

"Yes, that's fine, " said Chuck, who after three visits thought he knew the area quite well.

"Card or cash, Mate?"

Chuck handed over a note, " It is okay, keep the change,"

"You sure mate? Thanks."

Chuck walked the hundred or so yards towards the Triangle offices. He could see Clare along the road.

"Chuck!" she said, " It is a bit of a mess. Our building caught fire yesterday evening. Bigsy and I were inside when it happened."

"No one hurt?" asked Chuck.

"No - we got out okay - thanks to Bigsy. Although Jake was called by the fire alarm company, by the time he arrived it was all over."

They stood outside of the building, which had been cordoned off with some blue and white tape.

"I see the police have been, " said Chuck., " They've cordoned it off, are they still here?"

"No, there was just a small fire car here. They said they were checking that the fire was fully out. They've gone now. Jake says he's called for the insurers to come take a look."

"Where's Jake then?"

"We decided to adjourn to the pub at the end of the street. He's in there with Bigsy and Christina."

"I think I'll take a quick look inside before we go join them, " said Chuck.

He ducked under the tape and walked gingerly towards the front entrance to the office. He could see the side window broken by what looked as if someone had tossed a brick through it.

He pushed against the front door which opened easily. The Fire Brigade must have smashed their way in. The main office area stank of burnt wood and everything was coated in damp soot. It didn't look as if even the metallic computers had survived the scale of the heat.

Chuck looked across to the window that had been broken. There was no sign of a brick or anything solid. There was an indentation in the floor. It looked to Chuck as if it was the source of the fire. The heat had been sufficient to crack the concrete and left a rough clinker-like edge. The whole area was blackened, and it looked as if there was molten metal in the dip in the concrete.

"Thermate, " said Chuck, to himself. He looks around, and the source of the fire was unmistakably where he was looking. He could see that the blackened area formed an approximate sphere around the area, as well as where furniture items had separately caught alight.

He noticed that the doors were still intact. Despite the obvious flames, the fire integrity of the office had prevented more than smoke from spreading. Chuck could not tell the type of doors, but he knew that the cheapest fire doors lasted 30 minutes and he'd expect an office door to last for an hour, on average.

He deduced from this that the fire had probably tipped the alarm and then been quite speedily dealt with by the Fire Brigade.

He stood up and walked back to Clare, who was still waiting outside.

"It's a mess, isn't it?" she said still in some shock at the events.

"Yes, " said Chuck, " Let's talk to the others."

They walked the short distance to the pub. It was a half-timbered kind of affair, and inside was more reminiscent of a locals' boozer than anything that out-of-towner would frequent.

Chuck was initially taken aback - then he heard Jake calling.

"Hey Chuck, Clare, we're here." They had grabbed a large table by a window. Chuck and Clare joined them as Bigsy stood to say, " What'll it be then?"

They ordered and Bigsy made his way to the bar.

"It's a mess, isn't it?" Said Jake, " Not an accident either, Bigsy and Clare heard the fire-setter. We were trying to work out why and who?"

Christina looked towards Chuck, " An M14-TH3 incendiary grenade was the fire starter. Look I even found a piece of the casing."

She showed Chuck a piece of charred Orange casing. It still showed the lettering M14/EN/H -in purple letters arranged underneath one another.

"Yes, I thought so too, Thermate as the incendiary - those grenades make their own oxygen. They even work under water."

"I remember them, " said Christina, " We used to practice some things with NATO ones when I was in Bulgaria."

The others looked around. Bulgaria, another part of Christina's past emerging.

"How would anyone get hold of one of these?" said Chuck, " I thought London was supposed to be pretty tight on such things."

"It is, " said Clare, " It would have to come from a defence contractor or an army base."

"Well, I know I'm stating the obvious, " said Chuck, " But it has to be because of your trip to the listening station."

"But how would they follow us?" said Bigsy.

"Something I've recently discovered, " said Chuck, " That listening station isn't a fully US Government run facility. It might have some CIA, but it is actually run by Qube, which is a subsidiary of Raven. Now Qube might have some extra facilities that the US wouldn't ordinarily use."

"Such as?" asked Bigsy.

"Well, think about it. You and Christina go to Qube. You ask a few innocuous questions, Bigsy steals a badge and a lanyard. If I was Qube after that then I'd want to check out anyone unusual in the building."

"You both turned up with your phones. It doesn't take a genius to see that they have probably logged your phones on the way in through reception. I know it is now illegal, but they have probably used the same tech that is being used to track viruses and virus contact points, ever since that global pandemic."

Chuck continued, " Piece it together. They've got your photos, and your phone identities. All they need to do from their - wait for it - listening station - is to track your numbers. They can find where you live and where you work. I expect they were worried about the missing CIA badge. It's a very heavy-handed way to dispose of a badge, but that's probably why they did it at night. The spin-off is a warning to you that they can get pretty annoyed."

"And I suppose they don't really want to jeopardise their outsourcing gig with US DoD, either." Said Jake,

"Correct, " said Chuck, " although I'm wondering if there is also a sleeping partner involved? Some sort of further link back to Raven?"

"It would make sense, " said Christina, " And also explains this kind of extreme action. It's unusual nowadays to be flagrantly throwing bombs around on another nation's soil unless you want to be classified as a terrorist."

Christina added, " This was a clean operation, they did it the way we would. Quiet, tap the glass with a hammer, throw in an incendiary grenade and be away before it's even exploded. It is almost textbook. They'll have used a moped too, to get away. An automatic disguise with the crash-helmet and leathers. Probably a black-painted bike as well."

Chuck nodded as the other looked towards Christina. Chuck began to realise how she got the name Archangel.

"What are we going to do about the office then?" asked Clare.

Bigsy was sitting quietly tapping something into a laptop.

"I've found the perimeter video, " he said, " Two people, in leathers, on a motorcycle. They came along the road by the back of the building and then turned onto the front. Yes, a small hammer. It is just like Christina said."

"How far does that video go back?" asked Christina.

"Well, we should have about two weeks of it in a kind of endless loop. It only starts up when there's movement, " answered Bigsy.

"We'll need to go through it then, " said Christina, " Look for anyone loitering or looking suspicious - particularly in the last couple of days."

"Good thinking, " said Chuck, " They must have scoped the place in advance."

"They also seemed to know where to throw the grenade, " said Christina, " Although it's so powerful I guess anywhere inside would work."

"The irony is, they didn't get the badge, " said Bigsy, " It's still in my backpack. I never got around to transferring it."

"A lead then!" said Christina, " What's his name?"

"Her name, " said Bigsy, " Although I'll need to fish it out to remember, she was badged as CIA."

"Chertovskiy! We can take this head on, " said Christina. Chuck looked over to Christina, in a whole different way.

Jake interrupted, " I've spoken to the insurance people today and they will want to send someone around. To check if it really was fire damage. If so, then I think we'll get money to make good. If they sense foul play, I don't think they will want to pay anything, or it will, at least go on for ages."

"Okay, " said Christina, " I think I should go back to your offices this afternoon. We can make this job a whole lot easier for them."

"They said not to touch anything, " said Jake.

"No, of course, " said Christina, " But first I'll be making a side trip to B&Q."

"I'm coming too, " said Bigsy, " What's the opposite of frightened?"

The clean-up

Bigsy and Christina spent the afternoon at the Triangle offices. Christina seemed to know what she was doing as she carefully re-arranged a few pieces from the incendiary. She had insisted that Bigsy and her wear full DIY overalls inside, so they looked like something out of a crime scene or a science fiction thriller.

"This gear was so hard to come by during that viral infection, " said Bigsy, " And now we can get it at builders' merchants."

They had not gone to B&Q in the end, instead to a firm by the side of a railway bridge near to Borough Market. Bigsy had known it and was right that they seemed to stock everything that Christina needed. Overalls, goggles, brushes, cleaner fluid, paint, sand, rubber gloves, talcum powder.

"We just need a few makeup essentials now, " said Christina, pointing towards London Bridge station, "Trust me."

Bigsy had watched Christina at work. She'd poured the bleach onto the floor and let it run. She'd dropped various makeup items into the epicentre of the fire and set fire to a small carrier bag.

She'd switched on an office fan and let it blow talcum powder all over the room. Bigsy was coughing.

"That should be enough, " said Christina, " we've contaminated the scene well enough for any investigator to be confused now. See the epicentre is now a bag of cosmetics, which have caught fire and melted everywhere." There's new dust over everything from the talcum powder and I've left the container inside the melted plastic bag."

"What about the bleach?" asked Bigsy.

"Silly you, keeping a supply of bleach in the back of one of those metal filing cabinets. It must have burst and run out all over the floor."

Bigsy smiled, And the source of it all?

"A hot socket, " said Christina. "Look, this one here."

She pointed to where a desk light had been connected to a wall socket. She showed Bigsy the burnt wiring.

"See, faulty wiring in this old property, she said, " There's no way that you could know about it. When the inspector comes around we might have to help him find this, " she said, rather pointedly.

"And the broken window?" asked Bigsy.

"We should ride that one, " said Christina, "It could have been broken by the firemen. Fixing it will look way more suspicious."

I don't think I've ever been to a wrecked building to tidy up in quite this way, before, " said Bigsy.

"I studied a whole unit on it, back in Russia, " said Christina.

Anne-Marie Bristow

'Anne-Marie Bristow', it said, 'CIA Field Agent.'

They had all agreed to meet in Chuck's hotel room. He had offered it because it was so large. They had ordered some room service and were eating and drinking.

"We need to run a sting on that Field Operation out in East London, " said Christina, " I'm thinking of going with Clare this time."

"No offence, " Bigsy, " But I think we need to try another angle."

"Okay, none taken, " said Bigsy, " but why would you take Clare along?"

"Well, we read one another, " said Christina, " And she is kinda hot."

Chuck looked up, " I sense trouble brewing, " he said.

"Not exactly, " said Christina, " But I think we can put the frighteners onto Anne-Marie Bristow."

"Imagine if two FSB agents turn up at your front desk? Imagine if you are compromised as the one that gave the whole station away?"

"I think Anne Marie is going to want listen to us."

"Especially if one of us can talk like an FSB agent and the other one looks just like one, "

"Okay, " said Clare, " So I'm the one in a leather trench coat and dark glasses?"

She looked at Christina.

"No, too obvious, we'll dress you to look like a recognisable agent. I have just the person in mind, although you will need a ginger wig."

Christina moved over to Bigsy's computer.

"Type in Anna Chapman, " she said, " She's a spies' spy."

"Hah, " said Chuck, " She was traded back a few years ago I seem to remember, "

"That's right, but it was something like a 10 for 4 swap. She's the real deal, a honey trap who worked her way into high places. She even allegedly hired the now discredited Max Clifford to help zigzag her way out of accusations." Said Christina, " She was something of a legend with us, because she managed to keep her real name through just about all of it. And she wasn't field trained like we all are. She just spoke the languages and allegedly flaunted herself around the clubs."

Bigsy came back, " Here we are, here you are - you read it, Christina…"

Christina continued: "А́нна Васи́льевна Ча́пман, (That's Anna Chapman) born Anna *Vasil'yevna Kushchyenko* is a Russian intelligence agent, media personality, and model who was arrested in the United States as part of the Illegals Program spy ring.

At the time of her arrest she was accused of espionage on behalf of the Russian Federation's external intelligence agency, the *Sluzhba vneshney razvedki*. She had previously gained British citizenship through marriage, which she used to gain residency in the U.S.

"Em, am I supposed to be learning from this character profile?" asked Clare.

"Well, it says here that she was a catwalk model too and had her own TV show. She even had a UK passport, although that was revoked."

"Well, she's certainly hot, " said Bigsy, " I just found the Russian cover of Maxim, where she seems to be wearing Agent Provocateur lingerie, "

"Let me see, " said Jake, " Oh, yes, " he said, " I see what you mean, but what about that one with the chains, or that one with the red gloves? - What do we think? I'd say 10."

"Boys, " said Christina, " Concentrate! We need enough of the character of her to make Anne-Marie Bristow think Anna Chapman is back in town…And anyway look, this one of her posing with a Kalashnikov, she's holding it all wrong."

"Let's see, now, " said Bigsy, " However improbable this is, she seems to own a clothing fashion line as well. Should we dress Clare in some of the Anna Chapman line?"

Christina and Clare looked. They both shook their heads. "No, not good enough, they really don't look all that great, " said Christina, " and I don't think they would suit Clare either."

Clare looked around, " I'm not sure I like this idea, being dressed by committee, " she said.

"I agree, " said Christina, " Let's go to my apartment, we can discuss it between the two of us."

The others nodded, Jake leaned over to Bigsy and said, " Send me that link, would you?"

Snake-look leather belt

Clare and Christina were back at Christina's flat. They had poured a cool wine.

"How will you be with a wig?" asked Christina, " I'll admit I'm so used to it now that I don't even think about it."

"I reckon I could do it, " said Clare. "It's good then that we've come back to mine, " said Christina, " I've a few of the accessories tucked away here, "

She pulled out a large plastic crate from under the bed.

"Wow, party equipped!" said Clare.

"Less need for all of this, nowadays, " said Christina, " But I think we can use some of it for you."

"Look, we'll see if we can find some more pictures of her,"

They looked on the internet, but many of the pictures were of Anna in swimwear.

"I forget about all of the British tabloids sometimes, " said Christina, " Ready to exploit the female form."

"How about these?" said Clare, " It looks as if it is from a catwalk shoot."

"Excellent, " said Christina, " These are more like her day clothes, "

They both looked at the pictures. "This one, " said Clare, " Ironic that she is carrying a gun in it?"

"Do you think you could pull off that look? I think you could! It's a killer!" said Christina.

They studied it some more.

"Go on then, " said Clare, " Let's give it a go!"

Christina found a small leather jacket, complete with a faux fur collar. "There, " she said, " The first building block!"

"…And a wig, something like this one!" with a flourish she produced a shoulder length ginger wig.

Clare looked at it, pensively.

 "No. No. We'll get you your own one!" said Christina, " You won't have to borrow mine!"

"Now we need some tight black leggings. Then a brown metallic top, and a wide, brown snake-look leather belt."

"And makeup? - That pale pink lipstick…" tailed off Christina.

"Shopping?" said Clare, " Shopping!" said Christina, " We are close enough to Sloane Square around here."

"Okay, let's hit it, " said Clare.

Listening Station

*Although the Masons are not implicated
as an organization in CIA and military mind control,
connections in the network of doctors were
maintained in part
through high rank Masons.*

— Colin A. Ross, <u>The C.I.A. Doctors: Human Rights
Violations by American Psychiatrists</u>

Magpie

Christina and Clare were busy. They found the clothes, including a different snakeskin effect leather jacket which just screamed out to be bought.

Then back to Christina's trying it all on.

"Woooow. You look like one badass spy!" said Christina.

Clare looked in the mirror. She hardly recognised herself. She could be that Anna they had all been looking at in the internet pictures.

"Magpie!" said Christina, " You've earned the spy-name now!"

"C'mon, Let's go back to Chuck's."

They took the train. Clare couldn't believe the number of looks she was getting. Christina smiled, " I think you know how to work that look, " she said.

Inside the Mondrian, a couple of the check -in staff came forward, Clare realised that they thought she was someone famous and were trying to be A-list about the service.

"It's okay, " she said, " I'm already here, we are on the 11th floor."

"Would you like us to show you to your room?" asked the concierge.

"Um, that's okay, " answered Clare, then to Christina, " That's a first, being shown to the room when we're already checked in."

"A-list treatment. I expect they are looking you up right now, " said Christina.

They arrived at Chuck's rather elaborate room. Christina had the key and they let themselves in.

"Oh. My. God." Said Jake, " Clare, is that you! Sensational!" Bigsy looked up, " Wow, and that's for both of you by the way. We are in the presence of FSB greatness. Chuck, how could you allow this?"

Chuck looked over and grinned, " Nice work - you two should be able to scare the bejesus out of Anne-Marie. Only thing is, Clare looks a little younger than Anna Chapman"

"You mean younger and hotter, " said Jake.

They were outside of the American Listening Station, in Canada Water.

"Look, " said Christina, " A Wagamama's - perfect. Go get a table there in a minute and say it is for three of us. I'll get Anne-Marie to come outside of the building. It'll be much easier to talk there and gives us options for our getaway."

They walked into the Wagamama's and were shown to a long bench table.

Christina explained to the waiter that she had to go away for a few minutes but then she would be back with a friend. In the meantime, Clare ordered a drink.

Around the corner, Christina went to the Reception desk.

"Hi, I'm here to see Anne-Marie Bristow, but if you could say to her, I think she will prefer to meet me downstairs. My name is Katarina, Katarina Voronin."

"Would you like to be issued with a pass?"

"Oh no, that won't be necessary, perhaps you could simply call her, she knows what it is about."

"Hello, Yes, Ms Bristow, we have a …Ms Voronin here to see you. She says she will meet you downstairs at Reception."

"Yes, Okay, Right…She will be downstairs in about five minutes to meet you."

Christina thought to herself that she hoped that Anne-Marie looked like her pass card picture.

Christina looked around the lobby. There were no obvious signs of people closing in on her. She could see the ceiling cameras, none of them had adjusted focus towards her.

She had made the request seem innocuous enough. For a moment she wondered if Voronin had been a good choice of alias. It was the most intimidating, so long as they looked it up afterwards. She hoped that Ann-Marie didn't have as good a memory as Chuck.

Then, a few moments later, a youngish woman walked up to the reception desk. Christina guessed that she was maybe 22-23 years old.

"Hello, I'm here to meet Ms Varranan?" she said.

"Excellent, " thought Christina, " she hasn't heard of Katrina Voronin."

"Hello Anne-Marie, I'm Katarina. I've something to discuss with you but it's better that we pop outside. I've a table at Wagamama's. It is around lunch time."

"Oh, hello Katarina! I'm pleased to meet you. It all sounds very mysterious. Can I ask what it is about?"

"Look, " whispered Christine, " I don't want to get you into trouble, but I think I might have found something of yours."

"Oh, " said Anne-Marie, " I see, well in that case I'll be pleased to join you."

She looked over to the desk and called "Thank you, " Christina looked and did the same and they walked towards the double doors that led out onto the pavement.

"Thank you for agreeing to see me, " said Christina, " Only I think we have something belonging to you. We were aware that you might get into trouble if we handed it in in your lobby or posted it back."

"It's my badge, I assume?" said Marie-Anne, " I did get into some trouble actually, but they still issued me with another one. They said that if I found it I should hand it back. They are hoping I will find it, in any case."

They were already at the doors of Wagamama's. They stepped inside and the same waiter showed them to the table with Clare.

"This is my friend Anna, " said Christina.

"Hello Anna - but I guess you know my name already." Clare noticed that Anne-Marie checked her longer than was necessary. She assumed it was the outfit.

 "Yes, now here is the thing. We are not just two nice strangers, " said Christina.

"We are both working for Russian intelligence. For *Sluzhba vneshney razvedki* - The SVR. Your pass card has given us insights into the work being conducted at your building in Canada Water. In fact, you could say that other of our identities are a State Secret. Unlike yours, which you seem to have accidentally given to a foreign power."

Christina looked at Anne-Marie. She seems to be close to tears. Clare also noticed.

"Look, " said Clare, " We really don't want to get you into trouble, but we'll want a little help in return."

"No this can't be happening to me, " said Anne Marie, " I just wanted a life less ordinary than in Washington. My parents were all for me making a jump from the Homeland to somewhere foreign. I'd no idea that the English spoke a different language from we Americans."

"This is very simple, " said Christina, " This is a one-time deal. One time and we will be gone forever. You have my word on that and you can check me in the files when you get back if you don't believe me."

"We want to know what you are doing and who is running you in that Listening Station, " said Clare.

Anne-Marie sniffed and wiped her face with the paper serviette.

The server appeared, " Is everything all right?" he asked noticing Anne-Marie's crestfallen face.

"It's fine, " said Christina, " Our friend here just heard some bad news. Clare why don't you order for us all?"

"Vegetarian?" asked Clare, looking at Anne-Marie.

"No, thank you, " replied Anne-Marie.

Clare looked to the waiter and said, "In that case we'll have a chicken nikko with white rice, shirodashi ramen and teriyaki lamb and a bottle of chenin blanc cherry tree hill. We'll share everything."

Christina and Anne-Marie were both impressed that Clare could invent a selection so quickly, but then Christina remembered that Clare had been waiting for them for around ten minutes.

"So, you'll understand that we are offering to make this entire situation go away in return for a little information. You won't see us ever again, nor anyone else from the FSB in conjunction with this."

"We also know that you are supposed to log agent contact to the CIA, but rest assured we have made sure we are untraceable. If you log us, you'll only be drawing attention to yourselves."

"Why me?" asked Anne-Marie, " I've no status or profile in Minerva."

"That's the point, " said Christina, " FSB targeted you because you are below suspicion."

"It's simple, " said Clare, " You just need to tell us some things about the station and we'll be on our way and you'll have your pass back. By the time you've eaten the ramen, all of this will be over."

As if on cue, the first of the dishes arrived, with the bottle of wine. The server poured three glasses of wine and they set the bowl in the middle where each of them could pick at it.

"We need some side plates too, " asked Clare.

"I don't want to make this difficult, " said Anne-Marie, " But I don't think I know anything. The main operation is outsourced to Qube and seems to be a boiler house scam, in any case. I'm worried enough about this getting back to Washington. I dare not tell my parents what I have got into."

Christina actively listened to be able to feed some of what she had heard back into the questions. Clare was quite impressed.

"So, if Minerva is being run by Qube on behalf of the CIA, what are the boiler house scams that are being played?"

"Well, it seems to me that we are mainly tracking British politicians and senior business people. The only one I am aware of is named Bernard Driscoll - I think he is a government minister. Instead of conventional lobbying, they target these people in other ways, to get them complicit. What is the phrase? 'Moral suasion' - I think we millennials call it 'social engineering'.

"Then Qube lobbies the targeted individual for a new deal somewhere or other. Right now it seems to be something to do with Russia and Celarus. I think there is something being positioned."

"So, who is running the station then?" asked Christina, " Is it the CIA?"

Anne-Marie replied, "I thought it was, and that is how I got transferred here." It seems to be run by Qube though and some of us, mainly the more junior ones are being used as a front."

"Look - I don't want any trouble from this, nor for my parents or family. I don't think I have more to say to you though, " she looked long at Christina and Clare was trying to work out what it meant.

Christina looked at Anne-Marie and said, "One day you'll be able to tell the tale of how you met Katarina Voronin and Anna Chapman and were trying to recruit them. You can say that you had discovered that the shot at the GU7 summit in Paris was an attempt by the two of them working together. That you'd spotted them plotting in London and lured them into a trap. Christina pulled out her iPhone and instantly snapped a selfie of the three of them together.

"When we are long gone from here, I will send you this picture. You can do with it what you will, just make sure you use it to enhance your reputation. It's a tough life being in espionage, especially for a woman."

"Respect, " said Clare.

"Uvazhat', " said Christina.

"Thank you, " said a somewhat dazed Anne-Marie.

"Now here is your pass; remember we are two bad-ass ladies, so don't even think about double crossing us. Take a few minutes to walk around outside, then head back in as if nothing has happened.

"Don't take that pass in for a couple more days and if I were you, I'd find it somewhere inside the building, wedged under some paper on your desk or something. That way people will think it's just a silly mistake."

"Waiter, " called Clare and settled the bill.

"Okay let's all be on our way, " said Christina.

Young

"My god, " said Christina, " Anna-Marie was young!"

"Yes, I wasn't expecting that, " agreed Clare.

"I think we've scared her half to death, " said Christina.

"When she started talking about her parents and her family", said Christina, " She'll be back at the office looking us both up. She'll find Katarina Voronin and Anna Chapman, that's for sure."

"It'll probably start a whole new search for Anna around London, " said Clare, " You know, I think I'll miss her!"

They both smiled. "Now we've got to tell the boys what happened, " said Christina.

...

Back at the Mondrian, Chuck's suite had begun to take on the look of the Triangle office. Bigsy had 'just' added a few cables and boxes and there seemed to now be a printer as well.

"You can have stuff from Amazon delivered to a hotel room, as long as you're a high enough status of customer, " said Bigsy.

Chuck didn't seem to mind, as long as they kept the mess in his annex room, which was next to the main bedroom with its balcony.

"So, what happened?" asked Chuck, " Oh and well done, by the way!"

"It is some kind of set-up,' said Christina. "No wonder they were angry that we'd managed to infiltrate their premises. It seems as if the CIA originally set this up, but for whatever reason passed the running of it over to Qube. It's an outsourced listening station as we guessed. They've got some young CIA agents in to front everything; they are effectively interns, judging by the one we met. Then they are using the station - it's called Minerva - by the way - yes they are using it to pressurise various UK politicos and business people."

Clare continued, " Anne-Marie described it as like 'boiler room'. You know those scams where they keep calling old people and trying to trick them out of their money. Except in this case the boiler room plotting is targeting MPs and the like. I guess it's faster than lobbying.

Clare added, " Actually, Anne-Marie sounded pretty hacked off about the whole thing. She said she had moved from Washington DC. She was probably on a fast track over there. I guess you must do some international work to get further but then she is stuck with a seedy scam. Worse than that, she then gets compromised by two Russian agents, who she later discovers to have top profiles.

"It's not exactly her week. And all because of light fingers here, " She looked over to Bigsy.

"I'll try running Minerva as a codeword to see if it lights up anywhere, " said Chuck.

"Now, ever so politely, you may leave all your contraptions here, but I'd like to ask you all to leave until tomorrow morning, if I may." Chuck smiled and the others smiled back.

"Oh, it would be lovely to have an office with air-conditioning, room service and a view of the Thames, " said Bigsy

"Welcome to my world" said Chuck, eyeing the clock. Amanda would be back soon.

Blackbird calling

Christina's cell phone rang. It was the dead of night and she was back at her flat.

"Hello?" she answered.

"Archangel? It's Blackbird. We need to talk."

"Sure, by this line or in another way?" asked Christina, noticing that the number was from overseas, although she did not recognise the dialling code.

"This way is good, " said Blackbird, " Encrypted and VPN - Look, we've found out that someone may be looking for you."

"Who?" asked Christina, " I thought I'd covered my tracks pretty well."

"Yes, but this is someone you already know - Chuck Manners from the US Government. He normally operates as Black Ops - blowing things up - shooting things down. This time we think he has been tasked with finding you."

"So, do I need to move?" asked Christina. She did not want to give away that Chuck and she had already met.

"And do you know where he is?" she asked.

"We think he is in London; we are sending a couple of agents to find him - *аук и тупик* - They are a man and woman team from the Academy. The agents are already based in London, so they should be there almost immediately."

"How is Antanov?"

"Antanov is safely back to his home and family."

"There's something else: The other thing we have picked up is some chatter about a new US station somewhere in East London. We'd like you to see if you can find out anything."

Christina thought it interesting that Minerva Station was now breaking cover. Perhaps the bombing of the Triangle Offices had created the leak?

Vauxhall Cross

The next morning, Amanda was back in her SI6 office in Vauxhall Cross. She had filed a report about the Minerva Listening Station and another about Qube but had held off filing anything about Driscoll.

Even in SI6 she knew that the walls could have ears and that anything about Driscoll would be likely to get back to him.

By the afternoon, she was engrossed in another situation, when the phone rang.

"Hi Amanda, its Grace from GCHQ - I think I've found something."

"Hi Grace, it sounds intriguing, what is this about?" she asked.

"It's an interesting development, " Grace said, " We paid attention to that Listening Station you found out at Canada Water. You know, the one called Minerva. Your source was right, it is a boiler room.

Grace continued, "Several MPs are being approached, so it's doing the work of a lobbying machine, but without the usual detection and declarations."

"They seem to be operating it through some typical slush and sleaze approaches to the MPs and other company officials, " she said.

"For some, it's money, for others access to events and for a few - ahem -'Favours'

"It's a clever system though, because they can masquerade as CIA or MI6 while they are luring people into the snare. And there seems to be some level of additional secrecy applied by appearing as the secretive brotherhood of Freemasons."

"It's hard to pin it down, though. It seems to be operating as an outsourcer through the military contractor called Qube."

Grace continued, " I checked on Qube too, it's a subsidiary of Raven, and they have been mostly operating out of the US. They seem to get attached to any peacekeeping deals as quasi-militia and then, through Raven contracts, supply food, laundry, transportation and other life-cycle management services.

"It's notable that Raven has made its name in oil and energy provisioning and it doesn't seem to mind skating close to the edge. For example, it supplied four pulse neutron generators to Sudan after the US ceasefire. There's no match between funding and the supply of these devices, and it's not clear where Sudan would expect to get the foreign funds to buy one, let alone four of the devices."

"It smacks of baksheesh, " said Amanda.

"I'd say so, it looks like bribery on an industrial scale, " said Grace.

"But we are not sure who is running them?" asked Amanda.

Grace continued, " Well it's not us, and I don't think it is the CIA. I can't be definite about this, but if I had to guess for someone, then I'd point towards corporate corruption. Probably Raven permitting the operation of this through their subsidiaries."

She paused and then said, " I've been thinking about it. Raven have got most of the same capabilities as a nation state. Funding, R&D, manufacturing, run-rate production of energy, security forces, espionage and access to powerful people. It's like a pocket state."

Amanda considered what they had found. A corporation wielding state-like levels of influence and bridging political and geographic divides.

"We need to tread carefully with this, " said Amanda to Grace, " If we hint that we know what is happening it could trip some large-scale retribution."

"My thoughts too, " said Grace, " Once I'd realised that Minerva Station could be part of something huge, I pulled my own resources from the investigation. For the last couple of days, I have been working on this alone. And believe me, I've been hidden away underground inside the Core here at Cheltenham."

Chairman of the Board

Fortitude, Prudence, Temperance, Justice

Raven Board Meeting

Sir Charles Frobisher was attending the Raven's board meeting. He had brought another two experts on divestment with him Han Yoon and Brittany Krasnigor.

"They are both from Smooth Pebble, A Venture Capital company, based in Sand Lake Road, Palo Alto, " he said, introducing them to the room.

Han Yoon began, "Hi, my name is Han Yoon, we've a short session on divestment, to help Position Raven's latest move. Sir Charles has asked us along, because you'll want to put some small company thinking into your next big move.

As "Mark Twain put it: What gets us into trouble is not what we don't know. It's what we know for sure that just ain't so."

Han Yoon continued, " So we are here to position a few ideas. There is some PowerPoint as wallpaper behind the session, but we'd like you to take in the main ideas. And Charles asked us to challenge you all, so don't be shy!"

Brittany took over. She could see the attendees noticing the way she wore her tight-fitting blue dress with the tiniest sleeves and a high neckline. No jewellery, although some high-heeled computer patterned black-and-white shoes.

"The essence of commitment is making a decision. The Latin root for decision is to 'cut away from,' as in an incision. When you commit to something, you are cutting away all your other possibilities, all your other options. - That's what you are here today, deciding. About making that divestment."

She flicked the PowerPoint to a new slide. A picture of a fox and a hedgehog.

"You all know this picture, " she said, " It's a reference to 'Good to Great' by the well-known advisor Jim Collins, " But let's not forget that the wisdom is much older; "The fox knows many things; the hedgehog knows one big thing." That was Archilochus, Greek philosopher in 8th century BC."

"Can I stop you there?" said one of the Board, " I'm Bob Jones, Head of Acquisitions. This kind of strategizing wizardry might go down well in sunny California, but here we need practical advice and action."

"Okay then, you decide, " said Brittany, " I can take this up a notch. Let's look at the specifics of divestment."

Sir Charles intervened, " Please continue Brittany, but if you can get to the specifics, that would be wonderful."

She flipped through the slides to one entitled:

'Smart Divest'

"Okay, " she said, " Let's get to a few rules:

"1) Dedicate a team to divestment full-time, just as you do with acquisitions."

She could see they were still looking at her dress.

"2) Establish objective criteria for determining divestment candidates—don't panic and sell for a song in bad times."

A couple of them were doodling.

"3) Work through all the details of the de-integration process before you divest."

One was looking at his smartphone.

"4) Make sure you can clearly articulate how the deal will benefit the buyer and how you will motivate the unit's employees to stay on until the deal is done."

One of the doodles was a picture of her shoes.

"So, can I ask? Do you already have a framework like this in place?" asked Brittany.

"Absolutely, " said Bob Jones, " We have regular sessions to track process using a Red/Amber/Green tracker. As of now, we have - er… 17 Red. 14 Amber and 27 Green category items."

"That's great, " said Brittany, " but what happens when you miss a milestone or a target? - Why are you needing to use the Red Category so much?"

"Yes, " said Sir Charles, " We do seem to have quite a few Red items on the list? William, any comment?"

William Daniels, Head of Operations answered, " Well, we are pushing the line along, flattening the curve, getting rid of the lumps. It's a multi-dimensional situation. We have to matrix manage the situation across different business lines."

Brittany challenged, " But doesn't it look a little bit like a long straight line of green and then a suspicious bulge of Amber and Red? If this was a carpet, you'd have swept most things underneath, but then pushed them all into a big heap in the middle?"

Now it was William's turn to look aggrieved, " You misunderstand our process. We are able to track all of the critical events and put something in place to get on top of them."

"But how does that show up?" asked Brittany, " Slippage? deferral? What was your original timeline?"

Sir Charles spoke up again, " Yes, this project has slipped. There seem to be several areas that almost don't seem very keen to see it go ahead. It's almost as if they are trying to block it."

"Organisational Antibodies, " said Brittany, " They are the people who will feel threatened by the outcome from the divestment. People with comfortable positional power who are keen to see the initiative flounder."

Now it was Bob's turn again, " I don't think any of us are trying to stop this, you know, we, the Board are pushing for this to take place."

"So, is there a dedicated team?" asked Han Yoon.

A moment's silence.

"We are the dedicated team, driving this from the Board," answered Bob.

"Bluntly then, where's the single throat to choke if it all goes wrong?" countered Han Yoon.

They looked around the table. A younger looking attendee was scribbling furiously onto an iPad.

"I think Han Yoon has got a point, " said Sir Charles, " We should really have set up a specific team for this."

Brittany continued, " Used consistently, the four steps I outlined create disciplines to produce an internal sell-side capability that enables divestors to generate superior returns for their shareholders.

"Most firms - I'm sure you are included - You have sizeable corporate development organisations, elaborate acquisition pipelines, and extensive relationships with investment banks, which all drive buy-side activity.

"She looked around, several of the attendees were taking notes. The younger looking attendee was still scribbling earnestly on his iPad.

"In fact, as more companies—particularly the type we deal with - private equity firms—have focused on deal-making disciplines, buy-side returns have improved over the past few years.

"That's all very well, but your outfit tends to deal with smaller organisations. Raven is very large, more than your entire portfolio of companies, " said Bob.

"I might agree with your numbers, but you miss a point, " said Brittany, " The best divestors approach divestitures with the same level of planning and rigour that their counterparts in corporate development bring to acquisitions.

Brittany continued, " They have established sell-side teams, which are constantly screening their company's portfolio for divestiture candidates and are continually thinking through the timing and implementation steps needed to maximize value."

"Well we know which area we want to divest, and why, " said William.

"William is right, " said Charles, " There are special circumstances to our planned divestment. It is just that not everyone can yet see the advantages."

Han Yoon cut back in, " Obviously, it makes the most sense to sell a business while potential acquirers can still extract value from the operations and take steps to reignite profitable growth.

"Yet our observation is that when faced with the reality of a divestment many companies blow it. They hesitate yet are unable to support the level of investment required to transform the business. These companies hold on, often for many years, until the unit has lost much of the value it once had."

"Exactly, " said Sir Charles, " And we are hoping that the divested company will have considerable up-side once established."

"Hello, I'm Lucy Sidwell, from Corporate Treasury. You talk about up-side, but surely that only affects the divested company?"

"Not quite, " said Brittany, " If you can prove the multiple in a new business, then it can be factored into the sale price. You could even incorporate a share trade as part of the deal."

"But let us move on to the Plan for De-Integration. Once you, the board and the senior executives have decided to divest a unit, they must determine what type of separation will best meet the company's needs and then carefully think through the implementation steps required to generate the maximum value from the separation."

"Bob, has that been strategized by your unit? And William, do you have a tracker for those elements of the plan? You can see that without the two key building blocks you will have an opportunity for the institutional antibodies - the resistors - get a foothold."

"That's where a Force Field Analysis could be worthwhile, " added Han Yoon, "List your top people and identify whether they are for or against the divestment. See who can be converted, but as importantly, those people that need to be reassigned. Sometimes they are called 'the saboteurs'."

There was some shuffling of chairs after Han Yoon's last comment.

"I said we'd bring in these folks to challenge us. It's certainly giving us something to consider, " said Sir Charles.

"We need to talk about something that Lucy will be interested in, " said Brittany, " We need to make the separation pay. Corporations are not private-equity firms—they are not in the business of buying and selling assets. But they need to be just as savvy about how to structure a divestiture deal and whom to sell to. Here's the best thinking about the "how" and the "who" of divesting."

"Yes, that's right, and we mentioned it earlier, " said Han Yoon, "Once a company has decided that a unit is not vital to its core, it must determine how best to separate it out. That involves answering two important questions - cash or stock? And, all of it or part of it?

"In most cases, selling a business for cash makes the most sense. There are instances, however, when spinning off a division to shareholders can be a better bet—either because the seller has no use for the cash proceeds (and doesn't want to hold them for fear of becoming a takeover target) or because a spin-off would produce higher after-tax proceeds."

"Most of the time, it's easier to sell a whole business than to break it up into pieces, keeping some and selling others. In some cases, though, selling the whole business is not desirable or not feasible."

Brittany continued, " And, of course there is the important question of who will the buyer be? A couple of straightforward questions, I'm sure they are in your list, Bob?"

Bob remained silent. Brittany could see that he was annoyed at being outplayed by her, as presenter.

"First question: Who will pay the highest price? Typically, the company that makes the best offer is the one that views the property as the most strategic. But sellers cannot assume that buyers will intuitively understand their own strategic advantages, nor can sellers count on investment banks to tout the deal's potential effectively. The key to maximising the sale price is seeing the divested business through the buyer's eyes and tailoring the sales pitch accordingly. This "reverse due diligence" extends to identifying and quantifying potential cost and revenue synergies for potential buyers."

"Second Question: Is one buyer better than another from a strategic standpoint? In most cases, selling to the highest bidder will create the highest value for the divestor's shareholders. But not always. Divestors must be careful to account for the competitive threat posed by each potential buyer."

Sir Charles said, " I think we've sorted this questions out, haven't we?" He looked around the table. He sensed he could cut the atmosphere with a knife.

"William? Are we okay with this? Or do you haven additional comments?"

William muttered, " No, it's fine."

"What about you Bob?"

"If I'm honest, I think our own strategy team has laid out most of what Ms. Krasnigor is saying. I'm not sure any of it is new to us."

"Lucy? How about you?" asked Sir Charles.

"I'd like to hear something about the compelling logic of the deal. People like to ask 'What's In It For Me? – What's in it for Buyers and Employees?" answered Lucy.

Brittany answered, " Yes Lucy, you make a great point. The best divestors clearly communicate what's in the deal for all involved. This entails having convincing—and honest—answers to four questions:

"First: What actions should be taken to improve the profitability of the divestiture candidate or fuel its growth?"

Brittany realised the scribbler with the iPad had been selected as a minute-taker. She thought now would be a good time to say, " Er, don't worry to take notes. I've a presentation pack which I can send you across.

She continued, " Second: How long will it take the buyer to achieve the deal's full potential value? (The faster an acquirer can realize the increase in value, the more it will be willing to pay for the divested business.)"

Those two at the far end of the table were still staring at her dress.

"Third: How should the value that can be unlocked through divestiture be split between the buyer and the seller?

She clapped her hands together. The two starers both looked startled.

"Finally: How will we motivate and inspire the people in the business to keep it humming along until the deal closes (and beyond)?"

Brittany sat down, " Look, I think I've unpacked enough, and I can tell you were engaged and thinking about this during my talk. It's refreshing to know that Bob, William and Lucy have already got many of these points covered. I'd still recommend that you set up a separate team, but at least you know where you are heading with this."

Sir Charles spoke, " Well, I'd like to thank Smooth Pebble for their insights into our divesture and they have certainly given us food for thought. Let us hope our plans skim along the lake now- like a smooth pebble, rather than sink into it."

Dorothy, could you please show Han Yoon and Brittany Krasnigor back to my office now, and offer them some refreshments.

"Now, Next Item."

Grace Cathedral Hill

Dorothy showed Han Yoon and Brittany Krasnigor into the annex to Sir Charles' office.

They sat waiting for his return, but both keep quiet.

Around fifteen minutes later, Sir Charles returned,
" Sorry, we had a few things to wrap up in that meeting after you'd left. I can see that Dorothy has made sure you have some coffee. Come on into my office."

"What did you think?" asked Sir Charles, as he walked across to a small meeting table.

"I'm not sure that they were that pleased to see us, " said Han Yoon.

"I think you rattled their cages somewhat. Thank you - that was exactly what I asked you to do. To draw out their positions."

"We it is clear to me that Bob Jones wasn't a team player, " said Brittany, " He seemed very antagonistic, almost to justify his position."

"Yes, he is fond of asking questions like, 'what do we mean by analyse?' or 'what do we mean by 'strategy'? As a way to slow down the debate, he seemed to be doing it with you two, " said Sir Charles, " I'm afraid he may have to go."

"Then William. He was on top of a process, but it wasn't the right one, " said Tiffany, " It all looks business-like, but he's missed the main point, "

Sir Charles replied, " Yes I get snowed with diagrams and Excel charts from his department, but they never tell what is going along."

"I actually thought Lucy came up with couple of good questions, " said Brittany.

"I agree, said Han Yoon, " She seems to be treating it like a VC project and was following the money."

"Yes, Lucy is quite an asset to us here. Do you think I should move her to oversee the divestment project?"

"You could, " said Han Yoon, " But I'm aware of some extraordinary circumstances around this project, from my briefing with Michael Tovey."

"You know Michael…" said Charles, " I was forgetting - of course - he introduced your company to me."

"Yes, and he spelled out to me that you have some special interests running through the divestment, too, " said Han Yoon, " Look I won't beat about the bush…I might look Asian by descent, but I can still recognise a Masonic handshake."

"Ah yes, I thought the Communist Party had stopped Freemasonry in China?" said Sir Charles.

"Hmm, I'm American, " said Han Yoon, " From San Francisco actually. My Lodge is on Grace Cathedral Hill, opposite the Cathedral, actually. That is how Michael Tovey recommended us, He was in town for a VC thing, and we were both a little hungry, so we went to get hot dog, down the Hyde Street Pier."

Sir Charles frowned, " Yes, that's right, he called me up from San Francisco to recommend you. And he said you were a psychologist by training, Brittany?"

Brittany replied, " That's right, my presentation was designed to push a few buttons, see what kind of response we could get. Nothing fancy, but it seemed to work! And they never did ask about the hedgehog! "

Sir Charles said, " I think I know the answer - the fox is a cunning creature, able to devise a myriad of strategies for sneak attacks upon the hedgehog…Fast, sleek, beautiful, fleet of foot, and crafty – the fox looks like the sure winner.

"The hedgehog on the other hand, is a dowdier creature…He waddles along, going about his simple day, searching for lunch and taking care of his home…(but) despite the greater cunning of the fox, the hedgehog always wins. Roadkill excepted, of course."

"That's not bad, " said Brittany, " I won't give you the full answer now - not about that, anyway. But Lucy, yes, she could make a great PM for the divestment, except, as Han Yoon says, if you expect it to be Freemason-inspired."

Fake 'n ham

Bigsy was studying Bernard Driscoll's biography. He had found the entry in Wikipedia and was comparing it with a hatchet piece he had found in the Guardian.

"Bernard Driscoll has a small semi-detached in Ilford. He has had to flip it a couple of times with his bigger house out in the East Anglian countryside. It would be too embarrassing to reveal Fakenham as his residence and the tax relief and expenses available for the other property was so useful."

"Ha, Fakenham - you can't make it up!" sniggered Jake.

"Driscoll briefly joined the Labour Party in 1983 in Norwich but has stated that by the time he left to go to Reading University he was a Conservative."

"So, he flips in more ways than one!"

Bigsy read further, " Driscoll joined the Reading University Conservative Association and was secretary of Norwich North Young Conservatives. It says he helped to write speeches for Cabinet and Shadow

Cabinet ministers, although it doesn't mention which ones."

"What's the quote, said Clare, " 'If you are not a liberal when you're 25, you have no heart. If you are not a conservative by the time you're 35, you have no brain.' "

"Now, now, play nice Clare, " said Jake, laughing.

Bigsy continued, " When applying for a job at the Conservative Research Department he was told he was "insufficiently political" and "insufficiently Conservative", so he turned to journalism.

"All round, a bit useless then?" commented Clare.

Bigsy read, " Then close to home, he worked on the Norfolk Journal in Norwich, where he spent several months on strike in the 1989–1990 dispute over union recognition and representation.

"He got paid, though. It wasn't furlough pay exactly, but he took some sort of union position while the strike was running. A hired gun approach.

"During this time, he wrote a sympathetic biography of a couple of leading lights in the Tory party but was criticised when the books were released for using a ghost writer.

"I remember that, " said Jake, " That ghost writer went on to become a famous author, and in later interviews was asked about the Driscoll time. I think he said Driscoll was entirely 'hands-off" for the books and didn't really care for one of the politicians either. I think later Driscoll even got into some trouble about things that were included in the book."

Bigsy continued, " His pre-political career is interesting in that it suffered from the 'two-year problem', where he would only do anything for a couple of years before being asked to leave. It was symptomatic of someone that wasn't particularly good at anything but was given the benefit of the doubt after the first year's lame results but then went on to confirm the reservations in the second year."

"Oh yes, " said Clare, " We've all met people like that."

Bigsy continued, " Well, then Driscoll somehow inveigled his way to a position at Policy Exchange, a conservative think tank launched in 2002. He was also involved in founding the right-leaning magazine Particulars, to which he occasionally contributes. He was trying to build his credential as a thinker during this period."

Clare said, " The arrogance of the man. I mainly know of him from his tirades against women in the House of Commons. Using a kind of pompous bullying tactic. Thinks he's got a Headmaster power over everyone. I pity his poor wife."

Jake added, " Yeah, I remember when I was a journalist, the journos used to call him 'whip-boy'"

Bigsy continued, " Driscoll expressed admiration in late-February 2003 for New Labour Prime Minister Tony Blair because of the way he was handling the crisis in Iraq: 'As a right-wing polemicist, all I can say looking at Mr Blair now is, what's not to like?' Blair, he thought, was ' behaving like a true Thatcherite'. - It turns out later that the quotes he made were originally attributable to another Tory MP. Oddly enough they have stuck with him as if they were his quotes, right through to his entry on 'GoodQuotes.com' "

"As a result, he has almost no followers from within the House, commands no loyalty and is generally reviled. However, he is sitting in a Tory stronghold seat, with a majority of 25,000."

"What about scandals?" asked Jake, " There must be something?"

"No, not really, " said Bigsy, " You can hate him for his policies and his haughty attitude, but he is careful not to get caught. He also has some significant press machinery behind him, retouching anything that looks dubious.

"Here's an example; his swimming-pool in Norfolk needed re-equipping and he put it through as MP expenses. Then we hear how he needs steam therapy for a leg injury that was prescribed by his doctor and that anyway it had been an accounting oversight that he would reimburse in full. The Daily Mail was all over the story and showed Driscoll on crutches, which they said was during the time he couldn't get his routine therapy."

"There's an opinion piece in the Guardian about how Driscoll has reached such roles as Minister, with the thinking that he must somehow have friends in high places."

"So, what have we got?" asked Clare, " A noxious bully narcissist who has access to too much power."

"It seems to be a sign of the times, " said Jake.

Bigsy and Clare nodded.

Berry

Christina arrived at Chuck's hotel suite.

"You must have an infinite budget to keep this going!" she said.

"I seem to get by, " said Chuck, " The spoils of, ahem, Consulting!"

"I know that feeling, " said Christina.

"Yes, I know we are from different sides, but it has been interesting to meet you and to even realise that you are better - than the field reports!" said Chuck.

"I'll take that as a compliment, " smiled Christina, " And I'd like to offer one back - very similar. From one professional to another - I can see you know how to rock the role."

"Come on, come here. A hug, " said Chuck.

They hugged for several seconds.

"If the FSB could see me now!" said Christina, then she changed her tone.

"Look, Chuck, I've some unwelcome news for you, I think…"

Chuck looked suitably serious.

"My handler has been in contact. He was signalling to me that Antanov was safely back in position. But then he gave me some other information. He said that the FSB thought Chuck Manners was in London. That Chuck had got wind that I/Katarina Voronin was in town then he would be on to me."

"Well, we know that isn't the case, " said Chuck relaxing slightly, " If we were going to be fighting it would have started by now and we'd both have small-arms in this room."

Christina giggled.

Chuck realised Christina was armed. "Well, we'd both have small arms pointed at one another!"

"Yes, " said Christina, " So the FSB did what their bureaucracy dictates. They've sent a couple of agents to find you."

"What? I supposed I could have guessed that, " said Chuck, " To be honest, I think I've been having quite a good time here. Amanda, you, the Triangle folk and a really good mystery to resolve."

"Well, I think I'm warning you - much as it saddens me - that it is probably time for you to get the hell out of Dodge, " said Christina.

"I asked when the two guys were dispatched, and it was over a week ago. I know they will head for Central London and I think I could probably find them easily enough if I went to a couple of the gold-plated clubs in the West End."

"Have you got any names?" asked Chuck, " No just couple of code words. They don't sound very high up though, codenamed *аук и тупик* - auk i tupik - er that's Auk and Puffin.

"What's an Auk?" asked Chuck, bemused.

"I know them quite well, " said Christina, " They look a little like penguins, but are not even related. They spend most of their life at sea."

"So - go on then - tell me - what's your code name, Christina? It'd be useful to know in case I ever hear it in chatter."

Christina hesitated, then said, " It's Archangel."

"No way!" said Chuck. Christina could see the look of astonishment on his face, " I am in the presence of FSB greatness! My god - you have some exploits to your name. I thought Voronin was pretty high up there, but Archangel!"

"It's even *Архангельск* – Arkhangelsk in Russian, " said Christina, " You know something, I'm actually Icelandic, but I was trained in Russia and Bulgaria - this is for you privately, by the way, not for some dossier in the Pentagon. Now you'll have to tell me yours? Come on Colonel Manners."

"Ahem, it's not as good as yours. I'm usually called 'Berry' in dossiers. I've worked under a range of names in missions."

"Berry…wait that's Chuck Berry. I get it, " laughed Christina, " I suppose that's why you've no particular place to go?" she added.

"Not bad for a Russian!" said Chuck.

Christina remembered, " Okay - but as well as their code names, I can tell you that they are a couple; man and woman, who have been running deep cover for several years. Don't think of them as just troublesome though. They are deadly. I think you should move on, get lost again in your own cover. You must have some spare identities? It's time to use one."

Chuck nodded, " Thank you. Thank you, Christina, for this and for your generosity of spirit whilst here with us all. My pledge. If the chips are down, I'll still support you. That's from one professional to another."

"Likewise, " said Christina, " Sometimes it's good to have allies in unusual places., My pledge is also to you."

"Final hugs?" asked Chuck.

"Sure, " said Christina, " Until the next time!"

Occupational hazards

Amanda was back at the Mondrian.

"This is the fourth time I've been to the Mondrian, " said Amanda., " SI6 will begin to show an interest around now."

"What's been your story?" asked Chuck.

"I've told them I have an asset here, but that I don't want to divulge names."

"They are probably already following you, then."

"The operational unit responsible for that is run by Jim Cavendish. He and I have an extensive history. I've told him not to read anything into this. Sorry to say this, Chuck, but I fear we've run our course."

Chuck looked briefly mournful, " No, I understand, " he said. "Occupational hazard of the Life. I've also received a little whisper that I've been spotted by the FSB. I was thinking this would need to be my last day here.

"Give me something to take back, for my story - that I've been talking to an asset, " asked Amanda, " It can be related to that thing you are doing with those Triangle people. You know, the Minerva Station by the Dome."

"Yes, they are on to something. That place may be called Minerva, but it is more like her sister Medusa - you know, the one that could turn people to stone."

"Ah yes, hair of snakes and all that, I remember, " said Amanda.

"Well they seem to have identified that the Triangle team entered their premises and then they used some of the Minerva tracking technology to locate the Triangle offices and send them a message. A big message. Their offices were set on fire. By an American Army incendiary grenade. It isn't obvious to me that there's a direct link, but it is mighty suspicious."

"How can you know it was an American grenade?" asked Amanda.

"Oh, I've seen the evidence, they took part of the canister from the wreckage, photographed it and gave me a copy - it was military grade. An M14, and a very fast operation too. Tap the glass with a hammer, throw the grenade in and exit on a moped. A couple of minutes. Professional and slick. Someone like me did the job. Well, there were two of them on the video clip. A driver and bomber."

"Not entirely a CIA operational style?" said Amanda, " And way too sensitive if caught. Americans throwing bombs around London Streets?"

"I agree, " said Chuck, " They've black-Opp-ed this out. My guess is they didn't need to go far, what with all those Qube security services people around the place."

"That was what The Triangle people thought as well. They decided to go back for a second dig around Qube. It's good for both of us actually because these guys are freelance and clearly not working for UK or US governments. We get deniability, but results."

"This could work out well for both of us, " said Amanda.

Chuck continued, " So they still returned and put the frighteners on one of the CIA workers there. A pretty little thing called Anne-Marie. It sounds as if she got the job through her father's contacts; nothing like fast-tracking it via International assignments."

"However, a couple of the members of the Triangle managed to spook her and she did spill the beans. Minerva is running as a high-class boiler house to scam MPs and senior business players. We think it is cheaper than using lobbyists in a conventional manner and it certainly is stealthier."

"They got a name too, Bernard Driscoll."

"Driscoll, the MP? - Hah, he is too boorish to come up with any serious mischief by himself, they must be using some thick strings to manipulate him! I've had direct dealings with him - a loathsome bullying character and somewhat dim-witted, hiding behind pomposity."

"Well, this might be a chance to see his comeuppance!" said Chuck, " linked with Minerva and something involving Qube."

"Chuck, that is brilliant. I've got a great list of things to take back. Minerva, Driscoll and Qube."

"You know what, you shouldn't be thanking me, you should be thanking those guys that operate as 'The Triangle.'"

"I've noted that too, and I'm intrigued and more than a little bit thankful that you've stayed loyal to them."

"So, the night is yet young? We will have to plan how we extend our friendship when I'm back in D.C."

Chuck gets out of Dodge

The next day, Jake and Bigsy arrived at Chuck's room. Chuck was packed and looked as if he was ready to leave.

"Hi guys, look, I've piled up the equipment that Bigsy brought on the little table in the annex. I think you'll need a large suitcase or something to move it out of the room."

"Chuck - you're leaving. So suddenly too?" said Jake.

"I know, it was always intended to be a flying visit, checking in with a few acquaintances, but ever aware of the possibility that I'd get traced. D'you know that's what's happened, " said Chuck, " I've been put back onto a seek list but the FSB. They've sent a couple of agents to find me."

"What about Christina? She wouldn't do that to you, neither hunt you nor shop you, " said Bigsy.

"No, I agree, I'm certain that Christina was as surprised as anyone. Between you and me, she might just have tipped me off about the situation, " said Chuck.

"I'll be using another identity when I get back to D.C." Said Chuck, " I'm sure we'll all stay connected, in any case."

"Yes, Chuck, it's been pleasure, as always, " said Jake, slapping Chuck on the back.

"Yes, look after yourself and don't be a stranger, " said Bigsy.

"No Clare nor Christina this time, " said Chuck, " Please give them my regards."

For a moment Bigsy and Jake looked awkwardly towards Chuck, but then he said, " Time to haul ass, as we Americans say, "

"Yes, safe travels, " said Bigsy. Jake waved.

Chuck made his way between them, saying, "Oh yes, I've paid for the room tonight, so you've time to move out the gear." And then with a wave, he was gone.

"Wow, that was a turn-up, " said Bigsy. He knew Jake was a good friend of Chuck and of all of them he thought Jake would take Chuck's departure the hardest.

"We'd better move this gear out, " said Jake. Bigsy was already unfolding a couple of large blue IKEA bags from his habitually carried rucksack.

"Yes, if we can put all the small stuff into a couple of these, then one of us can carry the printer and the other one all the junk. If we can get it to the lift, then we can soon move it into a taxi around to mine, " said Bigsy.

"Yes, said Jake, or we could take it to the temporary Regus office that I've got for us."

"Office - that sounds good, said Bigsy, " Whereabouts is it?"

"Central, near the Institute of Directors by Liverpool Street. Ideal for the City of West End and pretty easy commute for all of us - Even Christina. - I thought it would be okay until we either refresh the Triangle Offices or, more likely, find something more modern."

"Cool, " said Bigsy, " When will you tell Clare and Christina?"

"They know already, " said Jake sheepishly, " I told them to go there today instead of coming over here to Chuck's"

"Right, then, " said Bigsy, " What are we waiting for?"

Driscoll Shining

Meet upon the level
Part upon the square

Soft power

Driscoll couldn't believe his luck. Marion had called him after the Formula One dinner. She'd said she was sorry that she had to rush away like that, but she realised that Bernard was caught up in some kind of conversation in any case.

She had asked to meet Driscoll again. This time at Berners Tavern, which Driscoll thought of as an exclusive and showy restaurant.

Marion had explained that ISMC had offered to provide a private dining experience there, but on the understanding that Bernard would take a few minutes from the occasion to listen to some ideas from ISMC.

Bernard had jumped at the chance. He knew that Marion Charlotte would be there on his arm and the location was simply one of the best in London.

Today was the date and he was looking forward to meeting Marion Charlotte before the occasion. He had been given a Loft Terrace room in the nearby London Edition, which he knew was one of the finest boutique hotels in London. Now he was meeting Marion in the intimate Punch Room before they made their way into the restaurant.

He had taken a seat and was sipping his way through a rather delicious speciality gin and tonic. Marion arrived and he felt a frisson of energy as she walked into the bar. The casual unflappable barmen missed a beat as Marion walked in, noticed Driscoll and walked across to greet him.

"Darling, " she said, " How lovely to see you, I don't know about you but I'm looking forward to this dining experience!"

Bernard nodded agreement and then watched as Marion sat down. She was completely in control of her surroundings and a waiter moved over to ask her if she would like a drink.

"I'll have one of your lovely Champagnes, " she said, and Bernard watched in fascination as she briefly scanned the menu.

"Do you know what? Why don't you choose? Something for both of us?" She handed her menu to Bernard."

He looked along the delicious menu options and settled on one of the sharing selections. "There, he said triumphantly, how about this?"

She looked at his choice, " Er won't that come rather large?" she asked and pointed to a more slim-line section of the menu.

"I think I'd rather go for this lemon sole, " she said and maybe a mixed leaf to start?"

Bernard put away his thoughts of 'Buccleuch Estate chateaubriand, baby parsnips and wild mushrooms' and started to concentrate on the 'sea bream in lobster sauce' instead.

Then he heard voices outside of the room. In walked a man and a woman, whom Marion seemed to know. "Darlings, " she greeted them, " So glad you could make it, and this is Bernard Driscoll, the MP and Minister."

She hugged and kissed them both in what Bernard noticed was the same way that she greeted him.

"Hello Bernard, " said the man, who made to shake his hand. Bernard noticed it was a freemason's handshake. Quite elaborate, he recognised it as the lion's paw of a master mason.

"My name is Miller; Miller MacDonald, he said with a clearly American accent, and this is my friend Trudi Hartmann."

Driscoll looked towards Trudi, who was smiling back. She was another stunner, who, to Driscoll, looked like a young Claudia Schiffer.

"Delighted to meet you both, " answered Bernard, " Although I'm surprised because I thought Sir Charles Frobisher would be here?"

"Ah, Sir Charles, yes he is a good colleague of mine, said Miller, " We are both at ISMC, although you can probably tell from my accent that I'm based in America - in Texas, actually."

"Sir Charles was unavoidably detained this evening and called to ask if I could take his place. Well I could hardly say no, what with such an awesome restaurant, two lovely ladies and a Member of Parliament for company!"

Bernard smiled.

"And I hear you like Formula One as well, I'm more of a NASCAR man, in The South you can't really avoid NASCAR and when I was younger, I lived in Dallas so the Texas Motor Speedway was never far away."

"I don't know so much about NASCAR, " said Bernard, " It seems to me that the drivers might get dizzy from only turning one way at the bends?"

"I know, they don't get paid quite as well as the Formula 1s, but to Southern ears it is reassuring to hear names like Earl, Jeff, Tony and Jimmie driving stink out of those cars."

"What instead of Max, Valtteri, Carlos, Sebastian, Fernando, Lewis, Jenson and Nico?" asked Driscoll, smiling, but feeling safe on one of his favourite topics."

"I used to be friends with Jamie Pollozini who is also a Formula One driver, " said Trudi, " His name sounds Italian, but he was from Perth in Australia, I remember he had an interesting nick-name."

"Oh, what was it?" asked Marion.

"I'll have to whisper, " said Trudi, " I know it's a bit rude to whisper, but so is the name." She stood, walked around the table to Marion's and whispered something in her ear. Then Marion whispered something back. They both laughed.

"Well, the girls seem to be having fun, " said Miller, " We boys need to have some too, but hey Darling, what shall we order? I'm thinking about the Chateaubriand?"

"You choose, " said Trudi, " So long as I can have it with Champagne."

The dinner proceeded and Driscoll came to see that Miller's exuberance somehow crossed into an altogether wilder side. Miller had tales of his sorority, of fishing in the Gulf of Mexico and of a penchant for classic sports cars. He was clearly well-heeled and well-travelled. In fact, Driscoll felt a little swamped by the anecdotes.

Then, Trudi excused herself from the table. Marion said she'd go along too.

That left the two men sitting across from one another.

"This is where the cigars would come out in my club in Austin. It's in a beautiful looking Antebellum building, with one of the few remaining statues of Robert E. Lee in the lobby. Most of Texas has now removed him from their memory, like some kind of Communist photo-coup. Yes, they took him off street signs, parks, pools and from the edges of the University in Atlanta. I'd put him as a smart man of his time. Opposed to slavery but accepting the social conditioning of the times which included 'be rude to slaves.' He also predicted that the war would be a long and bloody one."

Driscoll nodded. He didn't know much about the American Civil War, except the pieces he'd seen in that movie, what was it? Gone with the Wind. Burning of Atlanta. Sherman vs Hood. Someone set fire to the railroad boxcars of ammunition.

"Well, let's talk about something more modern, " said Miller, " I know you'll have been following the situation in Celarus. It's where we have a small ISMC outpost and where Raven are targeting to move Brant."

"Yes, said Driscoll, " Sir Charles referred to your presence when I met him the last time."

"I expect he mentioned the increased need to corral the effects around our bases. Like that situation in Iraq where the convoy was intercepted.

Miller looks at Bernard, " With you as the Minister for External Affairs, you can have a major influence on this and what happens next. The UK can either send politically sensitive troops into these areas, or with a little ingenuity can head off the problem, paving the way for infrastructure reconstruction and secure stability through the judicious sale of munitions.

Miller leaned towards Driscoll, " Your soft power influence behind the scene is all that is required to make this run along nicely. That's where we think you could be instrumental in stopping the violence and helping the trade position simultaneously.

Miller continued, " Bernard, this path provides opportunity for personal benefit without personal sacrifice."

Bernard was thinking; this was the second time he had heard ISMC make a similar offer.

"So, what, would I need to do?" he asked.

The Offer

"It's quite simple, really, " said Miller.

"Raven is divesting Qube. The recipient organisation is Brant, based in Brussels. There might be some challenges to this from Parliament, because it looks like another piece of Britain being sold off and too much like private security is running military situations."

Driscoll nodded. "No different from the Americans with their contractors running Basra and Helmand Province - DynCorp and Blackwater, to name but two. These keep coming across my desk."

"Admittedly so, but the situation with Qube is quite different, " said Miller, " It will be bidding fair and square for the construction contracts in Celarus and adding some value by building additional infrastructure within the original contract."

"Oh yes?" said Driscoll, " How can it afford to?"

"Quite simply, Risk and reward, Qube and soon-to-be Brant will have a tailored blend of military and construction expertise. Add that to the Raven energy knowledge and there's an unbeatable combination. We can construct bases and infrastructure as well as a new pipeline right across Celarus. It will completely deflect the Russian pipeline attempts to sell their energy to Europe."

"You said I'd be able to get some benefits from this?" asked Driscoll.

"Well there's two. One is purely reputational. You'll be the visionary that has seen the sense in the new endeavour and the benefits it brings to the British economy.

"Secondly, we plan to set up a kind of trust fund for you. It means you'll need a Driscoll Foundation or something which we can deposit money in. These won't be directly connected with your work as an MP but will be seen as an above-board humanitarian support for, say, the wellbeing of people in Celarus."

"What sort of deposits would we be talking about? " Asked Driscoll. "Well initially, maybe ten, to start it off. Then once the mechanism is established, we can look at maybe another couple each month. When the pipeline comes on stream, I guess that could increase, maybe to four."

"When you say 'ten' what do you mean, exactly, " asked Driscoll.

"Oh, sorry, ten million, I should have said, " answered Miller."

"And which currency are you describing?" asked Driscoll.

"Oh, sorry again - when in Britain - British Pounds, obviously."

"That's still quite a lot to take in."

"I guess that's all the upside, visionary fame and stealthy recompense. You'll need some sophisticated banking for this you realise, oh and don't worry about the Parliamentary speeches; we have some people that can help you with those."

"Is there any downside, apart from me discovering that I'm in an elaborate sting operation?" asked Driscoll.

"Well, yes, I should mention that too. How can I put this? There are not many people we have made these types of offer to. Those that accepted them are living very well. Those that didn't accept seem to have accidents soon after the offer was made."

"Ahah, now we get to it, a threat?" asked Driscoll.

"You could see it that way, or be like me, an optimist, and think of this leap of faith as one giant opportunity."

Parliamentary Debate

DIVESTMENT OF RAVEN CORPS
HC Deb 29 March cc1207-15

3.49 p.m.

The President of the Board of Trade
I beg to move, that this debate be conducted into the planned divestment from Raven Corps, of Qube into a new company based in London called Brant.

This is a short debate. It does not attempt to do everything, even in the field of monopolies, mergers and divestments.

It sets out to do what is most urgent and most necessary in the belief that we should not postpone doing anything until we can do everything.

The Minister for External Affairs (Bernard Driscoll)
The planned move is one part of the comprehensive programme for streamlining and modernising British industry, which is crucial to the economic survival of this country, and which the Government are determined to launch.

If we are to retain, as I believe we must, a large sector of private enterprise in the mixed economy of this country, competition is essential as one safeguard of the efficiency and progressiveness of that private sector.

The Raven divestment is conceived in the belief, which I think is common to all parties, that monopolies, mergers and divestments are not always bad.

Sometimes they are and sometimes they are not.

This truth was admirably expressed in that classical document, which wears well with time, the White Paper on Employment Policy, of May, 1944—a bipartisan, perhaps I should say a tripartisan document which said that, although "arrangements or combines do not necessarily operate against the public interest", " nevertheless "the power to do so is there"."

1208

Three valid criticisms have been made of the working of our present dual system of a Monopolies Commission, on the one hand, and a Divestment Practices Court, on the other.

The first is that it has all been too slow. The Monopolies Commission has not been able to work simultaneously on more than a very small number of inquiries; and each enquiry has tended to take years rather than months.

The watchdogs have barked, or prepared to bark, but meanwhile the monopolies have gone marching on.

We cannot let this situation arise for divestments, of which the Raven example if materially beneficial to the United Kingdom.

This situation breaks apart a behemoth, producing instead a more manageable beast and one that can be tamed by judicious oversight.

1209

But I should like to emphasise the value which we attach to the services of busy people in business and the professions who devote their time to this public work and to express our gratitude to them. [HON. MEMBERS: "Hear, hear."]

Where this firm (Raven) is really dominant in an important industry, controlling perhaps over half the market, we now have an ideal opportunity to see through changes which will reduce its size and potential impact within the control of the relevant sectors which it inhabits.

The smaller units produced - comprising a blend of Qube and Brant should be able to manage their new and diverse industry and successfully provide a positive Balance of Payments surplus to the United Kingdom.

Instead of an outflow of funding to the United States, we will see a new tax centre for Brant in London.

1210

Apart from those qualifications. however, I think that it is right that both professional and commercial services should be included within the scope of the divestment, though that does not, of course, mean that the Government have any present intention of rushing in to question the arrangements of the learned professions.

What the divestment does is to give the Government power to refer such commercial or professional practices to the Commission wherever this seems to be desirable and to use the powers contained in both the 1948 Act and the present Bill to restrain any practices which the Commission condemns.

1211

Mr. J. T. Spicer (West Loughton) Before my right hon. Friend leaves that point, in interpreting the intention of the Clause at a later stage will he pay particular attention to the effect on prices of cost accountancy and the very high fees which automatically are loaded in to inflated prices?

Mr. Driscoll I do not doubt that that is one of the considerations which we shall take into account, but it is not necessarily the only one. I note, however, what my hon. Friend has said.

Many divestments, as I have said, will be positively in the national interest and can probably be reasonably easily seen to be so. Others, however, might tend, or, indeed, even be deliberately designed, to derail competition, which, in the last resort, is the only real justification of private enterprise. The practical problem, I think we should all agree, is to sift the one sort of divestment from the other
1212

Mr. A. E. Sopels (Ditherington-in-the Marsh, South) If a public announcement is made that two companies want to divest and re-form, and the Board of Trade decides that it wants to intervene, in what period of time would it make its decision? Because there could be a long period of uncertainty while there was dithering in the Board of Trade.

Mr. Driscoll I am coming in a moment to the point of what the Board of Trade would do if a proposition of that sort were put to it.

I believe that the legal powers embodied in the Bill are sufficiently flexible in that they leave it possible for divestments to go forward in many cases with no investigation at all, but also provide for investigation either before or after the event as may seem desirable. Even, of course, when the Commission has inquired, and made its report, it will still be possible for the President of the Board of Trade of the day, who, I think, as responsible to this House, must be the final judge, short of Parliament itself, to accept or to reject the Commission's recommendations, but when action is clearly shown to be necessary Parliament will have the power, by affirmative Order, to prohibit or dissolve a divestment found by the Commission to be contrary to the public interest.

Next—and I come to the hon. Gentleman's question—the House may reasonably ask what criteria the Board of Trade will use in deciding which divestments should be referred to the Commission and which should be left alone.

1213

We have given some thought already to this question. Mergers are of very great variety, and I do not propose to attempt to spell out precisely the cases where the public interest might be at risk. One obvious case, I think, is where competition in a vital industry might be markedly reduced.

That is why we have provided, as an alternative to the criterion of monopoly, a size of assets test, so that what are called vertical or diversifying mergers could be investigated if the public interest required.

Divestments involving large firms are not, of course, necessarily harmful to the public interest. In judging all these cases, however, I would propose always to remember what divestment in certain cases can do to achieve greater strength for our economy at home and abroad.

1214

Sir John Cricklewood (Seven-Teeseoak and Gomply-Titheridge) Would the right hon. Gentleman say, for the purpose of clarification, whether the powers he has outlined apply not only to divestments covered by the Measure, but also to divestments voluntarily negotiated?

Mr. Driscoll Yes, certainly. They apply in either case where divestment would be the result of the operation.

Mr. A. Cokeburner (Dopley and South Trumsett) May I put a question to my right hon. Friend on that? My right hon. Friend will remember that one of the large items which gave rise to a good deal of agitation was big accounting firm divestments. Would those come under the scheme?

1215

Mr. Driscoll Yes, certainly. This is ground-breaking for a divestment but others may follow a similar path.

Forward to ROYAL ASSSENT
Noticed a typo? | Report other issues DIVESTMENT OF RAVEN CORPS
HC Deb 29 March cc1207-15

The Launch

"It's happening, " said Bigsy, " The divestment of Qube."

"They are setting up Brant just like your friend said, Christina."

"What, Elena?" said Christina, " That seems like such a long time ago."

"The mills of the gods grind slowly, but they grind exceeding fine, " chipped in Clare.

"I'm not so sure about that, " said Christina, " Where I come from the Gods can be pretty fiery tempered and run around wielding big hammers."

Jake continued, " Well anyway, it looks as if Driscoll has fronted the deal through a debate in Parliament. They've a green flag now to go ahead and split off Qube from Raven and to amalgamate it with Brant, just like Elena predicted. Another British Company becomes European."

Bigsy added, " Then remember what Nelson said, they will get rid of the people from Raven that have been transferred to Brant and start afresh with a new team. It's a classic outsourcer manoeuvre."

"So, is this some kind of Masonic move?" asked Clare, looking towards Jake, " Or is it something else?"

"It smacks of *Vzyatochnichestvo* - that's corrupt practices, " said Christina, " In Russian, we say *блат (blat)* , which is a is a form of corruption through a system of informal agreements, exchanges of services, connections, Party contacts, or black market deals to achieve results or get ahead.

"The *blatnoy (блатной)* run much of the *blat*. It has a criminal meaning in Russian and it relates to a status in the criminal world. It usually means a member of a thief gang, *(blatnoy/блатной)* itself means professional criminal in Russian."

"So, you are not saying the Russians are involved in this?" asked Bigsy, looking concerned.

"No, just that this corruption is as old as the hills. You English say 'You scratch my back, I scratch yours.' In Russian we say 'One hand washes the other,' " said Christina making her hands make a washing gesture.

"But the other thing is, if this was blat, there would be more to it. Split off the company, move the people, set-up a new boss structure. But you have to ask the question, Why? " said Christina.

"You think there is more to it?" asked Jake.

"There must be, " said Christina, " Someone is out to make a lot of money or secure a huge amount of power, otherwise why entrap Driscoll? Why set up that Minerva station?"

Financial Times

"Look here, " said Bigsy, " The FT is calling the Qube divestment from Raven creating Brant a financial triumph. Raven's shares went up by 7% and the Brant shares are already trading at nearly 2x their original predicted level.

"Think about that for a minute, " said Jake, " All the advisors and financiers to that deal will have underwritten it to some degree. The Brotherhood will all be coining it in."

Bigsy added, " The deal is led by Lucy Sidwell, from Raven's Corporate Treasury, she is a Board Member, but I seriously doubt that she would be a Mason."

"Yes, but there has to be another move behind the divestment, " said Christina. "Trust me, I've run security for too many of these kinds of operations."

Jakes's phone rang. "Oh, hello Amanda. How are you? Yes, it has been a while. Yes, Chuck did say you might call."

Jake walked to the whiteboard and wrote Amanda Miller in big letters.

"Yes, Yes, we were. I know, we saw it too. As a matter of fact, we were just talking about it."

"When? What topic? This isn't a hoax of anything?"

"Okay, I'll ask the others and ring you back. Goodbye then. Until later!"

He switched off his phone.

"Well that is an interesting development, " said Jake, " It was Amanda Miller from SI6. You remember when she detained me that time you - Clare and Bigsy - were gallivanting around Arizona?"

"Well she's been tracking the developments on Brant too and wants to talk. She mentioned something about a politician."

"Interesting, " said Christina, " Although I'm not sure I should be present. I get the feeling Amanda would feel the need to turn me in to some of her associates."

"I seriously doubt it, " said Jake, " I expect Amanda will treat you in the same way the Chuck did. Kind of Case Closed - based upon that other Russian name - what was it? Vanonin?

"Voronin, " corrected Clare.

"Okay, we'll all go then," said Jake, " I'll suggest to Amanda that we meet at the Riverfront, by the book sellers. It's a kind of classic spy movie setting, " said Jake.

"Not to mention Hugh Grant and Andie MacDowell in Four Weddings and a Funeral, " added Clare.

"Game on, " said Jake.

Four Theories and a Funeral

*"You come to nature with all your theories,
and she knocks them all flat."*

— Renoir

The Riverside

Amanda was already sitting at one of the small outside tables when Clare, Bigsy, Jake and Christina arrived.

"Wow, I get to meet you all!" said Amanda, " I know Jake from way back, but I think a couple of you were travelling around the American deserts when we were last involved together."

They all shook hands and introduced themselves. Bigsy made his way inside to buy some coffees.

"Clare and Bigsy, I've heard of, but I don't think I know you, Christina?"

"You might know me by other names, but we'll keep it simple today, " said Christina.

"You are not Voronin? Katarina Voronin?" asked Amanda, " Chuck was mighty respectful of you if that's the case! I seem to remember we captured you somewhere, and the case got closed?"

"That's more or less the same story that Chuck remembered, " said Christina, " But I can see I'll need another name change after this operation is complete."

Amanda paused looked closely at Christina and said, " Yes but the Archangel name will follow you around. I'm in the presence of a super-agent."

Christina smiled. It was good to know her reputation was even visible in London.

"They made part of Four Weddings and a Funeral outside here, " said Amanda. Jake and Clare nodded.

"Hugh Grant and Andie MacDowell, " answered Clare, " With Kristin Scott Thomas!"

"Yes - I hear you've moved to a new office?" asked Amanda, " After your other one was fire-bombed?"

"That's right, " said Jake, " Although we are keeping the exact circumstances reasonably low key for the insurance."

"So how could we be of assistance?" asked Jake.

"Look, I know you know Chuck Manners and he suggested that I contact you about all of this. I gather you have found an American Station working out of Canada Water, but outsourced to Qube- nowadays Brant? And that you've noticed something untoward about Bernard Driscoll?

"The American Station is, we think, the source of the fire-bomb to our offices. We think it was an American incendiary grenade. We suspect Qube of having a hand in it."

"Then Driscoll, we think someone is operating him to smooth the divestment from Raven of Qube to Brant. And we also think that it hasn't played out yet. We think there is something else in the works."

Amanda nodded, " I've been drawing the same conclusions. There's some heavy-handed Freemasonry in the mix, but I think that is just to camouflage whatever Driscoll is doing."

"You'll know he has been seen around Freemason parties lately, and heading off into small smoke-filled rooms?"

"We'd heard about some of this but can't tie it together."

"We think that Raven is pulling some of the strings here. American interests moving to make money from civil unrest. You know the model. Sell them weapons. Architect the unrest. Sell them peacekeeping. Sell them reparations. Harvest whatever natural resources they have.

"Syria is a case in point. It's a long time since the ceasefires, yet the embedded industries of Qube are still present. Occasional little skirmishes break out which prevent the US from pulling out completely.

"Now it seems to be positioning for Celarus. Brant are already present there.

"With the divestment/merger we can see Brant establishing a presence. Just as a few arguments break out along the border. It will be the usual American response. Fly some planes along to knock out perimeter defences. Then America will want to build a base. Do they build their own? Hell No. They get some builder in to do the hard work, building roads and MacDonald's cafeterias for the troops. Maybe an airfield and a few other security measures.

"Who will they call? Why Brant of course. Next things we see is Brant's share price rocketing as they land some big fat American orders for defence infrastructure. And if America can persuade a few NATO Allies to join in, then why wouldn't they use the incumbent suppliers?

"Ker-ching, " said Bigsy.

"Exactly, " said Amanda, " So you could say I'm eager to trace the lineage of the Brant deal up the chain of command. I can get as far as Driscoll, but then it stops.

"Well Driscoll has some weaknesses for 'the ladies' , " said Christina, " I met him at a Freemason Ladies' Night. I also met a couple of other escorts and was told about their head of arrangements, someone named Jennifer Sussex. "

"That's great, " said Amanda, " We can chase that link through. Try to pin Driscoll down."

"Do you think he's being rewarded for what he is doing?" asked Clare.

"Oh yes, he must be, and likely it is very well recompensed, " answered Christina, " The sort of deals I saw, the slush funds were immense."

"So, what's the move to be?" asked Clare.

"Do what we'd do. Scare him and turn him, " said Christina.

Popups

Bigsy's computer went into meltdown after he typed in the search for 'London Escort Agencies.'

He was trying to find the elusive Jennifer, or a link to any of the other women that had been present at the Ladies Night.

He'd drawn a complete blank, although he now had a comprehensive folder of potentially scary future dates.

Jake and Clare thought it hilarious, not to mention the range of new search terms that Bigsy seemed to have acquired.

"All of those little sidebar and popup adverts have changed from USB gadgets and back pain remedies to 'ladies looking for lurve,' " he added.

Amanda decided to use her contacts with GCHQ to try to trace what was happening in Celarus.

Grace had put together a briefing profile.

It was simple. The Celarus government was fragile. Their leader was under attack from the opposition and they were trying to encourage military leaders to join the new breakaway movement.

In the middle of this, Brant were building a new base for the Americans and the Americans in turn were providing security services to the Celarusian government.

It was rumoured that there was a massive pipeline deal in the works too and that Brant were front-runner for the construction.

"We've all the pieces, " said Amanda.

"I think we can add on something personal - there's his wife and daughter out in Norfolk. I doubt they know about Bernard's dalliances."

"Nor would they think him capable, " added Grace.

They both laughed.

"So how do we lure him for a meeting?" Asked Grace.

"He seems keen on the women, so I guess a conventional honey trap might be the way to go, " said Amanda.

"Won't he be suspicious?" asked Grace.

"He thinks of himself has a powerful man. What do they like to surround themselves with?"

"Oh okay, let's run with it, but whom?"

"Well, we could start with Marion Charlotte, I suppose, assuming she is more coin-operated than loyal to her prior masters?"

"Do you think he'd be suspicious of a call from her?"

"I think the only way to find out will be to approach her. We'll need some theatrics around it too."

Using Grace's links in GCHQ, they soon tracked down a London address for Marion Charlotte. Amanda planned a direct head-to-head confrontation with her.

Vzyatochnichestvo

Marion Charlotte's address was a smart building in West London. It was in a street of similar looking four story tall white painted building with huge pillars either side of a grand looking porch.

Amanda considered using SI6 for the approach, but felt, on balance that it would bet better to use someone from the Triangle offices. It would improve subsequent deniability and stopped any rumour from circulating that Driscoll was being investigated.

The Triangle team had decided that Christina would accompany Amanda, although they realised that this was a surprise twinning of a SI6 office with someone from FSB.

"Don't worry, " said Christina, I'll be scary if required."

They were outside the house and Amanda rang a bell which had neatly printed the name M Charlotte.

"Hello, " called the entry system, " who is there?"

"Hello, we are friends of Bernard Driscoll, " answered Amanda, " We come about the secret party we want to throw for him."

"Second Floor, " came the reply and a buzz.

They were in and would meet Marion Charlotte in a few moments.

"Come in, " said Marion. They entered an opulent and tidy realm. Fashionable pictures on the walls, decorative walls and sumptuous furnishings. It reminded Amanda of a cover-shoot.

"A glass of wine, maybe?" asked Marion.

"I'm surprised you have been able to find me here, I'm not even sure that Bernard has this address?"

"We got it from Jennifer, " replied Christina.

"Ah okay, I see, " said Marion, " She is not supposed to give it out. Security and all."

"Well we thought this was a special situation, " said Amanda, " We want to surprise Bernard, " based upon some of the little things he's been up to lately, " we want to offer him a big bonus."

"Oh, I see, " said Marion, " To be honest, if you want me to call him, you'll have been told my rates by Jennifer at MDA. I'm inclined to add surge rates for Driscoll though."

All three laughed at the reference to Uber's peak charging policy.

"So, what would it take to get you to invite him to what I promise will be a surprise party?" asked Christina.

"I'll write it down, " said Marion. She found some paper and a pen and wrote down what seemed to Amanda to be an excessive sum.

"Half in front and half after the deal?" asked Christina, " direct payments?"

"That will do nicely, " said Marion.

Gavvers

Marion had invited Driscoll to her surprise event. She was sure he had come along. She had told him it was a small private party to celebrate winning a modest award and that he would be her partner.

She had told him it was lounge suits and not very formal. They were meeting at La Gavroche in Upper Brook Street and would be dining in the Chef's Library.

Driscoll could hardly believe his luck that he was now being invited out by the lovely Marion. And this sounded like a more intimate session that some of the others which had a certain working bias.

Now that his Foundation was up-and-running and seemed to be accumulating a decent bankroll, he felt quite positive about all of this.

He arrived at La Gavroche and was shown through to the Chef's Library. It included an intimate banquette and table and looked as if it would hold about six people. He wondered who the others would be.

Marion was next to arrive, they greeted one another, and she sat next to him in the centre of the banquette.

"Who are we waiting for?" asked Bernard.

"Oh, you'll see, soon enough, " twinkled Marion.

They could hear footsteps from a small group and then four people entered, two men in suits and two pretty women.

"Here we are, all ready for the surprise!" said Marion.

The others moved forward to introduce themselves, Amanda Miller, Christina Hyde, Jake Lambers and Dave Shelley- but you can call me Bigsy."

"Champers all around?" enquired Driscoll.

"Now that's what I call an ice-breaker, " said Jake.

They sat around the rest of the banquette and on two smaller chairs directly opposite to Driscoll and Marion. Christina and Amanda were directly facing Marion and Driscoll.

"We haven't got the boy-girl thing quite right, " quipped Jake.

"No, this is fine, " said Christina.

"I remember you!" said Driscoll, " You were at the Ladies' Night at the Raven Hall? - You were on Gerhardt's table; I think you wore a deep blue gown."

Christina was silently pleased that the von Fürstenberg was still working its magic, even after all of this time.

"That's right, " she said, and pointedly looked towards her small rose brooch, the one that Antanov had given her, " I seem to remember that you were called away for a meeting with Sir Charles Frobisher?"

"Oh, you know Sir Charles?" asked Driscoll, unaware that anything was amiss. By now he had seen the rose and now noticed the symbolism of the triangular background.

He had been looking through those books that Gerhardt had provided. That symbol that Christina wore. It was The Ancient Mystical Order Rosae Crucis - AMORC. He was in the presence of someone well-connected.

He remembered that there was no religious connotation associated with this symbol; the Rose Cross symbol predated Christianity. The cross symbolized the human body and the rose represented the individual's unfolding consciousness.

"I can see you looking at the brooch, " said Christina, aware that Driscoll was once again staring at her for just too long.

She continued, "It has quite a history, dating back to 1500BC. It taps into a special gnosis, a secret wisdom. Thousands of years ago in ancient Egypt select bodies or schools were formed to explore the mysteries of life and learn the secrets of this hidden wisdom."

"Fascinating, " said Driscoll, " But I thought women could not reach higher degrees in the Masons?"

The waiter arrived. He introduced the dinner. Brought along some canapés. It was to be a tasting menu, matched with a sommelier choice of fine wines.

"You miss the point, Bernard, " said Christina, toughening her speech. "Together, the rose and cross represent the experiences and challenges of a thoughtful life well lived.

"Thus, by our name and symbol we stand for the ancient fraternity of Rosicrucians, perpetuating the true traditions of Rosicrucian movements from centuries past to the present day."

Amanda looked at Christina, she was a little startled that Christina appeared to know so much.

"Yes, said Jake, " The further one travels, the less one knows."

"That'd be George Harrison, " said Bigsy, sipping lightly at the freshly delivered champagne cocktails, " The Inner Light."

"Yes, said Jake, " Now Mr Driscoll, Bernard - we must decide whether to look within you, or whether we are better without you, " said Jake, riffing on the Beatles tunes.

Amanda cut in, " Bernard Driscoll, we have reason to suspect that you may be in breach of the Official Secrets Act, on several counts, which include:

"Conspiring to manipulate political events for personal gain;

"Creating a tax haven vehicle for the deposit of funds from a foreign undeclared source;

"Leaking government plans to a commercial enterprise;

"Manipulating bids to elicit a favourable outcome for a pre-selected supplier;

"Speaking, in Parliament, to pre-condition a foreign divestment for personal gain.

"This is preposterous, " interrupted Driscoll, " Marion, do you know anything about any of this?"

"Yes darling, I do, " she said, " surely you remember some of those conversations you had, with Raven Corps?"

The waiter reappeared. "Consommé de Volaille et Sot-l'y-laisse aux Epices d'Asie

That is Chicken Oysters and Broth flavoured with Asian Spices, " he announced.

Amanda cut in, " But then, Bernard, to our amazement, you set up the external foundation. You didn't make it too difficult for us, did you, Bernard? - Imagine naming it The Driscoll Foundation!? - Nothing like making it easy to cross-check."

"But I put that Foundation in Lichtenstein, " answered Driscoll, " Where it was assured of privacy."

Amanda replied, " Maybe you did, but the payments into your UBS account, held by the Foundation were sufficiently easy to cross check."

Amanda pulled a small black book from her bag. She opened it and read:

"Let us summarise - You received £10 million initially and then seem to have a £2 million run-rate. But the clincher is another set of payments. These all coincide with payments to Brant. The new American base in Celarus. The deal was for $234m, then the perimeter management $68 million and finally the new riverside docks was $48 million. Your Foundation has received, concurrently, $2.34 million, $0.68 million and $0.48 million."

Driscoll looked rattled.

"What if I deny everything?" he said.

"Well, the recording that Bigsy here is making won't go down so well in a Crown Court or The Old Bailey, I admit, but it will work just fine in my offices at SI6, " said Amanda.

Driscoll looked as if he was getting ready to make a dash for it, except he was sandwiched between several people around the table.

"Look, don't think about running, " said Christina, " I can do 100 metres in 11 seconds, although maybe not in these heels. But I am also quite accurate with a knife. Even one of these." She picked up a steak knife.

The waiter had been busy, and the next course arrived, " Salsifi Roti au Beurre et Amandes Salees - That's Whole Roast Salsify with Spanish Salted Almonds and Cornish Smoked Sea Salt, " he announced triumphantly.

Driscoll's chest sank. He could see he had been outsmarted.

"Will you be telling my wife about this?" he asked.

They looked at one another, Jake almost laughed. Even Marion smirked.

Amanda looked towards Driscoll, " Look, we know you've been duped. You will probably get a sentence of something like 30 years for this. But we are more interested in the even bigger players. I've a deal for you."

"I'm interested, " said Driscoll.

Christina was amazed at how quickly Driscoll had folded.

"Okay, you'll need to work your way up the chain of command. Who is the next level? Who gives you instructions?"

"I can already answer both of those, " said Driscoll, " Sir Charles Frobisher and then Michael Tovey, the MP - They wield significant influence in all of this."

"Okay, said Amanda, " We'll have to treat you as a mole."

"Mole? " Said Driscoll.

"It sounds better than a snitch, " said Bigsy.

"Yes, we will want to know what your organisation is planning, so that when needed we can run countermeasures. What you are doing amounts to terrorism. You are using clandestine means to subvert the course of the British Government."

The waiter looked interestedly at the group, as if he was trying to work out whether they were playing an elaborate game of Murder Mystery, " Saumon Marnine et Fume aux Sirop d'Erable that's Maple Cured and Hot Smoked Var Salmon with Crème Fraiche, Dill, Gherkin and Pickled Shallots."

Driscoll said, " I'd still need to look as if I was gaining from this."

"Agreed, " said Amanda, " but the UBS funds will be re-routed to an SI6 suspense account. You cannot be seen to profit from this."

"So, the price of my freedom is to turn me into a double agent?" asked Driscoll.

"That's right, " said Amanda, " But on this occasion you will be ideology free."

Jake and Bigsy looked at one another. They were both thinking that Amanda had just told Driscoll he was vacuous.

The waiter returned again, " Selle de Cabri Roti Jus au Thym et Olives - this time we present Roast Saddle of Somerset Kid Goat, Thyme Jus and Provencal Garnish."

Amanda continued, " Look and don't think you'll be able to wriggle out of this once you are back on Upper Brook Street. We've folk who can track you down very easily and we'd soon know if you were attempting an identity change."

There was pause.

"You know, this is really good food, " said Bigsy, " and the pudding is still to come."

"I'll want this tied down legally, " said Driscoll, " You make me an offer and I accept it and with it your ongoing protection."

"I'll have to see what we can arrange through SI6, " said Amanda.

"Vzaimnykh a ne Vzyatochnichestvo" said Christina, making a slight Russian pun of the words for reciprocity and bribery. She noticed something. That Marion appeared to chuckle too.

The waiter returned again, " Ossau Irraty aux Truffes and Cerises. That's Layered Ossau Irraty and Truffles, Cherry Compote and Walnut Bread"

"Wow, now for the cheese!" said Bigsy.

"Yeah, its sheep's milk cheese too, " said Jake.

"It must be strange, how some of us can enjoy this meal, whilst others are finding it difficult to swallow, " said Amanda, " I must say that this is delicious, and with the wine, well - sublime."

"I think I'll save myself for the French Toast, " said Jake. They had all noticed that Bernard's usually healthy appetite had, on this occasion, run out. He was leaving course after course of the food, although he seemed capable of consuming the wine.

"That's a good point, " said Christina, I think we should have a toast now, to celebrate our new understandings,

"May we suffer as much sorrow as drops of wine we are about to leave in our glasses!"

"Wow, said Jake, That's a bit heavy!

"Slavic, " said Christina.

"*Poyekhali!*" said Amanda, " See, I know a Russian toast too!"

"Em, that means 'Let's get started', or 'Go!' You'd normally say that at the start of a meal, not the end, " said Christina, " It was well-pronounced though, " She looked towards Marion who nodded agreement.

"Look and now here comes a French toast, " said Jake as the waiter re-appeared.

"The gentleman is correct; this is Pain Perdu, Rhubarbe et Gingembre - that is Glazed French Toast with Yorkshire Rhubarb and Crystalized Ginger, " said the waiter.

"Perhaps you could bring us some coffees now, please?" asked Jake.

"Certainly, " said the waiter, " The coffee comes with Petit Fours comprising Sable Breton, Apple and Cinnamon, Pate de Fruit, Extra Bitter Chocolate."

Amanda looked around the table.

Thanks to her renewed acquaintances and a resting FSB agent, they had caught a corrupt Cabinet Minister who was selling UK diplomatic positions for a grubby commercial gain. She mused that it could even be classed as treason.

She felt pleased with herself that they were even able to turn the situation to an advantageous one, where Driscoll would become a mole for the UK Government.

Wrap it up

They had reassembled at the temporary Triangle offices near Bishopsgate.

Christina, Bigsy, Clare and Jake were seated around a table.

"I think that ended well, " said Jake, " We managed to track down and stop a corporation that are doing bad things."

"Yes, because of the bribery of that rather sleazy Bernard Driscoll, " added Clare.

"And under the cover of the Freemasons, " said Christina.

"Have you seen this?" said Bigsy.

He held up the Daily Telegraph.

"I didn't know you could read, not from paper anyway?" said Jake.

"Ha-Ha - No, Look- Seriously, " said Bigsy, he pointed to an article on the front page. 'Cabinet Minister in Fatal Car Crash'

Bigsy continued, " It says that Bernard Driscoll was on his way from his constituency to his family home, when his car suffered a puncture and crashed off the road, into a ditch, hitting an electricity sub-station. According to the police reports he was not wearing a seat belt and they found that his phone was on, although the number was International. They are calling it death by misadventure."

Christina looked up, " I wondered, you know, that we kept Marion Charlotte in for the whole dinner. I could not quite place it, but I thought she noticed a couple of things that I wouldn't expect. When I spoke Russian and when Amanda did, I could see her look of recognition. I think we were played."

"What? Do you think that Marion was still actively working for Raven?" asked Bigsy.

Christina answered, " If so, then she would know that Driscoll was compromised. She could tell Raven. They could clean up after Driscoll's mistakes.

They had got what they wanted from him. And removing him would mean they didn't have to pay him any longer. But now I'm concerned there seems to be a Russian angle on this."

Jake said, " We'd better call Amanda Miller then and warn her. She would also be compromised."

"If there is a Russian angle, then I think it is organised crime rather than pure state, " said Christina,

" Russian organized crime or Russian mafia (российская мафия) otherwise known as Bratva (братва).

It is a collective of various organized crime elements.

Today, there are as many as 6,000 different groups, with more than 200 of them having a global reach.

"Criminals of these groups are often former prison members, corrupt officials and business leaders, people with ethnic ties, or people from the same region with shared criminal experiences and leaders. Some claim it is one of the best structured criminal organizations in Europe, with a quasi-military operation. Some say they are operating puppets in the White House.

"So, the Americans are pushing to get Raven installed in Celarus, under the name Brant. But you think there may be Russian influences there too?" said Bigsy, " That's one hell of a hot-spot".

Christina said, " Yes, I think we stumbled into something altogether more malevolent. I now have a feeling that Marion is about to disappear. If she was trained the way I've been trained, then she would know she was 'burned' and already be calling the FSB for a new identity."

"We'll need to take heed too and maybe lose our connections with this entire situation."

"Yes, at least you've been able to operate as unknown freelancers in all of this.

"It's people like Chuck, Amanda and me that get the scrutiny. We are the ones that people will watch."

Loud and clear

Sir Charles Frobisher sat in his ISMC office at Raven Corps.

 "Interesting, " he said, " How useful to get a microphone into their temporary office."

ARCHANGEL RAVEN'S CARD

Book 3 of the Archangel Trilogy

Ed Adams

a firstelement production

First published in Great Britain in 2020 by firstelement
Copyright © 2020 Ed Adams
Directed by thesixtwenty

10 9 8 7 6 5 4 3 2 1

A CIP catalogue record for this book is available from the British Library.

ISBN 13 : 978-1-913818-00-5
eBook ISBN : 978-1-913818-01-2

Printed and bound in Great Britain by Ingram Spark

rashbre
an imprint of firstelement.co.uk
rashbre@mac.com

Mailing list: https://mailchi.mp/9f0b30712620/ed_adams

To John and Georgina

who provide socially distant advice

Thanks

A big thank you for the tolerance and bemused support from all of those around me. To those who know when it is time to say, " step away from the keyboard!" and to those who don't.

To Julie for that kind of understanding that only comes with really knowing me.

To thesixtwenty.co.uk for direction.

To the NaNoWriMo gang for the continued inspiration and encouragement.

To John, for many hours of intense scrutiny, whilst I was delicately scoffing asparagus. To Georgina for cover ideas. To MJ Cullinane for the Crow Tarot. To Alexej Ravski for inspirational cover art.

And, of course, thanks to the extensive support via the random scribbles of rashbre via http://rashbre2.blogspot.com and its cast of amazing and varied readers whether human, twittery, smoky, cool kats, photographic, dramatic, musical, anagrammed, globalized or simply maxed-out.

Not forgetting the cast of characters involved in producing this; they all have virtual lives of their own.

And of course, to you, dear reader, for at least 'giving it a go'.

Books by Ed Adams include:

Triangle Trilogy		About
1	**The Triangle**	Dirty money? Here's how to clean it
2	**The Square**	Weapons of Mass Destruction – don't let them get on your nerves
3	**The Circle**	The desert is no place to get lost
	The Ox Stunner	The Triangle Trilogy – thick enough to stun an ox
		(all feature Jake, Bigsy, Clare, Chuck Manners)
Archangel Trilogy		
1	**Archangel**	Sometimes I am necessary
2	**Raven**	An eye that sees all between darkness and light
3	**Card Game**	Throwing oil on a troubled market
	The Archangel Trilogy	the above three in one heavy book.
		(all feature Jake, Bigsy, Clare, Chuck Manners)
Stand-Alone Novels		
1	**Coin**	Get rich quick with Cybercash – just don't tell GCHQ
2	**Pulse**	Want more? Just stay away from the edge
3	**Edge**	Power can't be left to trust
	Now the Science	the above three in one heavy book.

About Ed Adams Novels:

Triangle Trilogy		About
	Triangle	Money laundering within an international setting.
	Square	A viral nerve agent being shipped by terrorists and WMDs
	Circle	In the Arizona deserts, with the Navajo; about missiles stolen from storage.
	Ox Stunner	the above three in one heavy book.
		(all feature Jake, Bigsy, Clare, Chuck Manners)
Archangel Trilogy		
	Archangel	Biographical adventures of Russian trained Archangel, who, as Christina Nott, threads her way through other Triangle novels.
	Raven	Big business gone bad and being a freemason won't absolve you
	Card Game	Raven Pt 2 – Russian oligarchs attempt to take control
	The Archangel Trilogy	the above three in one heavy book.
		(all feature Jake, Bigsy, Clare, Chuck Manners)
Stand-Alone Novels		
	Coin	cyber cash manipulation by the Russian state.
	Pulse	Sci-Fi dystopian blood management with nano-bots
	Edge	World end climate collapse and sham discovered during magnetite mining from Jupiter's moon Ganymede
	Now the Science	the above three in one heavy book.

ARCHANGEL - RAVEN'S CARD

Secret Keeper

ἢ τὰν ἢ ἐπὶ τᾶς

Ḕ tằn ề ep" tâs

'Either with your shield, or on it'

annað hvort með skjöldnum þínum eða á honum

- *Plutarch*

Roberta

Christina was in the dark, underground vaults at Waterloo station waiting to see Roberta, the fortune teller.

Christina had originally visited Roberta in the Boxpark, where Roberta had a small gallery, and Roberta had given Christina some spirited advice, which had been useful when trying to understand the Raven situation.

Now Christina was standing in a crowded, bohemian bar, lit by fairy lights and waiting for Roberta's show to begin. They were all called through to a small black room, with rows of chairs arranged along the back wall. A black curtain marked the edges of a stage area.

With a flash of smoke, Roberta appeared as a pirate queen. Long, flowing brunette hair, a white bodice pulled tight with a leather corset and thigh-length leather boots. She carried a dangerous-looking sword which glinted in the spotlights.

"Of course you would," thought Christina.

Roberta winked when she spotted Christina in the audience of about forty people. She flashed the sword through the air and a pirate flag appeared. She held the sword aloft, and the flag rose above the point of the sword, then fluttering down where it cut into halves. Then, suddenly, the two halves became bats fluttering upward.

A woman behind Christina screamed.

"The next one to scream will see me use my pistol," she cried and as suddenly as the bats appeared, a flintlock pistol was now in Roberta's hand.

She holstered the weapon and slapped her thigh, in good pantomime style.

"Imagine two ships, she said, A tall galleon and a smaller frigate. The smaller frigate holds the pirates. The tall galleon has a larger crew but is slow.

At that moment a back projection appeared. On the left was a galleon and on the right was a frigate.

"What type of audience do we have tonight? Are they King's supporters or Pirates? Think hard about this. Which ship do you want to win?"

… The story telling continued, of pirates, wreckers all along the coasts of Cornwall and Devon and then some stories from the Spanish Main.

"… Who is for this King's ship? Point to the ship. And who is for the Pirates? Now you point. And you that have not pointed, you will feel the anger of the sea."

There were several shouts from around the audience, some of whom were being soaked with jets of water.

"Come here," said Roberta to one of the people who had screamed, "For you must face my pistol."

Roberta pulled the female audience member still wearing her raincoat forward.

"Stand still," she said, and pointed the flintlock pistol.

There was a loud crack and glitter fell from the ceiling. A gasp from the audience as her victim's coat swept away, revealing a pirate costume.

"Now sit yourself down and behave," said Roberta, "But look at the ships. The King's ship survives. The pirate ship is burning. We cannot spare the souls of the pirates. It will become a ghost ship."

There was a scraping of chairs and three others of the audience stood. They each had bedraggled pirate costumes and grey skins.

"Look, for we have new ghosts tonight."

"And now, a song."

Roberta used a flourish to produce a black and silver ukulele. She played and sang Pirate Jenny - The Black Freighter.

…" And now, the chorus," she sang.

"And the ship, the black freighter
With the skull at the masthead
Sails into the bay"

And later "…another chorus…"

"And the ship, the black freighter
With fifty long cannons
Opens fire on the town"

She sang the verses of the song and then, "…this time the chorus…"

"And the ship, the black freighter
Runs a flag up her masthead
And cheer rings the air"

And, after a rousing ukelele solo, "… And we all go down together…" Roberta winked to Christina,

"And the ship, the black freighter
Sails away out to sea
And on it is me"

The pirates in the audience clapped and cheered and the rest of the audience followed.

"That's Kurt Weill and Bertolt Brecht for you," said Roberta.

"Tonight, I've been Pirate Jenny - the Pirate Queen - and thank you all!"

She carved her sword through the air. The pirate ships vanished, and a full stage-width pirate flag appeared and fell to the floor.

More applause. Christina clapped enthusiastically. Roberta knew how to work it.

The audience filed out. Christina realised that these were short sets, in a 'Fringe-style' performance. A chance to get a taste of the artist rather than an extended show.

A tap on her shoulder. "You came along! - Christina? Isn't it? - I remember you - from the land of the ice and snow!"

Christina smiled, "Yes, a great show. How do you do those clever things with the sword?"

"I may have told you some trade secrets, but a magician never tells," answered Roberta, "Come on, a drink at the bar?"

"Sure," said Christina.

They found two seats at the bar and ordered two Sol beers, complete with lime.

"Did you find your ship of fools?" asked Roberta.

"Actually, I did," said Christina, "And I found out a lot of other things that I can link back to our conversation in the Boxpark."

"That's great," said Roberta, "I'm still there, you know, hanging on by good fortune!"

"Plus, this act, terrific," said Christina.

"Yes, and that's before you see our regular theatre show "Busy" or even see me serving in The Pure Ground - it's a coffee shop."

"Were those some of the actors?" asked Christina.

"Yes, and Celine from the coffee bar - they come along to support me. I can't properly pay them, but we all help one another out with our solo projects."

"Look - after the last time we met, I wished I'd given you something," said Roberta.

"What's that?" asked Christina, intrigued.

"Well, you had natural abilities - we talked about it then - I think I have something in my bag. Wait, a moment."

"This isn't another magic trick where I get squirted with water? " asked Christina.

Roberta fiddled with the catch of a small bag. It was like a miniature-sized suitcase.

"Don't look inside," she said, "You'll spoil the magic."

Christina looked away.

Then, Roberta produced with a flourish, "Ta-da!" she said.

Christina looked puzzled. "What is it?"

Stacked on the bar was something small. It looked like playing cards.

"It's Rider Waite, " she said, "Tarot. These are the real deal. Look…draw two cards."

Christina fingered through the deck, looking at the backs of the cards and pulled two.

"Place one by you and one by me."

She did as she was asked and placed them on the bar.

"Now turn them over."

By Roberta was the Magician, by her The High Priestess.

"I knew it. You have the power. You pulled two of the most powerful cards from the Major Arcana - for me, the Magician, for you, The High Priestess, signifying Intuition and Wisdom. Together for you these two represent Willpower, Creation, Mastery, Adaptation, and Divine Truth. They are the powers of an Archangel."

Roberta smiled, "Take them. Take this deck of cards, This Tarot belongs to you. It is telling me to give them up. It has found its owner."

Christina smiled. She kissed Roberta on both cheeks.

"Robert/Roberta. Thank you."

The Tarot

Historie de la magie, du monde surnaturel et de la fatalité à travers les temps et le peuples (1870) - Jean-Baptiste Pitois

The tarot trumps can be considered as being the principle scenes of ancient Egyptian initiatory "tests".

At one stage in the initiation procedure, the postulant climbs down an iron ladder, with seventy-eight rungs, and enters a hall on either side of which are twelve statues, and, between each pair of statues, a painting.

These twenty-two paintings are Arcana or symbolic hieroglyphs. The Science of Will, the principle of all wisdom and source of all power, is in them.

Each corresponds to a "letter of the sacred language" and to a number, and each expresses a reality of the divine world, a reality of the intellectual world and a reality of the physical world.

Such claims, started by early freemasons, have today found their way into academic discourse.

Part 1 – Path of Mysteries

Cross Town Traffic

*You jump in front of my car when you; you know all the
time that
Ninety miles an hour, girl, is the speed I drive.
You tell me it's all right, you don't mind a little pain.
You say you just want me to take you for a ride.*

*You're just like crosstown traffic, so hard to get through
to you.
Crosstown traffic, I don't need to runnin' over you.
Crosstown traffic, all you do is slow me down
And I'm trying to get on the other side of town.*

Jimi Hendrix

Ten of Swords

Failure
Collapse
Defeat
Backstabbing

(Reversed)

The Worst
The Depths
Inevitable End

Unwrapping

"Look, " said Bigsy, reading from the newspaper, "Cabinet Minister in Fatal Car Crash"

The newspaper rustled as he held it up.

Bigsy continued, "Driscoll was on his way from his constituency to his family home, when his car suffered a puncture and crashed off the road, into a ditch, hitting an electricity sub-station. No seat belt and they found that his phone was on. They are calling it death by misadventure."

Christina looked up, "I wondered, you know, that we kept Marion Charlotte in for the entire dinner with Driscoll. She noticed a couple of things that I wouldn't expect. When I spoke Russian and when Amanda did, I could see her look of recognition.

"I think we were played."

"What? Do you think that Marion was working for Raven?" asked Bigsy.

Christina answered, " If so, then she would know that Driscoll was compromised. She could tell Raven. They could clean up after Driscoll's mistakes.

"They had got what they wanted from him. The company divestment and the ability to operate in Celarus. Removing him would mean they didn't have to pay him any longer. But now I'm concerned there seems to be a Russian angle on this."

Jake said, "We'd better call Amanda Miller at SI6 and warn her. She would also be compromised."

"If there is a Russian angle, then I think it is organised crime rather than pure state, " said Christina, "Russian organized crime or Russian mafia (российская мафия) otherwise known as Bratva (братва).

…

Sir Charles Frobisher sat in his ISMC office at Raven Corps with Michael Tovey, the MP.

 "Interesting," said Sir Charles, "How useful to get a microphone into their temporary office."

"Just how did you manage that?" asked Michael Tovey.

"Well, it's all a matter of degree," answered, Frobisher, "I found a man who proved to be very helpful."

"Ah," answered Tovey, realising that Frobisher was alluding to his Masonic connections.

"Yes, and I've arranged with Brant Holdings that they will run ongoing monitoring of the office from Minerva Station, out in east London."

"Is that the CIA station out by the Dome?" asked Tovey, "The one that seems to pay too much attention to the indiscretion of MPs."

"That's correct," answered Frobisher, "Although I have a sneaking suspicion that we have been compromised. And what's more, I think it is something to do with the same people."

"There are too many of them to meet the same fate as Driscoll," said Tovey.

"I agree, although I'm not sure if it involves the full office, the way they were talking it seems to point towards an American ex-marine, someone named 'Chuck'. We don't know who that is though, nor where he has gone. We are not even sure whether its an actual name or a codeword," answered Frobisher.

"I've asked the people at the listening station to monitor for longer to see if we can work out what is happening. However, I hear that one of them, Jake Lambers, is already looking for a new office space - we could lose our access if that were to happen."

"Not necessarily, " said Tovey, "Wouldn't one of the members have an attractive property somewhere in central London? - We could lure them to that location but also ensure that it is fully equipped. What do you think?"

"Well, if someone would like to assist us with a very special offer to the group of them, one they would be crazy to turn down?"

"I'd imagine we could assist the difference in the cost. We could add something from Brant into the deal as a sweetener?" added Tovey.

"So long as they didn't know or suspect anything?" answered Frobisher, "The sound quality from here is really rather exceptional!"

They listened, as Christina was speaking.

"… Yes, Bratva is a collective of various organised crime elements. Today, there are 6,000 distinct groups, with over 200 of them having a global reach. They are everywhere.

"They say that the United States is operated by Russian oligarchs. I believe this, both from my direct education but also after having lived in a range of other countries.

"Criminals of these groups are raw material to the Russian criminal operatives. They are often former prison members, corrupt officials and business leaders, people with ethnic ties, or people from the same region with shared criminal experiences and leaders. Some claim it is one of the best structured criminal organisations in Europe, with a quasi-military operation. Some say they are operating puppets in the White House. Back in Russia, those in charge of the schemes are quite amazed that they have not been found out.

"So, the Americans have got Raven installed in Celarus, under the name Brant. But you think there may be

Russian influences there too?" said Bigsy, " That's one hell of a hot-spot".

Christina said, " Yes, I think we stumbled into something altogether more malevolent. I now have a feeling that Marion is about to disappear. If she was trained the way I've been trained, then she would know she was 'burned' and already be calling the FSB for a new identity."

Clare added, "We must take heed too and maybe lose our connections with this entire situation like Chuck has done."

Christina said, "Yes, at least you've been able to operate as unknown freelancers in all of this. It's people like Chuck, Amanda and me that get the scrutiny. We are the ones that people will watch."

"Or listen to," said Sir Charles, looking towards Michael Tovey.

Too good to be true?

Clare saw Jake staring intently into a computer screen.

"What's happened? Won't the inspiration come?" she asked.

"No, it's not that. I've been looking at so many offices I'm going slightly mad," answered Jake.

"Now that the insurance has come through and we have the option to sell the old plot for redevelopment, I'm keen to get us something even more central. Even with a lot of money we could end up stuck outside London if we are not careful. I asked Richard to give me a hand, and he's pulled in some favours from his agency, but most of them are further away from the centre. Look, Acton, Finsbury Park. We'd be further away than if we'd stayed in Triangle Works."

Clare looked at the properties on offer.

"I can see they are spacious, but not really what we are looking for. Ideally, we want central, good transport access, decent floor space, near to amenities, ideally some parking in case we need it."

"It is but a dream," answered Jake.

"Well, until this one came through… It looks a bit too good to be true."

He showed Clare the listing. She read out loud, "Well it has got security access, decent sized room; it is about 3 minute's walk from London Bridge train station! There's - wait a minute - riverside views towards St Pauls Cathedral. Amenities include - no way - two pubs downstairs, a restaurant, a pizza place, a wine cellar. This is bonkers, Jake,"

"I know, that's what I thought, I wondered if they had forgotten a digit in the pricing or something?"

"Yes, look at the neighbours. They are all rich financial services type organisations. Wait - Bigsy could commute to work by riverboat! This is amazing."

Just at that moment Bigsy walked into the office. "I could do what?" he asked.

"Look at this place - it's called Hay's Galleria - and has an office space."

"Hold on, I know Hays, it's just by London Bridge train station, " Quite an extensive complex of old tea warehouses that have been refitted as offices. They must go for an enormous sum?"

"I can get us a managed space in one of them here for a superb rate," said Jake, "Frankly it kicks everything else out of the way."

"Hays would be a top choice," said Bigsy. "London Bridge is on the Jubilee, with fast links to the centre, west end and to docklands. The middle of the building complex is a huge atrium with restaurants and bars everywhere. You can walk along the river all the way to Westminster. Borough Market is only about 10 minutes away - on foot! Take it! - Wait, what about the office space - is there room for expansion?

"Well, we could get four adjoining air-conditioned individual offices, an open plan area, break-out areas, a crash bar with kitchen and access to managed meeting rooms, all for what we were paying at Triangle Works. It says it is all Category 6a wired and wi-fi ready. There's perimeter security, CCTV, washrooms with showers, a downstairs 24-hour security and concierge and access to onsite services such as a laundry and food delivery services."

"Can I live here too?" asked Bigsy, "It sounds too good to be true."

"What about gym membership?" asked Christina, who had just arrived.

"No there's no gym… but wait, there's access via an underground walkway to a nearby commercial gym, with preferential terms."

"It also says that parking is limited but can be pre-arranged on demand."

"No good for a daily commute then," said Bigsy.

"And when did any of us ever do a daily commute by car?" asked Clare, "Oh, I know, never."

"Visitors might need it and we'd need to make an occasional van run, I suppose," said Bigsy, "but we'd be better with the transport parked away, like it is now."

"Okay, do I sense a consensus?" asked Jake, "If so, I'll make a call."

"Agreed!" said Clare. Bigsy nodded. "I'd say yes, if I had a vote," said Christina, "Although I was always taught to beware of deals that look too good to be true."

Jake picked up the phone.

Emily Karankawa

Pete Burr was sweeping through the recordings. He'd listened to Triangle Yard for the last couple of weeks and felt he was getting to know the people there. He could recognise their individual voices and the banter. Pete had decided that the banter for this group was altogether more respectful of one another than the banter he'd had on his last listening case, which was of the inside of a police station.

The police had been investigating some kind of politician sleaze and he was supposed to find pieces that referred to the charges against a certain MP. But oh, the language in that police station was over-ripe. He knew they were dealing with some shady situations, but there didn't seem to be an end to the depths that they would sink when calling one another names.

He was used to it now, and thankful that the name calling was only something distant. Pete had worked his way through a whole range of call-centre jobs, from the sleaziest low-end hustler roles- working from home and paid by results. Then he had joined a corporate financial services call centre - which was still a hustle. - He was fed automatically with numbers to call and offers to make, usually driven from scripts.

Oh - the names they had called him when he did that. He was pleased and relieved to be doing something now that seem to be in the national interest, although he couldn't work out why the bosses all seemed to work for the CIA, instead of GCHQ. Still, the pay was hugely better than in the previous roles and his French and Italian language skills had given him a further boost. He worked out he was already a ten-year veteran of call centres in one form or another.

He had been DBS'd - that was Disclosure and Barring Service checked when he joined and had to sign various papers of Non-Disclosure Agreement and Official Secrets Act, but he had decided it was easiest to say nothing about what he did at the listening station. If he was called upon to describe anything, he would fall back on his earlier time in a call centre.

When he'd talked to others that worked at Minerva, they had all said the same thing. Just describe the previous employment as if it was current. The pay was too good to accidentally crash and burn the opportunity.

The American bosses he worked with all seemed to be so young to be in charge of things. He wondered sometimes if there was another shadowy one behind the scenes running everything but had never asked.

If the Americans went out socially with the team, it was usually to one of the places around the Dome or across to Canary Wharf. It was just one stop on the tube and several of the Americans had said the living underground of the Isle of Dogs reminded them of where they lived in America.

He noticed that many of the Americans seem to have small apartments around Docklands, so he guessed they were all well-paid. He also thought they seemed to be as scared as the call centre operators about doing something wrong.

He had briefly dated one of the Americans, Emily Karankawa. He was surprised when he had discovered she was eight years younger than him, yet already a higher grade. He remembered being on a date and asking if her name was middle-European and registering her surprise as she said instead that her name was native American and that her people had lived in Texas for many centuries.

Her father had worked for a company called EDS which was big in Plano, Texas. Pete had to look up Plano on google and found it to the north of Dallas.

Emily had explained that her father was a big shot in EDS but then they had been taken over by Hewlett-Packard and then HP had sold them to another company. The company's name had then changed from a world-renowned company to a three-letter acronym and eventually to another name like Perspective or something.

Her father had seen his role slide down as each new company appeared and from once being at the epicentre of a company employing 300,000 people centred in Plano, he was now on the periphery of a company based in Virginia and close to Washington. The old, majestic waterside Plano Head Office had been closed.

He remembered Emily describing the situation,

"Yes, when Father's firm moved out to Virginia, it reminded them of what happened to the family name. We were descended from the Karankawa, " she explained.

"Yes, sorry I thought it sounded middle European," responded Pete.

Emily continued, "When a Spanish explorer Álvar Núñez Cabeza de Vaca washed up on a Galveston beach in 1528, he was met by the island's American Indian inhabitants— the Karankawa. "

"This encounter, which Cabeza de Vaca wrote about in his diary," she explained to Pete, "It was the first recorded meeting of Europeans and Texas American Indians."

She continued, "Then In 1685, French explorer René-Robert Cavelier, Sieur de La Salle, also met the Karankawa when he established Fort St. Louis near Matagorda Bay."

"These places have such exotic names, " answered Pete.

Emily continued, " Yes, Matagorda Bay is a large Gulf of Mexico bay on the Texas coast. It is a major estuary along the Gulf Coast of Texas and serves as the mouth of the Colorado River. There's even a ghost town of Indianola, which was a major port before it was destroyed by two hurricanes in the late 19th century.

" The bay is separated from the Gulf of Mexico by Matagorda Peninsula. Its shore, especially near the Colorado River delta, provides a habitat for a wide variety of wildlife. It can look beautiful there in the evenings, watching the sunset from Jensen Point. And all of this was Karankawa land.

"The Karankawa were historically one of the most powerful American Indian peoples in early Texas, but by the 1850s, their numbers had been so reduced that they were considered extinct."

He remembered she'd said something heartfelt to him, "I find it great, here in London, not be greeted with the kind of entitlement that permeates many American encounters. People in the US see my skin, my facial shape, my dark hair and even my name and sometimes a quiet racism emerges."

Pete had only dated Emily for a brief time. He found being with her was just too intense and intermingled work and socialising. They still got along, but he felt that Emily had found going out with him just as much of a challenge.

Knight of Wands

Action
Adventure
Fearlessness

Pete Burr

Pete Burr was concentrating now. He had been listening to the recordings from Triangle Works and a pattern was emerging.

Two names had emerged, Amanda and Chuck, both of which seemed to be linked to security services, but the name Chuck, or Chuck Manners seemed to appear the most frequently.

'Chuck' seems to be an American, and it sounded as if he was a one-time soldier, now working on black Ops. This would fit the bill exactly with what had been the discovery of the Minerva Station.

Pete had called his bosses and one of them had come along to listen to the discovery work. Her name was Olivia Lang and Pete knew she was another one of the young transferees from Washington.

"Hi Pete, " she said, "What have you got for me?"

"It's an American running Black Ops inside the UK. Counter to the intentions of Brant and Raven. I've some recordings here, which I've down selected into a single file."

"I think you know Emily, don't you?" asked Olivia, "We're quite good friends, actually. She says you are very reliable."

"That's right," said Pete, concerned about what else Emily and Olivia might discuss.

Pete played the recordings, and Olivia listened.

"Well, that's quite some work to piece everything together. It seems to indicate that 'Chuck' could be a player here, " said Olivia.

"Yes, or it could just be my editing, " said Pete, "But I like to think I've done a good interpretation."

"One approach we can take now is to run the name through CIA searches to see what we get," said Olivia, "We don't know yet whether it is an actual name or a codeword?"

"I think it is his name, unless we've started to give people two-part code names," answered Pete, "see he is often referred to as Chuck Manners. One time he was called Colonel Chuck Manners."

"That should make any search easier," said Olivia, "Look, can we keep this quiet now? I don't want half the station latching on to this or we'll have comms flying back and forth to Washington."

"That's smart, I agree," said Pete, "Let's see what we can turn up."

Mastermind

Pete had called Olivia Lang back for another meeting. He had been doing some routine intel gathering.

"It looks as if I have been able to track down Colonel Chuck Manners, mainly from routine HUMINT files," said Pete Burr. His boss, Olivia Lang, looked interested, "So spill,"

Pete continued, "He's a bit of a hero. He's been in many campaigns and a few clandestine ops. Here, take a look," They both leaned over Pete's computer. Pete noticed the pleasant fragrance that Olivia was wearing.

Pete began, "Manners has been in Afghanistan, shown as from 2001 and as part of the War on Terror and the War in Afghanistan. He was in the Resolute Support Mission. It shows that he was fighting against the Haqqani network and then later against al-Qaeda and the Islamic

Jihad Union. It doesn't say what role he played, although it also lists opposition to the Talibani Army, the Salafist extremists and the 055 Brigade. Whichever way you cut it, that would be intense."

"It sounds like groundwork too, rather than in planes?" asked Olivia.

"I'd think so, there would be some mention of hardware otherwise. They have been clever with their redaction too, because they have deleted all the dates - I suppose that assists deniability, although I suppose we could reassemble the dates from other records."

"Why would they do that?" queried Olivia

Pete continued, "It's an obvious way to disguise someone's movements and allows for little extra missions to be slipped in the gaps but conveniently not recorded."

Pete scrolled through the text for a moment, "Next he is shown as involved with the destruction of al-Qaeda and Taliban militant training camps, involved in the Fall of the Taliban government and the establishment of the Islamic Republic of Afghanistan under the Karzai administration."

Olivia picked him up on this, "'Involved with' is a somewhat vague term?"

Pete continued, "Yes, but 'destruction' isn't and suggests he was a shadow there doing something quite robust. I'm used to reading between the lines of these reports - even the redacted ones. Then there is a gap before he is involved with drone strikes in Pakistan."

"It also shows him in the invasion of Iraq and as Part of the War on Terror. It includes the invasion and occupation of Iraq and the Overthrow of Ba'ath Party government as well as the tracking and capture of Saddam Hussein."

"Capture?" asked Olivia.

"That's what it says, it doesn't mention anything subsequent," answered Pete, "Then the combating of insurgency during the rise of al-Qaeda in Iraq with its severe sectarian violence. It shows him assisting the reduction in violence and depletion of al-Qaeda in Iraq. And being an instrument in establishment of democratic elections and formation of new Shia-led government."

"So that could be the hunting down of some of the 'playing cards'?" asked Olivia, referring to the playing card decks of Iraqi suspects handed out to the US fighting forces.

Pete replied, "Yes, although in-between this he seems to have served on a missile testing range in Arizona and during this time he learned to fly several classes of aircraft and helicopters at Kirtland, Arizona."

Pete looked further down the screen. "Then he transferred to East Pakistan where he was involved with some of the insurgency in the Northern tribal regions of Pakistan and in Khyber Pakhtunkhwa. That included more drone attacks."

"Drones? Any particular types?" asked Olivia.

Pete repelled, "It doesn't say, although I think these would be the big ones, you know like Predators and Scan Eagles - and not just used for surveillance either. Used to hunt and kill. "

Pete was studying the file again, "Then he took off for Somalia where there were yet more drone strikes. I would say that Colonel Manners was a highly technically accomplished operator with a broad knowledge of combat territories and of drones, missiles and asymmetric warfare. "

"So, has he collected any medals during this time?" asked Olivia.

"Mainly the US and NATO service medals for some of the theatres he operated within," replied Pete, "Nothing that leaves an obvious trace or connection. I'd guess there's probably an Intelligence Star somewhere in Langley with his name on it too. But then, there is just this one hard-core anomaly. He was awarded a KBE for gallantry by the Brits."

"KBE - that's a serious medal - isn't it?" asked Olivia.

"You bet, A Knight Commander of the British Empire - He's officially a 'Sir' with that medal. - And it has been awarded for gallantry rather than merit, so he must have done something spectacular to get it."

"But nothing shown in the records?"

"Nothing. Nada. Nichts." Replied Pete, "Whatever it was must have been very secretive."

"Then he moved into Libya, where he worked for the overthrow of the Gaddafi government and the subsequent interim control by National Transitional Council(NTC). Despite diplomatic recognition of NTC as sole governing authority for Libya by 105 countries there was a lot of post-civil war violence in Libya leading to the restart of the main war in 2014."

"Colonel Manners seems to have cut loose by then though and it looks as if he then pops up in redacted reports, from London, Saint-Petersburg, Nice, Washington, Cali-Columbia and Paris.

"It says he was suspected of having got inside the violent drug cartel Los Urabeños, also known as the Autodefensas Gaitanistas, where he was trying to pinpoint Dario Antonio Úsuga David, also known as "Mao", the Colombian drug lord. That section is also redacted, but I suppose it ties in with Cali-Columbia."

Pete continued, "Then there's some other stuff about human trafficking and the Libyan refugee crisis , where he is thought to have run missions."

"These later reports position him as disrupter, designed to create waves which could ultimately bring empires down."

"What about private life, is he married, does he have kids?" asked Olivia.

"Divorced. He married a British woman, Melissa Skipton-Buxley, a member of the landed gentry. They had a child, Charlotte, aka Charlie. There is no reason given for the divorce, but I guess it must have been a consequence of Chuck's times away. I guess that's how he came to have a British passport too."

"Do we know anything else about Melissa?" asked Olivia.

"Well, for her it was a second marriage. She had married into wealth. Her first husband Anthony was a landowner with inherited wealth and made more money by selling off part of his estate to a builder. They built homes, schools and community building on the land, which seemed to enhance his reputation."

"Anthony was an ardent skier and had represented Britain in the Olympics. His love of skiing was what killed him. He was off-piste around Les Daiblerets, in Vaud, Switzerland when he crashed out. He was in a coma for a couple of days, but sadly died. I can't see how long afterwards Chuck met Melissa, but they seem to have got married about three years later. I guess Melissa liked her action-men!"

"And when did Charlie appear on the scene?"

"About two years later, but then they seemed to break up within another couple of years. According to Wiki, which lists the Skipton-Buxleys, the 'divorced second husband of Melissa' is also shown as 'estranged'."

"Wow, there's a book in there somewhere," said Olivia.

"Yes and it is noticeable that Chuck Manners would not even show up on a google search to this family record," said Pete.

"I see," said Olivia, "But now we see this Colonel Chuck Manners showing an interest in Minerva? We should be worried. I will need to escalate this. Please package your findings into a report for me, with a summary cover sheet."

Pete nodded to his 23-year old CIA boss.

Olivia climbs the pole

Pete wrote his report and summary of Chuck Manners and forwarded it to Olivia. She thanked him but said she would be tidying the summary sheet to make it punchier.

Pete had seen this before. He was all-too-aware aware of the Chilcott Report. How the Iraq Weapons of Mass Destruction report had allegedly been adapted by 'communicators'. He was concerned that his report into Chuck might be going through a similar process.

It was as he feared. The brigade of new millennials had worked it up into something altogether more sensational.

He read the new summary:

"Chuck Manners is a US-spy on British soil. A disrupter using a British passport to operate among the privileged classes. His range of skills made him an expert in asymmetric offensive measures, and he should now be considered a threat to the UK, USA and NATO-States. An immediate alert for his apprehension would be issued."

"Well," he thought, "The golden thread of justice of the Universal Declaration of Human Rights is not so obvious in this case. The presumption of innocence until proven guilty has gone missing."

Pete wondered if he had done the right thing, by telling Olivia as much as he had discovered. She was already spinning her way up the greasy pole by now. Still, there were still a few more things which he had later unearthed. He doubted whether any of the other CIA millennials would dig as deeply as he had done, preferring to review, extrapolate and surf from the existing report.

Pete was even beginning to wonder about the pages beyond the summary. Did anyone really read them?

A convenient truth

The repackaged report about Chuck Manners was soon in circulation at higher levels inside the CIA. Several CIA people in higher positions saw it for what it was. A piece of cobbled together spin. Some had worked with Chuck or knew of his prior exploits and were certain that he would not jeopardise his career in the ways suggested in the report.

A copy also found its way across to the Raven Offices. It was marked "For the eyes of Sir Charles Frobisher Only," It had already gained a mystic sheen by the time he opened it.

Sir Charles had called his Ruler, the Freemason and MP Michael Tovey. He knew that Tovey was not supposed to hold a Freemason degree or membership whilst in Parliament, yet the secrecy of the Masons would protect him.

"Hello Charles, so what have you got today?"

"Michael, Some interesting news from Minerva. We've a report on Chuck Manners."

"Yes Charles, I think I might have already seen it."

Charles was taken aback by this statement. If he had only just received it as an 'Eyes Only' report than how on earth could Tovey have already seen it?

"Yes, I received it yesterday, direct from Minerva. I think one of our Brothers works there and decided it was worth plucking from the routine delivery chain."

"We need to decide what to do," said Frobisher, " He sounds like a loose cannon."

"I think you know what to do," said Tovey, "And I'll expect to see another report when it is ready."

There was a soft click as Tovey hung up his phone. Sir Charles was left with a difficult problem to resolve. He called his fixer, Gerhardt Schmidt.

"Hallo, Schmidt hier,"

"Hello Gerhardt, we've a little problem to fix." He explained the situation with Colonel Manners and that he felt direct action would be required.

"I can find out what is happening," said Gerhardt, "It might take me a couple of days to gather the intelligence, but I've a wide range of options - especially as this is linked with Qube and Brant. Leave it with me."

Eight of Pentacles

Diligence
Passion
High Standards

Blackbird

Her phone woke Christina, trilling early in her apartment. She recognised the voice. It was Blackbird, her handler.

"Hello," she said, deliberately deciding to stick to English. She secretly wondered that now she had re-awoken the FSB beast, whether things would be as straightforward for her.

"Privet, Arkhangelsk, mogu skazat', chto ty predpochitayesh' govorit' po-angliyski. Ya prines vam interesnyye novosti."

"Yes, I would prefer to speak English, and what is the interesting news that you bring?" asked Christina.

"Well, you know I mentioned that I thought Chuck Manners was trying to track you? And that we had brought a couple of embedded agents in to look? Well, they have found out something," said Blackbird.

"Our agents - you remember the man and woman team аук и тупик er that's Auk and Puffin?"

"How could I forget them?" laughed Christina, "Although they never made any contact with me."

"Well, they continued to trace Chuck Manners until they finally caught up with him."

"And where was that?" asked Christina, intrigued at the thought of a near miss.

Blackbird continued, "They found out where he was working, but not where he was staying in London. Manners seemed to have a range of contacts spread across London, but аук и тупик could not even find out what he was doing. Well, it turns out that they have now intercepted a report from the Americans about him."

"At a listening station on the Thames, there's been some surveillance of an office that was used by Chuck Manners and a small team of other freelance operatives. The same station sent them as a hit squad into that team's prior office as a warning when they thought the team might have been on to something. To throw people of the trail, they used an American incendiary grenade."

"So you are telling me that these two agents were deployed for a live mission as well as to act as a tail?" asked Christina.

"Yes, to be truthful, the number of Russian agents in central London has diminished since the oligarchs gained power. They've bought up parts of the system for their own enforcement uses. Putin has just watched it happen."

So that implies that there are private armies out there now?" asked Christina.

"Yes, many of them. You know how street enforcement is managed in Moscow?"

"Yes, with small *Chastnaya armiya* patrolling the areas." answered Christina.

"Well, it is getting to be the same in London, and even down to the increasing costs. They don't want to be paid in roubles either, its USD, GBP and Euro all the way."

"I've seen some security in use. It's the flabby end of the GRU mostly. It looks as if the Silovik have been holding a fire sale to lose a few less-effective agents, " said Christina.

"Don't underestimate the security services though," said Blackbird, "They have a pretty tight grasp on things. Some would say they even have a grip on Putin."

"Ah yes, the Putin as a spook fan-boy theory?" asked Christina,

"Yes but watch out if offshoots of Wagner or Kramer turn up on the London scene. They are extremely dangerous," answered Blackbird

"The real 'men of force?' " asked Christina.

"Yes, not to be messed with," said Blackbird.

"What does this Listening Station have to say?" asked Christina, not prepared to reveal that she had already visited it.

"Well, they are putting together a dossier on Colonel Chuck Manners. It is nearly as impressive as yours, although he did more of his work in combat zones and only a scattering around in civilian situations."

"They are saying he needs to be brought in. There's not a strong reason, but he's being positioned as someone who knows the secrets of the Listening Station."

"Is the station one of ours? Asked Christina.

"Only indirectly, it has been set up with CIA fronting it and then uses the private contractor Brant to run it." Answered Blackbird.

"I see, we are supplying the staff into Brant?"

"We have a wrap-around Russian management structure for the station. Oh, the station is called Minerva."

"Roman goddess of wisdom, arts, poetry and notably, war," said Christina.

"That's right, myth has it she sprang from Jupiter's head and was borne fully grown and carrying armour." said Blackbird.

"Yes, and like all good Icelanders, I remember the stories of the gods. Minerva was a member of the Capitoline triad, a group named by the sacred Capitoline Hill in Rome, where Minerva is placed in a position of power and importance. The three gods were Jupiter- her father, Juno and Minerva." Said Christina, "I suspect there's a couple of other listening stations named Juno and Jupiter, somewhere in the world."

"Correct, and we are looking for them right now," said Blackbird.

"So what we get from your two agents is that Chuck Manners is wanted by the CIA, and that the CIA station in London is partly being run by Russian subcontractors?" asked Christina.

"That's right," said Blackbird, "And we just want you to sit tight at the moment. Let's see how the next stage of this plays out before taking any action."

"Okay, although can I meet аук и тупик - Auk and Puffin?" asked Christina, "I'd have a few questions for them."

"No, we want to keep the air gaps between you at the moment," said Blackbird, "Silent running."

Gerhardt

Sir Charles Frobisher's phone rang.

"Hello, Sir Charles, It is Gerhardt - I think I have tracked down what is happening with Colonel Chuck Manners.

"Someone from Minerva has already put out a hunt order for him. They have also dispatched two Russian operatives to find him. The two Russians have been tracking him for several weeks already, but their orders have been changed to terminate him now."

"I think you can let the system run its course on this situation," said Gerhardt.

"Whose orders are the Russians operating under?" asked Frobisher. He was mystified that there was already an order out on Chuck Manners.

"I couldn't find that out. The most likely would be the FSB, but I'm told these particular agents were partial to freelance work as well. I think their time in the west has corrupted their ideology."

Sir Charles considered for a moment. Minerva Station was supposedly being run by the CIA; Brant were positioned inside it as outsourcers. Someone was pulling the strings, but it sure wasn't him.

"This also seems somewhat clumsy," said Sir Charles.

"Clumsy?" asked Gerhardt,

"Maladroit, ungeschickt" answered Sir Charles.

"Ach Ja," said Gerhardt,"Unpassend - Yes I don't know who is running these agents, nor how they have issued a kill order - and I can't imagine it would be the CIA either - Colonel Chuck Manners is held in the highest regard inside the CIA."

"So now we have two loose cannons chasing one loose cannon?" asked Sir Charles.

Polystyrene peanuts

Back at the Triangle's temporary offices, Jake and Bigsy were unpacking a few containers of electronics.

"Do we really need all of this stuff?" asked Jake, looking at a Rode shotgun microphone.

"Oh yes," answered Bigsy, "That microphone, for example, is very omnidirectional. Great for picking up conversations. And look, I have some anti-surveillance equipment too. To stop people doing to us what we might want to do to them."

"Where do you get this stuff?" asked Jake.

"Literally, from the Spy Shop," answered Bigsy, "It's a place in Tottenham Court Road."

"What? Do they still have all those gadget shops along there?" asked Jake, "I remember when it was the place to go for hi-fi and TV equipment, before computers took over music and television."

"Yes, the spy gadgets thing has always been there too," answered Bigsy.

"Look at this," he plucked a large carton from a flutter of polystyrene packing peanuts.

"What is it?" asked Jake.

"I thought I'd get one for the new office," answered Bigsy, "It is a WAM-108t Multiband Wireless Activity Monitor. It is a high specification portable handheld multi-band detector for the detection and logging of all types of radio frequency devices. It provides coverage and logging of all radio activity in the surrounding area"

So, then, switch it on, "show what it does," asked Jake.

Bigsy quietly assembled a row of small antennae along the top of the unit.

"Right, here we go, but it shouldn't detect anything here, except our normal wi-fi and phone signals."

Jake was intrigued as Bigsy suddenly made series of 'silence' hand gestures to Jake.
    "Is everything okay?" asked Jake. Bigsy was shaking his head.

"Yes, its fine. Just as I thought. Nothing to report. Do you know what, all this unpacking has made me thirsty. Shall we go downstairs to the cafe?"

Bigsy was gesturing to Jake to go downstairs.

"Oh, Sure, Let's grab a coffee."

Bugged

"What was all that about?" asked Jake, looking towards Bigsy.

"Here, two lattes," answered Bigsy, "I can't be sure, but I think we are bugged."

"How so?" asked Jake.

"Well, that last gadget I was testing. It showed a huge amount of activity from a couple of spots in the office. Like there's a microphone been placed there."

"But how could that be?" asked Jake. "Since we've been in there, we've only had 'known' visitors and there's not been any perimeter alarms?"

"Yes, but we are in a managed facility," said Bigsy, "That means at night we have cleaners come around and in the day we might get someone visiting from the service desk."

"Can we track down the microphones?" asked Jake.

"Em, with four-thousand pounds worth of kit I jolly well hope so," answered Bigsy.

"Really?" said Jake, "I'd no idea those little gadgets were so expensive."

"Think about it…They help stop company secrets from being sold, so the guys that make them value price them," said Bigsy, "And I'd rather know that it works than build something that would leave a nagging doubt."

"Fair point," said Jake, "so what are we going to do about it?"

"A couple of things. First, we should see whether we can work out who is listening, and second we should stage an accident which somehow zaps the microphones, or at least their transmitters."

"We'd better tell the others too," said Jake.

"Not in the office though!" said Bigsy.

Mop-up operation

They were sitting together in the coffee bar across the street. Bigsy had just told Christina and Clare about the bugging. Jake returned with the coffees.

"What are we going to do to remove them?" asked Clare.

"Well, now I've found their base station, I think we have a simple solution," said Bigsy, "Whoever planted the devices gave each of them a big fat battery, which I reckon would last about a year. The signal from the microphone goes to a special base station outside one of our cupboards. It looks like an old landline telephone connector, to throw us off the trail. From there, it just sends the signal along the old telephone lines back to whoever is on the other end."

"Do we think there will be an accident of some kind?" laughed Christina, "Maybe a two-part demolition of the device?"

"Good idea," said Bigsy, "I can be quite clumsy with a mop and bucket.

"Okay, so one of us spills something on the floor, another one comes along with a galvanised steel bucket which just accidentally knocks the cover off the device. And oh dear, we've also dislodged the wires. It will all make sense to them listening to the recording too. Cause and effect - all innocent," said Christina.

"You've done this kind of thing before?" queried Jake.

"Maybe, but only in training situations," answered Christina, "Let's see now, what kind of sandwich should I buy? - One that is especially messy."

She settled for a BLT - Bacon, lettuce and tomato, which she said to the others represented the best payload for the upcoming mayhem.

They trooped back across to the office and Christina started to noisily unwrap the sandwich by the side of the cabinet at the foot of which was the phone adapter box.

"Oh no! I've dropped my sandwich all over the floor. The package must have been loose!" she cried and then Bigsy called out, "Hold on a minute, I'll get the cleaning mop."

He wheeled in a galvanised cleaner's bucket filled with soapy water and a rugged looking mop. Christina noticed he was also wearing a tool belt.

"Here we are, " he said, "I'll soon have this mess cleared up." He banged and crashed the bucket around a couple of times. Christina noticed that the top had already come loose from the phone adapter. Then she saw Bigsy snip through some wires. He replaced his cutters in the leather tool belt and continued the mopping sounds for another couple of minutes.

Then, gesturing to everyone for silence, he tiptoed around the office with his bug-detector.

Then, a thumbs-up.

"Well, that sea bit of a mess, but we've cleaned it up really well. I'd say we've made the office squeaky clean now, but I think we maybe need to check for any other dirt maybe once a week." Said Bigsy.

"Cool tool belt," said Jake, to Bigsy.

"Yes, brand new and leather - first time I've ever needed one," said Bigsy in reply, "I feel like I'm in some wild west show, instead of pushing a mop bucket around!"

Christina looked around. Everyone was looking relieved that they had removed the source of the bug.

"You know, I found out something today," she began.

She told everyone what she had heard about Chuck. She explained that she thought Minerva station was setting him up for capture. She also described the two people that had been chasing him and that they had a part in the fire-bombing of the original Triangle Offices.

"Well, maybe they did us a favour?" said Clare, "I mean I liked the old place, but if we are moving to Hay's Galleria then that is still a real step up."

The Lovers

Choices
Union
Love
Relationship

Kramer

"Something I can't properly understand," said Christina, "Is how Minerva is being run?"

"How do you mean?" asked Jake.

"Well, think about it. We know it is fronted as if it belongs to the CIA. We also know they are bringing in people from Brant to run most of it. Yet we know that the Brant people are being sourced with at least some Russian Agents."

"My handler, Blackbird, said that the big oligarch operated private armies were not present in London. I can see that is the case by the lack-lustre performance of the agents that I've seen. Auk and Puffin were the two firebombers. Neat work, but they still took an age to trace Chuck Manners and didn't make any connections between Chuck and the Triangle offices. Multi-lingual low-end workers in the Minerva offices - and incidentally being run by CIA children. It's all a bit *poshchechina* - er slap-dash."

"What's this about oligarch armies?" asked Clare, intrigued.

"As well as the Russian Army and the various Russian secret services, there's been some attempts at privatisation. For example, there is the Russian firm Wagner Group, which is a shadowy mercenary outfit waging secret wars on the Kremlin's behalf from Ukraine to Syria to the Central African Republic. It seems like something from a Tom Clancy novel.

"I visited one of their training camps once, " said Christina, "It was in the back of beyond, in Russia, sandwiched between the Ukraine and Georgia. They had a facility there. They called it a children's school, but it was a boot camp. We flew there by Anatov AN-148 from Vasil Levski National Military University in Bulgaria. It was a kind of away-day. We were told we were getting there on a MIL-26 so there was much relief when we found we would be on a jet plane with windows and seats instead of a helicopter with stretcher mounts and no view. The flight time was about two hours instead of what we guessed would have been 8 or 9 hours in the chopper."

"I was a little bit shocked at how basic the facilities were at Wagner. It was far more primitive that the capabilities we had at Vasil Levski NMU. We had a much better supply of weapon types, trainers and even the accommodation. Wagner was for tough guys and was all about the shouting with a loud frog voice over 22mm autocannon fire."

"Come to think of it, I was at that camp with Antanov Chekeryn. We had to stay there overnight, and we both decided to sleep out under the stars. - Yeah Yeah - stop it!" as both Jake and Bigsy moved in with questions.

"I'm going to try to call up Antanov for this one. He will have some inside information about this. He was pilot trained and would have gained other insights into the way the camp ran. Hold on while I try to reach him in Brussels."

She reached for her phone and they all waited to see whether he would pick up.

"Antanov - it's Christina - Great and how are you. Look, you remember the folk from The Triangle? I'm sitting with them now - but we are in a different office after the first one got fire-bombed."

"Yes, I know - cross town traffic - ninety miles an hour, is the speed I drive. Well - you remember that Anatov flight we did to *Mol'kino, Krasnodar Krai*? You remember, the one where they let you co-pilot part of the way back? Well, I'd like to describe the Wagner facility to the guys here and thought you could help me remember? Can I put you on speakerphone?"

"Sure Christina, hey guys, it sounds like you have been having some fun! Who is there? Jake, Bigsy, Clare? Chuck?"

"Hey Antanov - all of us except Chuck. He's in some hot water now and left London."

"Huh? I guess it makes sense. What about that woman of his? Does she know where he'll be now?"

Clare looked up, "Antonov - you are a star! I'll bet Amanda Miller has a way to find Chuck, we'll be on to it after this call!"

Christina asked Antanov, "So what can you remember about Wagner and Kramer?"

Antanov started, "Well, I think they liked to use names that were not particularly Russian - which is why they chose Wagner and Kramer. - The wagon makers and shopkeepers of middle Europe!"

He continued, "Putin has let Wagner and Kramer set up their outfits and a few smaller ones. They are born out of a need for plausible deniability in Moscow's military operations abroad."

" 'Plausible deniability' sounds like something out of a CIA movie," said Jake.

Antanov continued, "Take Wagner - Their contractors were at the forefront of some of the heaviest fighting in eastern Ukraine and Syria in recent years before hitting the headlines with their brazen assault on a U.S. military position in northeast Syria in February 2018."

Christina added, "There's been setbacks too, although Wagner seemed to herald a new reality, one in which it would form the spearhead of aggressive new Russian policies abroad, but it may be less influential than it seems."

Antanov continued, "Yes, the past few months have been filled with revelations about the group's reversal of fortune. A Russian independent media outlet Novaya

Gazeta revealed that three Russian military contractors killed in central Syria in mid-June were not Wagner employees but part of another similar firm, called Shield."

"Like the Russian dolls?" said Bigsy, "Contracts within Contracts?"

Antanov continued, "*Babushka* – Yes. The casualties were the first confirmed non-Wagner-linked Russian contractors killed in the country, a fact made more significant by their presence in the central Syrian desert, previously one of Wagner's primary operations zones in Syria.

Antonov's tone changed, "Remember that Wagner played a pivotal role in capturing Palmyra and Deir Ezzor in 2016 and 2017?"

"Yes, they were tough fights too," added Christina, "But what with another Russian private military contractor apparently muscling in on Wagner's turf there was then another report the following day which painted the group in an unflattering light. It's incredible to think the subcontracts of the Russian army would become as factional as they did."

Antanov continued, "Yes, that report was from Meduza, a Russian independent news portal who spoke with one of the Russian contractors deployed to Venezuela."

Antanov added, "When a group of contractors arrived in the country in January, it was widely reported that they were Wagner mercenaries, sent to the country to shore up President Nicolás Maduro's rule in the face of sustained mass protests. Russia could be looking away while this was happening."

Christina added, " Yes, but some Western analysts, not unreasonably, took the move to indicate Wagner's growing status as a Kremlin policy instrument to militarily bolster a key allied regime whose survival was in serious doubt, furthering Moscow's foreign interests while remaining at arm's length."

"Kremlin Policy instrument? Now things were getting serious, particularly as they had rumbled Wagner," said Clare.

Antanov said, "That's why the Meduza report suggested the opposite. Their source, a Wagner employee, revealed that he and his fellow contractors had served merely as security guards for Rosneft office buildings in Caracas during an unremarkable year-long posting."

"There's plenty of evidence of the same operations on the streets of Moscow, outside of the headquarters buildings of the big conglomerates. It would make perfect sense to an average Muscovite reading about it in the papers." Added Christina.

Antanov added, "But then, other interviewees, including a long-time Wagner employee, confirmed that Wagner itself has played no role in Venezuela, contrary to initial reports. The outfit has reportedly haemorrhaged experienced veterans to several other such groups, including the firms Shield, Patriot and Kramer in recent months, while it has lost its autonomy in decision-making and was downgraded to guard duty in Syria."

 Christina added, "Wagner became a shell of its former self, having had its wings clipped by the Kremlin and its most valuable personnel stripped away by competitors. Not quite what Putin had in mind when he first embarked upon the idea of deniable private armies."

Antanov continued, "Well, seeing Wagner being discussed publicly in the Russian press finally prompted some direct action by the USA. Wagner's confrontation with U.S. troops in Deir Ezzor marked the beginning of the end for the firm."

He continued, "When roughly 600 Wagner contractors, armed with tanks and artillery, launched an assault on a position of the Syrian Democratic Forces, a largely Kurdish militia force that had worked closely with the U.S.-led anti-Islamic State coalition, in northeast Syria.

Antanov added "What they may not have known is that U.S. advisors were embedded with the unit and promptly called for air support."

"Could those advisors have included Chuck?" asked Clare.

"Well, he did claim to be a disruptor," said Christina.

Antanov continued, "Wagner forces maintained the assault for a full four hours, during which U.S. artillery, airstrikes, helicopters, and even an AC-130 gunship hammered them. When the dust cleared, about 300 of the 600 Russians were dead or wounded, in the first direct battle between Washington's and Moscow's forces since the Vietnam War."

"Whew, so the US had launched a counterattack using aircraft and obliterated the quasi-Russian force. That would be some disruption," said Bigsy.

Christina added, "The most astonishing aspect of this incident was that it evidently occurred without being ordered by, or even fully known to, the Kremlin itself - an illustration of what happened when Putin allowed deniable autonomy to armed forces."

Jake added, "I can see that, not wanting to become implicated in the mess, but I bet Putin was furious that someone had acted with such stupidity as to fall into an American military trap."

Antanov continued, "Yes, but leaked telephone conversations revealed that Yevgeny Prigozhin, a man referred to as President Vladimir Putin's 'chef' who is believed to lead Wagner, ordered the assault after conversing with several Syrian business colleagues."

Antanov added, "And that this could all be self-interest. Prigozhin also controls a company with oil and gas stakes in the region."

"Ahah, so it was a greed-driven mission by Wagner!" said Bigsy.

Christina agreed, "Yes, Prigozhin himself was sanctioned by the U.S. Treasury Department for his role in Russia's 2016 U.S. election interference several times. I know from first-hand about the Russian click-farms. We even had one when I lived in Arkhangelsk."

Antanov added, "Yes, and this marks the time when Putin was looking towards soft influence rather than purely warfare to get what he wanted. The start of the cyber-warfare."

Christina added, "The disjointed response from official Moscow also suggests they were uninformed: It took a week for Kremlin officials to say that there 'may be citizens of the Russian Federation' not linked to the Russian armed forces fighting in Syria, before later saying that five Russians may have been killed, a number that later grew to 'several dozen' - still a long way short of the real number."

Antanov continued, "Sources close to the Russian Ministry of Defense said they were "simply stunned" when they learned the attack had occurred and that a deeply embarrassed Prigozhin then had to grovel to Kremlin officials that such an error would not happen again."

"I'm amazed that Putin didn't get crazy with Prigozhin after him doing something so stupid and revealing his corrupt hand," added Jake.

"It was a sign of the times," said Christina, "Corruption and pocket lining by Russian state officials with access to state industries."

She added, "This is where it gets interesting, vis-a-vis Brant. Viewed in this light, the Prigozhin's moves in places such as South Sudan and Mozambique appear almost pathetic, casting about desperately in a mostly futile search for opportunities that could come close to matching those they found in Syria and Ukraine. They had great opportunities but blew them."

Antanov nodded, " Yes, and the Russian model was not as sophisticated as an American one. The Americans would blow up everything, install a peacekeeping force and then set up contracts to rebuild everything damaged. That is the model that Brant and Raven want to operate in Celarus, for example."

Antanov continued, "Training a handful of minor militias in Central Africa and bidding, seemingly unsuccessfully, against Erik Prince of Blackwater fame for security contracts is a far cry from leading assaults backed by the Russian air force in a major civil war in the strategically sensitive Middle East."

"It shows a lack of imagination too," said Christina, "to just run the warfare but not the civil reconstruction - let alone the infrastructure."

Antanov agreed, "With a wealth of new competitors springing up, such as Shield, Patriot (allegedly directly linked to the Russian defence ministry), Kramer and Vega, Wagner's days as the top dog of Russian defence contractors are likely done and the waning of Wagner will elicit few tears in and around the Kremlin."

Antanov continued, "Wagner gets downgraded without major scandal, its personnel dispersed among similar groups, and its operations curtailed. It's punishment for Prigozhin, who was never one for the spotlight and not attempted to complicate matters in any remotely public manner, likely aware that doing so would only further jeopardise his position."

"Not least with Putin!" added Clare.

Christina added, "Out of Wagner's fall there is the opportunity for a new company to rise - Kramer springs to mind as the most likely. Wagner's fall has had few consequences for the Kremlin, which has no pressing need for a professional yet expendable military force."

"I agree," said Antanov, "Although I can't imagine Putin without a few useful strings to pull spread around Europe."

Jake questions, "So, with the Babushka dolls, do we think there is another layer? I was just getting my head around the Raven divestment of Qube, the merger of Qube into Brant and the stealthy outsourcing of a spy operation by the CIA to Brant. Now I'm wondering if there isn't a further wraparound of Kramer, which pushes the overall game to the Russians?"

Antanov Analysis Redux

"Can we position this against what is happening in Celarus?" asked Jake, "We know that Raven was up to no good when they hived off Qube to make Brant."

"Yes, although we thought this was Raven or Freemason inspired, with no strong thoughts about it being state-run," said Christina, "We'd found the link to the CIA but Anne-Marie who we questioned confirmed Minerva was running as a boiler house to blackmail and squeeze some MP influencers."

"I agree, it doesn't seem to set up a major foreign army outpost in east London," said Bigsy.

Antanov added, "The Kremlin has long jealously guarded the approaches to the security field, placing strict regulations on private security firms to maintain its monopoly on armed force in Russia."

"Hmm, there's still an ability to build up a private army on Russian soil though," said Jake.

Christina added, "We were taught that legally, Russia's various private military contractors do not officially exist: Their presence remains illegal under Russian law, with various false-start attempts to draft and pass new legislation on the matter to allow their registration."

Jake queried, "So how did Wagner develop in this legal vacuum, transforming from an ad-hoc project into a full-fledged private military, replete with Russian tanks, artillery, and as many as 5,000 service members?"

Bigsy added, " Yes, if Wagner is the beta test, then maybe Kramer or Brant will become the first full release?"

Christina agreed, " Yes. If Wagner became one of the most powerful force structures in terms of fighters and material in the Russian Federation, outside of the Kremlin's own security apparatus.

Antanov said, "So a new Kramer or Brant could start to challenge Moscow's central authority. These challenges are bound to grow as Russia lurches toward the uncertainty of life beyond Putin."

Clare said, "Instead of the image of an omnipotent autocrat brandishing all levers of power, Putin may be forced to lead Russia through a series of compromises and understandings among powerful elites, from businesspeople to bureaucrats, with the all-powerful security officials. He's built a system with powerful thugs running things but now they are building their armies, it could be the beginning of a power grab."

Christina said, "The struggles to carve out turf and eliminate rivals with five years to go until this watershed moment have already begun and are certain to continue to deepen as the next presidential election approaches. Putin's system, while stable and presenting the image of a monolithic entity to outsiders, is highly personalised. Russia's various security services are riven with factionalism, with the one controlling variable being their agreement to bow to the current president.

Christina said, "It is important to remember that it was not always this way: Putin's predecessor Boris Yeltsin had a famously difficult time controlling Russia's various armed services, and it took Putin years to bring them to heel and eradicate the various fiefdoms corrupt generals had established in Chechnya in the early 2000s, where trafficking in illegal oil sales became a popular pastime for commanders looking to enrich themselves."

Antanov agreed, "Firms such as Vega, Shield, Kramer and Patriot are a pale echo of what Wagner was at the height of its power, but they have a shining example of what they could one day become."

Christina smiled, "What remains of Wagner's service members are now acting as glorified bodyguards and mall cops. But its successors like Kramer will set their sights much higher—and in a less stable post-Putin future, that could pose a threat to Russian, and global security."

"Yikes," said Bigsy, "So we are all doomed?"

"Not exactly," said Antanov, "But there's a lot to unpack here. I always say to Christina that she runs at ninety miles per hour. This has just been another example. Now, I will sign off and tuck my children into bed. Night-night everyone!"

There was a click.

"Only ninety miles per hour?" said Jake.

Finding Chuck

Jake made the call to Amanda Miller at SI6. He had several past dealings with her including that time she had locked him up for his own protection and knew she would take the call. He was just slightly cautious about broaching the subject of Chuck to her.

"Hi Amanda," he began, "It's Jake, Jake Lambers,"

"Hello Jake, and, how are you?" asked Amanda. Jake was pleased that she at once recognised him, in amongst the hundreds of contacts she met in her role.

"Look, I need to talk to you about someone," he said, being suitably covert on an SI6 line, "It's a somewhat military matter."

"Can I meet you somewhere?" asked Amanda.

"Certainly," said Jake, relieved that Amanda had picked up on the delicate nature of the call, "The weather is nice. How about Jubilee Gardens?"

"That's very walkable for me, shall we say an hour?"

"Perfect," Jake was secretly delighted that he had a head of SI6 coming out to meet him at an hours' notice. He walked outside. He'd take a cab the short distance and if he was early, he could enjoy the sunshine.

…

An hour later, Jake could see Amanda walking towards the gardens. They were a large expanse of grass by the side of the London Eye. Londoners would sit on the curved walls next to the paths that cut through the gardens.

Jake could see the busy tourists walking in large groups along the embankment of the River Thames.

"Hello Jake!" said Amanda, "I've thought about your team a few times over the last few weeks."

"Well, this is about our honorary guest member, Chuck," said Jake, "And funnily enough, we first met him close to here. Just along Belvedere Road in the Sushi place. We didn't have a clue who we were dealing with back then."

"No, he's never told me how you all got intertwined, but I suppose he is a man of mystery."

"Well, we think he might be in some more trouble," said Jake, "And Clare thinks you might know how to contact him."

"Okay, you've got me," said Amanda, "We discussed a way to contact one another, where I'm static most of the time but Chuck moves around a lot."

"I'll respect your privacy on this," said Jake, switching into journalist mode, "But we think Chuck is being sought by a couple of Russian tracers."

"Tracers?"

"Yes, low level agents who have been tasked to find him," Jake looked serious, "If you remember that east London listening post, the one called Minerva? Well, we think its them that have requested a trace on Chuck."

"I'm confused now. The listening station was being operated by the CIA, in collaboration with Brant. Why would they put two Russians onto it?"

"That's what we thought, but we think there is already a hole in the Listening Station's security and that the Russians have access to what is happening. The Russians have been tipped off that Minerva is looking for Chuck and now want to get to him first."

Amanda nodded, "Okay. I think I can contact Chuck, to let him know. I don't know what he will do though, whether he will come in or go deeper into hiding?"

"Well, if you make contact, please try to find out his plans," said Jake, "and let him know that we are all- including Christina- rooting for him."

Yegorin protection

Amanda made her way back to Vauxhall Cross. She was scheduled on a video conference call with Jim Cavendish from SI6 and Grace Fielding at GCHQ.

They were discussing the case of Khramov Gavril (Gavy) Yegorin.

Jim Cavendish began, "After a bomb scare, Yegorin requested the protection of SO15, the counter-terrorism squad. Yegorin had once enjoyed the life in Moscow – high powered deal making, behind-the-scenes agreements, 'understandings' between friends in the Kremlin corridors of power. It was all good."

Grace continued, "Yes, then it looks as if the tide has turned. Yegorin is being squeezed. He asked for protection from the UK counter-terrorism squad. Like every good TV show cliché, his bodyguards found suspicious-looking boxes taped underneath his Rolls-Royce, and magnetically attached to the car used to transport his children to school."

Jim asked, "Do we think these were real, or was he trying to get our sympathy?"

Grace answered, "We don't know. The devices were real enough. Smart magnetics on the kid's car and a phone operated explosive on the Roller. UK were obligated to give him protection."

Amanda asked, "Could this be linked with that Minerva listening station out in south-east London?"

"We don't know. The profile of that listening station is confusing - fronted by CIA, staffed by Qube/Brant and possibly under Russian influence."

Jim added, "Well, as far as Yegorin goes, SO15 counter-terrorism squad has installed Yegorin's home with an attack alarm and perimeter protection. Frankly, he has enough security of his own. I think the alarm was a way for him to signal to those attacking him that he was linked with the UK security forces."

Grace added, "Let's not forget. Ten years ago, Yegorin was a Kremlin insider who'd manoeuvred to help bring Vladimir Putin to power. He would most likely be on someone's list by now,"

She continued, "Known as one of the Kremlin's financial advisors, he has been a master of the deals and the conjuring tricks that governed the way Russia operated."

Amanda agreed, " Yes, I had him pegged as one of Putin's untouchables. A member of Putin's inner circle that made and bent the rules to suit themselves, with law enforcement, the courts, and even elections twisted for their needs."

Grace added, "But now the Kremlin machine he'd once been part of has turned against him. He had become the latest victim of Putin's relentlessly expanding reach.

"The Kremlin had moved in on his business empire, taking it for itself. Television sketch shows and popular magazines show how Putin manoeuvres to take control, with prior owners of businesses taking a fall or disappearing in the process. We've seen some examples here in Britain."

Jim said, "Yegorin was smart and well-informed. When things stacked against him, he left Russia. First to France and then England as the Kremlin launched its seizure of his assets. Putin's men took the prestigious hotel projects the president had granted him in St Petersburg and in Moscow. Then his shipyards, among the largest in Russia, valued at $4 billion, were acquired by one of Putin's closest allies for a fraction of that sum.

Jim referred to his notes, "Then Yegorin's coal project, a huge coking-coal deposit in the Siberian region of Tuva, valued at $3 billion, was taken by a close associate of the Chechen president, for $150 million."

Amanda added, "Let's not forget, the manner that Yegorin acquired these projects in the first place is also a matter for question."

Grace added, "Yes, and so to put the boot in, Putin's men blamed Yegorin for the collapse of *Mezhdunarodnyy kommercheskiy* bank, that's *Mezhkommbank*, the international commercial bank Yegorin co-founded through his 'relationships' and that had once been the key to his power."

Amanda asked, "So were his relationships to the siloviks, or the blatnoy, or whom?"

Grace said, "We think, by definition, that Yegorin is a blatnoy - gangster - and his relations are to the silovik clans, but he has worked his relationships through the use of Freemasonry. It's not helping him much now, though."

Grace continued, "The Kremlin authorities were ruthless and opened a criminal case claiming Yegorin had caused the Mezhkommbank's bankruptcy by transferring $800 million from it to a Swiss bank account at the height of the 2008 financial crisis."

Jim said, "Yes, that's where it becomes very murky. The Kremlin paid no regard to Yegorin's claims that the money was his own. Nor that the takeover of the hotels and shipyards at a fraction of their value was the biggest reason for the shortfall in the bank's funds to creditors."

Grace said, "Honestly, it is hard to have any sympathy for Yegorin, it seems more like a case of rough justice."

Amanda said, "Yes, the state manipulated the rules against him to bring the bank down, unsurprisingly benefiting themselves. It is a typical story for a Kremlin machine that had become relentless in its reach. First, it had gone after political enemies. But now it is turning on Putin's one-time allies. Yegorin was just one of the inner circle to fall."

Amanda added, "But now the Kremlin is leveraging its campaign against him using the veneer of respectability of London's High Court. They know certain London lawyers can be coin-operated and so the Kremlin obtained a freezing order against Yegorin's assets, tying the tycoon up in knots in the courtroom along the way. Ever since Yegorin left Russia, the Kremlin has pursued him."

Grace said, "Yes, and we've been following the trail of breadcrumbs outside of Russia. Yegorin has links to Raven, via Brant in Celarus."

New Office

Jake decided to walk from his meeting with Amanda along the bank of the Thames towards the new offices in Hay's Galleria. He could do an early scout around to see whether there was anything they had missed. His general impression was that it was getting better and better.

Outside the building was a bustling glass atrium area. It had a range of small shops and cafes along it. It was all high-end and there was a discreet wine bar underground just along one side. At the end was the River Thames, with a tourist ship - The HMS Belfast - moored alongside and in the other direction there was a small dock where the Thames Clippers - high-speed glass-domed passenger boats came into dock. It was possible to go all the way to Chelsea or to Canary Wharf on the river, including passing right underneath the nearby Tower Bridge.

On the other side of Tooley Street was the huge conurbation of London Bridge complete with its myriad shops and hidden arches. There was also the tube line to the West End and across the bridge along the Thames was the start of the City of London.

Jake was surprised at the cost of the offices, which had been lower than he had expected, but the estate agent had told him something about a special offer because of the aftereffects of the recent pandemic's financial meltdown which had drowned the City for a while.

Jake wasn't convinced by the story but wouldn't argue because he was getting the offices for a bargain price.

"Hmm," said a voice," They look like pizzas hung on the wall." It was Bigsy appraising the corporate artwork supplied with the offices.

"Hi Jake, I thought I'd bring some of my electronics over, maybe give the place a quiet sweep," said Bigsy.

He was pushing a large black hard-shell suitcase until he had caught up with Jake.

"What have you brought?" asked Jake.

"A few bibs and bobs," explained Bigsy, "After I discovered those extra devices in the temporary offices, I thought we should look here too. I'm also replacing the wi-fi receivers with my own set. I can set the encryption and other general security settings. I just need to find the wiring closet…"

Bigsy disappeared off around a corner. Jake could hear him unscrewing something and realised that Bigsy could be happy for hours.

Ed Adams

The Fool

Innocence
New Beginnings
Wonder
Foolishness

Hekla

Christina was back at her apartment. Her phone rang.

"Hello?" she said; she noticed the dialling code was +354 - Iceland.

"Hello? Agnes? Aggi? It's Hekla here."

"Hekla? Guð minn. Hvað í ósköpunum ertu að hringja í mig? What on earth?"

"Hæ Agnes, ég held að þú myndir helst vilja tala á ensku nú á dögum?"

"Yes, Hekla, it would be fine to talk in English. This is a remarkable moment for me! I have not seen you since my family left Kjalvegur for the airport and to another world."

"But how on earth have you tracked me down?"

"It's a long story - Oh this is so exciting! - I am a big music fan of 'Ian and the Annalists' - Well, imagine my surprise when Ian posted an Instagram from Stuttgart airport, where he said he'd just met up with you. He showed you and another pretty lady and him in the middle. He called you Christina Nott and said you'd played together on some recordings in Amsterdam."

"But you still couldn't recognise me from that picture? queried Christina.

"No," but I also know Kristján Sigurðursson, who is something of a muso in Reykjavik. He told me he had run into you after a council meeting once and that he had later introduced you to some people in the business. He also told me you were going around with the name Christina Nott. I checked you out on YouTube and Spotify and that's how the connection worked. Then I contacted Ian, from the band and he sent me your number."

For Christina, this was the second time in her life that Hekla had set off warning alarms. The first time was when she fell through the roof of the wool-store and discovered Pabbi's listening station. That was when the entire family had to move suddenly to Russia to avoid detection. Luckily, Pabbi was a well-honoured jet-fighter pilot as well as an embedded agent and so they had been moved to a very comfortable apartment in Arkhangelsk, which is where Christina had learned about becoming an agent.

This time, she was concerned that Hekla had somehow joined the dots all the way from Reykjavik to London. If she could, then maybe someone else could also follow her.

"So, where are you now?" Asked Christina

"Well, here's the thing, I've booked a short break to London - you know to see the sights, but when I realised that you lived in London, Agnes, I thought it would be great to meet up again!" replied Hekla.

"Wow," that would be great, " said Christina, carefully weighing up options, "When do you get into London and where are you staying?"

"I fly in on Saturday," said Hekla, "And I'm staying at a hotel by Tower Bridge. It's called the Citizen M, I think."

"Citizen M? I know that hotel, I even walk past it sometimes. It can be busy but I think the location is fine and I've heard that the rooms are good. Why don't I meet you there? We can go out to somewhere pleasant in the neighbourhood. Just let me know a time when you arrive."

Hekla could hardly contain her excitement. "There's so much to talk about," she said, "It'll be brilliant fun."

Hilton Brussels Grand Place

Chuck's cellphone chirped.

He looked across. He was in the Hilton Brussels Grand Place, and his room seemed to be in the roof space of the hotel but with excellent views in all directions.

He was adjacent to the train station where he'd arrived from London. He had travelled on his Canadian passport and the name Charles Desjardins, which fitted with the Québécois origin.

He picked up the cellphone.

"Hello?" he said.

"Chuck? This is your friend in London."

He realised it was Amanda but that she was being cautious.

"No need to tell me where you are," she added, "But I think you would like to know something."

"You have my full attention," he said, aware that Amanda was giving signals that the line might be monitored.

"You might remember a couple of tracers in London? An auk and a puffin? They are looking for you for bounty from Minerva. Let me know if I am making sense?"

"Yes, that makes scary sense, except for one part. The auk and puffin are of a nation than the main Minerva station?"

"That is correct, we are trying to work it out. Some of your friends are also looking at the same puzzle. Even the musician."

Chuck could work this out. He was pursued by the two Russians who had first appeared in London. The Minerva Listening station had put out an alert for him. Despite it being CIA, it seemed that two Russians were chasing him. The Triangle team had his back and even Christina Hyde was stepping in to help him.

"Thank you. I liked it here, but I suppose I will need to move again," answered Chuck.

"I liked it 'there' too," answered Amanda.

"So did I, very much" replied Chuck.

Chuck weighed up the odds. He was in a good hotel, on the top floor, in a huge room. It was already late, and he was in one of the most well-secured areas in Europe, so close to the European Parliament buildings.

He would stay tonight and then prepare a plan for the next few days. He hated being on the run and would rather face-off to these two low-level agents.

He decided to sleep. But he would keep a pistol nearby.

Go Bag

Three in the morning in the Brussels Hilton and Chuck thought he could hear something. It was a small scraping sound outside his room. He was at once alert. Someone was trying to break in.

He knew that the suite he was in was too large for easy containment. He would need to take down the lighting and so he stealthily moved around unscrewing the side lights and switching off the main lights. Why did any luxury suite in a hotel have so many separate light circuits?

He felt in his 'Go Bag' and found his Night Vision Goggles. Armasight NYX-7. Expensive lifesavers. He could flip them down in front of his eyes and see like in daylight. If anyone tripped a light-switch, they would cut their amplification right down. Then he reached for two stun grenades and a neck tube.

He held the P226 in his hand in a confident way. He had even had time to add the silencer.

Now he had got the advantage, even if they were trying to break into his room.

He listened longer. There was still a scraping sound. These people were slow. He'd have a door opened in around three seconds. A hotel room with a swipe card? Come on.

Then the door opened slowly. He admired the clump of clothing he had put on the bed. In the dark, it looked as if someone was sleeping.

Then he heard two clicks. He knew the sound - they were shooting at the bed. They thought he was asleep. Then a shout. A rapid-fire rattle. He looked towards the door. Someone was entering with extreme prejudice. He looked towards the face. It was Christina. Talk about archangel vengeance, she had been firing a submachinegun which was now smoking from the heat she had unleashed.

"Christina- Steady," he called - She acknowledged him with a raised index finger and walked carefully towards the two assassins.

Chuck noticed that the gun she carried was tiny.

"Hey Chuck, I thought you might need some help," said Christina powering down from her onslaught,"Those two people were trying to kill you. Look at the state of that bed."

He realised that Christina was still jacked on adrenaline and from the sounds of the last few seconds.

"Thank you, you were amazing," he eventually said. Christina looked around. "I've made a mess in here," she said, "I hope you don't mind."

He noticed that Christina clicked small levers around the submachine gun but also that she loaded another magazine into it. He also noticed that she, too, was dressed in black. The two erstwhile assassins were dressed as if out for a walk around Brussels.

"It's going to smell awful in here, " she said, "do you want to come back to mine? I'm not sure how we are going to break this to the hotel management."

She led Chuck out of the room. He noticed that she kept the tiny submachine gun prepared under her dark coat as she walked to the elevator.

They were soon back at her room.

"I'll let you have the big fancy suites, I've picked a normal sized room for a regular guest," she said, "but it does have a minibar."

"So how on earth did you find me?" asked Chuck, "and how did you know all of that was about to happen?"

"I used my Russian intuition," said Christina, "First I went to a couple of Russian clubs in London. There's plenty around Belgravia and Chelsea. I found our two followers. They were not exactly low profile in London either. They had been given you as a mission but seemed to be enjoying the expenses that went with it. I soon found them and even got their real names. Then, it was a case of tracking them tracking you. To be honest, they were terrible. A couple of times I wanted to give them hints. But eventually they worked out that you were booked on a Eurostar to Brussels and they managed to catch the same train - as did I."

She continued, "I sat a row behind them and could hear them chattering away in Russian. They were planning how to get to you and I thought to myself at one point that they were making up a ridiculous plan because they had worked out I was listening. "

She shook her head, "But no, their plan was to follow you to your hotel, book in and then at around 3am to come to your room and shoot you in bed. Tap Tap."

Christina continued, "They didn't have night goggles, stun grenades, smoke or anything. They were just planning to break in and shoot you." She paused as if thinking, " Okay, they had silencers on their pistols - but that was it."

She smiled, "I thought there was no point in taking a penknife to a 'Chuck' fight so I brought along a sensible firearm. A Sig Sauer Submachine gun. An MPX Copperhead."

"Let me take a look," said Chuck, I've never seen one of these,"

"Maybe it's a bit of a girly-gun size-wise but its still got a 3.5 inch barrel with integrated muzzle brake, brilliant performance, great anti-recoil handling and is totally reliable. Oh, and it fits quite nicely into a medium sized Mulberry."

Chuck weighed it in his hand. "You know something, I'm gonna get me one of these. It's so compact yet devastatingly powerful."

They both looked at the gun. Then Christina said, "You were going to take them both with the P226 and the goggles? - Respect."

"Yes, I didn't have anything chunkier to hand, but I'd have managed it against those two."

"Look, what about tomorrow morning?" asked Christina. They'll notice a couple of bodies in your room and the bed shot to shreds."

"I suppose I'll have to put a 'no cleaning service' sign on the door for tomorrow, then buy an extra night and scarper," said Chuck, "Oh, by the way I'm Charles Desjardins here, over from Canada. And Christina - Thank You."

"Enchanté ," said Christina.

Galleria

Jake was trying to move the office to its new location before the end of the month. He hoped that they could save an entire month's charges if they were speedy. And anyway, the new office was nicer than the temporary one.

Across London, in the listening station, Pete Burr had set up new surveillance of the new office. It had been a mystery to him when the comms to the original office had suddenly cut out, although he had put it down to the intensive cleaning, which must have somehow dislodged the transmitter unit.

The new place had both microphones pre-embedded and an external circuit of CCTV, which meant he would finally get to see what these people looked like. He already felt he know some of them, but it would be good to see if his imagination was correct.

The CCTV was a boon too, and he didn't even need to use a clandestine link to get it. The cameras recorded a continuous feed to a cloud database and all he needed to do was monitor it. Fortunately, the cameras were also motion sensing, so he didn't have hours of dead airtime to scroll through.

Bigsy had been busy around the office too. He'd wired up the replacement wi-fi network and made a few other adjustments to the circuits. He did the universal signal for a pint of beer to Jake, who nodded and so they both walked towards the elevators.

"See what I mean?" said Bigsy, "Pizzas?" - he pointed to the artwork installed in the lift lobby.

"It's bright and cheerful," said Jake.

"I bet it costs a lot too," answered Bigsy.

"It's probably costed out by the square metre," ventured Jake.

They arrived at lobby level, waved to the security folk and were soon outside in the glass atrium of the Galleria.

They headed for one of the two adjacent pubs. It was already busy, but Jake staked out an outside table while Bigsy grabbed the beers. It would be very pleasant being able to pop out to sit along the river and watch the world go by.

"This is great," said Bigsy, returning with the two pints, "I think Louise the bartender is already starting to recognise me- she gave me the eye and poured these two pints despite all the tourists waiting."

At that moment there was a noise from the riverside and one of the large Thames Clippers appeared, getting ready to dock at the nearby pier.

"That'll be my commute," said Bigsy, "When I don't have to lug equipment around. I never thought I'd be going to work by boat."

"Look, I found a few things during my re-wiring. To begin with there's another collection of stealth microphones installed. This time they are per room and seemed to have been installed systematically. The ones at the last place were radio transmitters to that little box. These are a bit more sophisticated and are wired into the Local Area Network."

"So, we are being properly monitored?" asked Jake.

"Yes, that's right," said Bigsy, "And by the look of it by someone for whom no expense is too great."

"It points back towards Minerva, then?" asked Jake.

"That was exactly what I thought. Yes, they have added intelligent devices to our LAN this time. Not just the microphones, but also the CCTV cluster. It all records on movement and sound and send the recordings to the Cloud."

"What are we going to do about it? We can hardly have multiple cleaning accidents?" said Jake.

"It's lucky I was planning a few tweaks to the LAN, said Bigsy, and it is a case where their strength becomes a weakness. I brought a couple of spiders with me, in case I needed them for diagnostics."

"Nah, you've lost me," said Jake, "I know spiders can get through small holes and probably, like kittens, have something to do with the world-wide-web?"

"It's a little box we can plug into the LAN - You know, the wired Ethernet part. Then it gives us access to everything on the LAN. Intelligent boxes included. I wrote a script for the spider."

"What, Hamlet spouting spiders, whatever next!" laughed Jake.

"Yeah, it is a simple on-off switch. We can control all of the microphones and all of the cameras from a simple console. I'm going to add a couple of 'BigButtons' in the office."

"BigButtons?" queried Jake.

"Yes, they are what they seem. I'll have a BigButton to switch off all the microphones, another one for the cameras, and maybe a Blackout button, like they have in theatres, which will take everything offline. I just need to get back onto Amazon to find the products."

"That's brilliant," said Jake, "but it implies we can only control it from inside of the office?"

"I thought of that," said Bigsy, "I was planning to add OOBI to the network in any case as part of my Wifi update."

"Oobi-dooby-doo?" queried Jake.

"Yes, Out-of-Band Infrastructure management," replied Bigsy, "It's a simple idea. If you cannot get at the network because it is broken, then you can call it up over an 'out of band' service and fix the problem remotely. The most common service is 3.5G telecoms."

"3.5G doesn't sound very impressive, when everyone is talking about 5G and even 6G?" queried Jake.

"Yes, but that is the point, you don't need to be all fancy and high performance and just about every phone will work on a 3G link. So, a dumbed-down service is all you need to reboot - or as importantly to mute the network."

"Are you going to trust us with this?" asked Jake.

"I should think so," said Bigsy, "Just a case of remembering to switch off the microphones or cameras when something confidential is being discussed. I was even thinking of designating one of the rooms as a confidential room. If we do that, I can automate the shutdowns."

"Okay, and I assume the reason you are keeping the system online is to avoid suspicion?" asked Jake.

"Well, I looked at the costs of office space around here and looked at the tech they are providing, and I suddenly realised that there is no way we'd have been able to afford this location."

Bigsy looked at Jake, "It makes me think they've lured us here so they can keep an eye on us. I'll be exploring the rest of the wi-fi nodes running in the offices next to us, to see who our neighbours really are, " answered Bigsy.

Ed Adams

Hierophant

Tradition
Legacy
Society
Organised Religion

Yacht

Sir Charles Frobisher was enjoying life here on a yacht in Monaco. He needed the sunshades and was surprised when Ray-Ban had approached the Lucky Two yacht with a whole choice of complementary sunglasses to wear and to distribute to others boarding. Gerhardt ensured the crew came equipped with the right entertainment credentials, so the next few days should be a delightful break.

Every so often he was getting flashbacks of his time here last year, when they all visited to watch the Grand Prix. Even Bernard Driscoll, who had died in the car accident.

Still, Sir Charles had new people to entertain, and he was sure that Gerhardt would serve them up in the right order.

Sir Charles was quietly pleased that Gerhardt had gone for a smaller yacht this time. The so-called yacht used last time was gigantic. 106.5 metres long yet with accommodation for just 16 people. The crew to run the yacht numbered 36 although Charles acknowledged they were selected for their looks.

But somehow when in such a large yacht, it felt more like being on a cruise ship. Only 8 cabins, yet about 6 floors. A waterfall for heaven's sake! A helipad to use up some space. That yacht sat 'on' the water and Sir Charles could tell the difference.

This time the yacht sat 'in' the water so that people on the quayside could look across. It felt better to flaunt one's wonderful fortune rather than hide away behind reflective darkened glass.

"Champagne, Sir," bobbed one of the crew.

"Thank you, my dear, that will be lovely," he glanced across to the shore where he could see several people noticing the pretty crew member serving him the champagne. Yes, Gerhardt had got this one right.

"I tried a smaller craft this year," said Gerhardt, "That yacht last time was a monster, and although it meant we could invite more people, it was something akin to crowd control keeping up with everyone. This time we can bring them on in batches, which gives the impact but also keeps us amused with an ever-changing cast."

"Anyone famous?" asked Sir Charles,

"It's a tricky one," said Gerhardt, "The stars look as if they own the yacht when they get on board. It can detract from what we are trying to do. It is different with the models. They can pose around the yacht as much as they like. And there's always room for them on the sunbathing decks."

"I'm glad to see you have some guiding principles for all of this," smiled Sir Charles. He had just been offered a back massage by one of the crew.

Then another crew member came along with a phone. Sir Charles realised it was a satellite phone. They always seemed to make a conversation seem more important.

"Sir Charles, someone for you."

"Hello, Charles Frobisher here, how can I help you?"

A Russian accent: "Hello, Sir Charles. This is Vassily Turgenev. I don't think we have met, but I am acquainted with your recent problem."

"Hello, No, we haven't met; where did you get this number?" Sir Charles shook from his tranquil and champagne-fuelled yacht relaxation.

The voice continued, "Regrettably, you ordered a shooting expedition which resulted in the loss of two of my people. I have heard they were discovered in a hotel room in Brussels. This puts us in a tough position. One that might require your help in the future. How can I put this? Without your co-operation, we could see some very unfortunate things happen. Accidents or even more prejudicial situations."

"I'm not sure what you are talking about?" asked Sir Charles.

"Well, you'd better ask your fixer - I'm sure he can explain things to you. I will not demand anything today, but you'd better be sure that if you hear from me or one of my representatives again, then you follow the instructions."

There was a click. The line went down. The little screen on the phone played an animated 'Iridium' logo.

Sir Charles looked stunned. He was not used to having circumstances running away from him. He was usually the one pulling the rug from under others' feet.

Gerhardt looked over, "Is everything okay?" he asked.

"Not really, I've just had a call from someone called Vassily Turgenev. He claims to know something about the Colonel Chuck Manners situation. He advised me to ask you."

Gerhardt grimaced, "I was waiting for the right time to tell you about this, " he answered, " I felt it could put a dampener over this time with the yacht."

"Not as much of a dampener as when I get a strange Russian calling me on my satellite phone, you'd better explain."

Gerhardt told Sir Charles about the discovery of the two FSB people in the Brussels Hilton. That they were found in the bedroom of a Charles Desjardins.

"Okay, but that's not Chuck Manners, " said Sir Charles.

"Yes, but it is," replied Gerhardt, "He has multiple passports, and this is another one that he uses - it's Canadian."

"But how is it that two FSB - Russian- agents are involved in this?" asked Sir Charles.

Gerhardt replied, "They were freelancers. To be honest, I am not sure how they were ordered to go after Chuck. It did not come from us. I thought Station Minerva had ordered it. I was happy to have 'plausible deniability' and not to ask too many questions, but now this Turgenev is calling I suppose we had better know what is happening. And come to that, to know who Vassily Turgenev is!?"

Gerhardt could see that Sir Charles was becoming increasingly annoyed.

"Look," said Sir Charles, "We - and by that, I mean you Gerhardt - specialise in a form of nuanced suasion - we even refer to it as Kompromat sometimes. Now, it seems as if in one fell swoop, I've been caught by the Russians in exactly the same way. You had better resolve this - and fast."

Gerhardt didn't look his usually suave, relaxed self.

Icelander

Christina had said goodbye to Chuck at the Brussels hotel. They would both be going their separate ways again. She had done a similar codeword exchange with Chuck so she could stay in contact if needed. She also said she would tell Amanda that everything was back to normal.

It would break Chuck's link to Amanda in case they had used it to track him down. Now Christina's high priority was to get back to London to meet Hekla.

...

Christina knew the hotel where Hekla stayed well, and it was only about a fifteen-minute walk from their new offices in Hay's Galleria. Christina was not sure whether she would reveal that location to Hekla, until after they had met.

She walked into the hotel lobby and found a quiet area around the back. There were several men with laptops and a family were buying food from the open kitchen area in the middle of the Lobby.

Christina thought this would not be a bad place to work as a freelancer, with tables, desks and coffee on tap. But then she remembered her new offices across the other side of the river. Just a stone's throw away.

She had texted Hekla that she had arrived and now waited until they could meet. She wondered if she would even recognise Hekla after all of this time. Although Christina had been back to Reykjavik in the intervening years, it had always seemed a sad and lengthy side visit to go back to the old farmstead where she and Hekla were near neighbours.

Christina wondered how Hekla had fared, considering she had stayed in Iceland all the intervening years.

Then she saw someone appear from the corridor leading towards the lifts. Strikingly blonde and with the unmistakable knit of an Icelandic jumper. The vivid white pattern went around the front and over the shoulders. Christina thought she looked like an exotic creature here in the streets of London.

"Hekla," she called, and the blonde's head turned.

"*Ó guð minn þú ert ótvíræð*" she said.

"Wow, and you are pretty stunning yourself," said Christina, "Iceland has obviously agreed with you!"

"I like to think I carry some of Iceland with me when I travel," said Hekla, reverting to English.

Christina noticed she had an American accent when she spoke English.

"So how is it you decided to come to London?" asked Christina still thinking of Hekla as a country-girl.

"Well, a lot happens in these many years," she said, "But I realise that with my travelling I have only ever been through London, never stopped in it."

"Travelling?" asked Christina, intrigued.

"Yes, I know you have got around 'Christina Nott' - and well, so have I."

"Tell all," said Christina.

"Let's get a drink first," said Hekla, "We can charge them to my room."

"Okay, but I will want to show you London at some point!" said Christina.

They ordered two glasses of wine, chinked the glasses and said "skál."

"Right, well, a lot happened to me after you left 'forever' to go to Russia," said Hekla, "I must admit I was sad for several months after you had gone. But then Geir and Hanna moved in and I had some new playmates."

"Did you tell them about the wool-store?" asked Christina.

"Of course, it was big news to a small farm-girl. I elaborated the story and added some rockets and guns into the picture. Geir was most impressed. The strange thing was, we went to explore it, but it was empty. Just some wool bundles tied up in a heap."

"Ahah," smiled Cristina, "Have you heard of deep cover?"

"No, but seriously, was your father a spy?" asked Hekla, sipping at her wine.

"What do you think?" said Christina, "Sure he flew jet planes when he was younger and so there was always some gossip following him around. But think of it; he was running a farm. D'you remember, after you fell through the roof and we went to find him? What was he doing? Painting the water trough for the sheep. Now that's what a super spy would be doing, like James Bond."

Hekla smiled, and Christina noticed several of the men around the bar area look over to her. She had an ability to light up the room.

"What happened after the playmates?" asked Christina.

"Well, to cut a long story short, I discovered the Americans."

"Hekla!?"

"Well Geir became old enough to drive and would give me lifts into Reykjavik. We hung out around the Laugavegur and down by the Solfar - you know the Sun Voyager ship."

"Er - I haven't had my mind erased," said Christina, "although you sound like a *Lattelepjandi miðbæjarrotta!*"

Hekla laughed, " I see your grasp of gutter Icelandic hasn't diminished! Although we didn't think of ourselves as latte-sipping city centre rats, more as *fágun* - sophisticates!"

"It was easy to meet new people there too. The Americans would come off-base and their entire chat-up line consisted of "What are Icelandic women like?"

"They had all been given the same spiel about Icelandic women. You know the one about beautiful Icelandic women - there always seems to be quite a large number of foreign men that just hear the words 'beautiful Icelandic women', which they automatically translate to 'sexy Icelandic women' but don't seem to listen when words like 'strong, independent and feminist Icelandic women' come up."

"I became quite practiced at the art of men swatting. One of my friends around this time was an athlete. We'd sit together for a chat in a cafe and get hit on about a dozen times. She went in for the Olympics and for a laugh did Miss Iceland. It was incredible that no-one in the press and media picked up on her athletics. They all just focused on her beauty."

"Such difficult problems, being a hot female in Iceland!" smiled Christina.

"Well it was different with Icelandic men. Icelandic men are supportive and respectful. If something needs doing, they expect women to be able to do it just as well as them. Most men I know don't think about tasks as being male tasks or female tasks. It does mean that if you start dating an Icelandic man and you are out driving and the tyre goes flat, he'll probably expect you to know how to change it yourself. It can look rude when you have been elsewhere. Icelandic men don't go out of their way to hold doors open for women, or even to offer to pay for drinks - they normally expect women to be able to hold their own doors open, and pay for their own drinks."

"I've missed all of this by living in a very macho country through my formative years," smiled Christina.

"But hey, it seems that we've both turned out all right," said Hekla.

"So, what is this about Americans then?"

"Well, I finally succumbed to one of them. He was sitting alone in a cafe on Laugavegur - Sandholt's to be precise - he was reading a book and I had to sit at the table next to him. I could see the book was in English and that every time he got to the end of a page he would look up at me before continuing. So, I asked him if it was any good.

"Well, that stopped him in his tracks. He mumbled something and then said he wasn't sure yet. He'd only read the first few pages and had not been properly concentrating.

"' Here it comes' I thought, He is going to lay down a line now."

"Well. He didn't. Instead I asked him why he looked so unhappy."

"He snapped around a bit when I said that, but then he admitted that he was new in town and it wasn't like he was expecting. He'd come over from Texas, which I thought of as all oil wells and - well - like that Dallas show on television - but he said he was from San Angelo and had been transferred from Goodfellow Air Force Base."

"It didn't mean anything to me, but he carried on anyway. He said most people thought of Texas with oil wells and cowboy hats and big shoulders, but the part he was from was a rural farming area. His family farmed sheep and goats.

"I was somewhat surprised by this. I had never even thought about Americans farming anything as small as sheep and goats. Especially in Big Texas. Buffalo, yes, horses and cattle, but sheep and lambs?"

"So, he was a sheep boy, then."

"Stop it. Anyway, he introduced himself as Daniel Williams, and said he was a pilot. He flew the little jets that the Americans use. F-15s I think they are called. He said that he had been transferred to either Iceland or England, but he thought England would be too intense for him. He was part of some kind of NATO swap."

"He doesn't sound like fly-boy material?" suggested Christina.

"Yes, that was the thing, I expected him to be all Tom Cruise in Top Gun, but he was much quieter."

"Well, that's how I got to know him some more. He didn't have a good chat-up line, seemed a bit depressed, but had some potential as a fighter pilot."

"In other words, a Project?" asked Christina, "I do and don't like the sound of this."

"Well, you might not know that the Americans moved out of Keflavik a few years ago, but then, after a few Russian submarines circled Iceland and some of their planes flew around, Iceland decided to invite America back, but as part of some kind of NATO deal. Danny had to go on 'patrol rotations' which seemed to cover an awfully large area."

"Let me guess…You took him to look around the farm and pet the animals?" asked Christina, smiling.

"Ooooh. You are so mean... still ...I love it!" laughed Hekla, "That is exactly what I did. He had a car and could drive me to and from Reykjavik, and -well- we sort of fell in love."

"Hekla! - Nooo. Is he 'The One'?"

Christina looked at Hekla's fingers. A few Icelandic rings, but no obvious sign of marriage. She asked, "What did your parents think? Your dad could be quite fierce."

"Yes, he was to begin with, but then Mamma could see that we were smitten with one another and helped persuade Pabbi."

"Oh, it's so good to hear certain words like Mamma and Pabbi again," said Christina.

"Yes, there were also some practical aspects to consider. Danny had been driving back and forth from Keflavik, but now he could stay over without Pabbi getting emotional about it."

"Scusi me, ladies, my fren' and I were wondering if we could join you at this table?" came an Italian accent.

"No," chorused both Christina and Hekla, and then Hekla went on to add, "We are waiting for our boyfriends."

"Perfect, man-swatting," said Hekla, "Just like in Laugavegur!"

"So, is he the one?" asked Christina persisting.

"It all went wrong about a year ago," answered Hekla.

"His tour of Iceland finished, and he was due to go back to the USA, to his home base. He asked me to come with him."

"I wasn't sure, if I'm honest, and the thought of an adventure in Texas was the biggest pull. Danny was up there in my thoughts, but I worried that he was too much focussed on flying to the exclusion of all else. It was like he had a manic state. Something that I'd seen in that very first encounter in Sandholt's."

"I met his family. They were not what I'd expected. They were very loud, warm and affectionate, not at all like Danny. They lived on the farm and had dozens of friends and neighbours. Despite the Texan distances, it wasn't like the solitude that we had around Sprengisandsleið. And it was very hot."

"Danny and I had arrived without a plan, although everyone expected that we were (a) engaged (b) would get married in a big showy ceremony and (c) start having lots of children.

" 'Danny introduce us to the little lady, will you,' was a common request. My mind was starting to explode.

"They had a gun culture too. Everyone had a gun. The women carried small Derringer pistols - they called them Texas Defenders and even the teenager girls had pink pistols. Imagine buying a Glock handgun in 'Prison Pink'? That's exactly what one of Danny's sisters did!

"They wanted me to shoot weapons too; they didn't know about us on the farm and what we used to get up to. Christina. I think you were the best shot, but I was pretty good too.

"They took me out to a range near to their homestead. The targets were static and laughably close. I borrowed one of the brother's hunting rifles, it was quite like one of ours, but made to look like a carbon fibre boy's toy. Then I shot a double."

"Two bullets through the same hole?" asked Christina.

"Yes," said Hekla, "Some skills don't go away."

"They didn't believe it of course, and thought I'd missed with the second shot. Then they looked at the target paper. Oval hole. Two grease rings. A confirmed double."

She sighed, "They called it beginner's luck, so I said I'd try again. Remember this is over such short distances as well. Pause, listen to heart rate, breathe, Tak-Tak. I admit to certain relief when I realised I'd done it again."

The men didn't like it. Danny was different, but they saw it that a random foreigner had somehow done something that they all attempted unsuccessfully. And done it twice. I was now noted as a strong woman. I think Iceland has a history of strong women, since the women would have to stay at home while the men went out at sea and then the women had to completely take care of their farms on their own. Take care of the animals, do repairs, take care of the kids, clean, cook etc - and often their husbands and/or sons would die at sea, so they'd be left to continue on their own.

"Well, in Amer—i—cay, or in this part, the women may be strong, but they keep it to themselves. I kept getting referred to as 'my little lady' and 'ma'am' when I went out anywhere. No one meant anything by it, but it did stick in the claw.

"And the women folk had a lot of questions for me about children. Was I going to have a big family with Danny? They were questions I was not ready to answer.

"Danny's family were also Evangelical Protestants. I went to the church with Danny and his family one time at a place called Lakewood. It was like a weekend break. We drove for about six hours to stay in a motel, then went to the church. It was massive. Like some kind of rock stadium. I think it seated over 50,000 people - and that was every week.

"The guns, the church, the heat, the massive family. It was too much for me. I had to tell Danny and then leave him. To be honest, I think, when I did, that he was relieved. I don't think he'd thought any of it through and the pressures from home were cutting in on him. I sometimes think it improved his status there in Texas, bringing back a foreign girl-friend but then 'seeing the light' and picking someone else from local stock."

"And you know something, I was flooded with relief when I sat on the runway on the way back to Iceland. It was such a tangible feeling, like a whole episode had drained away and I could start to behave normally again.

"So I decided, all in all, it seems that Iceland is the best place in the world for women to live and work, and I can taste the difference in the air each time I come back to Iceland after having spent some time abroad."

Christina smiled, and Hekla continued, "I don't know exactly what it is, maybe it's the fact that there's no cat-calling on the streets, or that in the office where I work there's pretty much a 50/50 of men and women, or that it doesn't take more than 'no thank you' to shake off a guy that's hitting on you if you're not interested."

Hekla paused, sipped her wine and then continued, "I think it's all the little things. The fact that you go to a protest march and you see your little cousins there. And your friend's parents. Or that outside sport stadiums there are posters of female athletes as well as the male ones. Or that when the presidential elections take place, half of the candidates are female - and that fact isn't blown up. It just, is. And if you're walking down the street and some mother is breastfeeding her kid, nobody takes notice of it."

Christina smiled, Hekla was as intense and lovable as she had been when they played together as small children. She'd found a few new causes and gained some worldview too, Christina had expected her to be a child of Iceland but she realised that Hekla was an Icelandic woman of the world.

"But hey, Christina, I can see you are toned like an athlete- the way you move is like a cat - you are as elegant as anyone in the room and clearly cosmopolitan. You'll have to tell me about your last few years!"

"You'd never believe it, " answered Christina and started to pour out her edited highlights.

Vassily Turgenev

Gerhardt was pleased that he had arranged for the yacht Lucky Two to be based locally in Monaco. It would go out for a cruise to Nice or across to Cap d'Antibes and then back. Everyone enjoyed it - not too long for anyone and plenty of time to pose around at whatever port they arrived in.

Now the short times at sea played to his advantage. He could get on with finding out more about the Russian who had threatened Sir Charles.

He used the satellite ship phone called one of his contacts back at the ISMC offices in Frankfurt. Felix Rossmann would know more about Vassily Turgenev.

Felix spoke up, "Turgenev: This is all about the business of corruption. We all know there is a pervasive culture of corruption in Russia that persists despite efforts by the government and opposition activists. Remember Russia was 137th out of 180 countries in the last Transparency International corruption index."

"Russia tries to introduce anti-corruption measures without any will to implement them, without understanding why they should be done," Felix said.

But is Vassily Turgenev dangerous?" asked Gerhardt, "He threatened Sir Charles,"

Felix continued, "Very Dangerous, despite the trimmings around his name. A quick search shows that Vassily is a Doctor - A physicist with a string of diplomas and memberships of august institutions. I guess that affords him some respectability."

Felix added, "But, the Russians also use academic corruption to jumpstart careers. Plagiarized works have emerged as a routine way for Russians to develop careers in politics, medicine, academia, and law.

Felix continued, "Some members of the state Duma have diplomas that are nothing more than a printout on some beautiful paper conferring a degree to them in the name of some non-existent academy of science or non-existent university,"

"Yes," said Gerhardt, "That's all very well, but it doesn't trace why Vassily would threaten Sir Charles?"

Well, it seems to link back to an incident in Brussels a brief time ago. A couple of Russians were killed. I'm guessing they were 'employees' of Turgenev."

Vassily Turgenev is a friend of Putin. Low in Putin's structure, but an enforcer for Kasharin Timur Maximovich, who is the Head of Russian Infrastructure.

"Maximovich?" asked Gerhardt. "He's involved with the Celarus project."

Felix added, "You've got to remember that corruption has been commonplace in Russia for centuries and the labyrinthine Soviet bureaucracy and constant shortages has created a culture of kickbacks to get around the USSR's ubiquitous shortages of consumer goods - the infamous *blat*."

"Ah yes," Gerhardt nodded, "We are not the only ones to provoke moral suasion."

Felix continued, "Since Post-Soviet Russia we've seen the rise of oligarchs and 'wild-east capitalism' with few rules and threats of violence amid tumultuous political times."

Gerhardt asked, "So Maximovich, who we are talking to about Celarus has Vassily Turgenev, a friend of Putin, as an enforcer?"

Felix agreed, "Yes, and you can bet that Putin and Turgenev both go back to the same teams inside the KGB. Putin has kept long-term allies from those days and well into the FSB times."

"This corruption has found its way into President Vladimir Putin's Russia despite frequent pledges from Putin to tackle the issue. You'll have seen him wringing his hands on television, 'I, of course, feel responsible for this mess,' he says when asked about his role on corruption during a televised question-and-answer show with the public. And then he sheds a few crocodile tears and cranks it up to the next level."

Gerhardt summarised, "So here we have the perfect set-up. State-sanctioned skimming, under the watchful eye of Putin. Exercised by Maximovich and enforced by Turgenev.

"But Tima Maximovich has been a friend of Gavy Yegorin too. He's the Russian Freemason that the Kremlin is turning over at the moment."

Felix added, "Yes, but here's the thing - and why this is getting dangerous. If Maximovich falls out with Putin, he might also join the Yegorin statistics. There's around 40 prominent Russians who are victims of unsolved murders or suspicious deaths since the beginning of 2014, according to a list compiled by a well-known US newspaper in collaboration with a British journalist.

"For example, the list contains 10 high-profile critics of Russian President Vladimir Putin, seven diplomats, six associates of Kremlin power brokers who had a falling out — often over corruption — and 13 military or political leaders involved in the conflict in eastern Ukraine, including commanders of Russian-backed separatist forces."

"Two are connected to a dossier alleging connections between President Trump's campaign staff and Kremlin officials produced by a former British spy and shared with the FBI."

"I know you'll think I'm making this up but check it for yourself. Dig out the USA Today articles or run a search on Google. Twelve were shot, stabbed or beaten to death.

Six were blown up. Ten died allegedly of natural causes. One died of mysterious head injuries, one reportedly slipped and hit his head in a public bath, one was hanged in his jail cell, and one died after drinking coffee. The cause of six deaths was reported as unknown.

"They have become so frequent, that a Russian TV cartoon show even put out an episode showing Putin disposing of the people - it's even on YouTube. You just don't want to be on the wrong end of Putin or former Prime Minister Dmitry Medvedev's pointing fingers."

Felix added, chillingly, "We should regard Vassily Turgenev as just as dangerous and now he is also pointing his finger towards us."

Ed Adams

Eight of Wands

(Reversed)

Panic
Waiting
Slowing Down

Kompromat

The next day, Gerhardt could see the bubble of people as Sir Charles approached the yacht. He could tell that they were a fresh batch by their unbridled excitement at coming on board a luxury yacht for a trip around the bay. Gerhardt hoped that they would strike some useful deals in the process and even noticed that Nina, one of his earlier escorts in London was coming on board.

Sir Charles made a direct line for him when on board asking, "Gerhardt, so what have you managed to find out?"

"Sit down, Sir, I don't think you will like this," Gerhardt then explained what he had gleaned from Felix in the ISMC Offices in Frankfurt.

"This sounds outrageous, we are being played at our own game," said Sir Charles.

"Yes, and I think if our ultimate backer is Raven, theirs is probably The Kremlin," answered Gerhardt.

"Can we do anything?" asked Sir Charles, "I mean Vassily has not asked for anything yet."

"That seems to be the way it works. Kompromat. And strengthened because Vassily Turgenev thinks we have killed two of his operatives."

"Well, can we give him the name of the killer?" asked Sir Charles.

"Well, that's just it, we have a name, but we think it is false. Charles Desjardins, a Canadian. It looks as if he was packing some serious firepower too. Reports say that 22 rounds were fired in less than a minute."

"Blast, we have opened a Pandora's box, here," said Sir Charles, "You know what, I'm getting out of Monaco today. It will be safer for everyone if I've gone. I can say there's been a family emergency."

Gerhardt nodded, "Yes, Sir Charles," he realised he was left holding the whole situation.

"I'm going to catch a helicopter back to Nice," said Sir Charles, and then fly back to London."

Gerhardt was momentarily diverted by Nina, who came over and sat herself on his knee. She was prepared for sunbathing and felt quite delicious.

"Hello Gerhardt," she said, "We haven't met since that time in London; remember? The Freemason Ladies' Night?"

"How could I possibly forget?" said Gerhardt.

"Good," she said, "Then you remember that I work for Jennifer?"

She referred to the agency who brought many of Gerhardt's escorts to the variety of parties that he ran.

"Naturally, " he said.

"Well, this time I'm working for Vassily Turgenev. He asked me to deliver this message to you. I am to tell you that his men were sent away by Charles Desjardins and a Russian woman named Christina Hyde. He asked me to give you this photograph too."

She fiddled around with her phone and found a picture.

"It was taken by Vassily's third man, the one who waited outside for the other two to return."

"He says you will know what to do."

"Yes, you had better give me the picture," said Gerhardt. He looked at the woman in the picture and thought she looked somehow familiar, but couldn't think where he had seen her.

"I think the woman was at the same Raven function. She was wearing a beautiful blue gown," said Nina, "I met her briefly, and we said hello. She said she also worked for Jennifer."

Gerhardt remembered. He had held a lengthy conversation with her; she was there with another Freemason, someone called Antanov, who was high in the Masons. He remembered she wore a brooch denoting a top rank in the Rosicrucians.

Nina wriggled away from Gerhardt. She planted a soft kiss on his cheek. "Now you be very careful, playing with Vassily. He can be very rough," she said.

Gerhardt was pleased with this outcome. Now he had two names and could start the search for the people who had dispatched Turgenev's men.

Minerva

Gerhardt knew about Minerva, the London Listening Station. ISCM had been instrumental in the sale of Raven's Qube to make Brant which became the outsourcer to support Minerva.

Gerhardt could use some of the Minerva people to help him trace Charles Desjardins and Christina Hyde. He called up Brant to discuss an operation. Emily Karankawa was on the duty desk and took the call.

"We need to start full scale tracing for these two- Charles Desjardins - Canadian and Christina Hyde - Russian," he said, "Sir Charles will want this to be a top priority."

"Wait a minute, you want us to track a Canadian and a Russian, for no specific purposes?" asked Emily.

"There is a reason, but it's above your pay grade," said Gerhardt, pompously. He had always wanted to say that, and this was his big moment.

"No, I'm Duty Officer at the moment," said Emily, with a sense of humour failure at Gerhardt's last remark. She would not be pushed around by some arrogant sleazebag spouting Sir Charles' name.

"Look," said Gerhardt, "I'm sending you over a picture of them both together. - It will be on the station feed from ISCM," said Gerhardt.

"No," said Emily, still annoyed at Gerhardt's aggressive impatience, "If you do that then the entire station will see it."

"Good," said Gerhardt, "And it's too late anyway, I've just sent it."

"Now see what you can do for me, honey, will you?"

Emily was deciding what level of action to take against this nauseous man, but he had already hung up.

...

The photo arrived and was the subject of much mirth around the station. "Now we are getting unsolicited requests to trace people? This is truly bizarre."

Pete Burr was one of the people that received the picture, now tagged with a whole string of witticisms. He noticed something at once. It was one of the occupants of the Triangle offices. He had been listening to them for so long and now he had the camera feed, he was almost certain he recognised her. Christina - although he thought they talked about her with a different last name.

Pete had to decide whether to action the request, which looked like a very unofficial request. He put it to Olivia, his CIA- field boss.

"Look, he said, this iffy request that has come through from ISCM. I think I can identify someone. She's one of the group I've been monitoring for the last few weeks. Christina Nott or Christina Hyde. She is part of that Triangle Office that we are asked to bug, the one that is in Hay's now."

Olivia was delighted with this news. Not only had she been able to elevate the profile of Chuck Manners when they dispatched the two agents to terminate him, now she had another suspect lined up.

"Wait, though where was this picture taken?" she asked Pete,

"Er, in Brussels, according to the GPS data with it, it comes from the Brussels Hilton."

Olivia froze. "Is this the aftermath of the Chuck Manners situation?" she asked.

"I don't know," said Pete, "It just came in over the generic email with a FIND request for both of them."

"What is it dated?" asked Olivia.

"What? when was it taken, or when did we receive it?" asked Pete.

"No, when was it taken?"

"Three days ago, in Brussels, in the Hilton Grand Place," repeated Pete, "Carrefour de l'Europe 3, 1000 Bruxelles, Belgium, to be precise."

"The man then, is Chuck Manners," said Olivia, "He got away from us the last time, and this woman Christina must have helped him."

"Okay, so it is a lucky result?" said Pete, "Or unlucky for them," added Olivia.

Mil-38

Sir Charles was making his way to the Monaco heliport. He had been picked up from Port Hercule by a smart black Mercedes and the coolness of the car's soft interior helped to sooth his jaded nerves.

Inside the heliport he noticed the row of helicopters lined up, six almost identical ones in red and white and then, at the end in the last bay, an all-red and somewhat larger helicopter.

"This one is ours," said the driver and he walked around to open the door of the limousine.

Charles walked across the tarmac and as he did so, he noticed that there were already a couple of people on the helicopter. He turned inside and saw a considerable number of seats, far greater than he was expecting.

"It's okay, we struck lucky today with a Mil-38, said one of the men, they can carry up to 30 passengers. The little guys in here can only take six."

An air-steward showed him to a seat near the back. "It is for load distribution during take-off," she said.

Sir Charles thought about this but could not raise a question. Instead he took a glass of gin and tonic and waited for the clearance for take-off for the short ride back to Nice Airport.

"We'll be flying out over the bay," announced the pilot, "You will get a beautiful view, but it is mainly to reduce noise pollution."

The blades started to spin and then the 'copter took off. Sir Charles was still fascinated with how quickly everything changed as they ascended into the air above Monaco. He looked towards the Monte-Carlo Casino and then down towards the dock where he had been on the yacht a fleeting time ago.

The helicopter headed out to sea and Sir Charles looked out of the window at the view. Maybe he would get out from this. He was sure that Gerhardt would come up with something.

He was aware of some movement in the cabin. A tall, lean gentleman sat in the seat opposite.

"I don't think we've been introduced?" he said, "My name is Vassily Turgenev."

Sir Charles felt all the blood drain from his face. He was now sitting opposite the man that had threatened him..

"Hello Vassily, I didn't expect you here."

"And neither did my men expect Chuck Manners to be supported by a wild banshee with a submachine gun. You must have told him something or tipped him off that he was being followed. That work from that woman was terrifying."

"Now we need to make things even. My brother would not expect it any other way."

"Your brother?"

"Was one of the people killed. The woman with him was his wife as well as an agent."

"But don't worry, we have prepared something a little special for you. It's why we needed a larger helicopter."

He motioned to one of the other men sitting behind them in the helicopter. The man pulled out some cable ties.

"Always so useful, don't you think?" as the man pulled the cable ties around Sir Charles leg's and then two more around his arms.

Sir Charles had frozen. He was not resisting.

The man searched inside Sir Charles' jacket and brought out his phone, "Good, iPhone X, face recognition." He held it up to Sir Charles and the phone unlocked.

Sir Charles saw the man tapping some codes in, which he guessed disabled the security. He felt weak, knowing he was probably facing his execution.

"Didn't they teach you any self-defence in your role?" asked Vassily, "You makes it rather too easy."

"See what we has done? In a moment my men has to do some heavy lifting, The *Kabel'nyye styazhki are* attach to those rope and the other end of the rope has concrete blocks on them. You make excellent test to see how the *styazhki* can handle the pulling, although it says their breaking strain is over 2000 kilos. To be honest, I think your legs might break before the cable ties."

"Now, we only fly at around 2000 metres height, so you will take maybe 20 seconds to fall, by which time you'll be doing something like 700 kph. The sea does more than sting at such a speed."

Sir Charles was in shock, he looked as if he was about to have a heart attack. "So, thank you, please, to leave your phone behind and I'll say '*do svidaniya*.' "

Sir Charles was aware that the helicopter was now hovering. There was a sudden increase in noise as a door was opened and then he felt a sharp pull to his legs. Then he blacked out.

Inside the helicopter, one of the men closed the door. He looked down out of the window and after few seconds said, "*kosnut'sya zeml*"

"Yes - Touch Down," said Vassily, He was sending a short text to Gerhardt. Then he called to another of the men in Russian, "Make a copy of this phone and then throw it in the sea."

Shad Thames

Hekla looked at her watch. "Wow, is that the time? We have been chatting for hours!"

Christina grinned, "Yes, and just about everyone who was in here has changed since we sat down. We are in for the long haul."

She stared pointedly to a corner table where a slightly scruffy man was sitting working on his laptop. Dark-haired and crumpled clothes, he didn't have quite the 'expensive' look that many of the tourists or Londoners had that dropped into the hotel to do some work.

"Ha, you noticed him as well," said Hekla, "I get the feeling he has been staring at us for quite some while. I don't think it is about our looks either."

"We must find out some more about him," said Christina, "Call me suspicious, but I think he's here because of us."

"Agnes, you really meant it about being a secret agent?" asked Hekla, "Or is this just a wind-up?"

"Well, let's just see what happens." Christina stood up and walked to the kitchen area in the middle of the hotel lobby. She selected some kind of rice curry dish. Then she wandered back towards the man with the laptop.

"Oh, excuse me," she said, "Could you hold this for me for a couple of seconds. I need to adjust my clothing. I'm really sorry."

She held out the tray with the curry and surprised, the man held out his hands. Then she pulled in her belt by one notch. "Thank, you," she said as she took back the food. The man smiled, not certain what had just happened. She walked towards Hekla.

"He is following us," she said, "Or at least following me. I could see his laptop screen. The emails were in Russian. I'm not sure what he wants."

Hekla looked fidgety. "Shall we leave this area then?" she asked, " I know I'm staying here, but it might be better for me to look as if I am going somewhere else."

"Sure," said Christina, "But I'll see you back to here later. Look, I'll show you London properly tomorrow, but why don't we go to Shad Thames now, where I can show you some of 'Old London' that is right near to your door step?"

"This is your city, *elskan*," said Hekla.

"Babe!?" laughed Christina, "I haven't been called that in a while!"

"Let's go!" she placed the tray unceremoniously in the middle of their table and they both made for the exit.

As they walked outside, Christina could see that the untidy man was packing up his laptop.

Christina linked arms with Hekla, and they set off at a brisk pace.

"This is a great area, you know, over there is The Tower of London, which is where they keep the Crown Jewels. In the late 15th century, it was the prison of the Princes in the Tower. Under the Tudors, the Tower became used less as a royal residence, because it could not withstand artillery.

"Then it became a prison in the 16th and 17th Century when many figures who had fallen into disgrace, such as Elizabeth I before she became queen and Sir Walter Raleigh were held within its walls. Right now, we are in the notorious Tower Hill which is where more than 100 executions took place.

Hekla asked, "What is that glass bubble on the river side?

"Oh, that's the town hall for London. The built a new one on the riverbank to replace the one up by Parliament."

"Now we'll be going over Tower Bridge, which is one of the most famous landmarks in the world. We'll get a picture right in the middle for your friends on Instagram.

If you look back from her you get a splendid view of the tall buildings around the City of London.

"And I guess that one is The Gherkin?" asked Hekla.

"Yes, you are right, and on the other bank, in the distant - that big spike is called The Shard," answered Christina. She had avoided pointing out where their new office was located, although the area could be plainly seen from where they were walking.

"Then we can hang a left down into Shad Thames, which is such an interesting area of old London." Said Christina.

They climbed down some stairs.

"Wow," said Hekla, "This is like one of those TV shows about Charles Dickens!"

Hekla looked around. The area was filled with picturesque converted Victorian warehouses and had cobblestones underfoot. Above were overhead gantries connecting the converted warehouses. Many of the ground level buildings were converted into what Hekla assumed were high-end shops.

"The street's warehouses were used to store grain, fruit, sugar, coffee, tea, and spices from all over the world," continued Christina. She looked back over her shoulder and could see the untidy man was still following them.

"Yes, and the overheard walkways were used to roll barrels from one warehouse to another. The area used to have the nickname 'the larder of London'. "

There was a puff of brick which exploded above Christina's head.

"Get down," she said to Hekla, "It's the scruffy man from the hotel - he is shooting at us. Get flat to the ground."

A couple of tourists looked around as Hekla laid down flat on the pavement and Christina walked around in front of her. They were expecting it to be the start of some kind of impromptu London show.

There was another puff and more brickwork dislodged. Christina estimated the second shot had been closer, but then the man was using a handgun - maybe just a 9mm, so the accuracy was limited to around 50 metres.

She pulled into her handbag and Hekla gasped as Christina revealed the Sig submachine gun and quietly clipped in a 30 round magazine.

"Stay here," she said, "Do not move anywhere whatever happens until I get back. Squeeze more fully into that corner."

Christina ran off, leaving the Mulberry scattered on the ground.

Hekla noticed Christina really did move like a cat - even in heels.

Then she heard a noise like a ruler scraped along railings. Some tiny sound like nails being dropped.

And silence. No other tourists.

Then footsteps.

Christina had returned. She was breathing normally despite having just run around a 200-metre loop. No shoes though.

"He's gone, fell in the river actually." said Christina, "We are safe now. And Hekla, my dear, you are safe as well."

Hekla noticed that Christina's gun was still smoking. Then she saw Christina unclip the magazine and replace it with a shorter one.

Christina put the whole gun back into the Mulberry.

"Bayswater tote," she said, "It's a Mulberry icon. You can get a lot into it."

"Okay," said Hekla, "I'd almost forgotten what it's like to be around you, Agnes. Why I always had so many scrapes and bruises when we played around in the fields. Are you a bank-robber or something?"

"No," said Christina, "There were some people were after a friend of mine, over in Brussels. This man must have been a relative or something. He's gone now, though."

Hekla could hear police sirens in the distance coming across Tower Bridge.

"I guess some tourists saw what happened and dialled 999, said Christina. This area has seen its share of violence, what with nearby bombers and other terrorists. I'm sorry to have contributed to it. Come on, let's carry on with our walk."

Hekla looked a little shaken by what had occurred.

"You know something, Aggi, you have turned out even more bad-ass than I expected - I wasn't sure whether to believe you being an agent, but now I do. And, by the way, how did you get that gun into the UK?"

"You have to know the wrong people," said Christina.

Lucky Two

Gerhardt looked towards his phone. A text had just arrived from Sir Charles.

It said "zu wenig zu spät," Gerhardt was confused, he knew that Sir Charles didn't speak German and would therefore be unlikely to send him a message like "Too little too late" in German.

Sir Charles was all over ancient Greek. He wondered what Sir Charles had meant by this. He had heard Sir Charles say 'Either with your shield or on it' in the past, about the need for courage in their endeavours, but never this phase and never in German.

He called Sir Charles. It rang through to voice mail. He decided not to leave a message. He would see Sir Charles soon enough in London.

He looked at his watch. It was already getting late, time to turn in. He could hear the partying going on about the yacht, but he just wasn't in the mood. Nina's move on him had been tempting, but he knew he has a busy couple of days and needed to be sharp. With Nina it could easily turn into an all-night session and he was sure she would have brought drugs on board.

No. Self-discipline. Tomorrow they would make a quick sprint across to Nice, enjoying breakfast on board the yacht. Then back for a scenic arrival in Monaco and then he'd make his excuses and leave the yacht.

He settled down in his cabin for the evening. Outside he could hear the water lapping and the hubbub from the revellers on board. Apparently, they had just discovered another yacht with a party and were now combining to make something memorable.

He felt a bang to his head and awoke. No, he'd imagined the bang. He was just having a restless night. Too much coffee and booze in the day, probably. Then he heard another bump along the side of the hull. It could only be the yacht hitting the jetty. He dozed off again.

Bright sunlight. Morning. A hint of buttery croissants and black coffee. People moving around on deck. He emerged just as Nina was walking past his cabin. She smiled to him and quietly kissed him. He noticed she was already in her bikini but draped with a towel.

"I've been called away," she said, "Another party, you can come along if you like?" she kissed him softly.

"No, they have left me in charge of this group whilst Sir Charles goes back to London."

Nina looked at him darkly, "You'll regret it," she said, " I promise you'll have more fun with me, than stuck on this yacht."

Gerhardt patted her, "Be gone, oh Temptress!" he said, and she skipped off playfully toward the gangway back to the dock.

"Le capitaine appelle, dernière chance de partir pour le rivage. Captain calling, last chance to leave for shore,"

Gerhardt could hear the engines start. They called it a yacht, but it still had four motor engines.

With a whirr, they had left the dock and were pottering to the edge of the harbour, past the other huge luxury yachts. Anywhere else this yacht would be a head turner, but here it was lost in the mix.

Then as they pulled away from the harbour protection and the speed restrictions, the Captain opened the engines. This yacht could really move, leaving four white trails behind in the water. Gerhardt watched as Monaco became smaller. He was aware of a whistling sound, he looked over the side of the yacht and could see an orange bulge on the rear of the hull. It would be in line with his cabin. He wondered whether it was some kind of listening device. It was sure making a noise.

The yacht became an explosive yellow fireball, with fragments spinning away from the burning hull. The orange magnetically attached mine had done its duty. A MILA smart limpet mine, attached to the outside of the hull by a Special Forces hybrid Swimmer Delivery Vehicle. It was the type of computer-controlled mine used by US Navy Seals.

The mine was used in demolition. Those on neighbouring yachts could see why.

From his own yacht, Vassily Turgenev looked through his Zeiss image stabilised binoculars.

"Magnificent," he said, "So good of Sir Charles to put on a display for us."

Ace of Wands

Creation
Willpower
Inspiration
Desire

Frosted walls

Jake was sitting in the office in Hay's Galleria. He could hear the lift ping and then saw Christina and another woman get out.

They both looked slightly shaken and Jake walked across the main office space to greet them.

"Hello Christina, and hello 'Christina's friend'" he said.

"My name is Hekla, I've known Christina since she was Agnes, " answered Hekla.

"That must be a very long time ago, then, said Jake. "I've never heard Christina called Agnes. Katarina, yes, but Agnes? - Was this in Russia?"

"No, even before that, in Iceland," answered Hekla.

Christina looked worried.

"It's okay, I've pushed Bigsy's BigButton. There's no sound or vision at the moment. I still think we'd be better to go into the quiet room though."

Christina nodded and Hekla followed Jake into a glass-walled meeting room. Jake pressed a button and the walls frosted.

"You have a very smart office," said Hekla, "and it is in an ideal part of London."

"We have just been followed," said Christina to Jake, "It was a bad job. A bodged single operative with a handgun. 9 mm at best and at a stupid range."

"Where are they?" asked Jake.

"Gone," said Christina, "In the Thames. He fell in, with some encouragement from me. I think he was working alone."

"You must be one of Christina's friends," said Jake, "How much do you think you know about her,"

"Oh, I know everything about 'Christina' when she was young, well very young. Right up to when she left the farm and went to Russia. Then nothing for many years, until I discovered her because she had renamed as Christina Nott. Reykjavik is a small place. Everyone knows everyone else in Iceland."

"Are you in Christina's line of work?" Asked Jake. "Oh, no, I'm a journalist and freelance translator," answered Hekla.

"I was a journalist, I worked for the Street magazine, here in London," answered Jake, expecting a response.

"No, I don't know it, but then if I told you my magazines I don't think you would know them either. Okay, maybe The Manhattanite," said Hekla.

"I should think so, what do you write about?" answered Jake. Christina looked intrigued too.

"Well, I started writing about daily farming and the rural stories; it wasn't the main emphasis of The Manhattanite, but they liked to include some as feel-good factor moments in the magazine. I was originally based on a farm out in Texas, so it gave an intriguing off-beat story every week."

"What about cattle, cowboys and oil wells?" asked Jake.

"You'd be surprised," answered Hekla, "Then, because of my writing style, they asked me to do some sections for their on-line magazine. That's where I've stayed right up to now. It's part of the reason that I'm in London. Getting some colour to include in a piece about the President."

"Okay, so will you be discreet?" Asked Jake, " Look, I had to not tell anyone about Aggi's back-garden missile silo for years, " said Hekla, "So I think I can be trusted with this."

"Aggi!" exclaimed Jake, "There's a first."

"Yes," said Christina, "Quite a lot is coming out since Hekla arrived,"

"Okay, and the missile silo?" asked Jake.

"Hekla is making that up," said Christina, "We'll need to watch her!"

"Sorry," said Hekla, "I couldn't resist."

"Okay, Let's try to work this out."

There was a ping. They looked towards the elevators. Clare and Bigsy had just arrived.

"Oooh - secret squirrel," said Clare, then noticing Hekla, said, "Hello I'm Clare - you must be the friend of Christina?"

IIekla smiled, "Yes, 'Christina' - that is Agnes and I go back a long way - all the way to Iceland. We've just been in a scrape together. Just like when we were little. Only, I'd say the stakes were higher this time."

Christina turned to them all and said, "Yes, Chuck was fired upon in Brussels the other day and now I was shot at in London. I'm certain the two events are linked."

"What happened?" asked Bigsy, "Are you all right?"

"Yes, both Hekla and I are fine, although I've messed up some really good shoes and Hekla's coat is in a bit of a state. The gunman was terrible. Too feeble a gun and too much distance. Luckily I was carrying my little sub with me."

"Sub?" asked Clare,

"Submachine-gun," answered Christina.

"Of course," said Bigsy, " never be without one."

"I'm going to teach you all some self-protection," said Christina, "Not like the stuff you see on the television; the serious short-range stuff that works. Not now, obviously, but soon."

"So, do we know who set up these attempts?" asked Jake.

"We think the last person was a Russian," said Hekla, remembering what had happened in the hotel.

"I don't know about the ones in Brussels," said Christina, "They didn't say anything, and I was more concerned with getting Chuck away. I'm certain that these events were all triggered because of our visit to the CIA Listening Station - Minerva."

Hekla looked surprised at this latest turn of events, "CIA? It doesn't make any sense," she said.

Wild Child

"Okay," said Clare, " So we need to piece this together."

"We first found out about Minerva station when Christina and I met with Anne-Marie along at their building. Then they traced us and we think they torched the office.

"Somehow they have found out about Chuck and now they are chasing down Christina and Chuck, with extreme menace."

"The strange thing is that they seem to be Russian."

"I think the Russian influence comes from Brant," said Christina. "The CIA have outsourced their operation both here in the UK and over in Celarus. It's ironic that the

Americans are once more being run by Kremlin-supported oligarchs."

"What like the President?" asked Bigsy.
  "Allegedly," answered Jake.

"What about other links that we have?" asked Christina, "We had a way to get to Raven via the Masons and also through that separate company ISMC? - You remember - Sir Charles Frobisher and Gerhardt Schmidt. I met them both at the Ladies' Night occasion at Raven's building in London."

"Well, there's some news about Schmidt," said Bigsy, " I don't know how to tell you this, but he was on a yacht that caught fire in the Mediterranean."

"Caught Fire?" said Christina, "Or was torched?"

"I've only got this Associated Press report. It seems it was just leaving Monaco (as one does!) and then was on its way to Nice, when it caught fire. No survivors."

Christina looked at the article. "Let's dial it up on something French instead," she said as she typed 'Libération' into Bigsy's computer.

"See a more colourful French paper," with pictures, she said, " Look here is an article about the Lucky Two yacht. It says, according to eyewitnesses that the yacht exploded in a yellow fireball, while travelling at speed. This man was interviewed and said it reminded him of a missile strike, although there were no planes around. In other words, the actual damage to the boat was far more forceful than implied in the English language press clippings."

Christina continued, "Let me try a straight-laced French paper… Here we are, Le Monde. I will see if I can find the article… Yes, here. Same story as Libération, but an interview with a different yacht's captain… This one says the police are investigating what might be a multiple homicide. The captain says he knew the captain of the yacht too and would always describe him as a 'quelqu'un de sûr' - someone sure - hmm - it's like a safe pair of hands. "

Hekla spoke, "Are you sure you should be messing with these people? They sound like hardened criminals. I mean, we've been shot at and then a boat carrying others has been blown up! Christina, this is strong stuff even for the wild child."

Christina grinned, "Huh - *Villt barn*! I'd forgotten that nickname. Hekla, you keep reminding me of life on the farm!"

"It was never like this," said Hekla, "You know something, I'm going to call my foreign desk at the magazine, see if I can get something useful. Don't panic, I'm not going to print any of this, but my friend Irina Barnaby might be able to help us."

"Irina Barnaby?" asked Christina, "An unusual name."

"She's married to someone from Yorkshire," explained Hekla, "I think her name was Irina Koval before she got married."

"Is she Polish?" Asked Christina.

"Not exactly, I think she is from the Ukraine, actually, but she knows her Russian stuff too - especially about Putin and his cronies." answered Hekla, "Here; let me try her," she fiddled with her phone.

"Hi Irina, Yes I've got here- London. I will be able to see you in a couple of days. The flight was fine, and I am staying by Tower Bridge. Yes… No, I said I was going to look up an old friend first. We've already met and I'm with her right now."

"To be honest, I wanted to pick your brain, she has asked me about some Russian things, and I knew you'd be the best person to answer! Well, it is a bit complicated. How about we bring forward our meeting to tomorrow? I think it has a great tie-in for that side book you are writing, you know, the one about Russian Mafia corruption. Yes. Do you know ", she looked at Jake, "What is this place called?"

"Hay's Galleria," answered Jake.

"Hay's Galleria?" asked Hekla, "You do- that's brilliant, can we meet here tomorrow? I'll have my friend Christina with me, and maybe a couple of her colleagues."

"Yes, if you come into the Galleria, say 10 o' clock. There is a big metal sculpture of a ship. If we can meet there, I'll show you to a meeting spot. It'll be great to see you again. Sorry this is like work, but I promise you it is interesting."

Hekla clicked off her phone.

"Yes, Irina will meet us tomorrow, right here. She said she knew the area well, and that it is not even far from her offices."

Irina

At shortly before ten a.m., Irina arrived in Hays. She walked directly to the ship sculpture and Hekla could see her striding towards them. Inky hair arranged in raggedy looking cut, but entirely London fashion of the moment. A plain white tee shirt and dark jeans. A short colourful shawl draped around her neck. Christina recognised it as a nod towards a Russian shawl.

Christina smiled at her, and they introduced themselves. Christina spoke English, despite knowing that Irina would speak very good Russian.

"Hello Irina, I love that shawl, is it Russian?" she asked.

"Pavlovo Posad," she replied, "They make such happy, bright things."

Do you work around here?" asked Irina.

"Only just," answered Christina, "We move here a few days ago from near Hoxton."

"I see, staying with the hip crowd?" smiled Irina.

Hekla began, "Christina and I go back many years. To be honest I didn't think I'd see her again, but now, in these couple of days it is like we were never apart."

Irina looked intrigued, "How did you get to know one another?"

"We lived on adjacent farms in Iceland - then Christina moved away, " answered Hekla.

"Wow - it is so unusual to find old friends like that!" said Irina, "But I'm intrigued, what is it you wanted to know from me?"

"Can we show you to our office?" asked Christina. Irina nodded and the crossed the concourse in the Galleria to the entrance to the offices.

"Nice building," said Irina, "I'm over by London Bridge in the mini-Shard complex. "

Punching at smoke

"What do we know, then?" asked Christina to Irina, "About the structure of the way the Russians operate - Putin down?"

Irina began, "Well, to begin with, Putin's system of rule is still often described as a monolithic pyramid. In the eyes of society, Putin presents himself as an irreplaceable leader-statesman- the west call him a tsar-. It is him solely making key decisions."

"Yes, the big boss without whose agreement no decision can be made?" asked Jake.

"Precisely, Jake, it's what they want the western press to think, but I think such an understanding of ruling processes in Russia is one of the main mistakes which prevents the west from obtaining a deeper insight into the regime's origins and foundations."

"Oops so I'm wrong then?" asked Jake, smiling.

Irina continued, "Forgive me if I seem sharp-tongued, but the Russian authorities do not comprise a strict vertical structure, ruled by one person. The vertical image is nothing more than a propaganda cliché."

"The Russian authorities are a conglomerate of clans and groups which compete with one another for resources and power. Putin's role in this system remains the same—that of an arbiter and moderator."

Irina continued, "The clan structure is a key to understanding how the system works, and how it can have its finger in so many pies.

"You have to think of it now as Politburo 2.0 and the style of making political decisions has been shifting towards that of the USSR's Politburo. That would be at the hand of Putin, who you must remember was an unexceptional member of the KGB who has risen through the ranks.

"The result is something of an expert's class in influence strategy. There's the creation of national corporations in politics and economy coupled with one of the 'Politburo 2.0' specifics is that its members almost never hold joint sessions."

"Deniability?" asked Bigsy.

"Straightforward shady behaviour," said Irina, "Any investigation will always be punching at smoke."

Irina continued, "Then, like a form of Masonic lodge, the formal status of its members does not always reflect their actual influence when making decisions. And in terms of sheer influence, the 'Politburo 2.0' has amassed a number of elite groups which, to some extent, can be divided into 'power', 'political, 'technical' and 'businessmen'."

"Ah yes," said Jake, "Value solutions: Got a problem? Find access to a solution, define the corporate and personal value of that solution, gain access to power and make a plan for how to deploy. If Politburo has access to all the types you describe no-wonder it is unstoppable."

"Well, the little extra spice in this is the access to tactics, which could easily become strong arm," answered Irina, "and that is part of the challenge for even Putin. The groups support the 'Politburo 2.0', yet they constantly fight among themselves for influence and try get their members inside it," answered Irina.

Christina chipped in, "That's why they call it 'collective Putin'; he has to be the focus for many factions."

Irina nodded, "Putin is a symbol of this ruling system though he hasn't lost his role as an arbiter and moderator. There's a continuous struggle for power inside the Russian authorities which determines the outcome of decisions while Putin is constantly struggling to balance the powers."

Christina nodded, "Yes, the 'siloviks' - that is representatives of power structures - and the 'liberals' in Russia are at loggerheads."

Irina agreed, "Yes and make no mistake that the siloviks are quite ruthless."

"I think some of those liberals are also not what they seem," said Christina.

"So, have we unleashed this somehow in the Raven and Brant situation?" asked Bigsy, "I mean, look at the increasing number of incidents. There was our building catching fire, then there was Bernard Driscoll's car crash. Then they shoot at Chuck and now they've shot at Christina and Hekla."

Irina looked at Bigsy, "Incidents! I'd call that all out warfare!" she said.

Bigsy said, "Keep talking, I'll bring us some coffees." He disappeared off to their new kitchen area.

Christina replied, "Ha - Yes, Dmitry Medvedev, self-styled leader of the 'liberals' - he still behaves like a clan leader, except his clan is the Liberals. He criticised Russia's foreign policy only because it 'cost too much to the country'. And he received the support of another famous 'liberal', Alexei Kudrin, who said that soon foreign policy goals should be adjusted, but only to ensure stable investment."

Jake asked, "So who are the dominant clans controlling Russia?"

Irina answered, "In Russia, the most influential clan is that of Igor Sechin, Head of Rosneft and factual curator of the country's energy. Energy rights are a particular source of income for clan members and so the tie-in with Celarus has to be investigated."

Jake cut in, "So what we can see is that Celarus discovered plenty of oil - enough to disrupt the Russian supplies to Europe."

Bigsy returned, "Here we are, coffee for all plus milk, creamer and sugar - help yourselves."

Jake took a black coffee and took a sip, "Then Celarus made friends with the USA who 'helped' it by putting some small defensive platforms in country. An airstrip filled with F-15s and a couple of military bases filled with soldiers."

He looked at Irina and realised that she was not so aware of these recent developments.

Bigsy added, "Except the US DoD subcontracted out the building of the new airstrip, the barracks - complete with its own US-style shopping mall - and several defensive missile emplacements along the Celarus border."

Jake again, "And who did it sub-contract to?"

Bigsy replied, "Brant - i.e. Raven. Now we've seen that Brant is ostensibly American but seems to have an awful lot of Russian influence within it."

Clare carefully poured a small amount of milk into her coffee, "So we see a game of Russian dolls. Dolls within dolls manipulating events."

Bigsy nodded, "Yes because we know that Celarus wants to build a pipeline across into Europe. That would be might inconvenient for Russia, although a big ker-ching for Brant and Raven."

Irina agreed, " Yes, That's a fairly typical set of moves. It is hard to follow because the clan structure gets in the way. It means there are many self-interested moving parts. Probably still only Putin, Medvedev and Sechin really know what is happening."

"One of the factors in the Brant case was the introductions via the Freemasons," said Jake, "Christina and Antanov were first introduced into all of this via Sir Charles Frobisher at a Masonic meeting in London."

"That would have been the opportunity for a lure," said Irina, "A honey trap probably. Entice the unwary into a trap, compromise them and then force them to play along."

Hekla nodded, "I'm afraid one of the magazines I freelance for specialises in that kind of gossip."

Jake smiled, "Yes, when I worked for 'Street' it was about half the publication."

"The honey trap," said Christina, "That was the MP and government minister Bernard Driscoll, who pushed through the agreement for divestment of Brant- it had to go to Parliament because of its implications - and then Driscoll walked it through."

Christina continued, "We also know that Driscoll's, 'lure' was probably a woman known as Marion Charlotte."

"Not THE Marion Charlotte?" asked Irina, "She's all over the tabloids at the moment in some kind of Cabinet Minister scandal."

"Sounds like it," said Christina, "Although I must admit I've not seen it."

Irina sipped her coffee, "You will have to tread carefully with this. The siloviks will go in with all guns blazing - literally. The liberals are as dangerous, though possibly more subtle - think hypodermics instead of bullets. It is far more difficult to identify the leaders of the so-called 'liberal' clans."

Hekla noticed Christina frowning as she heard this.

Christina added, "The liberal clans don't lack competition, but avoid open fights as much as possible. That is why it is difficult to define their borders. All groups often act as allies rather than reckless opponents. This clear unity is the reason they are simply called the 'liberals'."

Irina looked into her coffee cup, "Overall, Russia's biggest businessmen act very differently – some are related to specific groups and are using their protection and lobbyism, while others successfully manoeuvre between numerous groups."

Irina sipped her coffee again, "But even most influential power centres in Russia show that Putin is constantly playing the role of an arbiter and manoeuvring to maintain his power. The contradictory system of rule he has created guarantees this."

Irina added, "Contradictions have become the source of Putin's power. They allow him to act in several political areas at the same time and maintain reliability despite dubious reasons for doing so."

"This has been brilliant!" said Jake, Bigsy and Clare nodded their agreement.

"So you, Irina, are planning to show Hekla around London in a couple of days?" asked Christina.

"Yes, that was our plan - a simple tourist jaunt to see some of the sights."

"Well, I was planning a similar trip with Hekla tomorrow," said Christina, "You know, we could combine and have one 'girls tour' of London. What do you think?"

"You know something, I was thinking just the same thing," Said Hekla.

"So how would you be fixed tomorrow?" asked Christina to Irina.

"That can work for me," said Irina, " We could meet here somewhere on the South Bank. My tube stop is London Bridge, anyway."

"This could be excellent!" said Hekla smiling, "Christina - will you be bringing your Mulberry?"

"You bet, " said Christina, "At the moment I won't go anywhere without it!"

Ed Adams

Two of Cups

Unity
Partnership
Connection

Christina Hunt

Christina was back at her apartment asleep. Her phone rang. It was Antanov.

"Hey Antanov, how are you?" said Christina.

"Ha, I'm good, kotyonok, just a little worried for you!" said Antanov, "Look, I've been hearing some things. I thought you'd better know."

"Kitten? Your poor wife," queried Christina.

Antanov continued, "I've been told that you were being hunted by freelancers. That they work for Brant. Brant is being run by one of the clans - However, the FSB found out about the situation and have ordered an immediate cease. It turns out that someone higher up and more important has got your back."

"But that's not all, the Roslavl Bratva clan that have been arranging this are being run by Tima Maximovich. He also runs Gasneft, which is one of the largest gas exploration and production companies in the world. He wants to intervene in the planned oil extraction and pipeline creation from Celarus.

"Roslavl Brotherhood? Roslavl - That's close to Celarus too, isn't it?" asked Christina.

"Yes, so maybe that's why his clan ordered a couple of other things too. One was the assassination of Bernard Driscoll. They issued a kill for him, then staged a car accident. I heard they set up a roadside stinger (you know those things with spikes) to puncture his tyres, cause him to crash off the road and they then calmly fitted two replacement tyres to his car before they drove off.

"That was not the only thing, though. They have been burning the evidence trail linking Roslavl to the original Raven deal when it sold off Qube and formed Brant. Sir Charles Frobisher was heavily involved in that situation and was targeted. He's not been seen for several days and the rumours are that he is in the bottom of the Mediterranean off Nice."

"It doesn't even end there - they went after Frobisher's fixer Gerhardt Schmidt and blew him up in a yacht close to Monaco. That made the news but seems to have been reported as an unfortunate fire."

"Yes, and they have also chased down Chuck Manners and me - with guns," said Christina, "but it didn't end well for them."

"Yes - I'd expect no less, but now you've been given a blanket immunity by the FSB you should be out of trouble. That doesn't affect Chuck Manners though - I hear they are about to plant evidence to bring him down."

"Do you know what kind?" asked Christina.

"No," said Antanov, "Except it sounded big. I think they must be really pissed off with him."

"Antanov, thank you, " said Christina.

"Hey, stay safe, zvezda moya," said Antanov.

"Don't let your wife hear you calling me 'my star'," laughed Christina, But what about you? You are okay and distant enough from all of this?"

"Yes, when I flew back to Brussels, I decided to take a roundabout route stopping in Amsterdam and catching a train for the last part. It's covered my tracks enough to show that I've never even seen you this time," answered Antanov, "Hey Christina - stay safe."

The line clicked. Antanov was gone.

Clare remembers something

Jake and Bigsy were sitting around a conference table. Clare was typing something into a laptop.

Christina walked in; she was wearing sunglasses.

"Hey babe," said Clare, "Was it a good girls' day and night out yesterday?"

"Oh yes," answered Christina, "Irina knows some amazing clubs too. We started with regular tourist things like a Clipper trip along the Thames. Then the walk around the South Bank. Hekla wanted to see some other main sights too, so we did some of it by taxi - around Westminster, Buckingham Palace for an Instagram moment, Trafalgar Square, Downing Street and then back along to the Tate Modern and across on the boingy bridge. Then a Clipper up to Battersea and had a look around the shops at Chelsea Bridge by the power station.

Another taxi down to Sloane Square and a look inside some of the high-end shops around the Square and a stroll along Kings Road. We got papped there. Someone thought we were a girl band."

"Did you 'do' Oxford Street and the West End?" asked Jake.

"You know what, we skipped most of it because both Irina and I thought it was too touristy. We went into Soho though, and that's when Irina's knowledge of the clubs really paid off. We avoided the nasty places and went into those where you walk up to a normal looking front door to someone's house, only inside it's a great club."

"We did the last part until around 2 am, but by then Hekla was flagging, so we bundled her into a taxi back to her hotel. We both came along to see she was okay and then I offered Irina a stopover at mine instead of going back home."

"It sounds full-on, " said Bigsy.

"I just wish we'd had a little more food to balance the alcohol. I'm a little frayed around the edges this morning, Irina can pack away the *wodka*," said Christina.

"It's nearly this afternoon," said Jake, smiling.

"See, I'm losing my grip on reality, "said Christina, "But I need to tell you all some things I found out from Antanov - he called me."

Bigsy hit the BigButton to mute the room's hidden microphones and cameras.

Christina began to explain what she had heard from Antanov.

"We'd better warn Chuck," said Bigsy.

"How will we get in contact - have you got a way, Jake?" asked Clare.

"Only that emergency thing where we put something onto the Triangle website and wait for him to call in," said Jake.

Bigsy nodded, "I can do that."

"Or we could ask Amanda Miller?" suggested Clare, "I think she and Chuck have been 'together'."

"I knew it," said Jake, " When Chuck was staying in London at that hotel - The Mondrian."

"Yes," said Clare, "I only inferred it, but Chuck looked suitably rumbled."

"Okay Jake, you have the most track record with Amanda…Can you give her a call?" asked Clare.

"Sure, " said Jake, "let me go to the quiet room to make the call," He walked across to another room.

"So, go on…. Last night… spill the beans, Christina, where did you go and what did you do?" asked Bigsy…

Roslavl Bratva Chatter

Eventually, Jake returned from his call with Amanda.

"Yes, she knows where Chuck is…He's moved out to Germany. He left the UK for Belgium and has then worked his way south. He's in a military barracks! Hiding in plain sight."

"According to Amanda, one of the Russian clans, the Roslavl Bratva run by Tima Maximovich are planning something. They want to put the finger on Chuck Manners and are about to frame him in some kind of terrorist incident."

Jake continued, "Amanda says she knows the Americans won't believe it and neither will SI6, but there will be such a high-profile news scoop that neither of the secret services will contain it."

"Do we know what kind of incident? Is there any way we could stop it?" asked Christina.

"No, we don't know either. Amanda has picked up the chatter from the Roslavl Bratva and says there has also been some significant buying of shares in Gasneft over the last few days. It has Maximovich's fingerprints all over it and Amanda thinks the event implicating Chuck will be utterly ruthless. "

Jake continued, "Amanda told me that Maximovich has considerable influence over the news media. The best example is through his wife, Natalia Maximovich, who still controls somewhat liberal and influential media outlets: notably the news agency Lavlbalt and the Saint Petersburg newspaper Peterburgskij Komsomolets."

"I told Amanda about Irina, and said she works partly for The Manhattanite. I said it could be a useful aspect when this needed to be publicised for what it is."

Jake looked down to his small black Moleskine, where he had been taking notes from the call with Amanda, "Lavlbalt and Peterburgskij Komsomolets can feed direct news from Russia into the western press machine, where it gets syndicated everywhere throughout the west. I can remember using Lavlbalt when I was researching stories about Russians owning football clubs in England."

Jake looked back at his black notebook, "Lavlbalt was almost shut down last year."

Jake looked around the room, "The agency was accused of violations and the court revoked its license. But after the aggression in Crimea, when a new wave of media oppression began in Russia, the Russian Supreme Court repealed the decrees of lower courts and reinstated Lavlbalt's licence."

Jake flipped a page, "Amanda also said that Maximovich became a representative of the Communist Party in the Parliament. It shows that in the Russian ruling system the most important role goes not to what party you are in (opposition vs. the ruling party) but what clan you belong to."

Clare nodded, "This ties in with what Antanov was saying yesterday. It shows the build-up of power through vice and then media messaging. An object lesson in corruption."

Christina asked Jake, "Barracks, you said. Do you know which one?"

"I Imm, said Jake, looking through his notes, "Not sure - Ah yes, here we are - 'Panzer Kaserne'."

Christina smiled, "Typical Chuck- you know what Panzer Kaserne means? Tank Barracks. At least he is well-fortified."

Bigsy googled it, immediately, "Unbelievable, it's in the same part of Germany that Christina and Clare visited recently. Where you met Oskar. And the Barracks might sound German, but it's an American base, taken over by the Americans from the Germans years ago."

Brussels

Christina had called ahead to Antanov. Now she was on the Eurostar again, still on tasks related to Chuck Manners. It would be strange asking Antanov to spy on the Russians on her behalf, to find out something which could only benefit SI6 and the CIA.

She knew that Antanov would be careful and was now intrigued that she would meet his family.

She climbed out of the train and onto the platform in Brussels. As she approached the gate, she could see Antanov waiting there.

"Hey Antanov! I wasn't expecting this!" she said, "Being met at the gate, truly an honour."

"Yes *kotyonok*," said Antanov, "I thought we'd better establish some ground rules before you meet Camille. Remember we are old acquaintances who worked in the same office in Arkhangelsk and that's it. We haven't seen one another in fifteen years, but as you were passing through Brussels you thought you'd say 'Hi'. Oh yes, and it is okay to be asking me some Freemason questions too."

"You'd better not call me 'kitten' then," said Christina.

"Fair point," said Antanov.

"Don't worry - if you do, I'll say it was my nickname around the office."

They walked out towards the busy taxi area at the station.

"No, we don't want here," said Antanov. "Let me show you around to the nearest hotel with a separate cab rank."

Christina smiled as he showed her to the Hilton. It was exactly the hotel that she had stayed in with Chuck a few days earlier.

They ordered a cab to Christina's hotel, which was confusingly called The Hotel, and turned out to be a modern skyscraper in the centre of Brussels.

"I've never been in this hotel before," said Antanov, "But it looks pretty good."

"Do you mind if I drop off my luggage before we talk?" asked Christina.

"Sure, I'll be in the bar," said Antanov.

Christina tapped the floor into the lift and was soon in her 12th floor room. It was light and airy, with fantastic views across Brussels. She placed her small travel bag on the bed, picked up her handbag and was soon back downstairs, where Antanov was staring into a long, cool-looking drink.

"So, what is all this about? Not still Chuck, by any chance?" asked Antanov.

"You are good," smiled Christina, "Yes he's being set up at the moment, we think it is by one of our very own Russian *blatnoy*."

"And who would that be?" asked Antanov.

"Kasharin Timur Maximovich of the Roslavl Bratva, " answered Christina.

"I think I told you about Tima when we had that phone call, " said Antanov, "Head of Gasneft - and guess what, he's a Freemason too! It is one of the ways he got such a rapid spread of influence in western Russia. As a matter of fact, it is quite big news at the moment, because Maximovich is trying to establish the twelfth lodge of the UGLR - That's the United Grand Lodges of Russia. He's been arguing that such a lodge would fit right in, being between Moscow and Sankt-Peterburg."

"Well, it would be good to find out what he has been planning for my friend Chuck. There's some kind of plot out now."

"I can quietly ask around, " said Antanov, "Like I've said before though, I'm embedded here in Brussels now, have a good job with the EU and a wife and family, so I'm not looking for your high speed thrills."

"Scream if you want to go faster," said Christina.

"I'm not screaming," replied Antanov, "But I will look around for you. It could take me a couple of days. You can enjoy yourself having a look around Brussels. There's the Grand Place - which is a big tourist square, the Mannikin Pis - a statue of a little boy pee-ing, some cathedrals, a few old residences and my favourite - The Belgian Comic Strip Centre which features Tin-Tin and The Smurfs. And if you feel like taking the tram, you could visit the Atomium; oh yes and a few brown bars too."

"I can't wait," said Christina, "No wonder those diplomats have such a good time here."

"And come around for dinner, Camille would love to meet you. How about tomorrow night?"

"Lovely," answered Christina.

The whale sorcerer

The next evening, Christina was preparing to visit Antanov. She had casually tuned the TV into a news channel and was vaguely aware of smoke shown curling upward.

She listened to the news reporter. It was some kind of research institute outside of Rudnya, in Celarus. The reports were of a large complex which had suffered an explosion, putting a chemical haze blowing from Celarus towards the Russian border. There were rumours that the institute had been working on synthesised coronavirus vaccines, which were less essential since the outbreak of the one-time global pandemic had been contained, but were still, nonetheless, important products.

Reports said the laboratory that had exploded held both the vaccine but also the original virus. A full-scale lockdown of the area had ensued, both in Celarus and across the border in Russia.

Christina noticed that it was the area of Russia where Kasharin Maximovich and his Roslavl Bratva operated. The distance to Rudnya was around 200 kilometres.

She walked downstairs and asked a cab to take her to Antanov's apartment in Brussels. The apartment was in the Européen Quarter and in a smart block.

Camille came to the door and greeted Christina and said, "Come in, come in, and welcome to Belgium! We don't get too many pop-stars coming around to visit!"

Christina proffered a hastily bought bottle of wine to her host and then saw Antanov with his daughter in the next room. It was a bright joint kitchen and living space and Christina noticed along one edge of it were a couple of laptop computers. She could just see into another room which looked as if it had been set up as an office.

"Hey Christina, welcome and let's have a drink, what would you like, a gin and tonic maybe? Or a vodka?"

Camille said, "Yes, I'll have a white wine please," and Christina nodded agreement," That sounds like a great idea."

"Look what Christina has brought us," said Camille," A lovely bottle of Chateau Le Prieure, Pomerol."

"Sounds delicious," said Antanov. What do you think, Lucy?"

"Daddy, I'm too young to know about wines. I'm only six. You have to be at least eight to know about wines," answered Lucy in very good English.

"That's right, now you show Christina your bedroom, and then show her how quietly you can read."

Lucy grabbed Christina's hand and pulled her towards the corridor and then into a bedroom swathed in pink and decorated with unicorns. "Okay, this is my room, but when an adult comes in it, the only way they can escape is to tell me a story…" asked Lucy.

Christina thought for a moment, "You know, I'm from the land of ice and snow, and we have some good stories there. Let me tell you one."

"What, like in Frozen?" asked Lucy.

"No - these stories are from before Elsa and Anna were even born."

Lucy snuggled into her bed and looked intently towards Christina.

"There once was a fearsome King Harald Bluetooth who intended to invade poor, vulnerable Iceland and so he called for his sorcerer to help.

"His sorcerer had a good idea.

"He said he would change into a whale to find the island of Iceland's weak spots."

"What was the sorcerer's name?" asked Lucy.

"Oh - Øyvind Kjelda Hvalrekinn," answered Christina, We can call him Walter, for short."

"And then each time Walter the whale-sorcerer tried to land, a *landvættir*, or "land wight," fought him off, thus creating the four guardians of Iceland."

"A wight in the form of a dragon protected Iceland's Eastfjords,

"In North Iceland there was an eagle ready for a fight.

"In the Westfjords, a bull was ready to fight the whale,

"and finally, in South Iceland, there was a giant ready to finish the job.

"Nowadays images of these wights are all over my country, Iceland, adorning the Icelandic coat of arms, certain coins and buildings."

"And the moral of the story?", asked Lucy.

"Good question - 'never forget where you are from'," said Christina.

"I like it, so show me Iceland on my globe…" asked Lucy.

She pointed to the illuminated globe in the corner of the room.

"Why it's here," said Christina, pointing to Iceland on the map.

"That's a long way from Belgium," said Lucy.

"It is, but I think the wights will also keep an eye on you here," said Christina.

"Are you keeping Christina locked away?" asked Camille, who had just entered the room, "I guess you have told a story already?"

"Oh yes," said Christina, and we've checked out where Iceland is on the globe."

"Goodnight Lucy," said Camille, kissing the child on the forehead.

"Bonne nuit maman," said Lucy.

They walked back to Antanov, who was uncorking a bottle of wine.

"I thought we'd save your one, Christina, but I hope you'll like this one," he smiled.

Camille said, "You'll have to tell me something about yourself, Christina, Antanov says you met in an office somewhere?"

Christina proceeded to tell her backstory, suitably edited to incorporate Antanov.

"But I guess you wanted to talk to Antanov about something to do with his Freemason friends?" asked Camille, " He knows I think it is all a bit like boys and their toys, when they go off into secret huddles with leather aprons and chisels."

Christina laughed, she could see that Camille and her shared some opinions about the Freemasons.

"Yes, but it can bring great insights into the actions of others," said Antanov.

"I was particularly interested in the moves that the Roslavl Bratva might make under the guise of the Freemasons," said Christina.

"What? Do you think that the masons are mixed up in that explosion in west Russia?" asked Antanov.

"It was in Celarus actually, " said Christina, "Close to the Russian Border."

"I heard something about it," said Antanov, "that Tima Maximovich sounds as if he could be implicated. They are trying to create a situation similar to the ones that the Americans sometimes create, close to a war zone."

"What is that?" asked Camille.

"Create disruptions to justify keeping troops in the area. If necessary, create a brand name for the peacekeeping initiative and then flood it with resources."

Camille said, "It all sounds a little calculated and quite disreputable. I hope your Freemason friends don't get up to those kind of tricks?"

"Not at all," said Antanov, "but unfortunately there are members of our team who are not as altruistic about the masons as I am and most of us are. They are trying to bend it to support their less-than-ideal behaviours. That Kasharin Maximovich would certainly not think twice about subverting the cause to meet his ends. Did you see the press conference?"

Christina shook her head.

"Well he is now alleging that the explosion was caused by a CIA-inspired Black Op, led by none other than your friend Colonel Chuck Manners. It will certainly have raised the hunt for him," said Antanov.

"It is what we predicted, yet I can't think why they would be so angry with Chuck," said Christina, "You know something, I was with Chuck here a few days ago, when they were shooting at him."

"Brussels is a strange town, what with all of the diplomatic incidents that occur here," said Camille, sipping the wine, "But I don't think I've heard of too many shooting incidents?"

"Are you involved with the EU?" Asked Christina.

"Yes, I've a role in the anti-corruption unit," answered Camille, "To be honest, most people think of things like cigarettes, fake medicine and some occasional smuggling of trademarked items. But we do look at embezzlement, bribes, corruption and so on, although it doesn't make for such good photos as piles of cigarette cartons or fake COVID-19 testing kits."

Camille continued, "Russia is a great case in point, I think the estimates of the level of corruption in Russia are around \$2.5 bn from 2014- 2107. Instead of the money going to the government, it goes to representatives from the government and other people in positions of power.

"Putin may have presided over Russia for more than 20 years, but the 'anti-corruption' measures are often the settlement of political scores, rather than a realistic pledge to end the corruption."

"In Russia, the bagman hasn't gone. There are still bags of currency routinely moved around." said Camille.

"What about the FBK?" asked Christina, referring to the Russian Anti-Corruption Foundation.

Camilla continued, "Yes, the Anti-Corruption Foundation, run by Russian opposition leader Alexey Navalny has skewered Kremlin insiders and ministry officials through their illicit and often exorbitant holdings."

Antanov added, "A real fight against corruption is impossible under Putin. His whole system is built around it. Every attempt to really take on corrupt officials has ended in nothing,"

Camille nodded, and looked thoughtfully towards her wine glass, "Secret European villas, mansions, luxury yachts, stored artworks, wealthy relatives, and private planes ferrying pet dogs to international dog shows have all been subjects of the foundation's investigations in recent years."

"Say Christina, would you like some more wine? And I'm sorry that Antanov has tricked us into 'talking shop' for the last half hour. I want to hear about your time as a pop singer - and get some of the inside gossip."

Antanov added, "Yes, but before we finish this conversation, we should also flag the alleged secret wealth of former Prime Minister Dmitry Medvedev. And then that FBK was quick to note that Medvedev's replacement Mikhail Mishustin has family holdings that far outstrip his past government salary as Russia's chief tax officer. "

Camille added, "If your friend Chuck has been picking at this, then I would not be surprised if they seek retribution. Predictably, the Kremlin has launched raids and criminal investigations against FBK, moves widely seen as revenge for the organisations investigations and calls for democratic change. It seems to me that they have singled out your friend in a similar way."

"Now, what was it like being on the road? Was it glamorous or just a succession of hotels in different towns?"

Part Two – Tournament of lies

It's the end of the world as we know it

A government for hire and a combat site
Left of west and coming in a hurry
With the Furies breathing down your neck
Team by team, reporters baffled, trumped, tethered, cropped

Look at that low plane, fine, then
Uh oh, overflow, population, common food
But it'll do, save yourself, serve yourself.
World serves its own needs, listen to your heart bleed

Six o'clock, TV hour, don't get caught in foreign tower
Slash and burn, return, listen to yourself churn
Lock him in uniform, book burning, blood letting
Every motive escalate, automotive incinerate

Light a candle, light a votive, step down, step down
Watch your heel crush, crushed, uh-oh
This means no fear, cavalier renegade and steering clear
A tournament, a tournament, a tournament of lies
Offer me solutions, offer me alternatives, and I decline

It's the end of the world as we know it
It's time I had some time alone
And I feel fine

Mike Mills, Michael Stipe, Peter Buck & Bill Berry, 1987,
Nashville, Tennessee

Ten of Swords

Failure
Collapse
Defeat
Backstabbing

Institute

Amanda Miller had seen the SPA report of the Institute explosion in Rudnya, Celarus. She knew that Colonel Charles (Chuck) Manners was described as the suspect and that it had turned into an international search.

She asked for the satellite scans over the area, which she received from GCHQ.

She was in a briefing room with Jim Cavendish, whom she had worked with for years.

"It doesn't look right," he said, "This has all the hallmarks of a stitch-up."

"I'm not even sure that there was actually an explosion at the site."

He zoomed into the satellite image, which fragmented as he went in for a close-up.

"There's not enough resolution to be sure," he said.

"Can we run proof of life?" asked Amanda.

"We are ahead of you," said Jim, "None of this adds up. Let's start with cellphone location data. The SPA - That's *Sankt-Peterburgskaya Analitika* report says there was no cellphone activity in a high-security portion of the Rudnyanskiy Institut Virusologii across the 'explosion' dates and that there may have been a 'hazardous event' during that period.

Jim sipped water from a glass, "Our analysis shows no direct evidence of a shutdown, or any proof for the theory that anything emerged accidentally from the lab."

"So, it could all be fake news?" asked Amanda.

"Yes, staged to make it look incriminating. Although it would need quite some influence for this to work," answered Jim, "If such a shutdown, it could be seen as evidence of a possibility being examined by U.S. intelligence agencies and alluded to by US administration officials, including the president — that a rogue US marine blew up a pathogen lab. From what I've heard about Chuck Manners this seems incredibly unlikely."

"So who could have orchestrated this?" asked Amanda.

"I can't say - officially, but I'd put the chances very high that it was local *blatnoy* Kasharin Maximovich. Consider that crime-lord Maximovich is active in the region. Then that the report was released by *Lavlbalt* and *Peterburgskij Komsomolets*, which are the two media outlets owned by his wife. The analysis seems to account for only a tiny fraction of the cell phones that would be expected in a facility that employs hundreds of people."

Jim continued, "Now what is interesting is that a different document from Lavlbalt obtained by NBC News says that an annual international conference entitled 'Genomic population structures of microbial pathogens' planned in the same lower-security portion of the RIV appears to have been 'cancelled and never took place'."

"It's tosh. The conference went forward as planned. There is even a YouTube screening from a couple of the sessions. The cameraman kindly swings the camera around before the session showing just how full the conference facility was."

"It makes us highly sceptical of the analysis, which is based on commercially available cell phone location data."

"Our own analysts in Cheltenham saw the document and said the data 'looks weak and some conclusions don't make sense.' "

"Earlier, U.S. intelligence agencies received reports based on publicly available cell phone and satellite data suggesting a shutdown at the lab, two U.S. officials familiar with the matter say. But after examining overhead imagery and their own data, the agencies could not confirm any shutdown, and considered the reports 'inconclusive.' "

"It seems this really is a case of smoke without fire. A staged explosion, pointing the finger to Manners, but no evidence. Someone could have burned some truck tyres on the roof of the Institute."

"And here's the thing. The RIV is a high-security facility next to an adversary nation and studying dangerous pathogens. It is a collection target for several U.S. intelligence agencies. Data gathered would include mobile phone signals, communications intercepts and overhead satellite imagery.

"Analysts are now examining what was collected in October and November for clues suggesting any anomalies. There's none. Normal traffic patterns on the roads. No exclusion zone. No emergency buildings erected. Nothing."

Jim continued, "So here's my more pragmatic view. First look at routine telemetry data around the facility. If it shows dramatic drop off in activity compared to previous 18 months, it would be a strong indication of an incident at lab and of when it happened. But it doesn't. Life goes on as normal."

"So, it's all a fake?" asked Amanda.

"Looks like it," said Jim.

"To be honest, the report we intercepted that contains much of this evidence has several things wrong with it. There's badging showing the source consultancy *Sankt-Peterburgskaya Analitika* that provided the analytics. It looks to us like the bedroom company of a freelancer. Even the logo is suspect. We re-mapped it over a commonly available clipart from Star Wars and it has a greater than 90% match to a Darth Vader graphic, albeit with some recolouring.

"Profiling by us says the report was written by a precocious teenage gamer, who legitimised it by copying the style from - wait for it- Cambridge Analytica."

Amanda laughed out loud, "Sorry - it gets more preposterous by the minute," she said, letting her relief that it wasn't Chuck escape.

Jim added, "Then the Americans kindly dropped a Scan Eagle drone into the area, admittedly on a short sweep. It showed workers going about their business in normal clothing. No airlock tent or other devices have been installed.

"Air surveillance of the car parks indicate they are as full after the event as they were before it.

"There's been no traffic re-routing around the site and no excessive amount of emergency vehicles clustered nearby. In fact, a confectionery factory fire about 100 kilometres to the south east received significantly more emergency traffic than this facility after the alleged attack."

"So, you are saying it's a made-up event?" asked Amanda.

"It sure looks that way," answered Jim, "And I've cross checked with our cousins in the US and they seem to think the same thing."

"So how do we get the event back into the news?" asked Amanda, "To show it is made-up?"

"Yes, - a real example of fake news, but all the more difficult to deal with. Ironically we will need to provide our report to a media feed interested in media manipulation." Answered Jim.

"I may have just such a contact," said Amanda.

Framed

Amanda called Jake, "Look, this is as far off the record as it gets."

"You were right to warn that Chuck was being framed. He is, and it is for that explosion in Celarus. We think it is the local clan there, but we've also got evidence that it is framing. There's the report that shows the explosion, which is being used as a basis for hunting Chuck.

"Then there's our report, done in collaboration with the CIA, and it shows that there's been no disruption to routine around the facility. That the explosion was Fake News. They even ran a conference there just after the explosions was alleged to have happened.

"I'm getting the reports cleaned up so you can have a copy. The Americans sent in a drone to cross check and found nothing. Our theory about the smoke is that some tyres were burned on the roof of the building. It was a really shoddy operation.

"I'm hoping you still have contacts in the press that can filter this out. We can do so from here but it will have SI6 fingerprints all over it by the time the report reaches daylight.

Jake spoke, "We didn't think Chuck could be up to no good. I've also got a contact from The Manhattanite who can help get this out. She'll be such a random source that no-one will be able to piece it together."

"Okay, best you don't tell me any more - plausible deniability and all that. Expect an email from me tomorrow! And take care!

The phone clicked - Amanda was gone.

Irina visits Raven

Irina had decided there was a story in the situation she had discovered with Hekla and Christina. She had left Christina's apartment early, found a coffee shop and shaken the mental devastation of the last night from her head.

Then she had walked into a nearby Marks, bought a new outfit and changed to be fresh for the new day. She'd read an article in Manhattanite about 'After date clothes' and now she was living it.

Now she had an interesting situation from across the pond, complete with a US-angle. She called and arranged to meet the Raven Press Office for a brief conversation about Raven, as part of a positive profile piece to cover Raven, Qube and Brant. She had explained it was for The Manhattanite market and to position Raven as a success story of a US company operating from London and spreading into Europe.

By afternoon she approached the Raven offices near to Heron Quays, in Bank Street, just along from Morgan Stanley and JP Morgan's two huge plate glass buildings.

Irina was frequently around the area although still realised that she could easily get lost if she took to the tunnels and shopping malls which threaded their way around most of the lower floors.

It reminded her of Seattle, Calgary or even Toronto, with an entire infrastructure of fairly high-end shops, cafes, restaurants and bars in the labyrinth layers of the construction. The captive audience of thousands of office workers meant that the mall levels teemed busy with shoppers, yet it was like a secret zone, rather than destination shopping for anyone. No, if you worked here, you shopped here, men bought fancy shirts and suits here. Women found the latest fashions and high-end shoe-porn.

Irina entered the lobby of Raven, tiled in a vivid black and white diagonal pattern. She was at once impressed by the huge golden raven in the centre of the lobby, inside a circle of gold. The sort of thing an Embassy would position, but less usual for a corporation. Then she noticed the two rows of flags, to the left and right of the auditorium. She soon spotted the American flag, a British one and also an EU ring of stars, but she was more lost with some of the others. French, German, Belgian, Netherlands, Russia, but there were a few with added symbols that she didn't recognise.

Then she looked up towards the ceiling. It had been painted a deep blue and showed small stars twinkling in it. In the centre a sunburst and at either end of the atrium a rising and setting star.

Irina was also intrigued to see a large 'G' in the middle of the starburst, and seven extra-long strands radiating to the edges of the ceiling.

Then she looked back to the raven. She realised that the circle was not a simple ring. It was a serpent or some similar creature with its tail in its mouth. She remembered she had once owned a ring with a similar depiction, which she had received as a present from Egypt.

"Hello," said an attractive woman with spiky blonde hair and wearing a dark business suit, "I'm Isabelle Eastwood, from Raven PR."

"Oh, how did you recognise me?" asked Irina.

"Not so difficult when you are wearing a visitor pass and staring towards the ceiling," answered Isabelle.

"It's themed to look like our Head Office in Central London, which is, in turn, supposed to resemble a Freemason Hall. It turns out our head office is slap bang in the middle of the Freemason area of London."

"So is the Raven organisation Masonic in any way?" asked Irina.

"Not so's one would notice, but it's like all of these Head Office traditions. I had to visit a finance house recently. It was in a grandiose hall, complete with marble pillars. It turned out the finance house had been a bank and had taken the marble and pillars as some sort of forfeiture from another bank out in Milan or somewhere. It's incredible how these traditions seep through London."

"Even, it would seem, quite modern areas like your building here?"

"Yes, this building was part of the Heron Quays development and I think was finished in around 2003. So, it is somewhat more modern than the old buildings in the City."

"I'm told our building there was built around the same time as the Freemason Hall, which means only built around 1930. Although the London masons go back much further to the late 1700s."

"You seem to know a lot about it, " said Irina.

"Want to know my secret?" smiled Isabelle, "I'm usually asked about it by visitors, so I've accumulated my knowledge. I reckon I can talk about the building all the way from the lobby to the meeting room!"

Irina smiled, "That's brilliant, and you know all about my magazine The Manhattanite? I have to do a similar spiel about it to many Public Relations people."

Isabelle confessed, "Yes, actually, I'll admit I usually 'borrow' the latest edition from our press pile in the office. I enjoy reading it and many of the articles seem to come from well-known writers. It is surprisingly cutting at times too, mixing its comic-book humour with quite dark articles about the state we're in. Yes, I'm quite a fan!"

Irina started, "I've been based in London for some time. I'm usually asked to do pro-American stories from across the Pond here. Right now I'm interested in how Raven is pushing American business into Europe from Britain, almost despite Brexit."

Isabelle smiled, "That'll make a great story, let's get a few ground rules straight about quotes policy and so on, then we can begin. I've got a couple of pre-prepared quotes here too, from a couple of the big bosses."

They were inside a main meeting room on a high floor. Irina recognised she was being given the five-star treatment because this would be a good PR scoop for Raven. Featured in The Manhattanite, with a positive piece about their business development.

Isabelle proceeded to show Irina paperwork about policy on quotes and publicity, and Irina listened. Isabelle was clearly proficient because she had brought several quotes and a couple of good backgrounder pieces with potential to be woven into the main article.

"This is all great," said Irina, "But I was hoping meet one of the head folk here too, to ask a couple of direct questions. Will that be possible?"

"You know how tricky that is," answered Isabelle, "And it tends to skew the piece too. It will be more about the individual than about Raven. It tends to make it into an 'About Mr X' instead of about the whole company."

Irina realised that Isabelle was a professional and a strong gatekeeper too. She would not be able to get past Isabelle without pushing more of her magazine's leverage. And the truth was that she was acting independently, so the leverage would not be forthcoming.

"Okay, well, I'll say 'Thank You' then," she said to Isabelle.

"I hope we've provided you with enough to create an interesting article," said Isabelle standing as if ready to leave the meeting.

"Yes, that's great," answered Irina, walking to the door.

In the corridor she could see a couple of men chatting. They were speaking in Russian, and Irina could hear their conversation.

"Yes, Vassily Turgenev is meeting with Tima right now. They are to see Miller McDonald at 2 pm. He wants to understand what has been happening"

Irina was now out of earshot and standing by the elevators. Isabelle pressed the down button.

"Yes - I have to accompany you whilst you are in the office areas," said Isabelle, "You've got one of those Visitor passes."

"It's okay," said Irina, "I'm used to it, and I always look for the restrooms in the lobby!"

Isabella smiled, "Yes and they do make the ones here pretty fancy to impress visitors! Check out the sofas and the makeup area"

They were back at ground level. Irina said her thank yous and prepared to leave the building. But maybe she'd just take a look at these facilities before she left.

Ball's Brothers

Irina decided she would call Hekla.

"Hey Hekla, how are you doing after our epic night? You had to cave around 2 am, but we couldn't keep going much longer."

Hekla replied, "Yes, you and Christina showed me every side of London in less than 24 hours. My head was reeling when I woke up - Oh and that library where we had to go through the bookcase into the Speakeasy! Brilliant. Oh - I already thanked Christina - I should have thanked you too!

"No problem. Look - your other friends are mixed up in something with that Raven company. Guess where I've been today? - Only along to their headquarters. I was thinking I could tell you and Christina about it, but wasn't sure where we could all meet."

"How about back in Hay's Galleria? It is close to my hotel and also close to where you work. If we met there we could link up with the others? And there's a good underground wine bar too. What time?"

How about an hour from now? We can meet in Ball's Brothers?" replied Irina.

"Okay, I'll call Christina and tell her the plan!"

…

An hour later, Hekla was walking into Ball's Brother, down some steps and into a series of vaults. Across the room was a smart-looking bar and a large selection of wine.

"Er - I'm not sure?" Said Hekla.

"Try this," said the barman smiling, "It's our house red but pretty good. Are you expecting anyone? If so, may I suggest taking a bottle."

"Great," said Irina, "Yes please, a bottle then, and three glasses to start."

The barman carried the glasses and bottle to a table and Hekla sat down to wait. A few moments later Christina and Irina arrived together.

"Hey Hekla, we saw one another upstairs! I see you already have the wine. Excellent."

"Is this going to be like last time?" asked Hekla, "In which case I think I'd better know now."

"Em, no, we both have to work tomorrow, so we can't get too crazy," said Irina - looking knowingly at Christina.

"Okay, let's admit it - we all had a great evening! - Even if it took a long time to recover."

"I've asked the others to join us," said Christina, "I hope that's okay?"

"Sure," said Irina, "The more heads to think about this the better"

At that moment Jake, Bigsy and Clare appeared. Bigsy noticed the bottle on the table, "I'll get some more glasses and another bottle," he said and walked across to the bar. Jake and Clare sat down.

There was a moment's silence, then Jake said, "The triple threat is back in town!" and everyone laughed.

"Hekla - you need protection from these other two," laughed Jake.

"It has always been that way around Christina. Minor bumps and grazes - now they just get bigger."

Christina smiled, "Well we all did very well, even Hekla singing that Björk song in the karaoke bar."

"Oh yes, said Irina, "I'd almost forgotten...'*Declare Independence! Don't let them do that to you!*' You had half the bar marching around in a column! Madness."

Bigsy returned, "So what's this all about?" he asked.

Irina proceeded to describe her visit to Raven. She described the inside of the building.

"Another Masonic building!" said Clare. The others nodded. Then Irina explained about the meeting but in particular about the two Russians she had overheard.

"They were clearly saying that Vassily Turgenev was meeting with Tima right now and then that they were due to see Miller McDonald at 2 pm."

"Tima - that's Timur Maximovich - the head of Gasneft and a leader of the Roslavl Brotherhood," said Christina, "Antanov told me about him when we spoke by phone the other day."

"So why would Turgenev, Maximovich and McDonald be meeting together?" asked Jake.

"Think about it," said Christina, "We've got Vassily Turgenev - who is Tima Maximovich's enforcer and the two of them are meeting with Miller McDonald. It can only be for some kind of strong arm tactic."

"Yes, and I've heard from Amanda Miller now," said Jake, "She says that there's some kind of alert out for Chuck. It is to do with blowing up a research institute, in Celarus. But all fake. Amanda has various items that prove it. She was hoping that someone could bring it into circulation. It would be a world scoop." He looked pointedly towards Irina.

Irina looked interested, "Okay, she said, I'm on the hook, let me see the material,"

"Sure thing," said Jake, "Amanda is getting it cleaned so that we can have it. I can let you have it by tomorrow."

"So, we can see it laid out," said Christina, "Raven must want some disruption in Celarus - it's good for Brant business. Who are you gonna call? The local hoodlums. That's the Roslavl clan, which is run by Tima Maximovich. So perhaps the meeting today between McDonald and Maximovich was to receive payment?"

"It's clever really, create disruption in Celarus, which only reinforces the US presence - and indirectly the Brant presence. In return get Chuck Manners framed for the disruption," said Jake.

Chariot

Self Control
Discipline
Inner Strength

Plain Sight

Chuck had hidden in plain sight while the search for him continued. He'd left Christina in Brussels and taken trains across Belgium and then Germany until he could reach a US Army base in Southern Germany.

He knew he could lie low for a while and would be in little danger of being captured by anyone.

He'd selected Panzer Kaserne and the nearby Patch Barracks, mainly because he was on good terms with the Patch Commander. The Barracks were constructed in 1938 for the German Army and the two bases were linked by a tank trail. The Americans took it over in 1945 and had developed the base ever since. Throughout the Cold War, it represented a forward position, close enough to the East Germany and consequently the Russian border.

Just as importantly for Chuck, Panzer Kaserne was directly served by the regular Stuttgart Bus service and two nearby light rail stops in nearby Böblingen. It meant it was straightforward to enter and exit.

Since the formal end of the Cold War, the US Army ran U.S. European Command (EUCOM) at Patch Barracks and United States Africa Command (AFRICOM) at adjacent Kelley Barracks located in Stuttgart. With the long history of American occupation, a whole subsystem of Americana had built up around the base, including schools and a vast US Military Exchange shopping mall, which traded in dollars.

In it, the Panzer Food court was a home-from-home for American soldiers with a Popeye's Chicken, Starbucks, Burger King, Pizza Hut, Charlie's Subs and a Bun-D. There was also a huge Auto Center and Auto rental adjacent to the mall.

Chuck knew that because of its geographic location, Germany was of particular strategic importance for the American Armed Forces.

Despite this, the number of U.S. troops in Germany had been falling and several bases closed. One reason for this was the shift in the United States' security policy, which increasingly focused on the Asia-Pacific region. The egotistical US President had cut European operations because of NATO spending grievances. Russia could hardly believe its luck.

By having his military identity card, Chuck was able to re-equip himself with a complete uniform. Consequently, he was able to wander easily around the base. The same identity card gave him access to accommodation and other facilities.

Chuck was prepared for the worst. He knew it would only be a matter of time before the people who had been chasing him in Brussels re-appeared. He'd also seen the television reports, which implied he had taken a role in the destruction of a research lab. He knew what they were doing. By framing him they were just ensuring that more people could legitimately come after him. It was only a matter of time before the US military would awaken.

A Black Hawk and an Apache

Christina was back at her apartment. The phone rang.

"Hello, is that Katarina?" asked a voice.

"Hello Blackbird," she replied, "Why do you call me by old aliases? What's wrong with my code name?"

"I have intelligence for you," answered Blackbird. "I know you have been talking to Antanov. He's told me about the Roslavl Bratva thing, in Celarus. We directly threatened Maximovich as a result. He's been getting too big for his boots and it has even come onto Putin's radar. We had to ask him to call off Vassily Turgenev from the direct hunting of you. I think he was relieved to have an excuse actually, you seemed to be terminating too many of his little gang.

"However, we heard that Turgenev has decided to still go after Colonel Manners as retribution for his brother who was killed in Manner's hotel room in Brussels a few days ago.

"Turgenev has discovered that Manners is on a US base in Germany. We've been told he wanted to send a helicopter with several of his men on it to hunt down Manners. The pretext is that Manners is wanted as a terrorist for destroying an Institute in Celarus."

Do you know when this will happen?" asked Christina.

"Not exactly, but they have only just got the military helicopter. To fly it into the base it needs to be American or European. I have the registration and can send it to you."

"Did you provide the chopper?" asked Christina, "Was it some kind of deal?"

"Yes - we said we'd provide it in exchange for Turgenev calling off the chase for you,"

"Nice to know I'm worth a helicopter!" smiled Christina.

"Well its a $6 million to $10 million helicopter, after all."

"And it took us a long time to provision it. We were looking for two helicopters in case you needed one. I found you a pilot too - your good friend Antanov Chekeryn. And you know something, Vassily Turgenev is getting a high mileage empty US Army painted

Sikorsky UH-60A Black Hawk and you get a fully armed AH-64E Apache Guardian."

"We have certain air superiority with that E series," said Christina, " I won't ask how you managed to get hold of a latest model American Attack helicopter."

"Let's say that Chuck Manners has some interesting friends," answered Blackbird, " You can pick up the Apache from Brussels. Not from the airport though, from a separate heliport to the south-west of Brussels. Antanov will know it. We've asked him to fly other missions from there in the past."

"What markings will be flying under?" asked Christina

"USAG - United States Army Garrison - which is useful because its a NATO base."

"I remember," said Christina, 'It's SHAPE, isn't it? Supreme Headquarters Allied Powers Europe."

"That's right, it sounds grand but its only got a couple of thousand personnel on the base there. Think of it as US positioning in Benelux."

"Ha yes. The Americans and their abbreviations Belgium, Netherlands and Luxembourg - all grouped together!" said Christina.

"Well, you'll be an unmistakable profile in the air with that attack helicopter, but as importantly, we've given you the IFF of the other helicopter which will be travelling in from Roslavl."

"So, we'll be able to see the other helicopter on its whole route?" asked Christina.

"Yes," said Blackbird, "Although they won't see you - actually with the 64E with all the latest Block III functions they won't be able to see you at all."

"Vassily was most insistent to get the 'copter into Celarus airspace - He wanted the bragging rights. He'll be loading it with some of his hardened soldiers with the intention to kidnap or kill Chuck Manners on the base in Germany. The helicopter won't raise suspicions and the men are going to be in stealth combat gear."

"So, they will be all in black?" asked Christina, "How many?"

"Well, the Sikorsky can carry 11 troops, so I'd expect there to be a full squad," said Blackbird.

"I'd reckon more like eight people, so they are not all tripping over one another. They will also be flying a long way before the mission and those Black Hawks are not as manoeuvrable as an Apache."

"Yes - although don't be deceived by the bulk of the Black Hawk, it is surprisingly fast - about the same speed as an Apache," added Blackbird.

"And a much bigger target," said Christina, "But I'm confused, why all of this help? Is Manners a Russian asset or something?"

"No, but you've managed to stumble onto a huge piece of gangster corruption from Russia. Putin's people at the top are quite keen to stop whatever the Roslavl Bratva are doing. Tima Maximovich may run Gasneft, but he is getting too big for his boots. And he has had Vassily Turgenev as his ruthless enforcer - one who would stop at nothing. If directed by Maximovich he would go after the top positions. I understand the Kremlin is keen to see the whole enterprise end. It is like what Putin is doing with Gavy Yegorin - stripping him of all his companies and his cash. Redistributing it all to his new buddies. "

"So where will we do this?" asked Christina, "If we start a firefight around the base all hell will break loose."

"I agree," said Blackbird, "we've been scouting the approaches to Panzer Kaserne and think we've found a couple of suitable points before the Black Hawk gets there."

"Their route will be through Poland, but they are likely to go north of Czechia, across Dresden and Nuremberg and south west. It means they will fly over dense woodland before they reach their destination. They can be routed to the north of Schwäbish Hall and then south west for the last part of the journey.

"The forests around that area are ideal for an ambush. Eichelberg's woodland would make an ideal spot."

"I'll run this past Antanov," said Christina, "Also to check whether he's confident enough for an Apache."

"He's flown Apaches before, and we've already discussed it with him. He agrees already with the plan. He says he just needs a good wingman to control the firepower."

"That'd be me then, " smile Christina. I remember they have a chain gun, but also carry Hellfire and Stingers? I assume we'll have the twin missile packs?"

"You will, Archangel, be armed to the teeth."

Strength

Courage
Conviction
Compassion

Designed for comfort

Christina had not expected to be in Brussels for so long. She had extended her hotel time and waited to hear from Antanov.

He called her on her phone, "You'll owe me after this one, It's tonight." he said, "I'd promised myself I wouldn't get involved in any more of the difficult stuff after I settled into being a regular mole at the EU."

"Have you told Camille?" asked Christina.

"What do you think?" asked Antanov, "Look, they've provided us with some combat gear at the helicopter. We will have to get changed into it. I don't expect us to be ground troops, but you never know."

"God, I hope they don't use Euro sizing," said Christina, "they are all about 2cm smaller than you think."

"No these are NATO F2 - suitable for Americans- designed for comfort. They come with belts and elastic," said Antanov.

"Okay - but more importantly, will our mission also extract Chuck Manners?" asked Christina.

"I've been given clearance to land in the Barracks, but we'd need to find a way to get Chuck to the LZ." Said Antanov.

"What time?" asked Christina.

"It's overnight, we take off from the airstrip here at 22:00. Contact is at 23:30 and we will be able to land at the barracks at 00:00 midnight. We'll be back here before 02:00 dark."

"IIow about Chuck? IIe doesn't know yet, does he?" asked Christina.

"No, we've left it to the last moment to inform him. Less chance of information leak."

"Okay, I'll call Jake, he can relay the message via someone else," said Christina, thinking of Amanda, but not wishing to name her.

She picked up her cell phone and dialled Jake. Bigsy answered, "Yes he's just popped outside for a moment – he must have forgotten his phone."

Christina explained the situation. Okay, "I'll go to find him so that he can tell Amanda. What time do you have there? You're one hour ahead aren't you?"

Christina agreed.

"I'll text ACK or NAK to let you know when it's all done," said Bigsy.

Christina smiled, trust Bigsy to overcomplicate YES and NO.

Stinger

They were at the heliport. There was a row of helicopters lined up. The Apache towered over the two domestic choppers. It was already dark although the apron was well-lit as they walked towards the helicopter.

They had allowed an extra three hours to prepare. Antanov wanted to check the chopper, Christina to familiarise herself with the armaments. They would also be told when the Black Hawk left Roslavl so that they would have a confirmed mission.

The IFF system in the Apache was already on and Antanov had selected the code of Turgenev's helicopter. The radar was colourfully alive with blips and Christina could see Antanov studying it.

"Yep, they left on time, they are on their way and logged a flightpath to the north of Czechia, as predicted. They are making good time, they must be flying at top speed," announced Antanov.

"What time do we take off for an intercept?" asked Christina,

"Like I calculated at 22:00," replied Antanov, "We want to be behind and above the Black Hawk. It should not see us because we'll be using this E-model's stealth mode."

The minutes ticked around. Christina remembered other missions where she had been expected to wait around, but they were usually when she was already in position, rather than having to fly to a position.

"Okay," said Antanov, "we're going,"

He fired the twin engines of the Apache and as they came up to speed Christina felt the adrenaline kick in.

"Lifting now," said Antanov and Christina watched the reverse ground rush as they cleared some trees and she suddenly saw the orange lights of distant Brussels.

In a moment they were on their way and Christina listened to the rhythmic chop-chop of the rotors carving through the air.

"Contact time will be about 80 minutes," said Antanov, looking across to Christina.

Christina looked again at the Stinger launch controls. They should be able to launch a pack of Stingers towards the target. She did not expect to use the chain gun, and the Hellfire was only for any unexpected ground developments.

"They are through Poland," announced Antanov, "Contact in 20 minutes. That's the advantage of flying a NATO copter, they can breeze across half of Europe in a way I'd never be able to, even in a MiG-21."

"I'm going to start a climb here, said Antanov, They are at 8,000 feet. I want to be at least 1,000 feet higher."

"Helicopters don't like really high altitudes, do they?" asked Christina.

"That's right, the pilot of the Black Hawk is flying at probably the high end of the safe hover zone for such a heavy machine. We can go higher but only hover to around 10,000 feet. Then the air isn't dense enough. But don't worry, I think I can take this up to 25,000 feet as long as we are moving forward."

"Anyway, I suspect he will start a slow descent from about where we are going to intercept him. There he is on my short-range radar now. We are on a merged plot. You can look at target acquisition. Fangs Out."

"That's easy on this thing. We have got ATR - automatic target recognition against an MSTAR database. It's already recognised the Black Hawk. It says we are still too far away for a lock, but you seem to be closing fast. I'm arming the AIM-92s."

"Will you fire one or two?" asked Antanov.

"I'll fire the double pack," said Christina, "Mach 2 towards the target. If it tries countermeasures, it will only have seconds to deploy. I still suggest you flip once we've fired."

"You worry about the targeting, I'll worry about the piloting," said Antanov.

"Okay, Missiles selected- Two Stingers, Payload primed, Target Acquired, Padlocked, Ready to fire, count of three, one, two, three, Fox Two, missiles fired, on track, seeking target, target hit. Target immobilised, target destroyed."

"Sierra Hotel, Roger that, moving into Mission Phase Two," said Antanov.

They saw a bright yellow fireball tumbling through the air towards the ground.

"Mission Phase One accomplished," said Christina. The assassins sent to find Chuck Manners had been destroyed. It had been the combined work of NATO, the US and the FSB, something that would not make it into any mission report.

"ETA to LZ is around 12 minutes, said Antanov. "I want to do a spot landing and be out of there."

"Okay, let's hope Chuck is ready for this."

Antanov proceeded to the floodlit H denoting the helicopter landing spot inside the barracks. The late model Apache would be certain to attract stares, and Christina noticed someone taking a cameraphone movie of the landing.

Then, she realised it was the same person running across the 100 metres towards the 'copter and clambered in through the side door.

"Hi Guys, Thank you for the ride," said Chuck, not sounding out of breath despite his exertion.

"Chuck!" said Christina handing him a set of green headphones, "Welcome on board."

"Where are we going?" he asked as he clipped on the headset.

"I've a flight plan logged to Berlin," said Antanov.

"What Tegel?" asked Chuck.

"No - Brandenburg, actually," replied Antanov, "You can disperse with the crowds there, or even take a train. Those people looking for you are gone. Thank Christina for that."

Chuck looked at Christina, "Thank you. That's twice you helped me. I don't know what to say."

"Just store it to pay forward," answered Christina, smiling, "They had sent a whole gunship of people after you this time. I think the FSB are about to send them a *prekratit' i otkazat'sya ot poryadka* - that's a 'cease and desist' order,"

"They are very ceased," added Antanov, "Courtesy of two Stingers."

Christina looked at Chuck in uniform. Here he was an American Colonel, with a silver eagle on his uniform, rescued in a NATO helicopter by an FSB officer.

Antanov revved the engines on the Apache. It was soon back at 2000 feet climbing over the countryside of Baden-Württemberg.

Disproving fake news

Irina played her part. The article was now out there about the staging of the explosions at the Institute. The Manhattanite decided to run the story on its website ahead of the publication of the weekly magazine.

They linked it to stories of fake news, of Russian manipulation and of the hold that the Russian Mafia had over world events. Irina was given a by-line, although so were two better known journalists for the magazine.

Christina recognised that much of the material came from Amanda Miller, although the sources had been anonymised or relocated.

Amanda looked at the copy now spread across several other newspapers, including the Guardian and the Financial Times.

The Guardian created an entire series of graphics to explain what had happened, which looked decidedly well-informed.

The question being posed was who was at the root of the manipulations? Someone on a conspiracy site had also linked the Black Hawk helicopter crash in Germany to the story, although most reports were of a military training mission into dense forest which had gone awry.

A plane spotter expert had produced an analysis of the crashes of Black Hawks, which indicated that an original run of 16 crashes caused the aircraft to be grounded, a further two had exploded or crashed into mountainside, with on one of the most similar crashes by an ROCAF (Republic of China Air Force) helicopter and another at Eglin Air Force Base in Florida. In both cases there were no survivors.

Amanda flicked over the helicopter diagrams but then noticed another small boxout in the Guardian account. It talked about the origin of the original plot. It mentioned that it could have been state-sponsored by Russia and hinted that a well-known Russian in exile in France could have been the source.

Amanda was intrigued by this line. Was someone referring to Tima Yegorin? The story passed the duck test. It walked like a duck, swam like a duck, quacked like a duck. Yes, it was a duck. A story or hint placed there by the Russians.

She decided to follow up via Jake, who facilitated the original story placement. He had been careful to protect his sources and it was better that no-one inside SI6 knew, in any case.

Two of Cups

(Reversed)
Imbalance
Broken Communication
Tension

Kremlin anger

Christina was in the office. Someone was calling her phone. She could see it was Fyodor Kuznetsov, her handler.

"Hi Blackbird," she said, cheerily.

"Hello Archangel," he replied.

"What's happening now?" asked Christina.

"The collateral damage from that helicopter escapade," admitted Blackbird.

"The Kremlin is furious with Yegorin for letting Vassily Turgenev mount that mission. They would not have cared if it had all gone right, but instead there's so much trouble.

"First, the discovery of the fake reports, which had been sloppily put together, Russia got the blame for that.

"Then, the hunt for Chuck Manners in the Brussels hotel. The two agents have been identified as part of a Russian team. More blame for Russia, this time running around with guns in the EU Capital of Brussels.

"Then the gunshots in London. A Russian agent has washed up in Tilbury, but it points back to the recent gun shots around Tower Bridge.

"And finally, a 'stolen' helicopter in US Army colours is flown across the Polish border and then into Germany, where it is shot down by a Sidewinder. The crew were all identified as Russian.

"These point to Vassily Turgenev working for Yegorin. The Kremlin are not taking a happy view. It is messing up their stealth influence strategies."

"Stinger, not Sidewinder," said Christina, "It was two Stingers that brought the Black Hawk down."

"It doesn't matter," said Blackbird, "Yegorin is likely to lash out now, to salvage his tattered reputation with the Kremlin."

"Or do something covert," said Christina, "To try to strike a bargain? - So what do you want from me?"

"I think you have done enough. The original aim was to disrupt Yegorin and to interfere with the Celarus plans. I think you have done both, admittedly with more sparks flying than ideal. Right now, I need to stop you from further activities. Now, nothing is pointing towards you, we need to keep it that way."

Christina put her phone down.

Almost at once Jake's phone rang.

"Huh, we are popular today!" said Jake, reaching across.

"Jake? It's Amanda, thank you for getting that story out, it will have helped to clear Chuck and thankfully SI6 are no-where to be seen."

"My pleasure," said Jake, "Although there seems to be even more discoveries in the versions published."

"Yes," said Amanda, "That's what I wanted to ask you about. Do you know who added the embellishments in the Guardian story. The part about a Paris-based instigator?"

Jake replied, "No, I wondered that myself. I know Christina has useful links in Paris, but she would have told me if she was planning to do something like that - she was as mystified as we are."

"Okay, well if anything around that story surfaces, can you let me know? Please." Asked Amanda.

"Sure thing," said Jake, "I guess you are relieved that the complete rescue mission played out so well?"

"Yes, even if Chuck has gone to ground again. I hear he was last spotted in Berlin?"

"Yes, that's what Christina said. She said Chuck would lie low until after the dust had settled. I guess clearing his name is one step along that path, but I don't know whether someone will feel vindictive as a result?"

"Yes, he's wise to stay out of sight for the moment. Thanks for your help."

Amanda hung up the phone.

She turned to Grace. "They don't know. I'm sure they don't know about Yegorin. That Yegorin is in Paris under pressure from the Kremlin."

"Well, we must see if we can put Yegorin under some additional pressure," smiled Grace.

Price of peace

At his home in France, Yegorin had been threatened by associates sent by Mezhkommbank's liquidator - they were threatening his family if he did not pay a $350 million 'price of peace', they told him, the price for making the Russian criminal case against him for the Mezhkomm bankruptcy go away. He knew it was around 1/3 of his liquid assets and that they would have calculated the same.

 In the UK courts, Yegorin had been incapable of operating because of the unfamiliar rules and procedures.

Yegorin was accustomed to backroom deals like in his Kremlin past, too accustomed to slipping through the rules and regulations because of his position and power.

Yegorin decided to contact Maximovich to discuss options. In particular, he would like to borrow Vassily Turgenev for a while, to assist him with drawing a strong line under previous events.

Convinced of the righteousness of his position, that he was the victim of the latest Kremlin asset grab, he believed himself above the regulations of the British courts.

He'd failed to stick to court orders related to an asset freeze and had burned through millions of pounds from an account he'd kept hidden from the UK court. He took a view that he could afford to pay Vassily Turgenev from the same source and that Turgenev's methods might be quicker and more effective than that of the lawyers.

He believed disclosure rules were beneath him; petty compared to the woeful calamity that had befallen his business empire, and only part of a Kremlin campaign to hound and frustrate him at every turn.

Maximovich recognised the handwringing by Yegorin but realised that the Kremlin's spotlight on him could also just as easily turn into a searchlight.

He decided to lend Yegorin his enforcer Vassily Turgenev and make other temporary arrangements. He asked around and was soon introduced to Anatoly Yaroslav, a Ukrainian with access to a fierce firepower.

The Kremlin had become adept at pursuing its enemies through the UK court system, while a PR machine was honed to fill the pages of the UK tabloids with allegations of the Russian oligarch's stolen wealth, even despite his wife's two media interests. Notably, a couple of influential newspapers (The ironically titled Independent and London's Evening Standard) were already in Russian hands, those of the disarming Evgeny Lebedev, son of the billionaire businessman and former KGB agent Alexander Lebedev.

The Kremlin had learned to navigate its way through the UK court system during its victory against Boris Berezovsky, the exiled oligarch who'd become a fierce critic of Putin.

Berezovsky was the fast-talking one-time Kremlin insider who had tried – and failed – to sue his erstwhile business partner Roman Abramovich, a close Kremlin ally, for $6.5 billion in London's High Court.

The judge overseeing the case took a dim view of Berezovsky's claim that he'd jointly owned one of Russia's biggest oil majors, Sibneft, and a stake in Rusal, Russia's biggest aluminium giant, with Abramovich, and that Abramovich had forced him to sell his stakes at a knockdown price.

The current Yegorin situation was like history repeating itself.

Though Berezovsky was recognised throughout Russia as owner of these concerns, the judge said she found him to be 'an inherently unreliable witness' and sided with Abramovich, who'd claimed that Berezovsky had never owned these assets; he'd merely been paid for providing political patronage. It later appeared that a stepson of the judge had been paid around £500,000 to represent Abramovich in the early stages of the case.

Now Yegorin was facing similar treatment although no stolen or hidden assets were found. No fraud claims had been launched in the UK, or anywhere else outside Russia.

Instead, on the basis of a Russian court ruling alone, the legal team had won a freezing order against Yegorin assets and ran rings around him while he sank under a multitude of court orders.

He'd been interrogated over asset disclosures and was found to have given false evidence over whether the sale of his coal business had been conducted by himself or by his son.

It did not seem to matter to the judge that the hard-luck story was that the sale had been forced through at a price that was less than one twentieth of the business's real value. What mattered was whether he had followed procedure and declared all the assets that remained under his control.

Marion

Christina had just seen Hekla back to the airport. Hekla was bubbling with enthusiasm for her brief time in London.

"I'm going to visit again, Aggi…you are still packing so much in - and this is even more exciting than discovering what was in the *Ullarverslun* back on the farm."

"Well that wool store didn't contain wool, anyway!" said Christina, and they both laughed.

"Safe journey!" said Christina.

"Stay safe and avoid mischief!" replied Hekla.

"As if!" answered Christina. They hugged and then Hekla was walking into the Border Control area.

Christina's phone rang, and she answered it, "Hello?"

"Hi Christina? You may not remember me, my name is Marion Charlotte."

"Of course I do, and how are you?" replied Christina.

"I've something I'd like to talk over with you. It relates to the business with Sir Charles Frobisher and Gerhardt Schmidt. Can I see you?" asked Marion.

Christina thought, "Yes, why don't you come to our office. But I don't want any funny business though. I need you to play it straight."

"I will, I will, Circumstances have changed," answered Marion, "You have my word. Look, I would also like to bring Nina Valentine along. You met her at the Ladies' Night."

"Sure, I remember, she was a friend of Jennifer's," answered Christina, remembering the name of the fixer who supplied the women to the Masonic event.

"Okay, let us make it tomorrow. I'll text you a time and location," answered Christina.

Ed Adams

Queen of Wands

Courage
Determination
Passion
Joy

Ladies of the Night

Christina had texted Marion with the address of the Cafe Rouge, close to the Triangle office. It had outside tables and served breakfast. She could meet Marion and Nina and could also bring along some reinforcements of her own.

She asked Jake, and he suggested that both he and Bigsy come along. "Bigsy will check for - you know - devices," said Jake.

"I don't want Bigsy patting down two women in the middle of Cafe Rouge," said Christina.

"Oh no, he's bound to have a gadget."

"I hope so," said Christina.

All three of them were sitting drinking coffees when Marion and Nina arrived.

Christina saw Bigsy's mouth drop. He was already in their spell. They all said their hellos.

"Bigsy, behave," whispered Christina, and saw him nod.

"Hello Marion," said Christina; she still remembered when Marion had worked for both SI6 and a Russian clan.

"Thank you for seeing me," she replied, "Nina and I have some news for you. First, let me tell you something. After that dinner with Driscoll, I realised you were some kind of agent, but I guarantee that I didn't pass Driscoll's part in the dinner back to anyone. I know he was killed, but as far as I am aware, it was nothing to do with me."

Christina looked at her, "You swear?" she asked, "Because we had you down as the most likely suspect."

"No, I swear," she said, "And it is the same for Nina. She was a best friend of Gerhardt and narrowly missed being blown up on that yacht."

"Yes, Gerhardt had asked me to stay on the yacht," answered Nina, "I declined and walked back to the dock but about half an hour later the yacht exploded in a fireball at sea. There is no way that it was faulty wiring. Someone must have planted a bomb on board."

"Then we heard about Sir Charles. We both knew him," said Marion,"He was a feature at those big events."

Nina continued, "I arrived in his party on the yacht which Gerhardt had hired. He was his usual buoyant self, but then suddenly decided he needed to go back to London. He walked off the yacht and was going to catch a helicopter back to Nice, and from there fly to London."

Marion nodded, and Nina continued, "We checked, and it looks as if he got onto a Vassily one-way special at the heliport. Vassily Turgenev is a ruthless mobster. He works for Tima Maximovich and is his enforcer. There's a couple of other well-known businessmen at the bottom of the Ligurian sea, courtesy of Turgenev."

"Did you have anything to do with those cases?" asked Christina.

Nina and Marion both shook their heads.

"You know how it is, we girls that work for Jennifer all talk to one another."

"*A ty russkiy tozhe ponimayesh'*?" asked Christina.

"Yes, I understand Russian, I'm originally from Odintsovo," answered Marion, in English.

"Yes, and I'm from Central Moscow, but I worked in Strogino District, " answered Nina.

"Odintsovo, Strogino - you are both really from Moscow then?" asked Christina.

"Yes, but like many of us, Jennifer Sussex offered us a path to the west and to more money. I knew Marion from when we both struggled to find a living around Strogino and she told me about Jennifer."

"Jennifer's agency - Miel Doux Artists - was only looking for the most attractive women and ones that could already speak good English. We were both selected to come over to London, where we soon discovered a Russian home-from-home although it was significantly better paid."

Nina said, "That's right, the Russians all wanted a second home in London, and were wealthy beyond anything that Marion and I could imagine. Of course, it was stolen money, when the Russian state divided up its natural resources and gave a healthy slice to each of the new owners of the means of production. The men - and for that matter the women - we met were all so rich that they didn't care about anything."

Christina said, "I know Strogino. It's where the dives and pub-crawl bars are situated. It must have been a huge jump up for you to go to London?"

Jake interrupted, "So, we get that you delightful ladies have 'a past', but what is it you want to talk about today? It can't be Moscow reminiscences?"

Marion continued. "Yes, now that we are in London, we are also approached by Jennifer to help out on the bigger and most prestigious events. Those are often hosted by Russians or people who are somehow connected but are often include British establishment people. You know, Members of Parliament, legal operatives, police officers, sometimes athletes, sometimes people from the media, occasional people from music."

Nina added, "Yes, the athletes and music people are usually referred to as 'The Talent' and are there to help bring in the people that are really of interest. The media are there, I think, as an insurance policy."

"Okay," said Bigsy, "So these are big events, in London and have a mix of the good and the great?"

"And the Talent and the Honey," said Nina.

"The Honey?" asked Bigsy.

"That's the ladies," whispered Christina, "Pay attention, Bigsy"

"Oh," said Bigsy, his face reddening.

"We've been asked to come along to a new event," said Marion.

"One where we think we can settle some scores," added Nina, "My friend Natalie was murdered on that yacht."

"We both know people who have been killed under the orders of Turgenev," said Marion.

"Now there's to be a Maximovich fundraiser run for Gavy Yegorin, in London, and Turgenev is being asked to run the security for it."

"I don't think I've heard of Yegorin," said Bigsy.

Christina and Jake both looked at him.

Christina started, "Khramov Gavril (Gavy) Yegorin is a main player. I say is. Was, more likely. He is out of favour with the Kremlin now. I think he is actually under lockdown here in London."

"Lockdown! Ha - you should see it!" said Nina, "He's got a huge house and a ready supply of girls. It's like one continuous party there."

Marion continued, "Yegorin had been forced to hand over his passports to the court and was banned from leaving the UK during a prolonged period of questioning over his asset disclosures as the Kremlin's lawyers tightened the legal net. They wanted to squeeze all the money and assets from him, in something speculated to have been sanctioned by Putin."

Nina interrupted, "And the London lawyers were all bandits too, padding their bills with non-existent work. Russian cases from Moscow's tycoons were easy pickings. Add on the PR firms offering to defend Yegorin's image for £100,000 a month.

Marion looked earnest, "The well-dressed Brits can be cynical about their money grabbing, but it is living off the wealth of gangsters and works its way right through the upper Establishment."

Christina nodded, "Yes, I have seen it a lot."

Marion continued, "Yegorin believes he is in the right about all the stolen assets that - as he sees it - unruly Kremlin underlings are trying to expropriate. Then the car bombs appeared although Nina and I think it was Turgenev or one of his buddies that planted them in the first place. It's ironic that Yegorin is now getting Turgenev to run his security."

Nina said, "We think that the Kremlin see Yegorin as a whistle blower. That is why they are trying to bring him down. Yegorin had long detected the growing influence of Kremlin cash in London. Long before the legal attack started, he said, he'd met a string of English lords who'd guffawed and shaken his hand and told him how great they thought Putin was."

Marion added, "That's a problem, because if Yegorin blows the whistle on some of these people, then Putin's carefully created little empire of influence starts to collapse. And not only here, the same links extend into Washington D.C. as well - close acquaintances of the President - you know what I'm talking about."

Bigsy was busy with his phone.

"Yes," he said, "I've just found this extract...It says 'Yegorin donated to the Conservative Party. All his former friends from the Kremlin kept relatives and mistresses in town, who they visited at weekends, flooding the city with cash' ."

He scrolled down on his phone, " As an example, there's this Transparency International report about his buddy Igor Shuvalov, who owns two apartments in Whitehall Court. It's a penthouse overlooking Trafalgar Square worth £11.4 million. The Washington Times has covered the controversy surrounding Shuvalov's alleged ownership of an enormous $9.4 million apartment in Moscow.

"Igor Shuvalov is married to Olga Viktorovna Shuvalova. The income of Shuvalov's spouse over two years amounted to more than 1 billion roubles: she earned 642 million roubles in 2009 and 365 million in 2008. She is a major business figure engaged in the sale of real estate in the Skolkovo Innovation Center offshore business, and trading in shares of Russian raw materials companies."

Christina added, "1 billion roubles is about 14 million USD, I think."

"Well, it's still a lot, even if it sounds more in Russian," said Jake.

Bigsy was concentrating, "Then there's Arkady Rotenberg, the Russian businessman and tycoon. With his brother Boris Rotenberg, he is co-owner of the Stroygazmontazh (SGM) group, the largest construction company for gas pipelines and electrical power supply lines in Russia.

Christina interrupted, "It is a comparable situation to Yegorin, except he's done what he was told."

Bigsy continued, "Rotenberg was listed by Forbes in 621st place among the world's wealthiest persons. He is a close confidant of president Vladimir Putin.

"For about ten years, he was formerly married to his second wife Natalia Rotenberg, who is about 30 years his junior and their two children Varvara and Arkady live in the United Kingdom with Nataliya."

"I remember Nataliya," said Nina brightly, "Stunning blonde socialite and quite intelligent. Around Arkady, she looked like his daughter. "

Bigsy continued, "It says they divorced in the U.K. While the financial details of the divorce are private, the agreement includes division of the use of a £35 million Surrey mansion and a £8 million apartment in London. The couple's lawyers obtained a secrecy order preventing media in the U.K. from reporting on the divorce, but the order was overturned on appeal."

Bigsy added, "Rotenberg spread the wealth around though. Igor, his son is a Russian billionaire businessman and Liliya, a doctor living in Germany but she is also the co-owner of the TPS Nedvizhimost which is an investment group that owns shopping malls and entertainment complexes in major Russian cities including Moscow, Sochi, Krasnodar, Novosibirsk and Ocean Plaza in Kiev, Ukraine.

Bigsy looked at his phone, "The list goes on and on, but as one last example, there's the deputy speaker of the State Duma, one of Russia's most vocal patriots, Sergei Zheleznyak, who has raged against the influence of the West, yet his daughter Anastasia has lived in London for years."

Marion added, "As Yegorin famously said, "They have sorted themselves out very well on this small island with terrible weather. In the UK, the main thing was always money. Putin sent his agents to corrupt the British elite.'"

Nina nodded, "The city had grown used to the flood of Russian cash. Property prices surged and then a series of privileged share orderings to PR and legal firms."

Marion added, "And now we are about to see Yegorin go fund-raising."

Fund raiser

"So, what is the purpose of the fundraising?" asked Jake.

"Leverage," explained Marion, "Yegorin has asked Maximovich to front a fund raiser. If they raise the money, then Yegorin could rise into the ascendency again."

"They will bring along a host of well-known names, most of whom wouldn't notice dropping a few million into the gift box for Maximovich."

"Yegorin can't do this in his own name because it is considered tainted, and anyone appearing friendly with him could also get unwanted Kremlin attention."

"So, what is the point of the money?" asked Bigsy, "It can't surely be simply to bail out Yegorin?"

"No, it will be about setting up a new investment vehicle, co-owned by Yegorin and Maximovich. The purpose of the investment will be to build the new pipeline in Celarus. Basically, to take control of the oil supply into Europe.

Marion said, "Right now, one of the ways that Putin acolytes get paid is by skimming the natural resource revenues that flow across Russia and beyond. It works out to around a 17% tax by all the oligarchs on anything that can be considered a raw resource. It funds plenty of amazing lifestyles. It is why many Russians diversify into property, football clubs and artworks. It makes their wealth relatively illiquid and launders it."

Christina said, "I know this from running security detail: A typical oligarch may have a small stack of apartments in London as well as a couple of show-off places. The 'stack' amounts to 'money at rest' but of course it is also increasing in value in line with the London property market. The Chinese are starting to do the same thing now."

Nina added, "So Yegorin could throw a big spanner in the works by building a pipeline that links the Celarus oil-fields to Europe. And by doing so, also push the US Agenda in Celarus."

Marion added, "Yes, it would massively annoy the Kremlin and could even spark some civil unrest, like the Russian blockade of Ukraine. The Ukraine move was an obvious one by Russia and led to power shortages and a ransom being conducted for extractive companies. In effect the companies were to be turned over to the state and could then be chopped up among the oligarchs. It's a series of well-rehearsed rip-offs and ones that Yegorin has played before when he was in favour. This time it is possible to see the same moves being used in Celarus against Russia.

"But won't Russia intervene?" asked Christina, "Throw some force around?"

Marion replied, "Yes - Russia could even bomb the partly built pipeline; it wouldn't matter to Yegorin by that time. All it would do would be to intensify the US interest in the region. There would be US and NATO forces crawling all over Celarus before you knew it. Look, the Americans have already established forward positions in Celarus and have Brant building the bases and infrastructure."

"What role do we have in any of this?" asked Christina.

Marion looked at Nina, "Neither of us have any contacts; we don't have access to the state, to police, press or anything. You've already demonstrated that you have high links, like when you visited me, Christina, with your colleague Amanda who said she was from SI6. That's heavyweight influence."

Nina added, "What we do have is invitations and access to the event - we know what it is, where it is and will soon know who is going to be there. We're also completely trusted on the inside."

Marion added, "Yes, and that's something we want to maintain, or we'll end up like Sir Charles and Gerhardt."

Damaged goods

Back at the office, they briefed Clare.

"We'll have to tell Amanda Miller about this," said Clare, "She should be able to mobilise some other help."

"Yes, and to see if she wants to gain anything from the situation," said Christina, "There's a way, you know. "

They conference-called Amanda, to explain what had happened. She invited Jim Cavendish to listen to the call.

Amanda was intrigued to hear Yegorin's name.

Amanda said, "Yegorin is damaged goods. This is substantial risk. He is being punished for trying to exit the tight-knit system that ruled Russia, the mafia clan which no one was ever meant to leave."

"Some say he lost his mind and thought he could leave and work on his own business. The order was given to destroy him."

Jim Cavendish added, "When he left the UK to go to France, Yegorin left behind a number of tell-tale signs. Detectives working for the Kremlin's lawyers raided his Knightsbridge office on a court order issued in the days after his disappearance.

Amanda continued, "His own security must have been terrible. Among the documents, there were several disc drives. On one of the disc drives were recordings from every meeting he held in his downtown Moscow offices."

Jim continued, "One of the recordings shows Yegorin's feelings about Putin and his role in bringing him to power. Yegorin is sitting in his office with Valentin Vitalievich discussing over dinner the tense state of affairs as Moscow hurtled through yet another political crisis.

Amanda said, "In the Kremlin's warren, the former KGB and security men who had risen to power with Putin had been jostling for position, bickering, and backstabbing in hopes that they, or their candidate, would be selected as his successor.

Jim said, "Yes, on the tape we can hear Yegorin and Vitalievich clink glasses and discuss the standoff. The uncertain succession brought back memories of when they'd assisted Putin's rise."

Jake said, "So they'd climbed the greasy pole, but slipped back down?"

Jim continued, "Yes, it seemed to them an age ago. Now they were seen as relics by Putin's KGB allies from St Petersburg. The system of power had changed and struggled to understand what they'd done.

"So, they knew early on, that their days were numbered?" asked Jake.

"Not really; I think they expected to hold on to their gains, not have the ex-KGB come after them to try to grab everything back," answered Jim, "In those days, Putin had appeared reluctant to take the leading role, and seemed malleable and compliant to those who'd helped bring him to power."

Amanda added, "But then, Putin's first term had been drenched in blood and controversy. It led to a sweeping transformation of the way the country was run."

"The writing was on the wall?" asked Bigsy.

"Yes, the bloody writing was on the wall," replied Jim, "Putin faced a series of deadly terrorist attacks, including the siege of the Dubrovka Theatre in Moscow by Chechen terrorists in October 2002 which ended with more than a hundred dead when the Russian security services botched the storming of the theatre and gassed the very theatregoer hostages they'd been trying to free. Putin's battles with rebels from the restive northern Caucasus republic of Chechnya had caused thousands of deaths, including almost 300 who died in a string of apartment bombings."

Amanda said, "Many in Moscow whispered Putin's security services were behind these attacks, not least because the result was a security clampdown that strengthened his power. We considered it a time of mayhem."

Jim added, "Yes, it was a new guard. Putin and the ex-KGB men who ran the economy now monopolised power and introduced a new system in which state positions were used as vehicles for self-enrichment. It was vastly different from the anti-capitalist, anti-bourgeois principles of the Soviet state they had once served."

"No wonder Yegorin is angry," said Bigsy.

"Yes, but we must not forget that he stole wholeheartedly from the Russian people and used Putin to originally secure his power base," said Amanda, "He is a nasty piece of work."

"I'm not sure how we'd fit into this mission?" asked Amanda.

"Well," said Christina, "I think you could make a huge gain if you played it right. Let me explain."

Best cards

Christina began, "Right now, we hold all the best cards. We know about Yegorin. We know he is on the back foot. That his own security was terrible. We also know that he is trying to do a deal with Maximovich.

"Together they can invite an entire group of celebrity Russians to their party in London. There will be A-Listers there too, and 'Honey'.

"We must manipulate the way the event turns out. Maybe round up a few Russians, including Yegorin," continued Christina.

"We'd need some strongarms to do that," said Clare.

Christina continued, "We need to let Maximovich escape. The plans of Yegorin will have been foiled. He won't be able to fund the pipeline, nor will he be able to raise enough money to recover his stolen assets. He will be seen by the Kremlin to have been discredited in both the east and the west's eyes.

"Yes, we need some highly disciplined strongarms if this is to work," added Clare.

Christina added, "Maximovich can emerge as a local hero. He will have rescued Russia without the need for more bloodshed. The status quo will have been maintained. A dangerous opponent will have been quashed.

"Maximovich should get promotion from this. Firmly into Putin's inner circle instead of teetering on the edge of it. And that is where we want him. A highly placed mole."

Christina continued, "We need to trap Turgenev too. He has proved to be a highly effective and brutal security enforcer for Maximovich."

Amanda added, "This outcome would suit both sides. For the Russians, it gets rid of the troublesome and one-time ruthless Yegorin and keeps the current balance of power in Celarus. There will not have been the money raised to build the new pipeline which keeps the oligarchs happy.

"For the Americans it also keeps the balance of power in Celarus, including the US troops and planes stationed there. For Raven, it gives Brant more work to do."

Christina added, "But with powers of persuasion over Maximovich, we can place a mole inside the Kremlin."

"So how would we deploy for such an occasion?" asked Amanda.

Christina said, "I think we have to let Yegorin talk Maximovich into it. They will set a day and then start inviting guests. They will also inform Jennifer Sussex who will mobilise the Miel Doux Agency to provide escorts."

Bigsy said, "Now when they do that, we can have some fun... We'll create a little something for the Minerva Listening Station - just enough to get them interested in the event."

Jake asked, "What about you, Amanda? Will you be able to bring some support to the event?"

"I don't think it will do any harm for us to monitor Yegorin at his place in France," said Amanda, " But to be involved in the main event, I'll need reasonable grounds," answered Amanda, "If there was a plot, or some contraband there, for example."

"Let us worry about that," said Christina, "I should be able to get something for you guys to 'discover'. Ideally, it needs to be something linked to Turgenev. We all have some scores to settle there."

Page of Swords

(Reversed)

Deception
Manipulation
All Talk

Black tie

Bigsy had prepared everything for what was to be the acting debut of the Triangle offices. As well as Jake, Clare and Bigsy, there would be Christina, Marion and Nina present. They had all talked over what they would say when Bigsy magically restored the communications link to the Minerva Listening Station.

Across in Greenwich Peninsula, Pete Burr wasn't certain what he was getting. He was still expected to monitor the Triangle offices from Minerva, but there had been almost zero activity. It was as if the communications had been cut off. Occasionally there would be some footage of people arriving or leaving the offices.

He had also noticed the chit-chat of office banter, but nothing was of any consequence.

Then, one day he saw Bigsy return into the main meeting room.

"I found it," he said, "It was a fuse, well, a power supply actually. The programmable power supply for the second comms cabinet had gone down."

To Pete, this was an explanation. Suddenly he realised what had happened at the offices. Some kind of unit had ceased functioning and cut off the signal back to Minerva.

"Yes, said Bigsy, "I've rebooted the unit. It is supposed to have intelligent management, but the management controller is on the same circuit. If the unit goes down, it can't tell anyone."

Unseen to Pete, Bigsy had just winked to the others. They were ready to put on a show for Minerva.

"So, what do we know about this gala event?" asked Clare.

Jake started, "Well, it's going to be the talk of the town. A-listers abound. They have got a well-known TV presenter to host the show, which is targeted towards Russian magnates with plenty of money.

"It's so blingy, they have ordered extra gold-painted chairs and ornaments. The gathering's official purpose is to raise money for worthy causes, but, it is all about Yegorin's business opportunity, fronted by Maximovich.

"In other words, to get the investors to build the oil pipeline across Celarus and into Europe."

Clare added, "Yes, but there's an auction to win lunch with British politicians, Cabinet ministers and economic operators."

Jake said, "Rumour says it is a replacement for the Presidents Club, which was the appalling club which closed its doors after an expose in the Financial Times."

Bigsy wrote down of a small piece of paper, "I hope they are getting all of this."

Clare shrugged, "I suppose it makes the event all the more appealing, if some of those invited know that other well-known people have already accepted."

Christina added, "It is so non-PC, but in the culture of certain people, this is entirely acceptable. They dress it up as a black-tie evening. And include a couple of well-known TV hosts to do slots."

Bigsy said, "There will be around 300 figures from British business, politics and finance and the entertainment included as well as 120 specially hired hostesses."

Christina said, "The task of finding hostesses for the dinner is entrusted to Jennifer Sussex, founder of MDA - Miel Doux Agency, an agency specialising in hosts and hostesses for what it claims to be some of the 'UK's most prestigious occasions'.

Marion added, " Yes, a couple of days before the event, Ms Sussex will inform the prospective hostesses that their phones would be 'safely locked away' for the evening and that boyfriends and girlfriends were not welcome at the venue."

Nina continued, "The uniform requirements are also more detailed: all hostesses should bring "'black sexy shoes', black underwear, and do their hair and make-up as they would to go to a 'smart, sexy place'. Dresses and belts would be supplied on the day. For those who met the three specific selection criteria ('tall, thin and pretty') the job starts at 4 in the afternoon."

Marion added, "Yes, in the Vinery, where a team of hair and make-up artists will prep everyone for the evening ahead. It needs great self-control, because unlike most hostessing assignments — you can drink on the job."

There was a crackling sound." Oh dear, said Bigsy, "That control box seems to have gone on the blink again."

Bigsy did a double check and then signalled to everyone that Minerva would not be able to hear them any longer.

"You know what, though," he said, "There's a perfectly good pub on the river waiting for us to debrief this."

The Horniman

They all left the office and moved to the pub.

Bigsy looked relieved, "Phew, that was some test of my technology and all of our acting skills!" he said, "Cheers everybody!"

They clinked their glasses together. Jake noticed that they were attracting quite a few stares, with the joint power of Christina, Clare, Marion and Nina in their group.

"Do you ever get used to it?" he asked, "The stares, you know…"

"Beautiful women are like flowers," Marion interjects. "They turn to the sun. But if they don't receive a certain amount of attention, they wither."

Jake added, "That simile has an 18th-century feel; it's about manners, after all, which are always most complicated in times of equality."

"I concur," Nina says. "The most attractive women expect an attentive gaze that doesn't imply anything other than someone saying, 'You're attractive enough to gaze at.' And the most rewarding thing is if that gaze is returned."

"What does a returned glance imply?" Bigsy asks.

"It implies," smiled Nina, "As they say in the New York State lottery: Hey - You never know."

Christina looked rueful, "Some women assume the male gaze is sinful, hurtful, and evil; that men can never look at women in a different way. But that's not what the gaze is about. Because a sophisticated man would not hesitate to gaze, and then he might be filled with regret and loss, and therefore gain self-knowledge."

Jake added, "Longing makes us sad, but at least it proves we're still alive. Which is why men like spring so much, for the short time it lasts."

"But did we do it?" asked Bigsy, changing the subject, "Did we make the story interesting enough for the listeners?"

"I can't imagine they wouldn't want to pass it on.," said Jake, "All that stuff about black shoes and sexy underwear - it's too salacious."

"Let's just hope they were recording and believed that bit about the fuse box or whatever it was that Bigsy was talking about," said Clare.

Pete Burr reacts

Pete Burr was listening. He was used to the daily ritual of finding a few files from the Triangle Office, seeing a few people come and go and the ritual of early morning office banter. Then, usually after they had all collected their first coffees from the kitchen, it would all go quiet.

This day was different. The one called Bigsy had found a technical hitch in a cupboard and was triumphantly saying he had fixed it.

That could explain why the recordings had been so weak from the offices.

Some kind of technical overload.

Today's meeting was coming through as clear as a bell. And there were a couple of extra people in the office too.

They seemed to be talking about a big event which was to be held in London.

A fund-raiser of some kind, but with some dubious added attractions.

Pete listened to the recording. There were many moments within it of interest.

- The missing Russian Yegorin's business opportunity, fronted by Maximovich.
- A new pipeline for Celarus.
- An auction for lunch with British politicians.
- That the event would be non-politically correct.
- TV hosts as comperes.
- Black tie event with 300 guests.
- 120 specially hired hostesses, wearing black shoes and told to wear black underwear.
- Jennifer Sussex, of MDA - Miel Doux Agency, to provide the hostesses.
- The Vinery, to prepare everyone with a team of hair and make-up artists.

But shortly after this the recording had stopped. Bigsy was implying that the control unit had failed again.

Pete knew enough to know that the Vinery was in the Lanchester Hotel, a very fashionable hotel in Mayfair. He had visited it once with his then girlfriend, for a company event. The ballroom was like something out of opulent Soviet Russia and the company had thrown quite a party. Yes, Pete could see this being the scene for some Grade-A frolics.

He called to Olivia Lang and she walked over with Emily Karankawa. Pete thought to himself that this could be awkward. He ran through a description of what he had heard, and Olivia looked very interested.

"This could be a great win for us, to bring down Yegorin, who is someone that the UK and Russian authorities have been hunting.

"It could even make up for that business with the American Colonel," added Emily, "You remember, where those two dead Russians were found in his hotel room and he escaped on a Canadian passport."

Pete remembered that although Emily and Olivia were friends, there had been an increased rivalry since Olivia had been slated for promotion but then had it taken away again after the Chuck Manners incident. Emily, on the other hand, had been consistently reliable and was now a grade higher that Olivia. Pete looked at the two women standing next to him. He thought of the description that one of the women in the meeting and used, 'Tall, thin and pretty'.

They both were.

"I've an idea," he said, "You could both infiltrate the event and collect incriminating evidence. Recordings to use as collateral."

They both looked at him, somewhat shocked.

"What, infiltrate as escorts? You have to be kidding?" said Olivia.

"No, think about it for a moment," said Emily, "They need 120 women for that evening. We know where it is, what is expected to go down and even who is hiring the extra support staff. If we wanted to put someone on the inside this could be the way!"

"No, I'm not doing it," said Olivia.

"Okay, I'll find someone else," said Emily, "I know we can make a difference to this operation. I will ask Anne-Marie Bristow."

Pete smiled; he knew Anne-Marie. She fitted the description too. Tall, thin and pretty.

Three of Coins

Teamwork
Collaboration
Building Together

Energy Sector

Back in the office in the Galleria, Bigsy had been busy researching the energy sector in Russia. He'd called everyone together for a PowerPoint presentation of his findings.

"This is terribly formal!" joked Jake.

"Well, there's a lot and I don't want to miss anything," said Bigsy, " I've cut and pasted the web pages into the deck - so it is a bit messy."

He clicked to the first image.

"The present Russian vertical structure of power has clear roots. Today, the political and economic structure in the country is usually referred to as a state corporation or a system of bureaucratic capitalism."

"It's a closed political system which is resistant to foreign attacks, the merging of political and economic elite and strategic areas of the economy controlled by a bureaucratic corporation and isolated from the influence of foreign capital."

"Yes, we were briefed on this when I was back at the Academy," said Christina, "The late Russian oligarch, Boris Berezovsky, said that seven bankers controlled about half the economy of Russia."

"That's right," said Bigsy, "When during Putin's first tenure a new model of government-business relations started forming, the dominance of the so-called oligarchs was replaced by representatives of the political elite who ran the five largest Russian gas, oil, transport and nuclear energy enterprises responsible for one third of the country's GDP. "

He showed a diagram of the enterprises which included a pie chart showing how much of the economy they made up.

Christina added, "I ran security details for some of them when they were meeting foreign businesspeople. Out of that came the term silovak. The term means a system when former members of power structures have high posts in the civil service and also perform important functions in major state companies and therefore can always employ administrative resources when dealing with business competitors. In Britain that clown of yours would say you'd say you have your cake and eat it."

Bigsy moved to the next image, "Yes, that was the trick, enterprises like Gazprom, Transneft, Sberbank, VTB Bank, Rusnano or even Rosneft have members from nearly all groups. Similarly, in the Government or Presidential Administration all clans compete."

Bigsy nodded and move to the next image, "This shows that Putin's Russia signals a new interaction between politics and business, where groups of political elite take over control of major businesses and strengthen the centralisation of the political system, because the idea of a strong Russia is the compulsory unifying element of the entire political elite."

Jake interrupted," So Putin has control and these semi-state businesses are happily skimming away a slice from the top of all the run-rate business."

Bigsy added, "And that's a considerable amount when you think of the types of businesses involved. Oil, Gas, Electricity, Finance."

Christina agreed, "Yes, Putin's policies were aimed at regaining the power from Yeltsin's old-man oligarchs - where necessary crushing the oligarch and substituting one of his own.

"The most English example I can think of was Berezovsky himself, who was exiled to Surrey, where he described that he would mount an opposition to Putin. Instead, in 2013, he was found hanged in his home. Open verdict was declared."

Christina continued "But dig back and you'll find other things. I happen to know he was targeted by FSB hitmen in 2007 and fled the UK on advice from Scotland Yard. Then he came back to the London Hilton where a hitman known to Berezovsky was detained and later deported back to Russia.

"Still with Berezovsky, there's the well-known case of the Polonium 210 killing of Alexander Litvinenko, which happened in 2006. Litvinenko was one of Berezovsky's closest associates and UK government sources suspected a Russian state sponsorship.

"I only know that 'Dmitry K' had been speaking openly about the plan to kill Litvinenko that was intended to 'set an example' as a punishment for a 'traitor'. And then shortly Litvinenko's death Russian Federal Protective Service officer - FSO - Andrei Lugovoy was called back to Russia.

"Then, in 2008, Berezovsky's close friend and long-time business partner billionaire 52-year old Arkady "Badri" Patarkatsishvili, collapsed and died in his bedroom after a family dinner at Downside Manor, his mansion in Leatherhead, Surrey, England."

Christina looked around the room, "Surrey is a dangerous county for Russian exiles. But don't you all look at me like that, this stuff is all known to SI6 and the police. They just have to choose whether to act or not. Sometimes there's a whole domino effect if one person is toppled."

Clare said, "I find it incredible that first Berezovsky's closest associates Litvinenko and Badri are killed and then he is found hanged."

"That is just one story, there are many others, like double agent Sergei Skripal and his daughter Yulia, famously poisoned in Salisbury with Novichok, " answered Christina.

Bigsy flipped the PowerPoint and continued, "The development of political oligarchic capitalism during Putin's rule took a turn towards state capitalism. That is what is happening right now as the Kremlin attempts to crush Yegorin."

Jake nodded, "And Putin made sure that in such a system the private businessmen keep control of their companies, but only after having accepted the fundamental condition – loyalty to the political system and loyalty to Putin."

"So, Putin created the New Society Agreement," said Christina, "With it, the state ensures the immunity of property rights and balance between different interest groups, and businesses pledge loyalty to the state."

Bigsy added, "Yes, it says in this report that Russian models of safe business and politics can be various: private businesses can benefit from 'hidden' protectionism (for example, the largest Russian oil company, Lukoil) or a company can be run by top-level bureaucrats and politicians (or their groups) even though formally it wouldn't be legal. This is how the second largest oil company, Rosneft, operates."

Bigsy found an item on the screen, "When Sechin became Executive Chairman of Rosneft, the company was only ranked sixth in the country in terms of oil extraction.

"But Sechin and Rosneft are said to be the ones who ruined the private company Yukos. Rosneft took over Yukos' main extraction centres and became the second largest oil company in Russia.

Christina nodded, "Yes. The Yukos case served as a message to all independent oligarchs and businesses about the new rule for the games set by the Kremlin.

"Simply, it was, 'Disobey at your peril.'

Christina added, "I was providing security to some of those early enforcement talks. The creation of Putin's ruling system was highly influenced by the state's growing interest in the country's economy and the appointing of politicians to the management of state companies or corporations."

Jake added, "It's not that different from what Raven was trying to do with Bernard Driscoll, nor the ways that the Minerva station is trying to gather Kompromat on British politicians. There must be a similar mechanism operating in Washington D.C. and targeted at the American establishment."

Christina continued, "That's where Putin has the leverage to control the competition between different groups of the political elite. And the control he uses to guarantee stability is corruption.

"In order to create a loyalty system and decrease the risk or regional separatism, he made a double move: on the one hand, he created the relations between annuity receivers and providers, on the other hand, he drastically expanded the bureaucratic apparatus – from 2000 till 2012 he increased the number of bureaucrats by 65%.

Christina added, "That price of corrupt relations is a sum equal to 17% of Russia's GDP. Nearly as much as the UK's VAT."

"What? and all of it is payola?" asked Jake, "The skimmed money is going straight into the pockets of the Russian elite?"

"Exactly," said Christina, "And then, in turn, to buy football clubs, shopping centres and large-scale apartment blocks in the west. Notably in London, but plenty of other spots as well. London is just, well, decidedly friendly towards the influx of money."

"That's right," said Bigsy, " I thought London was turning into Little Beijing, but it's still Little Moscow at the moment. All these Russians have their families living somewhere in London."

Christina added, "But when they say they need to crush someone in the name of patriotism, they say it sincerely. It's just that if it's London they're targeting, they will get their families out first."

Bigsy put up a London map, "There's plenty of well-heeled Russians living in London now, he said, Let's just zoom in on the Queen's back-garden."

He put up an aerial shot.

"Kensington Palace Gardens. Just behind Buckingham Palace, it includes Kensington Palace where Wills and Katie hang out. But look at their street. Compound of the Russian Embassy. Leonard Blavatnik, Roman Abramovich. The neighbours include the Mittals - the richest man in Britain and the Ecclestones, complete with their car turntable to avoid reversing.

Then he flipped to another chart, "A few years ago, an analysis by estate agency Knight Frank estimated that almost a tenth of all buyers at the top end of the London market came from the former Soviet Union. Rival estate agents Savills calculated that Russians like to buy the biggest houses of any group of purchasers. Average house prices in Kensington have risen eightfold over the past two decades, at least partly thanks to the influx from Russia.

"In 2011, a Ukrainian bought the world's most expensive flat – the penthouse at One Hyde Park – for £136.4m. Five months later, a Russian bought Park Place, a stately home near Henley-on-Thames, for £140m. Russians who acquired homes valued merely in the tens of millions barely deserved notice.

"Among those lesser buyers was a banker who moved to London in 2008. He and his family came on tier 1 investor visas, which provide successful applicants with residency in exchange for an investment (of, at the time, £1m) in government bonds.

"Over eight years Russian citizens made up 764 of the 3,396 people who paid for these so-called golden visas – making them the second largest group of applicants, after Chinese citizens.

"Of course, I don't have up-to-date figures and with the recent turmoil in the world I suspect things are changing, but it is still a good general indicator."

"So, live in London on proceeds from State crime in Moscow?" asked Clare.

Christina added, "I used to overhear people talking, when I was on security detail. They used to say - with absolute sincerity – how great it is they can get so rich in

Moscow. They go and work for the state to earn money. Ministers hand out licences to make money. And of course all this comes from the boss …

"The first conversation Putin has with a new state employee is, 'Here is your business. Share it only with me. If someone attacks you, I will defend you … and if you don't use your position as a business you are an idiot.' "

"These are now like people who have drunk blood. They can't stop. Now it is state officials who are the businessmen."

Moving parts

"There's a lot of moving parts to this," said Christina, "For one thing, we will need something to warrant Amanda being able to send in some heavies. Look, I don't want to risk asking my handler to get something. It will likely leak back that there is something happening."

"To insulate Amanda from this, I guess we'll need to use Chuck," said Jake, "Who has gone back into hiding."

"Not necessarily," said Bigsy, "Remember our old agreement regarding the website, where we can essentially call him like Batman?"

"Oh yes, I had almost forgotten about that," said Clare, "We should use it now. What was it we have to mention - A Square?"

Bigsy nodded, "Yes that's right. I will work it onto the home page. I'm quite sure that Chuck will see it."

"Then, who and how will we get to the event?" asked Christina, "I guess I can ask Antanov again, but I really don't want to get him involved."

"Maybe he could get us the invitation. We could send someone else in his place and you, Christina, could be the plus one. At least you will know what to expect."

"Good idea," agreed Christina, "You know, no offence, but I think this would be a good play for Chuck. He'd know how to handle himself if things got tricky."

"What about Marion and Nina?" asked Clare, "Won't they get invited anyway?"

"Yes, I expect they will, but I think we should not implicate them further. After all, they tipped us off about this."

"So how do we get close to the action? Invited into the main auction?"

"I don't know. If it is like the Ladies' Day, they will run it in the main event, but I have a feeling that for this there will be a side room somewhere and an extra layer of security, probably run buy Vassily Turgenev."

"Turgenev plays hard-ball, so I think we should be prepared for Amanda's team to help in that area," said

Christina, "We'll just need the reasons for Amanda arriving with force."

"I think you'll need some special comms too," said Bigsy, "I've been tinkering with some new walkie-talkies recently. They use Tetra, which is the same stuff as the police and emergency services, except there's all these extra bands. I think we could use a few slim-line hand sets for this mission."

"I thought Tetra made milk- cartons," said Clare.

Bigsy replied "No that's Tetrapak. Tetra is radio designed for use by government agencies, emergency services, for public safety networks, trains, transport, and the military because it keeps on working and goes through walls and tunnels and so on. To make it work properly, we will need to install a base station in a store cupboard or somewhere around the meeting zone. Then everyone, even the military, will be able to use it, provided we divulge our secret channel and key."

"That sound very useful," said Christina, "Now we just need the just cause for Amanda to go barging in!"

Two-helicopter household

Amanda had asked Grace Fielding at GCHQ to dig around on Yegorin. She called back on a video link.

"Hi," Grace smiled, "More about your mysterious Russians. Yegorin first gained French citizenship in 2009, and knew French law protected its citizens from extradition to Russia.

"Then he fled to the relative safety of his villa high in the hills above the bay of Nice, a fortress surrounded by an impenetrable high iron fence, a team of bodyguards and a battery of security cameras at every turn.

"Of course, he still had the entire French Riviera on his doorstep, so it was hardly a hardship to be in exile. Notably, he had a couple of helicopters, and would cross over to Nice Airport to fly to European capitals whenever he felt the need. We obtained the flight logs and he makes extensive use of the facility."

"A two-helicopter household?" asked Amanda.

"Yes, one for the family, silly. The villa is really high in the hills. Pretty but isolated," Grace smiled, "It was the arrival of Moscow rules in London, where the Kremlin could twist the legal process to suit its agenda, where the larger issue of expropriation of Yegorin's multi-billion-dollar business empire could be buried in the detail of rules."

"Lawyers tying people in knots?"

"Yes and getting rich in the process."

"Of course, Yegorin was no angel- in fact, he was one of the very bad people in the lead-up to Putin's power."

"But he's been erased from the photographs now?"

"Exactly, you'd be hard pressed to know he even existed. Curiously enough, Berezovsky gets most of the 'credit' for Putin's rise."

"And then there is the little matter of the missing money. It was not at all clear what had happened to the $700 million he'd been accused of siphoning from Mezhkommbank.

"A New Zealand trust he'd set up to hold tens of millions of dollars in properties, including his Chelsea home, was later found to be a sham."

Amanda said, "For all his flaws Yegorin insisted he had been caught in a Russian state vendetta pursued through the UK courts. The Kremlin seemed intent on quashing any notion that he'd ever been well-connected in the Kremlin, or that he could have any knowledge that could be damaging to it?"

Grace replied, "The people I have spoken to just say he was a blatant crook. But Yegorin had worked at the heart of the Kremlin and had been privy to some of its deepest secrets, including how it was exactly that Putin came to power.

"He literally knows where the bodies are buried."

"That's why the Kremlin is after him, then."

"To be honest, I'm amazed they haven't sent him a polonium parcel by now," said Grace.

"I'm equally amazed that he thinks he can make a comeback from this position."

Incoming

Jake's phone beeped; an incoming text.

"What's the matter, can't get enough of me?" asked Chuck in a text to Jake.

"Hi Chuck, we think you are in the clear now over that fake news about the Institute bombing. How would you like to get even? We've found the culprits and are planning to bring them down."

"Okay," said Chuck, "Let me get to you, New office isn't it?"

"Yes," replied Jake, "Let me send the address."

...

Ed Adams

Page of Coins

Ambition
Desire
Diligence
Craving New Venture

Carrying

Pete Burr was quite excited at the prospect of going on an assignment. It sounded as if it was to be to one of the most politically incorrect events in London for the coming year.

He'd had to draw a compromise, though.

When Emily Karankawa and Anne-Marie Bristow had applied to Miel Doux Agency, they had been accepted straight away, especially with their back-stories about working in public relations for a call centre. He had been a much tougher sell. MDA wanted females for the event. Initially he was turned down, but then it transpired that MDA wanted 12 men as well as the women. He had been shortlisted for a call-back and had to answer one awkward question about his orientation.

But he was now in and could go with the two women to the event. There was a strength in numbers which he was sure would prove useful.

The three of them had all proved somewhat sheepish about revealing their plans to Minerva. But if it worked the way they hoped, they were sure that they would each get a promotion.

They had also worked out how they would gather information. They had acquired some voice recorders which looked like USB sticks and could be attached to their key rings. They were perfect for the task and would not be confiscated by security in the way that a mobile phone might be.

Pete received the same information as the ladies about what to wear for the event. He was also expected to show up at 4pm, for an event that started some three hours later.

Chuck arrives at the office

"It's Chuck!" called Jake, excited to hear that Chuck was downstairs in the lobby of their offices.

"He's on his way up."

Chuck arrived, gave a brief slap on the back to Jake and asked," So what it this about? I guess you are still dealing with that Raven crowd?"

They walked into the office area and he greeted each of them with a smile, saving a smiling salute for Christina.

"So what is the mission?" he asked, looking at Jake.

"Well, it's party time," began Jake, "Gavy Yegorin will be in town at the party being hosted by Tima Maximovich, who is the Head of Russian Infrastructure. Here's the twist. Maximovich's usually enforcer is Vassily Turgenev, who is being loaned to Yegorin to securely manage the evening. Turgenev is the person who sent gunmen after you."

"Okay, I can see that," said Chuck, " But what is the purpose of the party? Not just for old times' sake?"

"No, it is to look for backers for an oil pipeline project in Celarus, to add to the investment to be made by Yegorin."

"That sounds distinctly dicey," said Chuck, "Yegorin is betting against the Russian state."

"He is, but he is also being hunted by them. This would be a fantastic way for him to throw a huge spanner in the works. If he can build the pipeline, then the Russians will lose a substantial slice of energy business."

"Energy business which the Kremlin oligarchs skim to make their own private money?" guessed Chuck.

"Exactly," said Jake.

"So, it is likely to be backed by others on the Kremlin hit list. As Putin is tidying the Kremlin, there must still be people who are looking over their shoulders, even now."

"Yes, although we think Yegorin will want look further afield. Non-Russian backers too. We think he has asked Maximovich to use his Masonic connections to pull in a wider audience. He went to Michael Tovey, MP to set up the invitations. Tovey suggested the same facilitators as at Raven's Ladies Day. ISMC seem to be handling the production of the event again, although it can't be with Gerhardt nor Frobisher."

"Why would Maximovich do this? - Get involved - I thought he was still in with the in-crowd at the Kremlin?"

"Yes, we thought so too," said Christina, "It is possible that Maximovich is trying to smoke out some of Yegorin's allies, which would make it easier for the Kremlin to know who to go after."

"So, I assume you involved Amanda Miller in this?" asked Chuck.

Jake added, "Oh yes, and she says she will bring SAS troops along. But, she says she will need a sound reason to intervene, like they are plotting a coup, or have some signs of terrorism in the building."

"What something like guns or explosives?" asked Chuck.

Jake nodded.

"Did I mention where I've been visiting?" said Chuck, "I needed to top up my supply of olives and hummus."

"Middle east?" hazarded Bigsy, "Or Borough Market?"

"Ha ha. It was Jordan and I discovered a little something extra whilst I was there. The Russians have been supplying Jordan with Barkas."

"What is it, a type of clothing?" asked Clare.

"No, it's a weapon," said Christina, "A hand-held grenade launcher. Very compact and made in Russia. Based on the RPG-32, I seem to remember."

"Top marks," said Chuck, "The Russian company Bazalt made them, but now supplies them as assembly kits to Jordan. They are called Nashshab in Jordan. They like them so much they built their own factory to manufacture them."

"And they are easy to get hold of?" asked Christina smirking.

"Let's just say the Jordanian security at the factory is a little less reliable than that in Russia."

"Chuck, does that mean you've brought a grenade launcher to London?" asked Jake, somewhat incredulous.

"No - I didn't bring it, I had it shipped, complete with Lithium battery warning stickers on it."

"You don't intend to use it at the party?" asked Clare still looking alarmed.

"No, I think it will make a remarkably interesting accessory though, something for Amanda Miller's people to find. The beauty of it is that the whole RPG-32 is small and would easily fit into a cupboard, with a couple of defused grenades. We can get it in a small wheeled suitcase."

"Excellent," said Clare, "Not that I'm condoning bringing high explosive into prestigious central London hotels, but this does ensure that Amanda can bring her SAS posse into town."

Jake said, "Now Chuck, we'll need you in a tuxedo for this event. Properly James Bond. Christina arranged for you to go along, under Antanov's name - Antanov Chekeryn. Antanov is a senior mason and used his contact with Michael Tovey to get us two invitations to the event. That's for you and Christina."

"So, I'll be going with Christina? Well, that will set the tongues wagging!"

Christina smiled, "And I assume we'll both be carrying?"

"Possibly," smiled Chuck, "Will you have that fancy little handbag of yours?"

"Possibly," smiled Christina in return

Part Three – Riddle of One

The Hangman's Beautiful Daughter

The natural cards revolve ever changing
Seeded elsewhere planted in the garden fair
Grow trees, grow trees

Tongues of the sheer wind
Setting your foot where the sand is untrodden
The ocean that only begins
…
Earth water fire and air
Met together in a garden fair
Put in a basket bound with skin
If you answer this riddle
If you answer this riddle
You'll never begin

Robin Williamson

Tower

Upheaval
Disaster
Foundational Shift

Through the Yard of Blonde Girls

Pete Burr arrived at the Lanchester. He was a little early but had black shoes and rather self-consciously he'd been out and bought some new black underwear. It has cost him a small fortune, because he'd first bought Hugo Boss. A three pack had cost him £36, but when he'd tried them on, he realised that the logo was vastly too prominent in white around the waist-line. Then he'd bought another set of three Armani boxers. They had the logo on the side, in a contrasting colour, but it was, at least, grey. He'd worked out that it had cost him £72 to get one serviceable boxer brief.

Now he was inside the Vinery, where everyone was to get ready. It was already busy in the room and several of the women were unselfconsciously changing into their evening outfits. The women had all been provided with the same outfits. A black dress, with a wide belt and see-through side panels. He noticed that some women were given red shoes instead of the black ones they had been asked to bring.

Then he noticed that a few of the women were asked to wear a different outfit. A black, sleeveless top, with a white collar and impossibly tiny shorts, together with a black leather belt. Then he saw one of the other men and he realised that the shorts outfit worn by the women was the same one that they expected the men to wear.

"Don't freak out!" said Emily laughing. She had just walked into the same scene of chaos, "You know you have the legs for it!"

Pete was taken away by one of the makeup artists. "My name is Lucy," she said, "Not bad, but I'll need to see your legs." A few minutes later Pete found himself in the outfit and Lucy peering at his legs.

"It's gonna have to go," said Lucy, and switched on a hair trimmer, "Usually I'd suggest wax, but we haven't got time here, so we'll use this and then some spray tan over there."

Another woman approached and left a box of disposable boxers for spray tanning. Pete was thinking about how little of this he had suspected a mere half hour ago.

"I see you are almost done," called over another guy, with blonde spiky hair. "It's a great way to get a makeover!"

Pete decided he'd not ever seen this many almost naked women at one time. Now he had to cross in front of them to the tanning area. That old Jeff Buckley song was flittering through his mind.

'Through the yard, through the yard of blonde girls.

Through the river and the sea.
Gold sharks glittering.'

Mercifully, he noticed that there was one booth marked 'Men' and several marked 'Women'. He was soon sprayed a uniform tanned colour and emerged, after cautiously putting his shorts and shirt back on.

'You've got innocence in your eyes.
Even in this world of lies, you're still hopeful.
Very sexy. Okay, okay.
Fear we may come.
Fear we may come.'

"You are lucky," said Lucy, "You get to wear flats. This outfit has white deck shoes. Go over there and collect some."

'Fear we may come.
Fear we may come.
So run, run, run, run, run, run, run.'

Lori Kramer and Audrey Clark must have attended something similar he was thinking.

He could see that Lucy was rushed off her feet as more of the hosts had started to arrive. He looked at his watch. It was only just four o'clock. Things were going to get busier. Then, as he walked back to a table with some bottled water, he caught a glimpse of himself in a long mirror.

"Oh. My. God," he thought, "This seemed like such a good idea."

To stay focused, he imagined Jeff Buckley's guitar sizzling and swirling and the way Buckley pronounced 'glittering' the second time.

Anne-Marie and Emily came across and joined him. They now looked almost like a stage act in the outfits that had been provided. He noticed that Anne-Marie looked a little tearful.

"This is exploitation on a grand scale," she said, "I'm shocked - this would never happen in Washington."

"I'm not so sure," said Emily, "There's a planet of lively bars between F and H Street and around the Logan Circle."

Anne-Marie looked back, "Despite living in D.C. I have only ever been to the H Street Festival in that area. It's a bit too edgy at night - I'll take your word for the misadventures!" she said. The others noticed she looked a little brighter.

"Oh and there's that Mansion on O - you must have been there?" asked Emily.

Anne-Marie replied, "I have - we went there as a family once. A whole row of houses knocked into one and then filled fit to bursting with artworks. I remember seeing some Lennon and a Janice Joplin piece and a couple of famous guitars, plus paintings and books, it was incredible - and exhausting in a good way!"

Lucy came over, "Time for the talk - No offline arrangements, no gratuities, no handling, you can drink as much as you like; this has to look disreputable but maintain a high standard. You get any trouble, find one of the women in red shoes, they will help you get out of it. It will get more ragged as the night runs. Think about the average man powered by two litres of wine - you have to be sweet as you tell them to sit down. Now put on these wrist bands."

She looked at Pete, "And the same rules for the men. Now practice smiling and looking happy, everyone!"

Bolo

It was arrival time at the event. Chuck and Christina climbed from their taxi and made their way to the main line for entry. Christina had decided to wear the same blue gown that she wore to Raven's Ladies Night, but this time with a bright red sash.

Chuck had already told her how stunning she looked. "And Chuck, you look very dashing in the tuxedo, said Christina. "I like the American touch of the bootlace tie."

"It's called a Bolo actually," said Chuck, "I got this one when I was in Albuquerque."

"I love the turquoise stone and the red and black motif on the surround," said Christina.

"Yes, it's quite powerful Navajo symbolism, I got it from my friend Tom, - his real name is Atsa Tahoma - that's

'Eagle by the Water's Edge' - Bigsy and Clare have met him, we were all in the desert together at the time."

They both looked at the line. Christina looked in her Mulberry bag. "Here, put this on," she said. It was the insignia that Antanov had left in her apartment when he moved out. Christina knew it signified high Masonic rank.

Chuck clipped it to his jacket and almost immediately a man approached him.

"Would you like to come this way?"

Chuck nodded and the two of them walked around to a side entrance. Christina was used to this now, although this time she noticed there seemed to be some heavier duty security on the doors. She could sense that one of the guards had a pistol too and caught in Chuck's eyes that he had the same thought.

To Christina's surprise, they were whisked past the security and directly into the event. Once again, the side entrance had jumped the queue and they were already in the thick of the reception.

"We'll need to find our table," whispered Christina. She noticed Chuck was checking the number of exits from the room and the likely location of any side rooms. She was doing the same and when she found their table she briefly walked across to take a look.

"We'll rotate ourselves 90 degrees, then we have a view across the whole room, she said and moved the name tags from the table to adjacent positions.

"There," she said, "That's much better."

Then she took her phone and surreptitiously took a snap of the entire table plan for the room.

A band struck up a fanfare, and then a Toastmaster walked out. He brought everyone to order and asked that they applaud the hostesses, who would be coming out right now.

More music as 'Good as Hell' by Lizzo blasted from the speakers and the hostesses sprang out, accompanied by cheers and whoops from the attendees. To Chuck's eye, they were all pretty although he could see that many looked as if they were students trying to earn a buck.

Christina noticed one in particular. She was Anne-Marie from the Minerva station. The plan back at the Triangle offices when they staged their mini play script had obviously worked. Christina wondered just how many from Minerva were present.

Emil Pozharsky

The Toastmaster had urged them all to be seated. Christina noticed that this event skipped the formality of the Ladies' Night.

She was on a table with Chuck and six others. Two of the couples were chatting to one another in Russian. The two men were talking about Maximovich's offer and commenting that the last time he'd suggested something the return for investors was an almost instant doubling in the share price.

She decided to speak to one of the wives. These women looked like wives rather than escorts provided by Miel Doux Agency. "This is quite an event!" said Christina brightly to one of the women.

"Yes, Emil insisted we come over specially for it," answered the woman, "We came in from Nice last night.

We are staying in this very hotel, so it won't be a long journey after the event," she said, "I'm Marisha and these are our friends Lev and Karine Oblonsky"

Marisha looked at Christina's brooch. "That's a very pretty brooch," she said, "Where did you get it?"

"Oh, my partner got it," said Christina alluding to Chuck, "He's quite high up in - you know - the Masons." She gestured towards Chuck and the insignia pinned to his jacket."

"Oh, I see, I don't think Emil has realised, let me nudge him."

She spoke some Russian to her husband, who suddenly looked around startled, "My goodness, My name is Emil Pozharsky - I had no idea, let me welcome you, I am in the Nizhny Novgorod Masonic Temple although nowadays I spend a good deal of my time in France."

Chuck smiled, "Nizhny Novgorod, ah yes, home of Maxim Gorky. But surely you should join the French Masons if you spend much time there?"

"I know, I should, but thankfully my contacts via Nizhny are sufficient, and still get me invited to this lovely event."

Chuck and Christina realised, but were too polite to say, that Emil Pozharsky and Lev Oblonsky must be others of the exiled Russians, in a comparable situation to Yegorin. Maybe there were seeds of an uprising against the Kremlin's use of strong arm tactics?

See Emily play

Emily had been paying attention since the event started. There were many people present and to her surprise many of the men had brought their wives. She wondered how much this would cramp the style of the others, but to be honest, she was rather pleased.

She had been allocated a table which contained two married couples and two other men who were with escorts. Behind her was a pair of large exit doors and in front of them stood a security man.

Her job was playfully keeping the table served and to be jolly at all times. There was an outer circuit of red-shoed hostesses whose role seemed to be to ensure the black-shoed hostesses were occupied all of the time, but that the guests were not crossing the line.

Between courses there was entertainment and a rather crude comedian had just come on.

Emily regarded it as respite and could look over to where Pete was looking similarly relieved. So far, she didn't think they had managed to find much of interest for their recordings. She looked further around the room but could not work out where Anne-Marie had gone. She must be working behind the scenes or something.

Emily decided that the lull while the comedian was on would be a good opportunity to look around. She carefully snuck over to the big double doors, pressed the bar and was soon in the outer corridor, itself a wide space capable of holding most of the participants that were now seated in the event.

She looked across the way and saw another door, which she entered. A small side-lit room, but with a coffee station ready for use. She was about to pour a coffee when she heard a noise behind her. It was the security guard from outside. He had followed her into the room.

Now she had to decide what to do. He approached her and she could only think to smile. Then he grasped her around the waist, and she realised what was on his mind.

There was a click as the other door to the small room opened.

"Vassily!" said the guard, "Yes, Igor, what are you doing away from your station with this pretty little thing? Didn't you read the emails? You know that the second ballroom is being used for the auction and that it starts in about five minutes?"

"And you, what is your name?"

"Emily," she answered.

"Well Emily, I think you had better accompany me into the other ballroom. We cannot have you telling everyone what is going on before we've had the meeting. But do not worry. We'll find a few more like you to join us after the meeting."

Emily followed Vassily Turgenev into the second large room. It was another ballroom but this one had been set up with chairs and tables in rows. Each table separated from others with a total of around 50 tables in the room.

Emily noticed several of what she assumed to be Turgenev's 'heavies' spread around the perimeter of the room. She resigned herself to being stuck in this room until after the auction or whatever took place.

Wheel

Fate
Karma
Destiny
Fortune Cycles

Criticism

"So why did you come over for this event?" asked Christina, looking first to Lev and then to Emil.

Lev Oblonsky replied, "For me, my entire life, the truth was equivalent to freedom. I earned money not for riches, but for freedom. How much can you really spend? But a certain independence gave me one thing: I don't need to lie."

This all sounded too good to be true to Christina. She wondered what was coming next.

But as the conversation continued, it became apparent the two men believed that the president had become surrounded by yes-men, all of whom proffered lengthy toasts to Putin, telling him he had been sent by God to save the country, while they served at his pleasure.

Yet it seemed to Oblonsky that these yes-men understood the deep hypocrisy of the system, the sham democracy represented by the Kremlin's ruling party, United Russia, and how deeply corrupt it had become.

"Look at the people around VV – that's Putin - who say Vladimir Vladimirovich, you're a genius!" Oblonsky continued, "I look at them—but realise that they don't believe in anything."

Emil Pozharsky added, "These new men understand it's all crap. United Russia is crap, elections are rigged, even the president is a gangster. They know all this, but then they go on stage and say how great everything is. They make toasts which are also total crap, total lies."

Chuck interrupted, "Do you think you should say these kinds of things in here? Someone might be listening."

Emil said, "No, this is the one place we can say these things. We've come along here tonight to support Yegorin. He's being chased by the Kremlin. The latest in a long line of people positioned to fall under the wheels."

Lev said, "Yes, these bratva gangsters sit and tell stories about how they have always been together, ever since they were sitting on the school-bench.

Emil added, "But at the same time the guys sitting in the office next door are saying, 'As soon as he comes out, let's finish him off.' It could be financial ruin, a death threat to his family, a murder or a staged suicide."

Lev said, "The ones who have power are stealing from all sides, and then they come out and speak about how Putin is fighting against corruption. I look at them and think, this is the end. VV was always asking, "What is that word beginning with s? Sovest – conscience."

Emil added, "They don't have time for conscience. They don't understand it. They forgot the word and what it means. They've gotten totally messed up."

Chuck looked intrigued, "But aren't there people here who are part of that system?" He asked, "Ruthless, and conscience free?"

Lev nodded, "Yes, I'm not sure why Yegorin is using Vassily Turgenev's people here for security tonight. They are people that will push you off a building and then go for a cool beer. To be honest, if I'd known that then I might not have come along."

Karine looked at Marishe, then said to Lev, "Lapochka, don't get too wound up about all of this. Like you said on the way here, we can always just leave if we don't like it."

Christina smiled at the use of Lapochka - sweetie pie - when Karine spoke to Lev.

Lev continued, "All the achievements of the Putin era so far—the economic growth, the increase in incomes, the riches of the billionaires that had turned Moscow into a gleaming metropolis where sleek foreign cars filled the streets and cosy cafés opened on street corners—boiled down to the sharp increase in the oil price during the Putin years, they agree."

Chuck asked, "But hasn't it got more difficult now? The Americans, The Saudis, NAFTA, manipulating the prices and disadvantaging Russia?"

Emil interjected, "In the 2000s, the oil price was $50 to $70, and we were happy. Then when it topped $150 the only thing they decided was to skim even more from the top. Enough skimming to buy stacks of apartments in

London or villas on the French Riviera. The state is doing nothing with the money. They could have transformed the country's infrastructure. But everything, all the money, all the materials, will be stolen if we build roads. Oligarchs put it into property because it makes it difficult to steal."

Lev continued, "In the 2000s we gave the boss such a smoothly oiled machine. Everything worked. And what did we get? We didn't understand that he wasn't going to drive things forward. I thought he was liberal, young"

Emil said, "But it turned out he was from a different species."

 Lev agreed, "Yes. They are different people. They are different, special people. This was something we didn't understand. The person who understood this very well was the prosecutor general."

Christina interrupted, "But surely for people to turn out this way they would have needed some special indoctrination?"

"Oh yes," said Emil, "The Akademies, which took the young children away and indoctrinated them. They learned how to play fast and loose with the truth and with many kinds of weapon and fighting skill. Probably most of Vassily's people have come through the Academy structure."

Lev said, "That's right. They had a tiered system. There were 'the grunts' who were the strong arms for enforcement. Then the more able people were made into various agent types and embedded. The elite were promoted and given code names and a licence to operate anywhere, often on fake papers."

Lev said, "Yes, the prosecutor general told me, 'You understand, the guys from the security services, they are different. Even if you were to suck all their blood out and then put on a different head, they would still be different. They live in their own system. You will never be one of them. It is an absolutely different system.' I'm afraid that it is where Vassily Turgenev comes from."

Chuck asked, "So Turgenev is a necessary evil?"

Lev said, "No, he is only plain evil. He has left a trail of bloodshed wherever he visits. I won't be surprised tomorrow to read about some kind of shoot-out in London if he is here running security."

Emil said, "The KGB - nowadays called the FSB and the GRU - had forged an alliance with Russian organised crime long ago, on the eve of the Soviet collapse, when billions of dollars' worth of precious metals, oil and other commodities was transferred from the state to firms linked to the KGB."

"So, it was all planned then?" asked Chuck.

Emil continued, "Right from the start, foreign-intelligence operatives of the KGB sought to accumulate black cash to maintain and preserve influence networks long thought demolished by the Soviet collapse. They would run secret meetings protected by the very best security and cut deals about how many percent they would take off the top."

Lev said, "Yes, It's true that for a time under Yeltsin the forces of the KGB stayed hidden in the background. But when Putin rose to power, the alliance between the KGB and organised crime emerged and bared its teeth."

"Are we sitting in the jaws this evening?" asked Chuck.

Anne-Marie is worried

The event continued. Chuck and Christina watched as everyone enjoyed fine wine, good food and dubious comedy acts. Then a band was announced. They would be playing a set for around 40 minutes.

Chuck and Christina looked around. This was surely the time when some of the 'investors' would be scooped up and shown to another session.

"Hello," said someone in Christina's ear, "I think we've met before."

Christina turned. It was Anne-Marie in her hostess outfit. Christina had to make a snap decision whether to blank her or not. One look at her face and she decided she would talk.

"Yes, but I think this place is a lot more dangerous than Wagamama's restaurant," she said, referring to where they had previously met.

"Look, I'm worried, can we talk, please?" Christina noticed how American Anne-Marie sounded.

"Let me introduce you to my colleague, he is also American."

Chuck turned and said, "Hello little darlin' what seems to be the matter?" He could see Anne-Marie almost burst into tears.

"Look I've got to keep busy," said Anne-Marie, or the women with the red shoes will be over. Can you look like you are asking me something?"

"Yes, in that case I demand that you show me the way to the ladies rest-room," said Christina, " I want you to accompany me the whole way there and then wait whilst I re-apply my lip liner."

Chuck smiled. This wasn't what he'd joined the US Marines for.

The three of them made their way outside, Christina looked suitably unapproachable and Chuck quietly glowered as he followed them. It had all the theatre of a domestic dispute being handled by one of the hostesses.

They made their way to the rest room and Christina pulled Chuck inside.

"Chuck, get in the cubicle, so you can hear us, but if we are disturbed, you'll be hidden," said Christina. Chuck guffawed as he locked himself into the cubicle.

"Okay, now tell me what is going on," said Christina, "Don't tell me you are involved with all of this?"

"Yes, I am. Look, you know I work for the CIA out at Minerva listening station. We heard that there was to be some sort of deal constructed here tonight, fronted by one bad Russian and supported by another. It links up with Brant and the work that is going on in Celarus. I came along with two of my colleagues to find out what was happening."

"Now, one of my colleagues, a friend named Emily has been apprehended by the security here. I know because I followed her when she went out to snoop around. She didn't know I was following but was soon caught by a guard, who put his hands all over her. Then I saw her being taken through into another room - it is the second ballroom - this place is huge.

"They said they would keep her there until after the meeting had taken place. They said it would be in a few minutes, so I ran back outside. That's when I recognised Katarina here. She was around at Minerva with Anna a couple of weeks ago." She sounded breathless as she continued.

"I knew, from what you had said that you were good in a tough situation and frankly I didn't have anyone else to turn to."

Chuck's voice came from the other side of the stall door. "Anne-Marie you have done so many things wrong. Things that would never stack up in a CIA agent's field book. Fortunately, this time you have struck lucky, so I think we will be able to help you."

"You said two of your colleagues. Where is the other one?" asked Christina.

"I don't know," answered Anne-Marie, "He's one of the men hosts here. He has on a tiny black top and some white micro shorts. There's only about twelve of them here. I guess I'd describe him as the one who looks most like a fish out of water,"

"No good," said Christina, "You'll have to find him yourself, I assume he is still in the main room. We're going to the other ballroom and will keep a lookout for Emily. Is she dressed like you?"

"Yes, and with long dark brown hair."

Christina called to Chuck, "You got that, let's get moving."

Chuck opened the stall and came out. He made directly for the door of the restroom.

"Wait!" hissed Christine, "Let me look first. Okay it's clear."

 Chuck was once again aware of Christina's guardian powers as all three of them emerged into a dark corridor and walked back towards the two ballrooms.

Dry run

Emily sat at the back and watched the second ballroom fill up. The security officer Igor was being kept busy by a door. Emily had already decided she would need to get away from him. She hoped that Anna-Marie or Pete would have noticed that she had gone.

She was sitting close to a small group of men, who were talking about the event. She decided that they were the organisers and finalising who would say what. Then a woman appeared, "Hello Trudi," said one of the men, "Hello Miller, you've been over here all the while?" she asked.

"Yes, Gentlemen- I'm Miller McDonald and this is Trudi Hartmann, from my Company ISMC."

"Ah, we have heard much about you," said one of the men, "My name is Khramov Gavril Yegorin, but you can call me Gavy."

"And I'm Timur Maximovich, call me Tima." said another man.

"And hello again, "said the last man, "You'll remember when we met at The House of Commons, Michael Tovey,"

"Ah yes the Member of Parliament, " said Trudi, "I'm pleased to meet you all."

"Let us check the running order then," said Miller McDonald.

Emily sat quietly, at least she should be getting all of this recorded on her covert microphone.

"I'll briefly open and then pass over to Trudi. She will paint a picture of the fantastic opportunity which this presents to this privileged audience."

"Then Michael can add something about what this means to the UK, getting the security of a pipeline to ensure regulated energy costs into Europe with the bolstered stability to the UK."

"I'd like to remind people that Brant is a spin off from the British Company Raven, too"

"Yes, although, strictly speaking Brant is Belgian," said Miller McDonald.

"Yes, but a British angle will go down well in the sales pitch," said Tovey.

"Right, then who? One of you Russian gentleman, I think. And this section should be partly in Russian too. You can recap over what has already been said and then add any additional Russian points as well. I suggest Tima presents the case, and we keep Gavy in reserve."

Tima looked at Gavy. "Are you okay with that?" he asked, "Yes, I know why, the Kremlin's ceaseless chasing of me won't do our case any good. It's better to come from you, Gavy."

"Right, that's settled, then when Gavy finishes I'll take over again and explain to everyone what they need to do. We'll have prospectuses and other paperwork stacked up at the back of the room."

Emily knew right away that the meeting had been rehearsed by Miller McDonald, Trudi Hartmann and Michael Tovey and that the others were being used to bring in 'colour and texture'. It was a setup.

King of Swords

Head over heart
Truth
Discipline

Tetra codes

Outside the meeting, Bigsy had been using the communication gear to listen to what had been happening. He had booked into the Lanchester the previous day and even arranged on-site parking for his small van.

The van was a 'Bigsy special', kitted out with a Tetra repeater station and several concealed microphones spread around the hotel. He had used his best High-Visibility jacket to walk the various devices in after Turgenev's people had run their sweep of the floor.

Additionally, he had had to improvise a cleaning bucket to contain the RPG-32 which Chuck had provided. Bigsy had never seen one of these grenade launchers before, but Chuck had assured him it was safe and that the detonators for the grenades had been removed in any case.

Bigsy had put the device in a cleaning cupboard, behind a row of cleaning products. He thought it was well-enough hidden for 24 hours unless the whole hotel went on a sudden cleaning rampage.

Bigsy sat in the back of the van with Clare and Jake. They had direct communication to Amanda and in turn Amanda was using the same Tetra communications to talk to the SAS soldiers parked around the corner from the hotel.

Amanda had retrieved a plan of the Lanchester, and the soldiers also had a copy. The exact position of the concealed grenade launcher was explained to the SAS team and the two ballrooms were both known together with the ways in and out.

All it would take now was a coded signal from Christina and they would deploy.

Sell it loud

It was time for the start of the principal event. The dinner had been served and now the investor recruits had been shepherded towards the second ballroom. Inside the ballroom, Emily realised that only a small percentage of the attendees were being invited and considered that the rest of the event must have been a camouflage to get these investors in.

Just outside, Chuck and Christina were drawing similar conclusions. They had to make a speedy decision about whether to be inside or outside of the event. They both decided it would be better for them to be inside but seated near to the back. Anne-Marie had pointed to Emily inside the room, although they both realised, she seemed to be the only hostess present.

"You'd better stay outside," urged Christina, "It will draw too much attention if you go inside."

They slipped in thought the doors, noticing that the security people were present at each exit from the room. Christina estimated that the security detail were all carrying concealed handguns, by the way they fidgeted with what were probably underarm holsters.

"Give the security detail the job of preventing pistols and what do they do?" whispered Chuck. Christina nodded. It could get very ugly in the room if anyone pulled a gun.

Christina still had her Mulberry, within which she still had her compact weapon of choice, the Sig Sauer MPX.

Bothe she and Chuck were counting the number of security people visible, but also aware of two double doors at the end of the room, which could conceal more gunmen.

"That's where they will have any heavy fire-power," whispered Christina, "This is a classic GRU strong-arm setup. They will probably have a sub behind those doors, and maybe a couple of rifles too."

"They say that London is pretty-much gun-free, yet somehow they seem to move in quite a lot of fire-power."

"Yes, it is dismantled and then sent in with high value goods - electronics and camera accessories. Who would notice an extra pole or two in a disassembled TV camera tripod, for example?"

They noticed some movement. The first of the speakers had come to the stage. Christina vaguely recognised him. Then he spoke with a strong American accent, "Hello, my name is Miller McDonald, from ISMC. Welcome everybody. We are here to facilitate this evening's event and this special privileged meeting for potential investors in this unique business opportunity."

"I recognise Miller McDonald," said Christina, "I didn't speak to him, but he was present at the Ladies' Night at Raven. I guess he was manipulating the occasion for Raven. They didn't have a special event like this though."

"Or not one that you were invited to?" asked Chuck, "Remember there's still around 200 people in the other ballroom."

"…and now let me hand you over to Trudi Hartmann, who can give you the facts and figures."

He left the stage, and an immaculately dressed woman crossed the stage. Christina admired her choice of outfit. Power dressed in a sharp blue tailored suit, with tan shoes. Hair worn down. The tiniest hint of jewellery.

"Darker hues to be taken seriously," thought Christina.

Trudi began to talk and explain the virtues of investment in the new pipeline. That this was no ordinary fundraiser, and everyone should expect to see their initial investment double within two years and then a healthy 18% yield every year that the pipeline was active.

"If it looks too good to be true, then it probably is too good to be true," whispered Chuck.

Next it was Michael Tovey's turn. He played the earnest Member of Parliament and offered praise that an erstwhile British company - Raven - was involved in the development of the new pipeline.

"He is being somewhat economical with the truth," muttered Chuck, "Raven sold off Qube and made Brant - which is a Belgian Company - they are trying hard to conceal this now."

"Although, ironically, probably half the security here are on Brant's payroll," whispered Christina.

It was Maximovich's turn. He took to the stage and spoke with a polished English, but still a Muscovite edge,"This investment will be a great opportunity for all of us, " he said, "we can support the realistic rebalancing of power. It will be like a blow to our oppressors. We can fight with financial measures instead of staging a coup. We don't need to use guns and bombs to shift the balance of power in Celarus.

Maximovich continued, "Even though we spend much less on security than other countries, this does not mean that we are ready to compromise our combat readiness. Our equipment must be better than the world's best if we want to come out as the winners. This is not a game of chess where we can sometimes accept a tie."

Chuck said to Christina, "This smacks of a declaration of conflict along the Celarus borders."

"Working with military friends continues to play a key role in securing peace in Celarus. Our American allies, including those deployed at the new Brant-constructed airbase and perimeter border stations — are guarantors of peace and stability in that country. We have also fielded other weapons systems as well and tested them during exercises and in combat conditions."

"I can't see how Maximovich has managed to get the agreement of America to play along with this. It sounds more like an elaborate bluff, " said Christina. She looked around the audience and could see they were lapping it up.

"Yes. He is saying that Celarus is armed to the teeth along the borders with Russia, with mainly American forces," answered Chuck.

Maximovich continued, "We can all see that the arms control regime is disintegrating, which is a serious concern. Since last November, Washington has been creating new ways with its engagement under the Treaty on Open Skies. The prospects of extending the New START are also under consideration."

"He's trying to play both sides," said Chuck, "He wants this new Russian-backed pipeline, but he expects the Americans to defend it."

Maximovich shifted forward on the rostrum, " All of this is taking place as the U.S. expands the capability of its global missile defence system. A well-defended pipeline will be assured if we take our diplomatic mission seriously alongside the development of business. "

"War-mongering," breathed Christina.

There was clapping and 'Eye of the Tiger' rose from the sound system.

"Wrong tune," said Chuck, "It should be Eve of Destruction,"

Cristina looked at Chuck. "Now?" she said.

"Yes. Now," Christina fiddled in her handbag and pressed the signalling button on her phone.

"They will be in here in 20 seconds," she said to Chuck, "We need to be as close to those doors as possible,"

She gestured to doors behind her, close to where Emily was sitting. They indicated to Emily to follow them as they stood close to the closed doors.

Then a bang. A flash-bang stun grenade had been thrown into the middle of the floor. The security guards looked around. A door at the other end of the room burst open, and as Christina had predicted someone came in carrying a machine gun.

Then four of the smaller side doors burst open together. Soldiers in black combat gear entered the room. There was a short chatter from the sub machine gun and then two separate shots fired followed by silence.

A loud voice came from a different direction to the speakers that had been used during the presentation.

"This is a Police Announcement. Everyone remain calm. This is a raid under circumstances outlined in the Police and Criminal Evidence Act 1984 (PACE). We have the power to enter premises and search them to either arrest someone, seize items in connection with a crime, or both."

Chuck was aware of several people moving towards the doors. He knew there would be even greater force outside. He could hear the rattle of firefight and the clink of metal as bullet cartridges hit the floor.

Everyone else remained seated, looking shocked, but as if this was some kind of extended floor show. Chuck noticed one person edging along a wall towards a door.

Emily stood and pointed to the individual. Emily called out to Christina and Chuck, "It's Vassily Turgenev!"

The man pulled a pistol and took aim towards Emily. There was a further rattle of bullets. Christina had fired cross the room towards Turgenev. He was now pinned back against the door, having been hit by several of Christina's bullets.

Christina dropped the weapon as three SAS men came over to her. "She's with us," barked Chuck. "We are the people you have been listening to on the inside. Chuck Manners"

The squad leader made a hand gesture to the other two men, who relaxed. "Colonel Manners?" He asked, "Yes, said Chuck - he saluted, "And she is my plus one."

Christina knew why Chuck had said plus one. It was a lot simpler than trying to explain why he was with an FSB agent.

"You'll need to check in that cupboard," said Chuck quietly, "You might find there's some explosive in there, brought by Turgenev and Yegorin."

The squad leader walked across to the cupboard signalling to a couple of his men to follow him. They gingerly opened the cupboard, aware that it might be booby-trapped.

Nothing. Just packs of cleaning material.

"Behind them," whispered Chuck, motioning with his head. One of the soldiers toppled a few of the cartons with his gun. Suddenly, they could see the Grenade launcher and on the floor a couple of grenades.

"It's enough to blow a hole through the wall of the hotel, or with the launcher it could rip a hole in Parliament or The Palace," said the squad leader.

Chuck looked around the room. The guests were being marshalled into one holding area and the security men into another. A military paramedic was wound dressing Turgenev, who looked as if he was in a bad way.

"We are getting clearance for emergency services to come inside," crackled across the radio.

Streets of London

Amanda Miller had been monitoring the whole engagement from outside, in a specially established communications vehicle.

Amanda had been asked to take Sir Stafford Peters along. The head of the Department for External Security on a live mission. This would never have happened in Bernard Driscoll's day.

However unheard of, the stakes had risen because of the complexities around this situation.

A CIA Listening station, Brant Subcontractors, Russian ex-KGB, Celarus oil fields and pipelines. American bases. A presumed terrorist device.

The price of gaining access to heavily armed British forces and a FALCON Communication unit was that Sir

Stafford had to sit in the same vehicle. The Army had done a smart thing and set up the unit to look like a film location shoot, which meant they had brought along a second huge caravan truck which included a lounge and a catering area. It was all parked in a side street around the corner from the Lanchester, on double yellow lines.

Amanda had heard the gunshots but could also hear Chuck talking and referring to Christina.

"They all seem to be safe, " she said into the Tetra, for the benefit of Clare and Bigsy.

"Roger that," replied Bigsy, pleased he could, at last, do outgoing comms from the Tetra radio.

"What have we got?" asked Sir Stafford Peters.

"Well, they have caught the organisers, embarrassingly including MP Michael Tovey. Thanks to Maximovich it looks as if they were inciting an uprising- we could even consider it inciting a military coup."

"The bomb successfully implicates Turgenev in something deeply unpleasant and Yegorin is now a spent force. We can bring him in, linked to Maximovich. Everything that took place is on the recordings, thanks to the recordings we gained from the hidden microphones."

Sir Stafford looked worried, "I'm just not sure how much of this we want to advertise as occurring on London's streets."

"Now we need to do a deal with Maximovich. Tell him we'll make sure that Yegorin and Turgenev carry the can for everything. Tell Maximovich that he is free to continue so long as he provides intelligence to us.

Explain that if he doesn't then we'll leak what he did to the Kremlin and he will then soon find himself in a similar situation to Yegorin."

"This is good work, Amanda,"

"Thank you, Sir Stafford."

Sun

Joy
Success
Celebration
Pleasure

Containment

Christina could see that the military had the inside of the ballroom under control and containment. Vassily Turgenev now had several paramedics tending to him. She assessed the gunshot wounds from afar and decided he would live. Her prime objective had been to stop Turgenev from letting off a shot towards Emily after she had identified him to the military.

"Turgenev and Yegorin have been captured, and most of Turgenev's men have been rounded up - at least the ones in the ballroom and through in that back room. It will be interesting to see how many of them come from Brant and have been supplied to this event," she said to Chuck.

Chuck nodded, " I think this will see the disgraced closure of the Minerva Listening station, in any case."

Chuck turned to Emily, who had regrouped with Anne-Marie and Pete. He couldn't help smile when he saw Pete's outfit.

"You three are very lucky to have come out of this without a scratch," he said, "You were playing with fire. But I suppose you'll need to think of a story now that will get you off the hook for being implicated through Minerva."

Anne-Marie looked at Chuck, "Look I don't know why you helped us, but thank you. I know your friend helped save Emily. We are regular US citizens caught up in something far bigger than we expected."

"Come, come now," said Chuck, "We know you work for the CIA and that your friend Pete works directly for Brant. We can cut you some slack, but you must co-operate."

"What kind of slack?" asked Emily.

"Well, we'll want to say that you helped us identify the bad people. That you gave a tip-off that Yegorin was here. That you knew about the terrorist plot."

"Most of that is true. We knew about Yegorin, although not that his enforcer would be using a bunch of Brant contractors to run security at this event. We didn't know about the explosive either."

"Well, you'd better start practicing your story," said Christina.

"Why do you want us to do that?" asked Pete, somewhat indifferent to the situation.

"Well, it's easy really. You can go down as part of the conspiracy, just another three names on the Minerva roll-call of disgrace, or you can come out of this as saviours of the situation."

"Why would you do this to help us?" asked Emily,

Christina answered, "Ask Anne-Marie, she knows me already from a small meeting at Wagamama's close to your offices. She knows that I am quite a tough lady and my friend here is even tougher. - But we do not want our names mixed up in this. If the story of what happened can be told with just the three of you, then it will be a much preferable outcome,"

"What that we worked it all out by ourselves?" Asked Pete, now looking interested, "This could be promotions all round, if we play the story right. Olivia will be pig sick that she didn't get involved."

Emily and Anne-Marie looked at one another and smiled, Emily spoke, "Oh goodness, Olivia might even be seen as a part of the problem!"

"Or we could save her and then she would always be indebted to us." added Pete.

Loose end

Once the area had been secure, Chuck and Christina and the three from Minerva could cross back into the other ballroom. There was a similar scene in the master ballroom. The SAS had moved in although the security staff had surrendered under sheer weight of numbers.

No shots had been fired and Chuck could see that there was unease rippling around the room. It contained many senior people. Both those invited by the Russians and an additional selection of captains of industry, MPs and A-listers.

Chuck noticed that the military presence in this room had been offset by Metropolitan Police, who had also run security tape around much of the area.

Chuck looked at Christina, "They'll want to process these people and let them go as quickly as possible... There's too many well-known faces in here."

Emily and Anne-Marie looked over to the left-hand side of the room. There were fifty or more of the hostesses sitting together on the floor. They both noticed how matter-of-factly they seemed to be taking it and realised that for the hostesses this must be part of a way of life. Pete spotted the blond guy that he'd seen on the way into the event.

"All in day's work, I just hope they pay us for the full time here," he called over to Pete. He noticed that Pete was with Emily and Anne-Marie and that they were able to move around freely with Christina and Chuck.

"You take care," said Pete, "Sorry I couldn't tell you, but I'm a special agent,"

The blonde guy looked incredulous, but then noticed Chuck's pistol, which he had placed back in a shoulder holster.

The entourage of Christina, Chuck and the three Minerva people slipped out through a side door guarded by a police officer. Chuck explained they needed to speak to the controller of the operation, Amanda Miller.

...

Evidence

Once outside, Chuck looked for the military security detail. He saw one officer and engaged him in conversation. Then he walked back to the three from Minerva.

"Look, I've arranged for you three to be taken to a secure area. You will be guarded there until the heat from this dies down. You are not under arrest and are free to walk at any time, but understand me, you will be better in the Army's care for the next 24 hours. The holding area is inside the Lanchester. Three hotel rooms, upper floors I'm told."

The three looked at one another, "Well I'm in," said Pete, "Is room service included?"

Then Emily, "Well it does sound like a sensible idea, me too."

And Anne-Marie nodded her agreement.

Chuck heard them talking, "Yes, room service is included, but no booze, I'm afraid. Enjoy your stay."

Christina said, "Good, that's one less thing to worry about, Let's find Amanda now, and Bigsy, for a debrief."

Christina pulled her smartphone from her bag and texted "All OK. Meet at Amanda's location." The message would travel to Bigsy's comms van, also containing Jake and Clare.

They reached the street and walked to where they knew that Amanda had parked her convoy of vehicles.

"It looks so different now," said Christina, "with all these military buzzing around. Before it looked like a typical London street with a few film trailers parked along it."

Chuck agreed, and they both made their way to the now overtly guarded entrance to the hospitality vehicle.

Chuck gave his details to the sentry, and they listened as there was some communication interplay. The sentry then waved him and Christina through towards the entrance of the caravan.

They climbed a couple of steps and then entered a well-decorated environment. At the far end, around a small table were sitting Amanda and a suited man who they took to be Sir Stafford Peters.

Amanda and Chuck were still both in their finery and so the effect was more of a James Bond entrance rather than two combat veterans entering the room.

Amanda stood as they entered.

"Chuck, Christina, Well done! - You do not look as if a hair is out of place! That was an amazing operation."

"Yes," agreed Christina.

They all looked over to Sir Stafford. It intrigued Christina to know whether he felt it had been good value for money.

"Indeed, a very well-executed operation," he said, "And now we have Maximovich where we need him. As for the Yegorin and Turgenev, they will get what they deserve. And we can close Minerva Station, which was a cheeky attempt by the Americans to get on our soil in any case."

"Yes, all of that is good," said Christina, "But I'm still suspicious. In the Nordic stories of *Þiðrekssaga* there's a dragon. Sigurd can slay it, and smear his skin with its blood for protection, but he must always watch out for the sword Mimung, which can still cut and defeat. And for the shape-shifting that Sigurd may choose in order to get his way with Brynhild."

"That's like The Ring Cycle?" said Amanda.

"Yes, but you see my point. There's still someone running this, beyond Maximovich, Michael Tovey or ISMC."

"It's not over 'til it's over," said Bigsy.

"I agree," said Amanda, "We will need to interrogate the principal players to find out what they know."

Ed Adams

Hanged Man

Sacrifice
Suspension
Release
Martyrdom

(Reversed)

Stalling
Fear of Sacrifice

Mainstream Media Attention

They all soon discovered that they could not run a major assault on a famous landmark hotel in London, without it attracting the MSM – the mainstream media and getting cut-through.

Amanda had sought advice from a PR Agency to cover what information they released, and a selection of slightly posed pictures of SAS soldiers going about their business. Amanda's intention was to deflect the event's cut-through potential by getting it classified as terrorism on London's streets.

By doing so, she would capture Turgenev and be able to dispense rough justice. Yegorin would also fall squarely under UK jurisdiction with these charges and be less likely to gain a Russian extradition, which would anyway send him to his doom. Yegorin would understandably play along with this, being caught somewhere between the devil and the deep blue sea.

The PR Agency said the story had wrap-up potential.

The Agency suggested a positioning speech, by someone in authority and the next day a press conference was conducted with The Mayor of London. It was a passionate speech about the event and emphasised that Londoners had brought it all under control. The event was characterised as an incitement towards a coup and the plotting of a bomb placement.

There was tribute paid to the police and special forces who intercepted the conspirators and then to the emergency services for their swift, professional response.

The large swathe of attendees in the master ballroom were mysteriously absent from the story. It was briefed that there was a coincidental second event occurring in the master ballroom.

Ominously, wording was added that there will be more armed and unarmed officers on London's streets in the days ahead to reassure everybody as they go about their normal business. Londoners owed the police and security services a huge debt of gratitude.

Then, "Terrorists have tried to sow fear, hatred and division in our city before. They have never succeeded and will not succeed now. London will not be intimidated or cowed by terrorism.

"Rather, we will redouble our efforts to stand resolute, defiant and united in the face of such evil. Terrorism is an act of complete cowardice and we will pursue and bring to justice anyone who might have offered support."

"There will be earnest questions for the government to answer in the weeks ahead about how this plotting could have happened and whether it could have been prevented."

"I will continue working closely with the police, authorities and government to reassure our communities and ensure that all possible measures are put in place to protect Londoners. I have no doubt that in the coming days Londoners will once again show the world exactly why our capital is the greatest city in the world. We will not let anyone divide us or disrupt our way of life. We will defend our values—and we will never let the terrorists win."

Interrogation outcomes

Amanda had called the Triangle members to her offices in Vauxhall Cross.

"This is exciting!" said Clare, "We are going to Spy Central."

"It's less exciting if you've already been held there for several days," replied Jake, remembering his time detained there when Clare and Bigsy were travelling around Arizona with Chuck.

Christina and Chuck had assessed their chances of getting in and out of SI6 without being detained on 'other matters', but Amanda had given her word.

They all met Amanda in an entrance lobby, where Amanda asked each them to be photographed and issued with badges. "You'll need to be accompanied," she said, "Everywhere, I'm afraid."

They moved through the building's security system and were eventually in an upper floor meeting room.

"The system will record this automatically. There's nothing I can do to stop it," said Amanda.

"Would you like me to stop it?" asked Bigsy, "Only I have this little app on my phone that duplicates IP addresses, it'll confuse the heck out of your devices in here and they will all hang."

"Thanks, but no thanks," said Amanda, "We should really have confiscated that on the way in."

"You did take my other two phones, " said Bigsy, "that scanning booth on the way in is surprisingly efficient."

"Okay, this is my colleague, James Cavendish and we've another colleague Grace Fielding on the Polycom."

"Hello," said Grace's voice.

"Hi," chorused several of the attendees.

"Right, let's get to it."

Amanda began:

"Slide 1: What we know. We have seen the attempts to break into the commercial arrangements of Brant. The sell-off from Raven was extraordinarily successful and investors in Brant made about double their original stake holding."

"Slide 2: Brant's shareholding has reduced, because of the early profit-takers, but there seems to be several large blocks still held. It includes the sizeable block holding by Gasneft, a Russian company."

Slide 3 : One of the largest business opportunities for Brant is in Celarus, a country that borders western Russia. Oil discoveries there were made by American exploration and the United States agreed to place US planes and military in Celarus.

"That's American planes right along Russia's borders," said Jim

"Slide 4: Unknown forces have been creating some interference in Celarus. There have been acts similar to those affecting Qube in Syria. Skirmishes which ensure the continued presence of the American forces."

"Qube was the offshoot of Raven which was made into Brant when Raven divested Brant," said Jim, "They were operating in the same way."

"Slide 5: Brant offers a range of services. Oil exploration, extraction, packaging, movement, trading - these are the same services as Raven. Then it offers security services (that's a quasi-military force) and construction of large infrastructure. Like the pipeline building, but also military camps and roads."

"The old idea to blow up place and then repair it is a well understood American business model from the early 2000s," said Jim, " a kind of Kellogg Brown & Root and Halliburton type of manoeuvre."

"Oh yes, the Iraqi oil wells, featuring Mr Dick Cheney," said Chuck.

"Slide 6: Brant has other interests too; it appears to be supplying the outsourced contractors to the CIA Minerva listening station in east London."

"And yes, these outsources seem to be coming with a distinct Russian flavour?" said Jim.

"Slide 7: And Minerva has been used continuously to target British MPs and Captains of Industry - faster than lobbying, using sleaze and slush to compromise them."

"Slide 8: So, who is pulling all the strings? Why would Brant be positioned to win the contracts in Celarus? Who really owns Brant? The Belgians? Raven? Or the Russians?"

"Well, Raven even seemed to be using the Freemasons," ventured Christina.

"No, too obvious, a smokescreen," interrupted Grace from the speakerphone, "It's a clever idea, and can bring in contacts, but then someone else is taking over the manipulation. Meanwhile we can all run off to try to investigate the tirelessly secretive Freemasons."

"I think I agree with that, " said Christina," My friend Antanov was none the wiser about any plans by Brant of anything to do with Celarus or Russia."

"Slide 9: Our questioning of persons of interest," continued Amanda., "These are the 'net nets' from the interviews. What everyone said, boiled down to a line or two - I'm going to hand over to Grace for this part."

"Okay," said Grace,

"Slide 10: old players. I wanted to start with the people who were involved when this all started.

"1) Bernard Driscoll- the rude and hapless Minister who was compromised by the efforts of ISMC, acting on behalf of Raven. We think he was killed by the Roslavl Bratva run by Tima Maximovich. If so, that would have been orchestrated by Vassily Turgenev.

"2) Sir Charles Frobisher - threatened by Turgenev. Then disappears after saying he is going on a helicopter flight to Nice airport from Monaco. Likely death at sea caused by Vassily Turgenev.

"3) Gerhardt Schmidt - blown up, with seven others on a yacht off Monaco. Almost certainly an American smart mine attached to the vessel. Suspect Vassily Turgenev.

"That just about rounds up the deaths under suspicious circumstances. We could add the fire bombing of The Triangle Works in Hoxton to that list and the couple of attempts to shoot Chuck Manners."

Christina interrupted, "The attempts on Chuck were from FSB agents. Low level - their code names were Puffin and Auk. They worked with another agent, who also shot at me near Tower Bridge. I think the body was washed up near Tilbury."

"Oh," came Grace's voice, "I had no idea it involved you, Christina. You are not on cameras nor give any trace. It looked as if the extensive firepower used in both cases was a 9mm submachine gun?"

Christina said, "No comment."

Grace continued, "Let's move on to the captures from the Lanchester. Slide 11:"

"4) Vassily Turgenev - a nasty piece of work. Has no direct connection with Russian intelligence, but has been an enforcer for mainly Maximovich for around ten years. There is a bloody trail left from his endeavours. In interrogation he didn't give us much, except when he was under Midazolam because of the severe injuries from 9 mm bullets in the Lanchester.

"Under the tranquillisers, he rambled, but did that he had been pleased to even the scores with Driscoll, Frobisher, Schmidt and a couple of other names. He described the yacht explosion as one of the best fireworks displays he had seen. He described the Driscoll car crash as hilarious - something from Mr Bean."

"5) Yegorin - a true Russian gangster - one of the people that put Putin into power. He calls Putin 'VV', by the way."

"VV - Vladimir Vladimirovich," said Christina.

Grace continued, "Yes, and now Yegorin plays hard-done-by saying that metaphorically the Kremlin have held him by his ankles and shook him. They want all his hard assets, and his money. He's put the money into various hiding places and that has just made the Russians madder. That is why they are pursuing him through the English Courts. They seem to think that they have some kind of hold over elements within the legal profession. That and excellent PR outlets for what they see as 'the truth'."

"He said metaphorically, but I could see Turgenev trying exactly that ankles trick, " said Christina.

Grace answered, "Yegorin wanted to cut a deal with us, because he is frightened of extradition to Russia. He says his time will be limited if he goes back. We are leaving him to hang for a while longer," said Grace, "And hold that thought about influencing the English Courts and the link back to Minerva.

"6) Michael Tovey, MP - Now that was interesting. At first he made out that he had been dumped in a similar manner to Driscoll. Our people believed him until they unearthed a significant Foundation Fund in the Caymans. He had made the same stupid mistake as Driscoll and was funnelling money into it by a well-known bank. We think Tovey is further up the decision tree than he is letting on.

"7) Miller McDonald, MVP in ISMC- This is the outfit that has facilitated the various celebrity events. They seem to be more or less a fixer to Raven. Gerhart Schmidt also worked for them. Miller, a Texan, seems to be quite high up in the company, but aside from fronting the event in the Lanchester seems to be clean.

"He certainly looked like a tanned, drive-by handshake to me, " said Chuck, thinking back to the presentation.

"8) Trudi Hartmann, a VP from ISCM and a close ally of McDonald. Some say they are sleeping together. She gave the introduction presentation for the oil pipeline investment, but otherwise seems untouchable."

"She was polished, has the moves and the power dressing to add credibility to the session. They also gave her some time to position the arguments," said Christina.

"Slide 12: The others - Yes - while we were processing everyone at the event a few other names surfaced. A

Marion Charlotte, who said she knew and had been out with Driscoll and had met Chuck, Christina even Amanda.

"Then there was Nina Valentine a friend of Marion, who seemed to know Gerhardt Schmidt, Maximovich and Yegorin. She said she'd never forgive Yegorin for blowing up the yacht in Monaco. She said she was supposed to be on it and her friends were, plus Gerhardt. Oh yes, and Nina also knew all of you, from visiting the Triangle in Galleria.

"And a curious turn up was a couple of people from Smooth Pebble, which is a kind of Californian PR agency. Han Yoon was the SVP and said he had coached Raven's board on ways to handle the divestment to form Brant. He also knew Sir Charles but wasn't aware he was missing.

"Then there was Brittany Krasnigor, a very self-confident American, who had met the Raven board at the same coaching session as Han Yoon. She was surprised that Smooth Pebble were invited to the London event, but decided to come along 'to see the Brits at play' as she put it.

"Ha," said Jake, "Is she a psychologist or something?"

"Great guess," said Grace, "Behavioural Psychologist, PhD, from Harvard.

"She said she hadn't said anything to Han Yoon, but had been darkly disturbed by the Raven pre-divestment meeting. She reckoned that Frobisher and the other had deliberately put a 'B-Team' on to lead it. She said it was like passing the rudder of the ship to a blind captain. She reckoned that there were other games afoot and that

Raven to Brant was just the opening move of a more complex game."

"The Narrenschiff - Ship of fools, " said Christina, "A friend of mine told me to watch out for it."

"But wait - there's still one person we havn't talked about," said Grace.

"Saving the best for last?" asked Jim.

"Yes, you could say that," answered Grace, "But I'll pass the deck back to Amanda."

Amanda continued, "Slide 13: Kasharin Timur (Tima) Maximovich, who is the Head of Russian Infrastructure. He was asked to set up the Lanchester session for Yegorin and did so because of Yegorin's leverage towards him. "

"Leverage? Friendship or threats?" asked Christina.

"Probably all of the above, Yegorin knows, literally, where the bodies are buried," answered Grace, "It was because of Maximovich's inflammatory speech that we could send the SAS into the meeting. We needed something as well as the discovered explosives which implicate Turgenev, but the speech could implicate one or both of Yegorin and Maximovich."

"Creating the prisoners' dilemma?" asked Jake, "Who betrays whom?"

"No, they will both treat it as 'every man for himself', said Amanda, "They are caught too tight and both could expect execution by Russia if they play their cards badly."

Jim said, "That's where Maximovich has an escape. He can say that he was setting a trap for Yegorin and Turgenev. That it was best to find the anti-Kremlin Russians and this was a quick way to flush them out in a single sweep. We can even help write the script for him."

Amanda added, "Then the Kremlin would be very pleased with Maximovich and move him to the inner circle for such a daring act. Especially as it looks as if the Kremlin had no hand in it."

"That's how we can position a threat over Maximovich and ask him to become our mole."

Ed Adams

Judgement

Reflection
Reckoning
Awakening

The Maximovich trade

Maximovich had been placed in a secure detention centre, out in the Surrey countryside. A sweeping drive led to the main building, which was a repurposed stately home.

Amanda and Jim Cavendish arrived and walked through the large wooden door, with a smaller door cut into it. Amanda glanced to the door frame. Sure enough, a ring of small circular indentations. Apotropaic marks cut into the door to ward off evil spirits.

"Look - these ward off the witches," she said to Jim. He glanced over, "As long as they ward off the Russian bogey men too," he said as they walked in.

"We are here to see Maximovich, " explained Amanda flashing a badge, " We are Amanda Miller and Jim Cavendish."

"Ah yes, Ms Miller, Please, come this way. You'll be entering the secure part of the site, so be prepared for some security rigmarole. I expect you'll be used to it, coming from Vauxhall."

They walked through a metal detector and then into a small cubicle where they were body scanned.

"All good, you can leave your phones in the secure boxes and then follow me," said the guard.

They were both issued with freshly printed computerised badges.

"Here's the lanyards for the badges, they are proximity sensitive so they will let you through doors that you are allowed to go through. Just watch out for a green light - not a red light which means stop."

They walked through a couple of corridors including one which smelled of fast-food and then another of detergent. A sharp left turn and they were in a small lobby area with three metal doors.

"It's like one of those quiz shows," quipped Jim.

"He's in here," as the metal door swung open revealing another locked door.

"You will need to use your pass for the second door," said the guard.

They entered and could see Maximovich seated at a small table. His arms were out in front of him and appeared to be chained to the table via a small metal loop.

"More questions?" he said, "Haven't you got enough answers already?"

"Hello Tima," said Amanda, "This time we come with a deal for you."

"I don't do deals," he started.

"Well, you'll have to listen in any case. We want to set you free. But there is a price. So far no-one knows that we are holding you. Outside you can be seen as the man that brought Yegorin to justice. It will play well in the Kremlin and could save you from being chased the way of Yegorin."

"We know he has got something on you," bluffed Jim, "We even know what it is, but we won't be talking about it to anyone."

"Not if you play along with us," continued Amanda, "We want you to tell the Kremlin that you orchestrated the raid. That it was to catch Russian dissidents. They will believe you."

"I've been waiting for this," said Maximovich, "You English are so predictable. There's a price for me turning against Yegorin."

"Yes, but if you don't, you'll be turning against your families." said Jim.

"Blah-blah-blah, I've done this stuff too you know, let's cut to the chase. I'll need money and a safeguard," said Maximovich, "Both Yegorin and Turgenev go to Russia. You deport them on terrorism charges. Maybe trade a few people the other way?"

"That would represent death to Yegorin," said Jim.

"He can take his chances. I have stuck out my neck for him with this last thing. Look where it has got me. I need him off the scene. And Turgenev, for that matter. Otherwise he'll send a surprise package around to my home."

"Surprise package?"

"Yes, a gunman or a bomb. Maybe some poison. He's not that particular. Then I can go to the Kremlin. Say I engineered the take-down. They will believe me, but only if I'm not missing for too long. A week in hiding after that Lanchester incident is believable. Then I need to surface in somewhere like San Tropez. I can explain everything about hiding. But you'll need to get Yegorin and Turgenev moved fast. And offer me a sweetener, for the inconvenience. Maybe a million a day in detention. There. That's my offer."

"That's too much," said Jim.

"Okay, I'll be kind, Dollars. Final Offer."

Amanda and Jim remained poker-faced. They had been given a budget for this by Sir Stafford Peters. "Twenty million is the maximum. That's Pounds."

So far they were on day six. A couple more to fix everything. Eight days was eight million US, at the exchange rate that was about £6.4 million.

"Okay," said Jim, "We agree. How do you want to do this?"

"I want someone Russian that I trust to pick up Yegorich and Turgenev. Helicopter from the field behind this building. To an airstrip - military is fine - then on to Moscow. A Russian plane. I want to hear from the pickup they have all arrived. Then, show me a fund transfer, get me a private jet to LFTZ-La Mole out by Saint Tropez and we are done."

"Okay, although we'll want you to stay in contact after that."

"I understand, you expect me to be a double. But I need to be careful first. You only want infrequent high-value from me. Not lots of noise. Are we done?"

Amanda and Jim rose. They decided it was best to leave when Maximovich thought he was on a high.

Kamov Ka-60

It was early morning. Amanda and Jim waited on the field behind the stately home for the helicopter to arrive. They had done everything that Maximovich had asked. They had even transferred the £6.4 million to a bank account in Liechtenstein. Now there were two more things left to do.

To move Turgenev and Yegorin back to Russia via helicopter and then onwards by private jet to Sheremetyevo airport.

Then, some eight hours later, to move Maximovich to an airstrip from where he could catch a private flight to Saint Tropez, where he would resurface with a great tale of sunshine and powerboats and an additional $8 million in his pockets.

The Kamov Ka-60 circled once and then landed.

"Noisy," said Chuck, and Christina nodded. She was having flashbacks to when they used similar helicopters in Archangelsk to make short runs into the Dvina Bay and the White Sea, where they would stop on the flatlands of the Dvina River delta to practice various kinds of military field craft. It was where she had first met Antanov, when he piloted the craft to take their unit back to the Academy.

They looked out and saw Amanda and Jim shepherding Turgenev and Yegorin to the helicopter. Turgenev still looked in a bad way. He had sustained four bullet wounds to the leg from Christina. Only her shooting accuracy had kept him alive. Yegorin looked as if he was quietly going mad. He had let his beard grow long and his hair looked wild.

"He looks finished, " said Chuck quietly and Christina nodded. From a distance they could see Amanda and Jim saying a last few things to the pair as they climbed aboard the helicopter.

A large metal door was slid closed, with Christina thinking she did not remember that the door there even closed on the ones they had used in Russia, and then the helicopter started to rise in the air.

Christina's phone rang. It was Blackbird.

"Archangel. The helicopter ride is a trap," he said, in Russian, "Maximovich has got a word outside, to his new enforcer, Anatoly Yaroslav. Yaroslav is to take the plane down. We heard it today because we have been monitoring Yaroslav's line."

"Why are you telling me this?" asked Christina, also speaking in Russian, "Do you want me to stop it."

"No," he said, "I want to make sure you are not deciding to take a ride for old times' sake. Riding shotgun. You know the kind of thing."

"No, my feet are both on the ground," replied Christina.

"Yaroslav has access to firepower," said Blackbird, "It will be final."

Blackbird hung up.

Christina looked at the helicopter which had circled once before taking its heading towards the airfield where the jet was waiting. She looked around the field. There were several outcrops of trees. In the distance she could hear metallic scraping. Then a loud bang and she noticed the orange flash from behind the treeline.

She and Chuck watched as two white finned missiles headed towards the helicopter. There was a bright light as the first one struck and then a second orange light as the second one reached the target. Three or four seconds later the sound arrived, ominous and loud. A mix of explosion and metal sheets being torn apart. Then a short pause and a further noise as the helicopter hit the ground, or, as Christina gauged it, hit some trees in the middle distance."

"That was a Pechora, I think," said Chuck, "Where does anyone get one of those in Surrey? This is like the wild west."

Christina nodded as she looked toward Amanda and Jim. They were both running to the same part of the field where Christina and Chuck were standing, so they could get a better view.

"It must be Maximovich, " said Amanda, "He didn't want to take any chances. That was ruthless."

Jim nodded, "We will have to cover this up from the public," he said, "But it does still reinforce Maximovich's position with the Kremlin."

"Who do you think did this?" asked Amanda. Christina kept quiet.

"We need to find out who Maximovich has hired to replace Turgenev; he seems to be from the same barrel," said Jim.

"Do you think Maximovich knows what has happened?" asked Amanda.

"I mean he's in that building and that explosion was so close he could hear it."

"No, he's got some kind of link to outside," said Jim, "Maybe it is through his wife."

"Do we have any way of capturing the launch vehicle?" asked Amanda.

"If that was a Pechora 2M, they have the advantage that you can pull curtains along the side of them and apart from the odd-looking forward cab, they look like a regular haulage truck," said Chuck, "It'll have melted into the traffic."

"What would a soviet SAM be doing in Surrey?" asked Jim.

"I know, I was wondering the same thing," answered Chuck.

Saint Tropez

They decided not to talk to Maximovich before his departure. Eight hours later another helicopter arrived, this one a sleek modern-looking business craft with a Gatwick address on the door.

The original timings were to allow time for the other Russians to get back to Moscow.

Maximovich walked out.

"I think my reputation will be good for the Kremlin," he said, "And that there are no loose ends. Now I must find my sunshades for sitting outside Le Sénéquier."

He climbed aboard the helicopter, which revved for takeoff. Amanda, Jim, Chuck and Christina looked on as it took off, circled and then flew away, in the same general direction as the other craft had done during the early morning.

They waited until it was a tiny speck on the horizon and then moved back towards the house.

"Job done!" said Chuck, "Except for the tidy-up."

Christina looked towards him, "I'm not so sure," she said, "I can't help think there's still something else here. That we have not followed the whole trail, even now."

"I worry that the route leads into Moscow," said Amanda.

"Or maybe that is what they want us to think?" questioned Christina.

"Well, they've burnt all the links, that's for sure," said Chuck, "I think we must be careful now, because Maximovich seems to have traded up for his enforcer. Anatoly Yaroslev seems even more menacing than Turgenev."

"What about your friends?" asked Amanda, "The ones that work in that Triangle thing?"

"They'll want to know what happened, that's for sure," said Chuck.

"And probably over a few beers," added Christina.

"There should probably be some closing theme music about now," said Chuck.

"I can hear it," said Christina.

Providence at a top table in London

It was a busy reception. Drinks, canapés, a few celebrities, including some A-listers. Songs from a well-known pop band. An inspirational speech from a well-known football team manager.

Off to the side was a compact room. In different times they would have filled it with cigar smoke. Nowadays just the dark-suited men.

"We still need Brant, " said one.

The others nodded.

"Who can we use to manipulate it?" asked the second voice.

"Someone we can control. A puppet."

"I have the very person, a clean skin, " said a third voice.

"Well, let's invite him into the club." Said the first voice, as if concluding the discussion.

Ed Adams

Your Cards

World

Fulfilment
Harmony
Completion

Ed Adams

Judgement

Reflection
Reckoning
Awakening

www.ingramcontent.com/pod-product-compliance
Lightning Source LLC
Chambersburg PA
CBHW050951180726
48291CB00006B/1784